Nancy Crampton

Olen Steinhauer, the *New York Times* bestselling author of *The Tourist* and six other novels, is also a two-time Edgar Award finalist and has been shortlisted for the Anthony, the Macavity, the Ellis Peters Historical Dagger, and the Barry awards. Film rights to *The Tourist* have been optioned by Warner Brothers for George Clooney. Raised in Virginia, Steinhauer lives with his family in Budapest, Hungary.

Visit him online at www.OlenSteinhauer.com.

The
NEAREST
EXIT

ALSO BY OLEN STEINHAUER

The
NEAREST
EXIT

OLEN STEINHAUER

Minotaur Books
New York

This is a work of fiction. All of the characters, organizations, and events portrayed in this novel are either products of the author's imagination or are used fictitiously.

THE NEAREST EXIT. Copyright © 2010 by Third State, Inc. All rights reserved. Printed in the United States of America. For information, address St. Martin's Press, 175 Fifth Avenue, New York, N.Y. 10010.

www.minotaurbooks.com

The Library of Congress has cataloged the hardcover edition as follows:

Steinhauer, Olen.
    The nearest exit / Olen Steinhauer.—1st ed.
      p. cm.
    ISBN 978-0-312-62287-9
    1. United States. Central Intelligence Agency—Officials and employees—Fiction. 2. Undercover operations—Fiction. I. Title.
    PS3619.T4764N43 2010
    813'.6—dc22

                            2009047486

ISBN 978-0-312-62288-6 (trade paperback)

10 9 8 7 6 5 4 3 2

Za
SLAVICU I MARGO

There are three emergency exits on this aircraft. Take a few moments now to locate the closest one. Please note that, in some cases, the nearest exit may be behind you.

The
LAST FLIGHT
of HENRY GRAY

7890

MONDAY, AUGUST 6

TO TUESDAY, DECEMBER 11, 2007

1

When DJ Jazzy-G hit the intro to "Just like Heaven," that Cure anthem of his youth, Henry Gray achieved a moment of complete expat euphoria. Was this his first? He'd felt shades of it other times during his decade in Hungary, but only at that moment—a little after two in the morning, dancing at the ChaChaCha's outdoor club on Margit Island, feeling Zsuzsa's lips stroke his sweat-damp earlobe . . . only then did he feel the full brunt and stupid luck of his beautiful life overseas.

Eighties night at the ChaChaCha. Jazzy-G was reading his mind. Zsuzsa was consuming his tongue.

Despite the frustrations and disappointments of life in this capital of Central Europe, in Zsuzsanna Papp's arms he felt a momentary love for the city, and the kerts—the beer gardens that Hungarians opened up once they'd survived their long, dark winters. Here, they shed their clothes and drank and danced and worked through the stages of foreplay, and made even an outsider like Henry feel as if he could belong.

Still, not even all this sensual good fortune was enough to bestow upon Henry Gray such intense joy. It was the story, the one he'd received via the unpredictable Hungarian postal service twelve hours before. The biggest story of his young professional life.

His career as a journalist thus far had rested on the story of the

Taszár Air Base, where the U.S. Army secretly trained the Free Iraqi Forces in the Hungarian countryside as that unending war was just beginning. That had been four years ago, and in the meantime Henry Gray's career had floundered. He'd missed the boat on the CIA's secret interrogation centers in Romania and Slovakia. He'd wasted six months on the ethnic unrest along the Serbian-Hungarian border, which he couldn't give away to U.S. papers. Then last year, when the *Washington Post* was exposing the CIA's use of Taliban prisoners to harvest Afghan opium that it sold to Europe—during that time, Henry Gray had been mired in another of his black periods, where he'd wake up stinking of vodka and Unicum, with a week missing from his memory.

Now, though, the Hungarian post had brought him salvation, something that no newspaper could ignore. Sent by a Manhattan law firm with the unlikely name of Berg & DeBurgh, it had been written by one of its clients, Thomas L. Grainger, former employee of the Central Intelligence Agency. The letter was a new beginning for Henry Gray.

As if to prove this, Zsuzsa, who had been standoffish for so long, had finally caved to his affections after he read out the letter and described what it meant for his career. She—a journalist herself—had promised her help, and between kisses said they'd be like Woodward and Bernstein, and he had said of course they would.

Had greed finally bent her will? In this moment, the one that would last a few more hours at least, it really didn't matter.

"Do you love me?" she whispered.

He took her warm face in his hands. "What do you think?"

She laughed. "I think you do love me."

"And you?"

"I've always liked you, Henry. I might even love you someday."

At first, Henry hadn't recalled the name Thomas Grainger, but on his second read it had dawned on him—they had met once before, four years ago when Gray was following leads on the Taszár story. A car had pulled up beside him on Andrássy utca, the rear window sliding down, and an old man asked to speak to him. Over coffee, Thomas Grainger used a mixture of patriotism and bald threats to get Gray to wait another week before filing the story. Gray refused, then returned home to a demolished apartment.

July 11, 2007

Mr. Gray,

You're probably surprised to receive a letter from someone who, in the past, has butted heads with you concerning your journalistic work. Rest assured that I'm not writing to apologize for my behavior—I still feel your articles on Taszár were supremely irresponsible and could have harmed the war effort, such as it is. That they didn't harm it is a testament to either my ability to slow their publication or the inconsequence of your newspaper; you can be the judge.

Despite this, your tenacity is something I've admired. You pushed forward when other journalists might have folded, which makes you the kind of man I'd like to speak to now. The kind of journalist I need.

That you have this letter in your hands is evidence of one crucial fact: I am now dead. I'm writing this letter in order that my death—which I suspect will have been at the hand of my own employer—might not go unnoticed.

Vanity? Yes. But if you live to reach my age, maybe you'll be able to look upon it more kindly. Maybe you'll be able to see it for the idealistic impulse I believe it is.

According to public records, Grainger had run a CIA financial oversight office in New York before his fatal heart attack in July. Then again, public records are public for a reason—they put forth what the government wants the public to believe.

Around three, they fought their way off the dance floor, collected their things—the seven-page letter was still in his shoulder bag—and crossed the Margit Bridge back to Pest. They caught a taxi to Zsuzsa's small Eighth District apartment, and within an hour he felt that, were his life to end in the morning, he could go with no regrets.

"Do you like that?" Zsuzsa asked in the heavy darkness that smelled of her Vogue cigarettes.

He caught his breath but couldn't speak. She was doing something with her hand, somewhere between his thighs.

"It's tantra."

"Is it?" He gasped, clutching the sheets.

This really was the best of all possible worlds.

I will now tell you a story. It concerns the Sudan, the department of the CIA I preside over, and China. Unsurprisingly for someone like you, it also concerns oil, though perhaps not in the way you imagine.

Know too that the story I'm about to tell you is dangerous to know. My death is evidence of this. From this point on, consider yourself on your own. If this is too much to bear, then burn the letter now and forget it.

Afterward, when they were both exhausted and the street was silent, they stared at the ceiling. Zsuzsa smoked, the familiarity of her cigarettes mixing with the unfamiliarity of her sex, and said, "You will bring me along, right?"

All day, it hadn't occurred to her that the story had nothing to do with Hungary, and Hungary was the only country where her language skills were of any use. He would have to fly to New York, and she didn't even have a visa. "Of course," he lied, "but you remember the letter—it's dangerous."

He heard but didn't see her snort of laughter.

"What?"

"Terry is right. You are paranoid."

Gray propped himself on his elbow and gave her a long look. Terry Parkhall was a hack who'd always had an eye for her. "Terry's an idiot. He lives in a dream world. You even suggest the CIA was in some way responsible for 9/11 and he hits the ceiling. In a world with Gitmo and torture centers and the CIA in the heroin business, how's that so unimaginable? The problem with Terry is that he forgets the basic truth of conspiracy."

Self-consciously, she rubbed at her grin. "What is the basic truth of conspiracy?"

"If it can be imagined, then someone's already tried it."

It was the wrong thing to say. He didn't know why, because she refused to explain, but a definite coldness fell between them, and it took a long time before he was able to fall asleep. It was a staccato sleep, broken up by flashes of Sudanese riots under a dusty sun, oil-streaked Chinese, and assassins from Grainger's secret office, the Department of Tourism. By eight he was awake again, rubbing his eyes in the poor light coming in from the street. Zsuzsa breathed heavily, undisturbed, and he blinked at the window. There was a pleasant ache in his groin. He began to have a change of heart.

While Zsuzsa couldn't be much use tracking down the evidence behind Grainger's story, he resolved all at once to make her his partner in it. Did tantra change his mind? Or some indefinable guilt over having said the wrong thing? Like her reasons for finally sleeping with him, it didn't matter.

What mattered was that there was a lot of work ahead; it was just beginning. He began to dress. Thomas Grainger himself had admitted that his story was shallow. "As yet I have no solid evidence for you, except my word. However, I'm hoping for material very soon from one of my subordinates." The letter ended with no word from his subordinate, though, just the reiteration of that one crucial fact, "I am now dead," and a few real names to begin tracking down evidence: Terence Fitzhugh, Diane Morel, Janet Simmons, Senator Nathan Irwin, Roman Ugrimov, Milo Weaver. That last one, Grainger claimed, was the only person he could trust to help him out. He should show the letter to Milo Weaver, and only Milo Weaver, and that would be his passage.

He kissed Zsuzsa, then snuck out to the yellow-lit Habsburg morning with his shoulder bag. He decided to walk home. It was a bright day, full of possibility, though around him the morose Hungarians heading to their mundane jobs hardly noticed.

His apartment was on Vadász utca, a narrow, sooty lane of crumbling, once beautiful buildings. Since the elevator was perpetually on the blink, he took the stairs slowly to his fifth-floor apartment, went inside, and typed the code into his burglar alarm.

He had used the money from the Taszár story to buy and

remodel this apartment. The kitchen was stainless steel, the living room equipped with Wi-Fi and inlaid shelves, and he'd had the unstable terrace that overlooked Vadász reinforced and cleaned up. Unlike the homes of many of his makeshift friends, his actually reflected his idea of good living, rather than having to compromise with the regular Budapest conundrum: large apartments that had been chopped up during communist times, with awkward kitchens and bathrooms and long, purposeless hallways.

He flipped on the television, where a Hungarian pop band played on the local MTV, dropped his bag to the floor, and took a leak in the bathroom, wondering if he should begin work on the story alone or first seek out this Milo Weaver. Alone, he decided. Two reasons. One, he wanted to know as much as possible before sitting down to whatever lies Weaver would inevitably feed him. Two, he wanted the satisfaction of breaking the story himself, if possible.

He washed up and returned to the living room, then stopped. On his BoConcept couch, which had cost him an arm and a leg, a blond man reclined, eyes fixed on a dancing, heavy-breasted woman on the screen. Henry's mouth worked the air, but he couldn't find any breath as the man turned casually to him and smiled, giving an upward nod, the way men do to one another.

"Fine woman, huh?" American accent.

"Who . . ." Henry couldn't finish the sentence.

Still smiling, the man turned to see him better. He was tall, wearing a business suit but no tie. "Mr. Gray?"

"How did you get in here?"

"Little of this, little of that." He patted the cushion beside him. "Come on. Let's talk."

Henry didn't move. Either he wouldn't or couldn't—if you had asked him, he wouldn't have known which.

"Please," said the man.

"Who are you?"

"Oh, sorry." He got up. "James Einner." He stuck out a large hand as he approached. Involuntarily, Henry took it, and as he did so James Einner squeezed tight. His other hand swung around, stiff, and chopped at the side of Henry's neck. Pain spattered through

Henry's head, blinding him and turning his stomach over; then a second blow turned out the light.

For a second James Einner held Henry, half elevated, swinging from that hand, then lowered it until the journalist crumpled onto the renovated hardwood floor.

Einner returned to the couch and went through Henry's shoulder bag. He found the letter, counted its pages, then took out Henry's Moleskine journal and pocketed it. He went through the apartment again—he had done this all evening but wanted a final look around to be sure—and took Gray's laptop and flash drives and all his burned CDs. He put everything into a cheap piece of luggage he'd picked up in Prague before boarding the train here, then set the bag beside the front door. All this took about seven minutes, while the television continued its parade of Hungarian pop.

He returned to the living room and opened the terrace doors. A warm breeze swept through the room. Einner leaned out, and a quick glance told him the street was full of parked cars but empty of pedestrians. Grunting, he lifted Henry Gray, holding him the way a husband carries his new wife over the threshold, and, without giving time for second thoughts or mistakes or for casual observers to gaze up the magnificent Habsburg facade, he tipped the limp body over the edge of the terrace. He heard the crunch and the two-tone wail of a car alarm as he walked through the living room to the kitchen, hung the bag over his shoulder, and quietly left the apartment.

2

Four months later, when the American showed up at Szent János Kórház—the St. John Hospital—on the Buda side of the Danube, the English-speaking nurses gathered around him in the bleak fifties corridor and answered his questions haltingly. Zsuzsa Papp imagined that, to an outside observer, it would have looked as if a famous actor had arrived in the most unexpected place, for the nurses were all flirting with him. Two of them even touched his arm while laughing at his jokes. He was, they told Zsuzsa later, charming in the way that some superstar surgeons are, and even those few who didn't find him attractive felt compelled to answer his questions as precisely as possible.

They began by correcting him: No, Mr. Gray hadn't come to St. János in August. In August he'd been taken to the Péterfy Sándor Kórház with six broken ribs, a punctured lung, a cracked femur, two broken arms, and a fractured skull. It was there, over in Pest, that he'd been pieced back together by an excellent surgeon ("trained in London," they assured him) but had not woken afterward. "The fracture," one explained, touching her skull. "Too much blood."

The blood had to drain away, and though the doctors held out little hope, they transferred Gray to St. János in September to be observed and cared for. A small, wiry-haired nurse named Bori had been his primary caregiver, and Jana, her taller friend, interpreted everything she told the American. "We have—had—hope, you understand? The damage to the head is very bad, but his heart continue to beat and he can breathe on his own. So no problem with the small brain. But we wait to see when the blood will leave his head."

It took weeks. The blood did not completely drain away until October. During that time, his bills were paid by his parents, who came from America only once to visit but made regular bank transfers to the hospital. "They want to take him to America," Jana explained, "but we tell them it's impossible. Not with his condition."

"Of course," the American said.

Despite his condition stabilizing, the coma persisted. "These things, they are sometimes a mystery," another nurse explained, and the American gave a sad, understanding nod.

Then Bori blurted out something and raised her hands happily.

"And then he wakes up!" Jana translated.

"That was just a week ago?" the American said, smiling.

"December fifth, the day before Mikulás."

"Mikulás?"

"Saint Nicholas Day. When the children get boots full of candy from Nicholas."

"Fantastic."

They called his parents to deliver the good news, and once he was able to talk they asked if he wanted to call someone—perhaps the pretty Hungarian girl who'd come to visit once a week?

"His girlfriend?" the American asked.

"Zsuzsa Papp," said another nurse.

"I think Bori is jealous," said Jana. "She falls in the love with him."

Bori frowned and asked rapid, embarrassed questions that everyone refused to answer with anything but laughter.

"So Zsuzsa came, did she?"

"Yes," another nurse said. "She was very happy."

"But he was not," Jana said, then listened a moment to Bori. "I mean, he is happy to see her, yes, but his mood. He was not happy."

"What?" asked the American, confused. "He was sad? Angry?"

"Frightened," said Jana.

"I see."

Jana listened to Bori, then added, "He tell his parents not to come. He say they are not safe, he will come home hisself."

"So that's where he went? He went home?"

Jana shrugged. Bori shrugged. They all shrugged.

No one knew. After four days of consciousness, just two days before this charming American arrived looking for his friend, Henry Gray disappeared. Not a word to anyone, not even a good-bye to the heartsick Bori. Just a quiet escape in the late afternoon, once all the doctors had gone home and Bori was in the break room eating her dinner.

The memory of losing her favorite patient wet Bori's eyes, and she tried to hide them with a hand. The American looked down at her and placed his own hand on her shoulder, provoking jealousy in at least two of the nurses. "Please," he said. "If Henry does get in touch with you, tell him that his friend Milo Weaver is looking for him."

That was the way Zsuzsa understood the event when Bori called her at the offices of *Blikk*, a popular local tabloid, to pass on the information about the friend. Then Zsuzsa went to the hospital and approached Jana and the others for their versions.

Had the hospital visit been the only sighting, she would have tried to find this Milo Weaver. As it was, he kept appearing, and what struck her was that each time he appeared, though his questions remained the same, his manner and history changed.

With the nurses, he was a friend of Henry's family, a pediatrician from Boston. At Pótkulcs, Henry's favorite bar, the two Csillas talked of Milo Weaver, a chain-smoking novelist based in Prague who had come down to crash at Henry's place. To Terry and Russell and Johann and Will and Cowall, all of whom he'd easily tracked down at their regular café haunts on Liszt Ferenc Square, he was Milo Weaver, AP stringer, following up on a story Henry had filed last summer on the economic tensions between Hungary and Russia. From a Sixth District cop, she learned that he had even arrived to speak with his chief, representing Henry's parents' law firm, and wanted to know what had been learned about their son's disappearance.

Before his vanishing act, Henry had made it clear to her: Trust no one except Milo Weaver, but tell him nothing. It was a riddle— what use was trust if it meant silence? "You mean you don't trust him?"

"Maybe. Look, I don't know. If someone can toss me out of my window only hours after I got that letter, then what protection can any one man offer? I just mean that you should talk to him, but don't tell him where I am."

"How can I? You won't tell me where you're going."

Despite what Henry might have thought, Zsuzsa wasn't about to follow his words blindly. She was a good journalist—a better journalist than dancer—and knew that Henry, for all his momentary fame, would always be a hack. Fear kept objectivity an arm's length from him at all times.

So when her editor called to tell her that an American film producer named Milo Weaver had come to the office looking for her, she reassessed her position. "Did you tell him how to find me?"

"Jesus, Zsuzsa. I'm not completely corrupt. He left a phone number."

It was a way. The safety of the telephone would allow her all the distance she needed for a quick vanishing act, as quick as Henry's had been.

Even so, she didn't call. This man named Milo Weaver had too many professions, too many stories. Henry's golden letter had said to trust him, but there was a world of difference between Milo Weaver and a man calling himself Milo Weaver. There was no way for her to know which was which.

She did have some information on him; she'd scoured the Internet months ago, after Henry's attempted murder. A CIA employee, an analyst at a fiscal oversight office—assumedly the same clandestine Department of Tourism that Thomas Grainger had run. At the time of Henry's attack, though, Weaver had been in a prison in New York state for some financial fraud—"misappropriation" was the most specific word she could track down. There were no photographs anywhere.

So she settled on silence, which was just as well since she had nothing to tell. That Henry had woken from his months of sleep with weak muscles and a dry mouth and the utter conviction that *They* would soon be after him—yes, she could share these facts, but anyone looking for Henry would know them already. The details of his attack? Henry had run through what he remembered many times to be sure she had it all. He'd even begun exposing his own flaws, crying as he apologized for having lied to her: He never could have used her on the story.

"You think I didn't know that?" she'd asked, and that finally ended the embarrassing tears.

She stayed at a friend's house in the Seventeenth District, took the week off from work, and even skipped her regular weekend slot at the 4Play Club. She avoided all the places she knew, because if he was any good, this Milo Weaver would already know them, too.

Despite the measure of paranoia, her exile was refreshing, because she finally had time to read, which she mistakenly devoted to Imre Kertész. With a secret agent looking for her and Henry gone, reading the Nobel Prize winner just made her think of suicide.

On the fourth day of what she was starting to think of as her vacation from life itself, she had coffee with her friend, then watched from his window as he left for work. She left the Kertész novel by the television and showered, then dressed in some fashionable sweats. She'd decided to go out—she would have her second coffee in a nearby café. She packed her phone and Vogues in her purse, grabbed a coat, and used the house keys on the front door. Standing on the welcome mat, silent, was a man about six feet tall. Blond, blue-eyed, smiling. "Elnézést," he said, and the perfectly pronounced Hungarian *Excuse me* distracted her briefly from the fact that he matched the nurses' lush descriptions of Milo Weaver.

It came to her, but too late. He'd reached out, hand tight over her mouth, and shoved her against the wall. With a backward kick he closed the door. He glanced to each side as she tried in vain to bite his fingers, then struck him with her purse. She shouted into his palm, but nothing useful came out, and with his spare hand he ripped the purse from her and threw it at the floor. He only needed one hand on her mouth to keep her still; he was remarkably strong.

In English, he said, "Calm down. I'm not here to hurt you. I'm just looking for Henry."

When she blinked, she felt tears running down her cheeks.

"My name is Milo Weaver. I'm a friend. I'm probably the only useful friend Henry has now. So please, don't scream. Okay? Nod."

Though it was difficult, she did nod.

"Right. Here goes. Quiet, now."

He released her slowly, twitching fingers hovering in front of her face, ready to go in again. She felt the tingle of blood flowing back into her sore lips.

"I'm sorry about that," he said as he rubbed his hands together. "I just didn't want you to panic when you saw me."

"So you attacked me?" she said weakly.

"Good—you speak English."

"Of course I speak English."

"You all right?"

He reached for her shoulder, but she turned before he could touch her again and headed into the kitchen.

He was right behind her the whole way, and as she took out a can of Nescafé and a box of milk with her unsteady hands, he settled against the door frame and crossed his arms over his chest, watching. His clothes looked new; he looked like a businessman.

"What's the story for me?" she asked. "Pediatrician? Novelist? Lawyer? Right—film producer."

When he laughed, she turned to face him. The laugh was genuine. He shook his head. "Depends on the situation. With you I can be honest." He paused. "I can, can't I?"

"I don't know. Can you?"

"What did Henry tell you?"

"About what?"

"About the letter."

She knew blocks of the letter by heart, because for those few days in the hospital, after waking, Henry had demanded she help him remember. His fractured memory had bonded with hers, and they had been able to reassemble enough of it. For reasons of oil, the Department of Tourism, which employed brutal "Tourists" like this one, had killed a religious leader—a mullah—in the Sudan, which had sparked last year's riots. Eighty-six innocents had been killed.

Yes, she knew plenty, but she still wasn't sure about Milo Weaver.

"Just that there was a letter," she said. "There was a story in it. Something big. Do you know what it said?"

"I have an idea."

She said nothing.

"The man who wrote the letter was a friend. I was helping him uncover evidence of an illegal operation, but he was killed. Then I was kicked out of the Company."

"What company?"

"You know what Company."

To avoid his heavy stare, she turned away and set water to boil, then found a bowl of brown sugar cubes.

He said, "The letter told Henry to trust me."

"Yeah. He did say that."

"And what about you?"

"The letter wasn't meant for me," she said to the spoon she dipped into the Nescafé granules, measuring them into cups and spilling some on the counter. He didn't answer, so after a moment she turned again, then dropped the spoon. It clattered against the tiles. He had a pistol in his hand, a small thing no bigger than his fist, and it was aimed at her.

He spoke quietly. "Zsuzsa, you have to understand something. The truth is that if you don't answer my questions, things could turn very bad. I could shoot you in the extremities. I mean your hands and your feet. If you still didn't want to talk, I could keep shooting, a little farther in each time, until you passed out. But you wouldn't die. I'm no doctor, but I do know how to keep a heart beating. You would wake up in your friend's bathtub, in cold water. You'd be scared, and then you would be more scared because of the knife I'd take from that drawer behind you to make more pain. This could go on for days. Trust me on this. And in the end I'd get all the answers I needed. The answers that would only help Henry."

His easy smile returned, but Zsuzsa's knees went bad—first one, then the other. They buckled, and she sank to the floor, her limbs useless. Nausea hit her, and she leaned over, waiting for her break-fast to come up.

Staring at the tiles, which were filthy this close and sprinkled with coffee, she heard something click against the floor, then a rattling, scratching sound. The pistol slid into view and stopped against her hand.

"Take it," she heard him say.

She covered it with her right hand, then used her left to push herself up. He was still in the doorway, still leaning casually, still smiling.

"It's yours," he said. "I'm not going to do anything at all to you. I just want you to know that I can be trusted. If you think at any point that I'm fucking with you, just raise that and put a bullet in my head. Not in my chest—I might get you before you pull the trigger again. In my head," he said, tapping the center of his forehead. "That way, it'll all be finished." He got off the door frame. "I'll be waiting in the living room. Take your time."

It took twenty minutes for her to gather her wits and face him. She considered calling for help, but her friend didn't have a landline, and one glance into the corridor told her that Milo Weaver had picked up her purse on his way. When she passed the front door, she saw the dead bolt was locked and the key had been removed. So she emerged with a tray of two coffees, sugar, milk, and a pistol. She found him on the couch, flipping through the Kertész. "Baffling," he told her.

She placed the tray on the coffee table beside her purse and house keys. Then, remembering, she took back the gun and slipped it into the front pocket of her sweatshirt. "Kertész? You know him?"

"The name, sure. But I mean your language." He looked at the page again and shook his head. "I mean, where does it *come* from?"

"The Urals, maybe. No one knows for sure. It's a great mystery."

He closed the book and placed it on the table, then dropped a sugar cube into his coffee. He sipped at it. He had all the time in the world.

"You want to know about Henry."

"I want to know where he is."

"I don't know."

He took a long breath, then drank more. He said, "I know you were at the hospital before he ran off. Four days in a row, staying hours each time. And you're telling me he didn't mention he'd be leaving?"

"He did say that. He didn't say where."

"Certainly you have some idea."

"He called someone."

"There's something," said Weaver. "Who?"

"I don't know."

"What phone did he use? Yours?"

She shook her head. "One of the nurses'. He wouldn't use mine."

"Why not?"

"The same reason he wouldn't tell me where he was going. He didn't want to put me in danger."

Weaver thought about that, then grinned as if something were funny.

"What?" she said, worried.

"I just don't know how he's going to follow the story alone. Doesn't he want my help?"

She had been standing all this time, the small gun remarkably heavy in her pocket—or perhaps it was just the weight of her fear of it. She didn't like this Milo Weaver. He had none of the charm or sexiness everyone else talked about. Perhaps this was just how CIA men were. They were motivated by their missions, and whatever slowed them down—a terrified lover, perhaps—could be kicked around as needed.

Still, she did have the gun, didn't she? That was something. That, in CIA language, was trust. As she settled on a chair, she took the pistol from her pocket and placed it on her knee.

"Of course he wants your help," she said, "but he said that no one man can help him now. Not when the whole CIA is trying to kill him. He doesn't expect your help anymore."

Weaver seemed confused. "What does that even *mean*?"

"You tell me. Maybe you can also tell me why it took four goddamned months for you to come here and offer help. Can you do that?"

Weaver thought about it, his face settling into a blank stare. Then he set the cup back down on the tray. He stood. Zsuzsa stood, the pistol in both hands.

"Thanks," said Weaver. "You have my phone number in case he gets in touch?"

She nodded.

"Don't underestimate me, and make sure he doesn't either. I can help him get to the bottom of this, and I can protect him. Do you believe that?"

Despite everything, she did.

"Can I have my gun back now?"

She wasn't sure.

His smile returned, and she thought she caught a measure of that famous charm. "It's not loaded. Go ahead and shoot me."

She stared at the pistol, as if by looking she could know. Then she pointed it vaguely in his direction, but pulling the trigger was a far thought. Finally, Weaver stepped forward and snapped the pistol from her hand. He pressed the barrel into his own temple and pulled the trigger. Twice. Zsuzsa flinched as two loud clicks cut through the room, and later she would realize that the most frightening thing that morning was that Milo Weaver didn't flinch at all. He knew the gun was empty, but still . . . not flinching seemed somehow inhuman.

He scooped up the keys and let himself out. She watched him from the window as he left the apartment building and crossed the dead grass. He was speaking on a cell phone, no expression, no hesitation in his stiff shoulders or his relentless gait. He was like a machine.

Part One

JOB NINE

SUNDAY, FEBRUARY 10
TO MONDAY, FEBRUARY 25, 2008

1

He felt that if he could put a name to it, he could control it. Transgressive association? That had the right sound, but it was too clinical to give him a handle on it. Perhaps the medical label didn't matter anyway. The only thing that mattered was the effect it had on him, and on his job.

The simplest things could trigger it—a bar of music, a face, some small Swiss dog crapping on the sidewalk, or the smell of automobile exhaust. Never children, though, which was strange even to him. Only the indirect fragments of his earlier life gave him that punch in the gut, and when he found himself in a freezing Zürich phone booth calling Brooklyn, he wasn't even sure what had triggered it. All he knew was that he had lucked out: No one answered. An early breakfast somewhere, perhaps. Then the machine picked up. Their two voices: a minor cacophony of female tones, laughing, asking him to please leave a message.

He hung up.

No matter the name, it was a dangerous impulse. On its own, it was nothing. An impulsive—maybe compulsive—call to a home that's no longer home, on a gray Sunday afternoon, is fine. When he peered through the booth's scratched glass at the idling white van on Bellerivestrasse, however, the danger became apparent. Three men waited inside that van, wondering why he'd asked them to stop here, when they were on their way to rob an art museum.

Some might not even think to ask the question, because when life moves so quickly looking back turns into a baffling roll call of moral decisions. Other answers, and you'd be somewhere else. In Brooklyn, perhaps, dealing with Sunday papers and advertising supplements, distractedly listening to your wife's summary of the arts pages and your daughter's critique of the morning's television programming. Yet the question returned as it had so many other times over the last three months: How did I end up here?

The first rule of Tourism is to not let it ruin you, because it can. Easily. The rootless existence, keeping simultaneous jobs straight in your head, showing no empathy when the job requires none, and especially that unstoppable forward movement.

Yet that bastard quality of Tourism, the movement, is also a virtue. It leaves no time for questions that do not directly relate to your survival. This moment was no exception. So he pushed his way out, jogged through the stinging cold, and climbed into the passenger seat. Giuseppe, the pimply, skinny Italian behind the wheel, was chewing a piece of Orbit, freshening the air they all breathed, while Radovan and Stefan, both big men, squatted in the empty rear on a makeshift wooden bench, staring at him.

With these men, the lingua franca was German, so he said, "Los."

Giuseppe drove on.

Each Tourist develops his own personal techniques to keep from drowning—verse recitation, breathing exercises, self-injury, mathematical problems, music. This Tourist had once carried an iPod religiously, but he'd given it to his wife as a reconciliation gift, and now he was left with only his musical memories. As they rolled past the bare, craggy winter trees and homes of Seefeld, the southern neighborhood stretching alongside Lake Zürich, he hummed a half-forgotten tune from his eighties childhood, wondering how other Tourists dealt with the anxiety of separation from their families. A stupid thought; he was the only Tourist with a family. Then they turned the next corner, and Radovan interrupted his anxiety with a single statement. "My mother has cancer."

Giuseppe continued driving in his safe way, and Stefan used a rag to wipe excess oil off of the Beretta he'd picked up in a Hamburg market last week. In the passenger seat, the man they knew as Mr. Winter—who toured under the name Sebastian Hall but was known to his distant family as Milo Weaver—glanced back at the broad Serb, whose thick, pale arms were crossed over his stomach, gloved fists kneading his ribs. "I'm sorry to hear that. We all are."

"I'm not trying to jinx anything," Radovan went on, his German muddied by a thick Belgrade accent. "I just had to say something before we did this. You know. In case I don't have a chance later."

"Sure. We get it."

Dutifully, Giuseppe and Stefan muttered their agreement.

"Is it treatable?" Milo Weaver asked.

Radovan looked confused, crammed in between Stefan and a pile of deflated burlap bags. "It's in the stomach. Spread too far. I'm going to have her checked out in Vienna, but the doctor seems to know what he's talking about."

"You never know," Giuseppe said as he turned onto another tree-lined street.

"Sure," Stefan agreed, then went back to his gun, lest he say something wrong.

"You're going to be with us on this?" Milo asked, because it was his responsibility to ask such things.

"Anger helps me focus."

Milo went through the details with them again. It was a simple enough plan, one that depended less on its mechanics than on the element of surprise. Each man knew his role, but Radovan—might he take out his personal troubles on some poor museum guard? He was, after all, the one with a gun. "Remember, there's no need for casualties."

They all knew this, if only because he had repeated it continually over the last week. It had quickly become a joke, that Mr. Winter was their Tante Winter, their old aunt keeping them out of trouble. The truth was that he had been through nearly three months of jobs they knew nothing about, none of which had claimed bystanders. He didn't want these recruits ruining his streak.

This was job number eight. It was still early enough in his return to Tourism that he could keep track, but late enough for him to wonder, and worry, about why all the jobs had been so damned easy.

Number four, December 2007. The whiny voice of Owen Mendel, acting director of Tourism, spoke through his Nokia: *Please, go to Istanbul and withdraw fifteen thousand euros from the Interbank under the name Charles Little. You'll find the passport and account number at the hotel. Fly to London, and in the Chase Manhattan at 125 London Wall open an account with that money. Same name. Make sure customs doesn't find the cash. Think you can handle it?*

You don't ask *why* because that's not a Tourist's prerogative. Simply believe that it's all for the best, that the whiny voice on the line is the Voice of God.

Job two, November 2007: *There's a woman in Stockholm. Sigfreid Larsson. Two esses. She's at the Grand Hôtel on Blasieholmshammen. She's expecting you. Buy her and yourself a ticket to Moscow and make sure she gets to 12 Trubnaya ulica by the eighteenth. Got that?*

Larsson, a sixty-year-old professor of international relations, was shocked but flattered by all the fuss made over her.

Jobs for children; jobs for third-rank embassy staff.

Number five, January 2008: *Now this one is sensitive. Name's Lorenzo Peroni, high-scale arms dealer based in Rome. I'll text you the details. He's meeting with a South Korean buyer named Pak Jin Myung in Montenegro. I want you on top of him from when he leaves his apartment on the eighth until he returns on the fifteenth. No, don't worry about mikes, we've taken care of that. Just keep up the visual, hone your camera work.*

As it turned out, Pak Jin Myung was no arms buyer but one of Peroni's many mistresses. The resulting photographs were more appropriate for English tabloids.

So it went. One more impotent surveillance in Vienna, the order to mail a sealed manila envelope from Berlin to a Theodor Wartmüller in Munich, a one-day Paris surveillance, and a single murder, at the beginning of the month. That order had been sent by text message:

L: George Whitehead. Consider dangerous. In Marseille for week starting Thurs.

George Whitehead, patriarch of a London crime family, looked about seventy, though he was in fact closer to eighty. No bullets were required, just a single push in the hotel steam room. His head cracked against the damp wall planks; the concussion knocked him out for life.

It hardly even felt like murder.

Others might have been pleased by the ease and inconsequence of these assignments. However, Milo Weaver—or Sebastian Hall or Mr. Winter—could not relax, because the ease and inconsequence meant only one thing: They were onto him. They knew, or they suspected, that his loyalties did not lie entirely with them.

Now this, another test. *Get some money together. Ideally, twenty million, but if you can only get five or ten we'll understand.*

Dollars?

Yes, dollars. You have a problem with that?

2

Stefan, perhaps because of nerves, began to tell them about a beautiful girl he knew in Monte Carlo, a dancer who earned an excellent living having sex with animals, which Stefan believed to be the secret French vice. That, too, ruined Milo's inner sound track, and he told the German to shut up. "Give Radovan the gun."

Stefan handed it over.

Giuseppe said, "Just about there."

Milo checked his watch; it was nearly four thirty, a half hour before closing time.

Giuseppe drove through an open gate and across gravel to where three Swiss cars were parked in front of the museum, a nineteenth-century villa once owned by Emil Georg Bührle, a German-born industrialist who had earned part of his fortune selling arms to Fascist Spain and the Third Reich. He left the van idling. A middle-aged couple left the museum, and behind their van, beyond the stone wall, more couples moved along the sidewalk on Sunday outings.

"The four I said, okay? They're close to the front. We don't have time to shop around."

"Ja, Tante," Stefan said as they stretched black ski masks over their heads. Giuseppe remained behind while the others climbed out. Radovan clutched the Beretta against his thigh, and the three men crunched over gravel to the entrance.

When scouting this and four other museums the previous week, Milo had noted the lack of real security, as if it had never occurred to those responsible for the E. G. Bührle Museum that someone might love art a little too much, or just want some easy money. There were two guards in the front, retired Swiss policemen who didn't even carry sidearms. It was Radovan's job to neutralize them, and he did so with gusto, shouting in his heavy accent for them to get on the floor as he waved his pistol around. Perhaps sensing that this was a desperate man, they sank immediately.

Stefan pulled the ticket clerk out from behind her counter and forced her down beside the guards as Milo checked for patrons. There were only two left—an elderly couple in the first room. They stared at him, baffled.

While Radovan kept watch over his prisoners, Milo and Stefan took out their wire cutters. The first snip set off a piercing alarm, but this was expected. Ten minutes, he had figured, minimum. A Monet, a van Gogh, a Cézanne, and a Degas.

With their heavy glass covers, the paintings were unwieldy, so it took both of them to hustle each to the van, while Radovan paced menacingly. Seven minutes into it, Milo tapped Radovan's shoulder. They all withdrew.

Giuseppe laid on the gas.

This, of course, was the easy part. Four paintings worth over a hundred and sixty million dollars in less than ten minutes. No corpses, no injuries, no mistakes. Face masks, the minimum of conversation, and a white van out of town.

Giuseppe kept to the speed limit while behind him Radovan and Stefan slipped the burlap bags over the paintings and chatted about details of the job, the way they might discuss pretty girls they'd met on vacation. The expressions on the guards' faces, the ticket clerk's admirably shaped ass, the old couple's strange air of ease as they watched the robbery take place. Then, without warning, Stefan leaned forward and vomited.

He apologized, but they'd all been through enough jobs to know there was often one person whose nerves finally took control and emptied him completely. There was no shame in it.

Giuseppe got them out of Zürich proper by a confusing sequence of turns he had charted out beforehand. Only once they'd reached the eastward road to Tobelhof did the rigor relax, and for a brief minute they had a peaceful view of the forest rising toward the peak of Zürichberg. A moment of naiveté, as if this peace could be theirs. They passed through Tobelhof's scattered farms, and by the time they reached the urban landscape of Gockhausen, the feeling was gone.

They reentered the forest on the far side of the town and took a left onto an unused dirt road where, a half mile in, a VW van and a Mercedes waited for them in a clearing. They got out and stretched. Radovan gave a Serbian curse of glee—"Jebute!"—before they transferred the paintings to the VW. Giuseppe doused the interior of their white van with a canister of gasoline.

Milo removed a soft leather briefcase from the trunk of the Mercedes. Inside was six hundred thousand dollars' worth of used euro bills in small denominations, divided into three Tesco grocery bags. If asked, he would have explained that they'd been liberated from a drug dealer in Nice, but no one asked. He distributed the bags and shook their hands. He thanked them for their good work, and each told him to call whenever he had another job. Milo wished Radovan luck with his mother. "It took a long time," said Radovan, "but I've finally got my priorities straight. This money will pay for whatever she needs."

"You sound like a good son."

"I am," he said without a hint of modesty. "As soon as a man loses touch with family, he might as well put a bullet in his own head."

Milo gave him an appreciative smile, then shook his hand, but Radovan wouldn't let go.

"You know, Tante, I don't really like Americans. Not since they bombed my hometown. But you—you, I like."

Milo wasn't sure how to take that. "What makes you think I'm American?"

A big grin filled Radovan's face. It was a familiar one, that knowing and vaguely condescending smile prevalent among Balkan men. "Let's just say your German accent is lousy."

"Maybe I'm English. Or Canadian."

A laugh popped from Radovan's mouth, and he slapped Milo's arm. "No, you're American, all right. But I won't hold it against you." He reached into his pocket and handed over Milo's worn passport. He winked. "Sorry, but I like to know who I'm working with. Tschüss."

As Milo watched the Serb proudly join the others at the car, he thought how lucky they both were. Had he lifted something that could have connected Milo to his real name—not this Sebastian Hall passport—Radovan wouldn't have made it out of this forest, and he didn't feel up to killing anyone today.

Once they were gone, he reversed the VW a few more yards away, then walked back and lit the van's upholstery with his Zippo, leaving the doors open. He lit a Davidoff for himself and waited until the red flames had spread, turning blue as they began to melt the dash, filling the interior with poisonous smoke. He put the cigarette out on his heel, tossed it into the growing inferno, then returned to the VW and drove away.

Farther south on the A2, which would eventually take him to Milan, his phone vibrated on the passenger seat. He didn't need to see PRIVATE NUMBER on the screen to know who it was.

However, the voice was not Owen Mendel's. It was deep yet airy, like an educated man still clutching onto his progressive youth. The code, though, was the same.

"Riverrun, past Eve."

"And Adam's," he answered. "Who are you?"

"New, that's what. Alan Drummond. And you, I believe, are Sebastian Hall."

"What happened to Mendel?"

"Temporary placement, until they found me. Rest assured that I'm here to stay."

"Okay." Milo paused. "This isn't just a call of introduction, is it?"

"Please. I don't do those. I'm right to business."

"Then let's get to it."

This Alan Drummond, his new Voice of God, told him to go to Berlin, to the Hotel Hansablick. "The instructions are waiting for you."

"You know I'm in the middle of something."

"I should hope you are. Just take a few days."

"No clues?"

"I think you'll find it self-explanatory."

Two hours later, in a suburb north of Lugano, he transferred the paintings to a garage he'd rented the week before and secured with a combination lock. Because of their weight, it took a while. There was a single fluorescent light overhead, and in its surreal glow he took a moment to examine the paintings uncovered. It was a shame, because according to the plan he'd cobbled together only two of them would return to the world. He lit another Davidoff and tried to decide which would survive and which would not, but couldn't. Count Ludovic Lepic and his two daughters gazed back accusingly because they believed they would never be seen again, and perhaps that was true. Degas had immortalized them in oils nearly a century and a half ago, and at some point a master of industry had picked them up and his estate had hung them for all to see. Next week, with a bit of gasoline and this Zippo, they, or two others, would vanish, as if they had never been.

He locked up and drove on, leaving the Swiss southern Alps for the industrial Lombardy plains. The air outside his window was cold and clean, but in the late-night Italian darkness he could see nothing of the peaks behind him. It was past midnight when he reached the wet, tungsten-bright streets of Milan, and on Viale Papiniano he wiped down and abandoned the VW. He caught an hour-long night train to Bergamo, then a shuttle bus to Orio al Serio Airport, which had an eight-thirty flight to Berlin, the earliest one in the region. He'd left his last tote bag in a Zürich Dumpster before joining his crew for the job, and now carried only what filled his pockets—his pills, Davidoffs, passports, cash and cards, cell phone, and a single keyless key ring with a small remote. He boarded with his Sebastian Hall passport and took a seat over the wing beside a tired teenaged boy. He popped two Dexedrine to stay awake. Once they were in the air, the boy said, "Vacation."

"Excuse me?"

The teen, an Italian with impeccable English, grinned. "The

song you're humming. 'Vacation,' by the Go-Go's." He was clearly proud of his knowledge of a song forgotten by most people by the time he was born.

"So it is," Milo admitted. Then, despite the drugs rattling his nerves and the flash of those answering-machine voices laughing in his head, he passed out.

3

They'd called in early November to ask if he'd be interested in returning to the field. "Your record is excellent, you know." That had been Owen Mendel, full of baffled praise—baffled because he didn't know why this excellent Tourist, who'd even moved on to six years of administration, had been kicked off the Company payroll. Mendel had obviously been left with a severely edited file. "It's up to you, of course, but you know what kind of budgeting pressure we're under these days. If we could get some experienced people like you in the field, we just might make it."

A nice sell. The Company wasn't doing him a favor; he was the Good Samaritan.

He'd known, from the moment he heard Owen Mendel's voice, exactly what would follow. Yevgeny had prepared him. "You'll say yes, of course, and after some refresher course you'll be vetted by the jobs you do. A few weeks. We'll make no contact during the probationary period."

A "few weeks" had grown into three months. Even the great Yevgeny Primakov, secret ear of the United Nations, hadn't figured on that. Nor had he figured on the kind of job that Alan Drummond, Mendel's successor, would assign him in Berlin: a final, impossible vetting.

It was five days after the Zürich job, a little before nine on Friday morning, and he stood on the cold, gusty grounds in front of the Berlin Cathedral. He was caught in the funk of a muddy post-drunk anticipation, trying hard not to look like a vagrant, but it was difficult. All night he'd sought solace in a vodka-based honey liqueur called Bärenfang, but it had only added to his sickness. The rumble of rush-hour traffic rolled toward him; a tour bus with Augsburg plates swerved onto Karl-Liebknecht-Strasse and gasped to a stop not far away.

A white spongy envelope had awaited him, and once he'd gotten it from the Hansablick clerk in exchange for a tip, he'd taken it with him on a long walk, a subway ride, and another walk to a dusty, nondescript pension in Friedrichshain, a bohemian district of what used to be called East Berlin.

Two photographs, from different angles, of a pretty olive-skinned girl, blond from a bottle. Girl: fifteen years old. Adriana Stanescu, only child of Andrei and Rada Stanescu, Moldovan immigrants. On the reverse of one photo:

L0 2/15

Kill the child, and make the body disappear. He had until the end of the week.

He'd burned the instructions Monday, and since then shadowed the Stanescus, examining the details of their lives. Rada Stanescu worked at the Imperial Tobacco factory, while her husband, Andrei, drove under the banner of Alligator Taxi GmbH most evenings. They lived in Kreuzberg among Turkish families and gentrifying Germans, not far south of Milo's pension.

What of the girl, Adriana, who'd been scheduled to die? He'd followed her to the Lina-Morgenstern High School, where her friends were a mix of German and Turkish students. He'd found nothing out of the ordinary.

Don't ask—another Tourism rule. If a girl is to be killed, then she is to be killed. Action is its own reason.

He began walking to the cathedral's ticket office, where the Bavarians from the bus were beating their hands, sending up clouds of breath, waiting for the window to open.

Each morning, Andrei Stanescu dropped off his daughter one block from her school. Why one block? Because (and he read this from her expressions, from the shame in her father's face) Adriana was embarrassed that her father was a taxi driver. Between the drop-off point and school, along Gneisenaustrasse, were six apartment-building entrances and the always-open car-sized entrance to a courtyard. In the afternoon, she returned to him along that same route, always alone. The courtyard, then, was where it would have to happen. If it happened at all.

Every Tourist has a past, and Alan Drummond knew all about those two things that, had the budgets been more favorable, would have barred Milo from Tourism: his wife and daughter. Drummond knew that this seemingly simple task would be more difficult for him than storming the Iranian embassy in Moscow.

Clearly, his suspicions had been right—the department still didn't trust him, and all the jobs that had come before were mere preparation, a three-month incubation before his rebirth into Tourism. An extended test, really, culminating in job nine: an envelope, gray Berlin skies, and the desire to snuff himself rather than see this little job through.

If he'd had no daughter, would it have been easier? He made a conscious decision to not dwell on that, but his brain ignored him. He wondered, foolishly, how many evil acts it takes to make a person evil. Six? Eighteen? Just one? How many had he committed?

What does the Bigger Voice say?

Stop.

He needed to know why. Why Adriana Stanescu had been condemned to death.

He'd picked through their garbage, tracked down bank accounts, took some time to shadow the Stanescus' acquaintances, working around the clock. The only spot on their records was an uncle, Mihai, who worked in a bakery near the Tiergarten. He'd twice been arrested for bringing Moldovans illegally into Germany. A human smuggler, but small-time; otherwise, why would he rise at four each morning and not leave work until after four in the afternoon, flour dusting his hair and stuck to all his hard-to-wash spots?

By all appearances, the Stanescus were precisely what they seemed: a hardworking immigrant family with a lovely teenaged daughter.

Yet even as he investigated, he prepared. On Wednesday, he visited a bar not far from Alligator Taxi's central office and struck up a conversation with Günter Wittinger, a young driver who'd been with Alligator only one year. He'd introduced himself as someone looking to break into the business, someone who needed advice. Despite what Radovan had said, his accent was good enough for this to work. Six beers later, Sebastian lifted Günter's Alligator ID, then slipped out while the man was in the toilet.

By Thursday—which (he saw by the incongruous pink hearts filling store windows) was Valentine's Day—it was prepared. He knew the way in and the way out. The method of execution and the method of disposal. He had the tools—the coarse wire, duct tape, a large roll of plastic, a backsaw—but when the cashier slipped the saw into a stiff paper bag, he nearly collapsed, imagining its use.

Though he could go through all the motions, the fact was that he was ruined. He was no longer Sebastian Hall, Tourist, but Milo Weaver, father. Then he broke all the laws of good sense and called his own father.

It was irrationally stupid. If his Voice of God found out he was whispering secrets to a senior UN official, he'd be dead. Even the old man became short with him on the phone. "You don't *need* me, Misha. You just think you need me."

"No, I do need you. Now."

"It's a simple thing. You've got it all planned out. So go do it."

"You don't understand. She looks just like Stephanie."

"She looks nothing like Stephanie. This girl is twice Stephanie's age."

"Doesn't matter," Milo said, because now he knew. "It's done. Our deal is finished. I'm not killing that girl just so you can have your source."

Milo noticed that parental responsibility had done nothing to move the old man. This, though—the threat of losing an informer within the CIA—led Yevgeny Primakov to sigh and say, "Meet me in the Berliner Dom at nine in the morning. We'll join the crowds."

Before leaving that morning, Milo had scrubbed down the Friedrichshain pension and thrown away his toiletries and the two changes of clothes he'd picked up at KaDeWe. No matter what happened, he'd decided, today he would be finished with this damned city. To ensure that no one back at the Avenue of the Americas could follow his treasonous path, he'd taken apart his phone.

Now it was nine, and the Bavarians were trickling inside.

He approached the ticket window. The vendor, an old woman who'd lived in Berlin since its former life as three hundred and fifty square miles of rubble, squinted suspiciously when he said he wanted to see the church. He looked as hungover as he was, but his five-euro bill was clean enough.

4

Somehow, Yevgeny Primakov had gotten into the cold church before him, though Milo had entered just behind the last Bavarian. The old man was standing beneath a window topped by a biblical painting and the beatitude *Selig sind, die reines Herzens sind*. Blessed are the pure of heart. Milo's alcohol-stunted vision wasn't strong enough to read this, but he'd visited the church before and knew it was there.

His father didn't bother looking at him. He stood with long, knotty hands clasped behind his back, gazing up at the painting. It had been five months since their last meeting, and Yevgeny Primakov was exactly as he remembered him. Thin white hair; fragile frame; thick eyebrows and a tendency to swipe at his cheek with the forefinger of his left hand. The same exorbitant suits, which he imagined were de rigueur at all his United Nations functions. Milo, who was taller with dark features but the same heavy eyes, could never imagine aging to look like this.

That previous meeting had been like this one—an unconscionable risk. Milo had been out of jail less than a week when, late one night, frustrated and drunk, he climbed out of his Newark apartment's window, crawled down the fire escape, and snuck into the opposite building where his twenty-four-hour shadow had been holing up. He knew the face—the young surveillance operative had been on him since the bus from prison—and knew who he was working for. He unlocked the man's door with a screwdriver and a homemade pick and found him dozing on a cot beneath the open window, beside a video camera with a stack of tapes and a telescopic microphone. Fast-food wrappers and cups were scattered across the floor. He woke the kid with the screwdriver to his neck and said, very quietly, "You'll tell that Russian bastard to meet with me within forty-eight hours."

"Er . . . Russian?" the kid managed.

"The one who pulls your strings. The one even the UN doesn't know is doing its sneaky work. You call him and tell him to bring everything on the senator."

"What senator?"

"The one that cost me my family."

Thirty-five hours later, Primakov had met him in that same dirty room, overdressed as usual, and criticized his description of the man in question. "No," Yevgeny told him in Russian. "You cost yourself your own family, by being a liar." He'd brought along the file on Senator Nathan Irwin anyway.

Not that it told Milo much that he didn't already know, because someone like Irwin made sure the crucial details of his otherwise public life remained private. The senator had been behind last year's Sudanese debacle—the murder of a Muslim cleric, which had led to riots that had claimed more than eighty lives—and his desperation to cover it up had led to more deaths, among them two of Milo's close friends, and prison time for Milo. "This man may be at the top of your grievances list," Yevgeny had said, "but that doesn't mean he's responsible for all your life's disappointments."

Now, five months later, the old man stared up at the painting that had caught his fancy and spoke to the figures, again in Russian. "I've been looking into this. It might be retribution against the uncle. The baker. You didn't check on him, did you?"

"He's had some trouble with the law. I watched him. He's clean enough."

"Well, I did more than watch. Mihai Stanescu's involved in immigrant affairs. He works with incoming easterners and sets them up with jobs. That's how the girl's family got here. Sometimes he sneaks them in. He's got connections with the Russian mafia in Transnistria—which is another way of saying he's got government connections. I'm guessing he's using those immigrants to transport heroin into Germany."

Milo didn't quite believe it. "So? Why kill his niece?"

"Maybe he's been warned. Maybe the kid's involved."

"She's not."

"So you keep saying."

"I'm right, Yevgeny."

His father didn't answer immediately, because three Bavarians materialized close behind them and whispered in awed tones, gesturing up at the painting, one waving his camera around. Once they'd moved on, he said, "You know as well as I do that it would take a lot longer than a week to find out why your people want some girl dead. Just because New York won't tell you doesn't mean there isn't a reason."

Milo didn't bother answering, because the subject had moved beyond argument by now. No evidence would sway him.

Primakov turned to look at his son, though at first he focused past him to take in the milling tourists sprinkled throughout the cathedral. His focus drew back, and he frowned. "You look absolutely terrible, Misha. You stink."

"Perils of the job."

Primakov turned back to the painting. "My opinion? You're probably right. This girl has nothing to do with anything, and her death will serve no one's interests. Except, of course, your immediate supervisor's. Who is he?"

Even now, Primakov was trying to extract what he could. "Alan Drummond."

"He's new, then? I thought Mendel was running it."

"Drummond says he's gone now."

"And this Drummond is . . . ?"

"A voice on the telephone."

Without turning to face him, Primakov said, "You didn't check up on the voice on the telephone asking you to kill little girls?"

Milo stared at the back of his father's head. "Yale. Marines—Afghanistan for two years. Moved to the Company in '05. Arms Control Intelligence Staff. Requested transfer to Congressional Affairs the next year. Can't say how he got to Tourism. Friends, I suppose."

"Who's he friends with?"

"Don't know, but it can't be nobody."

Primakov swatted at his cheek. "It makes sense, then. Mendel's been vetting you the slow way. Easy jobs. This Drummond takes over, and he wants to show his government sponsors what a big shot he is; he wants Tourism up and running. So he looks at your file and notices your daughter. Ideally, he'd find a six-year-old for you to take care of, but that's a lot to ask anyone, even a Tourist. So he doubles the age and pulls out a random name."

"Then what I said stands. It's finished. I'm not killing some kid just to clear my name with New York."

"I'd suggest you think about it first."

"I've been thinking for a week, Yevgeny." He paused. "Mother won't allow it."

The old man swiped at his cheek again. "Been hearing her voice again?"

"Occasionally."

The fact that his son was listening to a dead woman didn't faze Yevgeny Primakov. "You don't have to kill her, you know. You said they want no traces, no body. Disappearance is enough."

"Hold her in a basement somewhere? Thanks for the help."

He turned to leave, but Primakov caught his arm, and they walked together down the southern aisle. "You're strung out. Pills again?"

"Not many."

"We need you healthy, Misha. I don't want you buried yet. Neither does Tina. Have you talked to her?"

Quick, elastic memories stretched into his head. That last meeting with his wife—November, the day after the Company came calling. Their counseling sessions had been circling around the same arguments, never moving forward. Trust—that was the issue. Tina had learned too much about her husband. No one, she'd explained in front of the therapist, likes to feel like the fool in a relationship. Over the weeks he'd seen no sign of forgiveness, so he said yes to the Company, and the next day announced his new job with the vague descriptor *field work*. The therapist, noticing the sudden chill in the room, asked Tina if she had something she felt like saying. Tina stroked the corner of her long, sensual lips. *Well, I was going to suggest he move back in with Stef and me. That's off the table now, isn't it?*

The worst timing.

"Misha?"

The old man was grabbing his shoulders, pulling him deeper into the shadows.

"No need to cry over it, son. She's still your wife, and Stephanie will always be your daughter. There's plenty of hope."

Milo wiped his cheeks dry, not even embarrassed anymore. "You don't actually know that."

The old man grinned; his dentures were a blinding white. "Sure I do. Unlike you, I've been stopping in to visit my daughter-in-law and granddaughter."

This surprised him. "What did you say?"

"The truth, of course. I told her all about your mother, how she died, and why you kept your childhood, and me, a secret."

"Did she understand?"

"Really, Misha. You don't give people enough credit. Least of all your wife." He rubbed his son's back. "She knows you're not able to get in touch now. But when you're able, I think it wouldn't be a bad idea to call on her."

It was the best news he'd gotten in months. For almost a minute, Adriana Stanescu ceased to exist, and he could breathe. Still hungover, yes, but his feet were stable. He cleared his throat and again wiped his face. "Thanks, Yevgeny."

"Don't mention it. Let's go fix your little problem."

5

They left five minutes apart, taking separate routes to an apartment near Hausvogteiplatz and its flower-petal fountain. The renovated two-bedroom on the third floor was registered to a Lukas Steiner, marked on the mailboxes Milo passed on his way up. When he asked, Primakov was elusive. "Steiner's a friend, even if he doesn't know it. Luckily, he's on holiday in Egypt. And no," he added when he saw what was in Milo's hand, "you can't smoke in here."

It took them two hours and a pot of coffee to hammer out a suitable plan. More than once, his father would stop and say, "Look, I know you don't like it, but killing her might be the only option."

"It's not an option."

Primakov seemed to understand, though his understanding failed him now and then, and he restated his opinion with different words. Finally, Milo struck the dining room table in a childish fit of anger. "Enough! Don't you get it?"

"But really, Misha—"

"You think I could ever go home again if I did that?"

This obviously hadn't occurred to him, and he let it go.

The old man occasionally asked casual questions about his life, though since a Tourist's life is the same as his work, he was in effect requesting intel on his son's jobs. Milo was too exhausted to bother lying. Besides, the man had saved his life last year, and the sooner he handed over information the sooner he'd be free of that debt. "A robbery. Should be wrapped up in a few days."

"Robbery? What is it, diamonds? Some politician's boudoir?"

"Art museum."

As he stirred his coffee, Primakov seemed to enjoy the images those two words provoked, and then he didn't. He soured visibly and placed the spoon on the counter. "Zürich?"

"Yes."

Primakov sipped his coffee. "This is the problem with the world, you know."

"Is it?"

"No one thinks about the bigger picture anymore, just his own gain. Robbing an art museum is like robbing a library; there's no integrity to it. Great art hangs in museums for the betterment of society, for the man on the street."

"For the proletariat?"

"Wipe that smile off your face. It's the social contract you've broken. Not that you care, and not that they care in the Avenue of the Americas. Whose idea was it?"

Milo had seldom seen him so angry. "Mine. I needed to collect money. This was the easiest and quickest way I could think of."

"Easiest and quickest?" Primakov let out a rare but bitter laugh. "You've got a Degas, a Monet, a van Gogh, and a Cézanne—the biggest art heist in Swiss history. How do you expect to sell those off? You think no one's going to notice?"

"Let me worry about that."

"Oh yes," said the old man. "I'll let you worry about it, because to you those paintings are just a pile of money." He shook his head. "If I'd raised you, you'd know better."

"If you'd raised me, Yevgeny, we wouldn't be here in the first place."

They returned to the plan. Its initial steps had never been in question—Primakov agreed that Milo's scheme to lure Adriana into the courtyard between her school and her father's taxi was suitable enough. The question was what would follow, and how quickly Primakov could arrange things on his side.

Very quickly, it turned out. As a man who commanded his own intelligence unit hidden within the folds of the United Nations' baroque superstructure, who could act with relative freedom because so few knew his office even existed, Yevgeny Primakov only needed to make two calls.

They decided to put the plan into effect that afternoon.

Milo filled his coffee-bitter stomach with garlic chicken from a Chinese diner, then picked up a ten-year-old BMW 3 Series with enough trunk space from outside a drab office block in Berlin-Mitte. It took about forty seconds for the Company-issue remote on his key ring to find the right combination; the car bleeped and unlocked. He slipped inside, pulling the door shut, and forced open the panels around the ignition tumbler with a screwdriver he'd lifted from Lukas Steiner's apartment, connected the cables, then used the screwdriver to turn the ignition. He pulled out into the Berlin traffic. Hopefully the job would be done before anyone noticed the car was missing.

He was in Kreuzberg by four, parked inside the courtyard on Gneisenaustrasse. The apartments that looked down on his BMW were full of young professionals, most of whom would be at work. For fifteen minutes, he sat behind the wheel, waiting. When a retiree wandered in to use the trash bins, he lay down as if searching for something that had dropped under the passenger seat.

By the time the students were released from their imprisonment at four thirty, he had used a T-shirt to wipe down the seats, steering wheel, gearshift, and handles and then taken his position by the courtyard entrance. The broad street, cut down the middle by a median of leafless trees, was packed with shops, and nearby he noted a small Sri Lankan and Indian restaurant, the Chandra Kumari, its strong scent filling the street. Then, farther down and across the street, he spotted a navy blue Opel sedan with Berlin plates and two Germans inside, looking intensely bored.

It was that, the look of boredom, so intense that it could only be fake, that caught his eye. Then the familiarity. It took about a minute to figure it out: Earlier in the week, while surveying the Imperial Tobacco factory where Rada Stanescu worked, he'd seen that same car. The same two men who, from their dress, hair, and glasses, looked German. One young—late twenties—the other somewhere past fifty. The same men. The same boredom.

He fought the impulse to jump back into the safety of the court-yard. Instead, he glanced at his watch and thought it through. Only two people knew where he was—Yevgeny and his new master, Alan Drummond. Of them, only Drummond had known where he was earlier in the week.

Alan Drummond still didn't trust him, and so, rather than as-sign another Tourist or depopulate a curious embassy, he had asked the Germans to run a casual surveillance. *No, not a terrorist, just a potential problem. All we need is a report on his movements.*

This, of course, was another level of the vetting. If the Germans saw him molesting a schoolgirl—or worse, killing her—they wouldn't sit idly by as the crime was committed. Drummond, like any mani-pulator, was raising the stakes of his final exam. Whether or not Milo had the stomach for the job was one thing; Drummond also wanted to know that he had the chops for it.

Despite a fresh wave of anxiety that tickled the Chinese food in his guts, this changed nothing. If the plan went properly, his minders wouldn't prove more than a distraction, Alan Drummond be damned.

Adriana Stanescu, it turned out, was not a stupid girl. Despite being ashamed of her parents' professions, she knew, as most chil-dren do, which of her parents' commands made sense. Not speaking to strangers, for instance—Adriana had been taught that one. When Milo said, "Entschuldigung," *Excuse me*, she only hesitated in mid-step, then continued. He tried again. "Adriana. Your father, Andrei, told me to pick you up. He's stuck over in Charlottenburg."

When the girl stopped, her little backpack, emblazoned with a manga superhero, bounced against her thin back. She turned to him. "Who are you?"

She was a clean-cheeked beauty, beautiful in an entirely differ-ent way than his own daughter, but that made it no easier. "Günter." He took out the Alligator Taxi ID, on which he'd pasted his own picture. "Look, all I know is Andrei said you'd prefer if I parked out of sight. Maybe you'd be embarrassed by the taxi, I don't know.

Anyway," he said as he shot a thumb over his shoulder, "I'm right in there if you want me to drive you home."

Adriana considered her choices, and perhaps it was the shame of her embarrassment, the fact that even her father's co-worker knew about it, that made her nod. "Okay. Danke."

He politely let her go first, a gust of sweet children's perfume filling his nose as she passed. He watched the Japanese cartoon character bounce as they entered the courtyard and left the Germans' field of vision. He slipped on a pair of leather gloves. Though coffee and lunch had cleared away his hangover, he still felt sick, and that little animated creature—what was it? a mouse? a dog?—just made him queasier.

Once inside the courtyard, facing three parked cars, Adriana stopped and turned around. "Where's your taxi?" She wasn't afraid, just curious.

This was the hardest part, the messy part. He'd toyed with the idea of telling her everything, but she wouldn't believe him. Of course she wouldn't. She would put up a fight, scream, bolt into the street. She no doubt remembered the story of Natascha Kampusch who, surviving eight years of imprisonment after being kidnapped at the age of ten, had finally found a way to escape just two years ago.

The only answer was force. So when she said, "Where's your taxi?" he smiled and raised an arm to point. As she turned to look again, he stepped closer, clapped a hand over her mouth and nose, and reached an arm around her stomach to grab her right elbow. He lifted her high, her legs kicking, muted squeals leaking from between his gloved fingers, but she was small enough for him to carry to the BMW as he sought a point four inches down from her elbow, a pressure point called Colon 10. Once by the trunk, he kept up the pressure, squeezing her stomach, pressing the nerve in her arm, and cutting off her air. Any one of these points, if dealt with violently, could have knocked her out, but he didn't want to hurt her. So he did all three at once, until her kicks slowed and she fainted.

He turned her limp body around and listened to her breaths. He pried open her eyes—bloodshot, but okay. She would be unconscious for no more than ten minutes.

With her body over one arm, he popped open the trunk and laid her inside. He quickly used a roll of duct tape to seal her lips and bind her feet and ankles. Once finished, he made a mistake: He paused to look down at her again. He took in her entire length, folded carefully into the trunk, and his stomach convulsed. He slammed the trunk and ran to the driver's side. He got the door open and threw himself across the seat. He waited, but in the end his stomach was stronger than Stefan's had been.

From his first *Entschuldigung* to this moment, two minutes had passed.

He backed out of the courtyard, made a U-turn at the next corner, then drove south. At the intersection of Gneisenaustrasse and Mehringdamm, he passed an Alligator Taxi with Andrei Stanescu behind the wheel, looking at his watch. In the rearview, the Opel sedan pulled slowly into the road and kept a steady distance behind him.

It took fifteen minutes to reach Tempelhof Airport's long-term parking lot. By then, Adriana had awakened, as he had expected she would, but during the fast drive down the B96, he hadn't heard a thing. Only when he slowed at the entrance and stopped to take an automated parking ticket did he hear her kicking against the walls of her tiny prison. His stomach went bad again, but he kept it under control, and once he'd parked, the sound of her struggling seemed incomprehensibly loud. He got out, leaving the car unlocked and the screwdriver in place. He followed her noises to the trunk. He took out his wallet and flipped through it as if counting cash, but said in German, "Adriana, it's going to be okay. Nothing will happen to you. In a few minutes someone else will take you out. Go with him. He's here to protect you."

If it weren't for the duct tape, Adriana Stanescu might have shouted German or elaborate Moldovan curses at him, but all he heard was wordless moans and three sharp kicks of her bound feet against the inside of the trunk. He ran to catch an airport shuttle arriving at a nearby stop. Just beyond the stop, the Opel had pulled into a space but kept idling. At the sight of Milo running toward the bus, the car backed out again. He moved to the rear of the half-full bus and watched the sedan follow him to the airport.

6

Milo had nearly expected failure, but since any good Tourist's travel plans are often thrown awry, failure didn't concern him. In fact, a part of him wished for it—perhaps at the airport ticket booth (had there been a person handing out tickets), or in the parking lot (had the German shadows decided to check his car before shadowing the bus). If failure stopped him in his tracks, he could end the pointless game. Not only this particular job, but all jobs, forever.

It didn't fail. The Germans followed him to the mostly empty airport—it was scheduled to close down later that year—and took notes as he bought a ticket for the next departing flight, to Dortmund. He depended on his Sebastian Hall papers too much to risk them, so he used his emergency documents—a U.K. passport that gave his name as Gerald Stanley, resident of Gloucester.

They watched him wait for the 6:50 P.M. departure. Out in the lot, he knew, his father parked beside the BMW, opened the trunk, and with the help of some friends transferred the struggling girl to another car in order to save her life.

His shadows tired before boarding began. He imagined that they were going to check out the BMW, but it would now be empty.

Yet by the time he was on the plane, taxiing down the old Tempelhof runway, his surety faded. Would Yevgeny keep his promise? It was a big responsibility: Keep the girl hidden for a month or

two while the police searched for her. The parents could make honest cries of despair, and after the attention had died down Yevgeny
would contact them. The child is fine, he would say, but the only
way to get her back safely is to keep her a secret, to leave your lives in
Berlin and move away—perhaps return to Moldova—under new
names, where you can live together in peace. Yevgeny would take care
of the particulars—the passports, transportation, visas if necessary—
but he would have to be assured of their silence.

A telling detail from their debate had been Yevgeny's doubt that
the girl's parents would be willing to leave their lives for the sake of
Adriana. "Of course they would agree to it immediately, but later,
when they're trapped in some lonely town far from Western civilization, don't you think they might change their minds? Contact old
friends and family?"

It told him that Yevgeny couldn't imagine sacrificing his own
future for the sake of either of his daughters, much less for the out-
of-wedlock son who'd caused him more grief, probably, than he had
been worth. As his plane crested cloud, Milo wondered if the old
man, after some consideration, would realize what trouble this plan
was and decide to end all their problems with a bullet.

He would have to see for himself. In a few weeks, he decided, he
would demand to visit the girl.

Exhausted, he burned the Alligator ID and his Gerald Stanley
papers in Dortmund and spent the night in a hotel as Sebastian Hall.
He also put his phone back together, but no one called. In the morning, he bought a change of clothes in the Westenhellweg shopping
center, rented a car, and drove through the Ruhr, where industrial and
once-industrial cities like Bochum and Essen passed; then the landscape turned to farmland as he continued into the Netherlands. By
Saturday afternoon, he'd reached Amsterdam, turned in his car, and
boarded a bus heading to Belgium. Only once he'd taken a room at
Antwerp's Hotel Tourist that evening did he pick up some German
newspapers. The only sign of Milo Weaver's trail of destruction was
a brief update, on the arts pages, on the lack of progress on the E. G.
Bührle theft. There was no mention of Adriana Stanescu—the Berlin
police would be waiting seventy-two hours before raising the alarm.

He ate a dinner of beef stewed in red wine with pearl onions, the obligatory french fries, and two half liters of Vondel brown ale. The meal left him tired again, so he climbed up to his meager room. Before sleep came, a cell phone melody jolted him.

"Yeah?" he said irritably.

"Riverrun, past Eve."

"And Adam's."

"Nice job, Hall. We've even heard of it over here. The family's been hounding the police."

"I'm glad you're pleased."

"None of us can figure out where you put her. In Kreuzberg?"

"Ask me no questions, Alan."

"I am asking you, Sebastian."

The lie came out smoothly because it had been practiced. "There was a second car in the courtyard. That's where I put her. After your Germans left me at the Tempelhof gate, I doubled back. I picked up the car and drove her out to the countryside."

"What Germans?"

"The ones you sent to watch over me."

Drummond paused, perhaps wondering about the uses and misuses of irony. "You lost me. I didn't send anyone."

"Doesn't matter. It's done."

"It might matter. If someone's following you—"

"No one's following me now."

Another pause. "Where are you?"

It was a pointless question, as Drummond's computer charted the location of all his Tourists' phones. "Antwerp."

"You'll be heading back to Zürich now?"

"Yeah."

"First thing when you arrive, drop by the Best Western Hotel Krone. There'll be a letter for you."

He rubbed his eyes. "Listen, I've got things to prepare."

"Won't take long, Hall. Trust me on that. Just follow the instructions and you'll be done in no time."

The line went dead.

7

From hotel to hotel, the trip took nearly nine hours, placing him in the Best Western's arid lobby by six Sunday evening. He drove most of the way in a Toyota he'd picked up on an Antwerp side street using his key ring, then dumped the car just over the Swiss border in Basel, wiped it down with a towel he found in the trunk, and took an hour-long train to Zürich Hauptbahnhof, where the previous night's snow had blackened into mud.

He gave his Tourism name to a demure desk clerk with tight, tired eyes and received an envelope with SEBASTIAN HALL scribbled across it. As he headed back to the front doors, he realized he was being watched by a man and a woman, placed strategically at opposite ends of the lobby, wearing matching dark suits, one clutching a *Herald Tribune*, the other an *Economist*. They watched him stop at the doors, where he read the note. One word: *Outside.*

He found a spot on busy, cold Schaffhauserstrasse, beyond the reach of some inconspicuous security cameras at the next corner. The two lobby watchers didn't follow him out.

It only took five minutes. A gray Lincoln Town Car made wet sounds through the dirty snow as it pulled up to the curb. The back door opened, and a man not much older than him—maybe forty—peered out. That now familiar voice said, "Riverrun, Hall. Get inside."

He did so, and as the car started moving again Drummond said, "We finally meet like civilized people." He gave a tight-lipped smile but made no attempt to shake hands.

He was young for a Tourism director, and his dark hair was long enough to be pulled back behind his ears—far from his time in the marines. He had reading glasses in his shirt pocket and a broad, all-American chin.

"Pleased to meet you, sir," Milo said, watching the lights of Zürich pass by. "You in town just to see me?"

"You'd like to think that," said Drummond, still smiling. "No—Kosovo's proclaiming its independence soon. I'm in for a little discussion with some representatives."

"Should be heated."

"You think so?"

"Depends on our policy. Serbia won't take it sitting down. At least Kosovo waited until the Serb elections were finished. If they'd done it beforehand, the nationalists would have swept the vote."

The smile vanished. "I wasn't too sure about you, Hall. I got some wind about you causing major havoc last year. Enough that I wouldn't have brought you back. You're too . . ." He snapped his fingers, but the word wouldn't be summoned. "Your Tourism career ended seven years ago with—the reports tell me—a breakdown. Then you moved into administration and—I'm just being honest here, you understand—and your record in the Avenue of the Americas was not particularly stellar. As for the way it ended . . ." He shook his head. "Well, you were accused of killing Tom Grainger, my predecessor." He squeezed his lips together and cleared his throat. "Anything to say about all this?"

Milo didn't have much to say, because, looking into Drummond's smug face, he lost all desire to impress the man. He tried anyway. "I was cleared of those charges."

"Well, I *know* that. They do let me see files now and then. It was another Tourist who killed Grainger."

"Yes."

"Now, that Tourist—him, you killed."

"You seem very well informed, sir."

"I've got facts, Sebastian. Plenty of them. It's the messiness that troubles me. A Tourism director dead. A Tourist. Not to mention Terence Fitzhugh, the Senate liaison . . . *suicide*, if you trust the files."

"Angela Yates," said Milo.

"Right. An embassy staffer. She was the first to go, wasn't she?" Milo nodded.

"All this messiness. All this blood. With you at the center of it."

Milo wondered if he'd really been summoned to Zürich to be accused of murder again. So he waited. Drummond didn't bother speaking. Milo finally said, "I guess you'll have to ask Mendel why he brought me back."

"He didn't tell you?"

"Something about budgets."

Drummond stared at him, thinking this over. "Messy or not, you're enough of a pro to be let in on a few things. Last year's budget problems have intensified, and Grainger turning up dead did nothing for us in Washington. It seemed to echo all our enemies' arguments. That we're irresponsible and expensive, financially and in terms of human lives."

"Sounds about right, sir."

"Sense of humor. I like that. The point is that by now when we lose a Tourist we don't have the resources to replace him. In Mendel's estimation, you had at least been trained before, and all it would take was a relatively cheap catch-up course."

"I was cut-rate."

Drummond grinned.

"How many have we lost?"

"Tourists? Enough. Luck isn't always on our side."

That struck Milo as an entirely banal way to explain away the deaths of human beings, but he set aside his annoyance and turned to the window as they merged onto a highway, heading out of town.

"Last year," Drummond said, "when things went sour for you, was there anyone outside the department who knew the details of what happened?"

"Janet Simmons, a Homelander—she learned a lot. I don't think she got the whole story, but she's smart enough to put some things together."

"We've vetted her," Drummond said. "Is that all?"

Yevgeny Primakov knew everything, but that was a treason he didn't feel up to admitting. "She's the only living person. She and Senator Nathan Irwin."

"The senator knows everything?"

"Of course. He was the one behind the Sudanese operation."

"You know this?"

"No real evidence, but yes, I know it."

A pause. "Senator Irwin's the only one keeping the department alive. I don't think we need to worry about him. We can thank him for any operational budget we still enjoy."

Milo realized with dismay that the senator was quite possibly Drummond's government sponsor, the friend who had landed him his new job in Tourism. But all he said was, "Do all these questions have a point? Sir?"

Drummond cleared his throat. "Look, Hall. I didn't call you here to play around with you." He produced a looser smile, to show how human he was. "I called you because you did an excellent job in Berlin. I had my eye on you, you know."

"So did the Germans."

"You keep saying that. Did they have the German flag plastered across their foreheads?"

"German haircuts."

"Well, I hope they didn't take useful notes."

"I'm sure they didn't."

"Good," he said, then looked at his hands, which Milo noticed were unusually red. "I knew it was going to be a hard one. For someone like you."

"Hard, how?"

"It being a girl."

Milo tried to appear bored. "The job itself was child's play."

"I'm glad you feel that way. And the other job, the financial work?"

"Should be wrapped up by the end of the week."

"Good. Because it raised some eyebrows in Manhattan when you requested that six hundred grand."

"You have a pen and paper?"

"Check the armrest."

Milo opened the leather armrest that separated them and found two bottles of Evian, a stereo remote control, and a pen and pad. He wrote down a twenty-one-digit code, and when he handed it to Drummond he wondered what kind of circulation problem caused his redness. Another medical question. "Here's the account's IBAN. Money should be there by Thursday. Harry Lynch knows how to withdraw it without leaving fingerprints. Is Harry still around?"

Drummond looked confused. He still hadn't learned the names of his underlings at the Avenue of the Americas.

"Doesn't matter," said Milo. "I just need one thing from you."

"What's that?"

"The name and number of the insurance adjuster working on the E. G. Bührle theft."

Drummond got him into focus. "Oh." He nodded, finally understanding. "Very good. I'll send that to your phone." He ripped out the page and folded it into his shirt pocket, thinking this over, then muttered, "It's a pity."

"Pity?"

"That we have to do this. This kind of thing. But Ascot wants to run Tourism into the ground. Bleeding us, at a time when oil prices are driving airfares into the sky."

"So that's what this is about. Keeping the department running."

"We do what we must to stay alive."

Milo considered asking if it was worth it, keeping alive a secret department that even Quentin Ascot, the CIA director, wanted to erase. It was a moot question, though: All government departments work on the basic understanding that their existence is enough reason to continue existing. Out the window was the blackness of countryside.

"You going to tell me where we're going?"

Drummond followed his gaze. "Two weeks ago, in Paris, the embassy got a walk-in."

"French?"

"Ukrainian. Name's Marko Dzubenko. He was in town as part of an entourage for their internal affairs minister. He'd been in town only three days when he came to us."

"Employer?"

"SSU," he said, referring to the Security Service of Ukraine. "He made no secret of it, particularly once the staff threatened to kick him out of the building. He wanted us to know he was an important defector."

"Is he?"

Drummond shrugged theatrically and settled against the far door. "Only if he's trustworthy, and for the moment I don't believe anything he tells us. Not until we know more about him. At this point we've just got the basics. Forty-six years old. Kiev University—foreign relations. Joined the secret police when he was twenty-four, then moved into intelligence after the Russians left. Paris was a coup for him—his previous trips were to Moscow, Tallinn, Beijing, and Ashgabat; that's in Turkmenistan."

"I know where Ashgabat is."

"Of course you do. But it was news to me."

"What rank is he?" Milo asked.

"Second lieutenant."

"Not so bad. Why does he want to leave?"

"That's the question, isn't it?" said Drummond. "According to him, it's personal gain. He's being stifled at home, skipped over for promotion, while the new capitalists are making millions. He says capitalism has cheated him. From the looks of his accounts, it's at least passed him by." Drummond pursed his lips. "He wants a new life in America, but what does he have to buy it with? Marko's trips were trade based, and that's largely what he had for us. Ukrainian trade secrets?" He smiled again. "The man actually thought that would buy him a life in America!"

Alan Drummond's mirth lasted a few seconds longer than

expected, then drained away when he saw his guest wasn't encouraging it. Milo said, "Well, there's a reason we're sitting here talking about him. And it's not Ukrainian exports."

"It's not," Drummond muttered. "He spent a while giving us reams of useless information, most of which we had already. He saw we were fading fast. So he panicked and pulled out his wild card. He said that there's a mole in the Department of Tourism."

Silence followed, the engine rumbling beneath them. "Did he actually say those words?" asked Milo.

"He knew about the department and specified the mole was there."

While the department liked to think of itself as existing in a parallel universe of absolute secrecy, Milo knew a few people who had figured out its existence—but they had been allies and friends. "The Ukrainians have someone inside? It's hard to swallow."

Drummond shook his head. "Marko claims it's a Chinese mole."

"Chinese?"

"The Guoanbu."

Milo stared at him.

"Short for Guojia Anquan Bu, their Ministry for State Security."

"I know what the Guoanbu is," Milo said, irritated. "I'm just confused."

Drummond ignored his confusion for the moment. "When he mentioned Tourism, as you can imagine, the agent in charge of his interrogation was baffled. No idea what Marko was talking about. So he went up to the embassy's security director, who was just as baffled. In fact, he was going to write Marko off as a nut job and dump him somewhere, but to cover his ass he sent a query to Langley. It landed on the assistant director's desk, and he came directly to me. Gleefully, I might add. A mole is just the kind of thing Ascot would happily use to hang us. So I sent one of ours to talk to him, and we shipped him here."

"Why not to the States?"

"He'll get there eventually," said Drummond. "I want you to listen to him first."

"Why me?"

"Because his story concerns you and everything that came raining down last July. And the only thing in the files on it is one single-spaced page that goes out of its way to not say a thing. Which makes me a fucking ignoramus."

"Really?" Milo asked, not sure he could trust that Drummond was so ill informed.

"Believe it," he said sourly. "Dzubenko has told me a novel compared to the haiku I was handed when I took over."

"Wait a minute," said Milo, raising a hand. "How does a Ukrainian second lieutenant learn about a Chinese mole in a secret CIA department? How does this make any sense?"

"Luck," Drummond said. "Over the last few years, the Chinese have been pouring agents into the Ukraine, and Marko spent some time with them. He doesn't like them very much."

"And they told him about their mole? Come on, Alan. Besides, the Chinese almost never invest in long-term double agents."

"I know this," he said, "but don't be so quick to doubt it."

Milo peered out at the blackness again, then looked at Drummond. "I'm getting a sick feeling of déjà vu. Last year a friend of mine was accused of sharing secrets with the Chinese. It wasn't true, and maybe if I'd known that from the start she wouldn't be dead now."

"This was Angela Yates?"

Milo nodded.

After a moment's reflection, Drummond said, "Listen to what he has to say. I don't want to believe it either, but if his story checks out, then I'm going to have to clean the department. It's not the way a new director wants to spend his opening weeks, but I won't have a choice."

Milo's hand twitched; he was catching Drummond's itchy agitation. "Well, then? Who is it? Don't tell me he held that back."

"He has no idea. From his story, it could only be in administration. A Travel Agent, most likely. Not a Tourist."

Milo rubbed his knees. Travel Agents collected and sorted intelligence from Tourists and tracked their positions. A mole among their ranks could pass on anything. "Who else have you called in?"

"Just Tourists. Our driver, and some extra help—I got them from the war on drugs. I've also collected some folks from other departments for analysis and background checks. I'll get you their phone numbers before sending you off again."

"Am I going somewhere?"

"You're always going somewhere, Sebastian. If your chat with him works out, you'll be checking on some of the Ukrainian intel Marko's been giving me. It might not be outstanding stuff, but it's another way to vet him, and if it isn't legitimate it'll give me extra reason to doubt the mole story."

"I'm not much of an interrogator," Milo admitted. "You should call in John. He's rough, but he gets results."

Drummond stared at him a moment, as if shocked by the suggestion. "This guy came to us. I'm not going to have John fit those electrodes to his tits just to hear him scream." He sniffed. "Really, what was the department like before I came along?"

"You don't want to know," Milo said, then took a box from his pocket and dry-swallowed two more Dexedrine.

8

Despite a broad stomach and thinning black hair, Marko Dzubenko was a young-looking forty-six. He wore a faux-silk shirt with rolled-up sleeves, the collar open to expose an Orthodox cross buried in chest hair, watching the German edition of *Big Brother* as he chain-smoked. The only sign of age lay in the gray stubble that ran along his jawline.

Milo stuck out a hand as he approached. "Good evening. I'm here to ask some questions."

His handshake was hot and dry. Instead of returning the greeting, Dzubenko shook a smoldering Marlboro at the television. "Great show, no?"

The television camera was angled high in a corner of a kitchen, and two pretty twentysomethings were arguing. "Never got around to watching it."

"Great show," he repeated. "I am for the Melly. I would easily do her."

"Marko?"

"Yeah?" he said to the television.

Milo picked up the remote and turned it off. Dzubenko rubbed his eyes with the heels of his hands. "Motherfucker. I am already answer you fuckers' questions, okay? Twenty fucking times!"

Suppressing the urge to strike him, Milo switched to Russian.

"And you'll continue to answer the questions, or we'll beat you, sodomize you, then dump you naked in the bad part of Mogadishu."

Marko's head jerked back as if he'd been slapped; then he smiled and put out his cigarette. "Finally. Someone who speaks Russian with balls. Want a cigarette?" He lifted the pack.

Milo preferred his Davidoffs but knew how sharing cigarettes created an instant bond between Slavs. He produced his lighter and lit Marko's first, then his own.

He settled on a chair that he recognized from old trips with Tina through IKEA. Then he recognized the sofa Dzubenko sat on. In fact, the whole lower floor of this two-story farmhouse outside Frauenfeld, not far from the highway, had been fitted with that Swedish company's functional furniture. Around the house lay acres of cold, flat field, empty save for four Company guards with infrared binoculars. Upstairs, in a room the size of a closet, Drummond was watching them through video monitors. By morning, he would have a transcription of the whole conversation, with English translation.

"So, Marko. I hear you've got a story about the Chinese for us."

The Ukrainian stared at the black television and shrugged. "They tell you about all the hot Kiev information? Man, you can worry about the Chinese all you want, but it's the Kievskaya Rus' you should really worry about."

"Trust me, we are worried. But I'm here about the Chinese. You want to tell me how a man like you learns of a secret Chinese plot?"

Dzubenko glared at him, as if his word couldn't be doubted, but said, "Biggest intelligence organization on the planet, so what do you think? Guoanbu. The motherfuckers are all over Kiev now. It's getting like Chinatown. They know how important we are, how we're positioned. Russian fuckers on one side, European Union on the other—it all rubs."

"Friction."

"Exactly," he said, using his cigarette to point at Milo. "I've got respect for them—don't get me wrong. They spend money on their people, place them all over the world. They're *smart*. But that doesn't mean I have to like it when they take over my hometown and my hard-ass bosses start treating them like princesses they've got boners for. Know what I mean?"

Milo didn't, not exactly—he hadn't been in the Ukraine since the nineties, and the Guoanbu hadn't gained a foothold there yet—but he could imagine. "Look, I'm just surprised the Chinese shared their secrets with a Ukrainian second lieutenant."

"It wasn't like that," said Dzubenko. "It was at a party. On Grushevskogo Street."

"The Chinese embassy."

"Of course."

"What for?"

"What?"

"Why was there a party?"

"Oh! Chinese New Year. They've got their own, you know."

"So do Ukrainians. What date?"

"Beginning of the month. February 7."

"And they invited an SSU second lieutenant?"

Dzubenko frowned at his cigarette and chewed the inside of his mouth. "You're trying to get a rise out of me, but it's not going to work. I'm sure of the rightness of my position."

"I'm just trying to understand, Marko."

"It was my boss. Lutsenko. Bogdan Lutsenko. He's a colonel—you can check on that in your files. He was invited, and he asked if I wanted to come along. I said, *Why not?* But I didn't know, did I?"

"Didn't know what?"

"How it would make me sick to my stomach, being there. And that Xin Zhu would be there soaking up all the attention."

"Xin Zhu?"

"Guoanbu," Dzubenko told him. "Don't know his rank, but it must be high up. He's a fat fucker. Big as a cow. Carries himself like some fucking sheik. Half his entourage were slant-eyes, the other half were my bosses, laughing at all his jokes."

"What kinds of jokes?"

"Russian jokes. China's full of those jokes, I guess. It didn't hurt that he told them in excellent Russian. Plays on words, that sort of thing. Had them in stitches. You know what it looked like to me?"

"What?"

"Like the defeated fawning over their new masters. That's what it looked like to me. So I went out on the terrace and started smoking, waiting to go home. I got through two cigarettes before he came out to join me."

"He?"

"Xin Fucking Zhu."

Milo allowed an expression of surprise to slip into his features. "You're fucking kidding me."

"I am not. He brings his fat ass outside. It's cold, you know, but he's still sweating. Glowing from all the attention. That's why he came out—inside, he'd melt. He lights up and we get talking. And the guy *is* funny, I have to admit. Even drunk—and the guy is really drunk. We talk about Kiev, and he tells me some of the places he likes. Not tourist shit—no. Some of the best clubs, the ones you have to look hard to find."

"He goes out dancing?" Milo asked doubtfully.

"Ha!" Dzubenko spat, imagining that. "Please. He goes out looking for hot chicks, what else? We share war stories about girlfriends. Very funny, that guy. He convinces me to come back in, and I end up staying until after midnight. Fun time."

Milo stared at him, waiting, but Dzubenko didn't seem to want to go on. "Well?"

"I'm not saying another word until we get some vodka in here."

"Sure," Milo said, then switched to English. "You hear that? Get us some vodka!"

It took about two minutes. They heard trotting on the stairs, then the door opened just wide enough for Drummond to place a bottle of Finlandia and two shot glasses on the floor. The door shut. Milo poured shots and handed one over. "Budmo."

"Hey," Dzubenko answered, then added in English, "Mud inside your eye."

They each put back two shots before Milo said, "Is this when it happened? You got the story at the embassy?"

"Hell no! You think Xin Zhu's a complete idiot? That was the next week. I get a call from him, and we head out to Tak-Tak, one of his favorite clubs. Usually, guys like him, they'll end up at the Budapest Club, maybe Zair, but Tak-Tak? Shit, *I'd* never been there. But Zhu walked in like a king. They know him there. It's the one place he can go where he's the only slant-eye. We get a booth in the corner where we can watch the girls and talk in private. Then he starts drinking. I like to drink—don't misunderstand me—but this Chinaman puts them away. Unbelievable. I guess because he's so big he can take it."

"So he wasn't drunk?"

"Oh, he was drunk. Easily. He just didn't pass out."

"Did you?"

"For a few minutes, yeah."

"And he talked to you."

"Like we were brothers. Want to know what I think? I think the fat bastard is lonely. I mean, he can't really trust anyone under him, and he's afraid of those above him. So he works his intrigues all by himself."

"He told you this?"

"I'm a good judge of character."

"But he told you about his intrigues."

"A little, yeah. But it wasn't until the end of the night, when he was really wasted, that he told me this thing that's got your friend excited. About the mole he's been running in the fucking-secret American Department of Tourism."

"Tell me about that, please."

"Certainly," Dzubenko said. He raised his shot glass, then drank. "When I told Zhu he was making this up to impress me—really, Department of *Tourism*? What kind of name is that?—he immediately broke it down. The administration of the Department of Tourism is organized into seven subject areas. One supervisor and nine Travel Agents for each section." He grinned. "I stopped him there—*Travel agents?* I said. That's when he told me they were kind of like analysts, collecting information from Tourism's field agents, who are called Tourists. There are sixty-three of these guys, these Tourists, spread around the world."

Sixty-three—not even Milo knew that number. Drummond could verify it later.

"He said that the Department of Tourism was the dirtiest part of America's filthy intelligence machine."

"And he said he had a mole in this secret department?"

Dzubenko nodded and held out his empty glass; Milo refilled it.

"He offer any evidence of this?"

"Well, I've got some experience in this sort of thing. Learning what's true and what's not."

"I imagine you do."

"Sure. I knew that with this fat fucker the best thing was to play on his vanity. I told him he was a liar. I told him no one would have a secret department with that kind of name, certainly not the Americans. They'd call it Alpha Bravo. Or Operation Free-Fucking-Eagle. Something like that. We had some girls with us by then—so we talked in English—but in Russian I'd tell the girls he was a big fat liar. You see what I was doing? I was using his manhood to get the evidence from him."

"Extremely clever," said Milo. "I suppose he rose to the challenge."

"You suppose right. First he made me swear to keep my mouth shut—this was just for me. Then he told me about one of the Tourism Department's operations, in the Sudan. One that was supposed to cripple China's oil supply. This was back in July, and—get this—it all surrounded the Tiger."

"The Tiger?" Milo asked, feigning ignorance.

"Come on! You know, that famous assassin. The one who killed the French foreign minister a while back. He was hired by the CIA." Dzubenko shook his head. "Now, Zhu started with this, which made me doubt him right away, but then he slowly told me the whole story."

"Which is what you'll do for me right now."

For the next hour, Dzubenko told it as he remembered it. He told it the way one tells a story he's had to repeat often in recent days, playing with red herrings and side characters, knowing that the essential focus will not be lost. He began with the assassin, Benjamin Harris, otherwise known as the Tiger, and his surrender to a man from the department named Milo Weaver, with a message: *Someone has killed me with the HIV virus, and I want you to find him*. "But that wouldn't be enough, would it? Not for any Company agent, least of all someone from this fucking-secret department." Dzubenko was right about that; it hadn't been enough to get Milo moving. It had taken more. It took the untimely death of an old friend, Angela Yates, and its connection to the Tiger, to make him act. Dzubenko took a drag off his Marlboro. "People are all the same. We need a personal reason to get our asses off the couch."

He told how an agent in the Department of Homeland Security decided Milo was responsible for Angela's death, and he had to go on the run. "From Disney World—can you believe it? He was there with his old lady and his kid. Tina, that's the wife's name. The daughter was called Stephanie. He had to leave them behind and go black."

Dzubenko knew about the other players: the Tourist James Einner, the Russian businessman Roman Ugrimov, Diane Morel from French intelligence, and the Tourist Milo had killed, Kevin Tripplehorn, aka, many other names. He knew that it all connected to an attempt to destabilize the Sudanese government by blaming the murder of a radical cleric on the Chinese, who had significant oil interests in that country. Zhu told Dzubenko that the murder itself was one thing—the mullah had been a pain for everyone—but the riots that followed were the real crime. *Eighty-six is the official number*, Zhu told him, *but more died. Innocents. Even a few of our own people, working in the oil fields. There was no need for that.*

Zhu knew, further, that the plot had been instigated by Thomas Grainger, then head of Tourism, now deceased, as well as Terence Fitzhugh, also deceased. Both of whom had been directed by a certain senator, Nathan Irwin of Minnesota.

"That was a fuck of a messy month. Don't get me wrong—we have plenty of messy months ourselves, but we expect a little less bloodletting from the CIA. I mean, you guys have a real budget. It should lead to less corpses, no?"

"It should," Milo said, all the feeling drained from his limbs. This man knew everything.

"But there was one thing Zhu couldn't figure out, and it irritated him. This Weaver guy. He was the one who figured out what was going on, and as a result everyone wanted him. Homeland Security wanted him for murder. The Company wanted him dead so the story wouldn't get out. *But this man*, Zhu said, *he lives the most charmed of lives. He survived.* That really confused him. He said Weaver spent a couple months in prison, and his marriage fell apart, but he did survive. Now, not only was he still living and breathing, he was even working for his old employer again. He wanted to know how he pulled off that trick. You know what I told him?"

"I don't," said Milo, "but I'd like to know."

"I told him this Weaver character was obviously working with the bad guys himself. Because the bad guys are the only ones who ever survive. Zhu thought that was pretty funny."

The truth was that Yevgeny Primakov had helped him stay alive, and it struck him that the question of whether his father was a good guy or a bad guy was just a matter of perspective.

He'd had enough. It wasn't just that the Chinese knew ninety percent of what had happened last year; it was simply hearing it again, described so vividly, and the way Dzubenko's words brought back all those mixed feelings of confusion and anger and despair. He stood and offered a hand. "Thanks, Marko. You've been a big help."

"So now will you move me to Wisconsin?"

"Wisconsin?"

"I have a cousin who lived there for two years. The most beautiful place on earth. The best women, too."

"I didn't realize," said Milo. "We'll see what we can do. You need anything else?"

Dzubenko looked at the full ashtray and the vodka bottle. "Another carton. Maybe some tonic water for mixing—my stomach's starting to hurt."

"Maybe you need some food instead."

"Tonic's fine." He picked up the television remote. "It's good, you know."

"What?"

"Your Russian. Not that teach-yourself-Russian bullshit most of you Company guys use."

"Thanks."

Dzubenko turned on the television and added, "Poka," an informal good-bye.

"Poka, Marko," Milo said, and as he closed the door behind himself, he heard a German talk show hostess ask, with utter earnestness, *You mean that, after all the things he did, you slept with him again?* The studio audience let its contempt show with a synchronized *Boo*.

9

Drummond was coming down the stairs. "So?"

"It all fits."

They stepped onto the dark porch, and cold, erratic gusts hit them. In the distance, against the glow of headlights on the highway, the silhouette of a guard stood smoking a cigarette. In the foreground, the Lincoln started up, but Drummond didn't bother stepping down to the grass. He didn't say a thing, so Milo said, "He tells me we have sixty-three Tourists in all. Is that about right?"

"Don't you know?"

"I used to know how many we had in Europe, but that was my focus. Grainger never shared the big number."

"It's the number we're supposed to have, yes." He coughed into his hand. "This is some serious bad news, but I want to vet him more before freezing things."

"Freeze?"

"I don't want the Chinese picking off our Tourists for sport. If we do have a mole, then I'm using the Myrrh code."

Myrrh was the universal recall, the order of last resort. "Shouldn't you wait for a second source?"

"Dzubenko is the second source."

"What?"

Drummond chewed on something, perhaps the inside of his

mouth. "As soon as I got his story, I started asking around. Any Chinese intel on double agents. There were a few leads, but these kinds of rumors are a dime a dozen. They always sound convincing until you ask for compromised material, then they dry up. But a friend over in Asia-Pacific told me about someone they've got in the Guoanbu. A woman. She'd been in the Third Bureau, which deals with Hong Kong, Macau, and Taiwan, for a couple years. Nice, solid source for low-level intel. Then, in late December, there was a personnel shuffle, and she ended up in the Sixth Bureau, counterintelligence, and a small office on the outskirts of Beijing, run by one Xin Zhu."

"You're kidding me."

Drummond shook his head. "Don't get too excited. Zhu runs his department like al Qaeda runs its operations—in cells. Each individual works on a fragment, completely insulated from the person working at the next desk. This discipline is kept in check by the knowledge—or rumor, it doesn't matter—that a percentage of them are only there to spy on the others for the boss. Sounds like a dreadful place to work."

Milo didn't bother saying that it sounded familiar. "She does have some access, though, right? We could backtrack the intel that crosses her desk."

Again, he shook his head. "Nothing she's worked on has dealt with any Western sources. Zhu kept her with her specialty, and the best she gets is occasional dirt on Macau and Taiwanese politicians. Only once did she come across what you and I are interested in. Once. And that was just blind luck, and lust. A couple weeks after she started working there, Zhu's own secretary, An-ling Shen, began showing interest in her. She let him take her out one night. He's an insignificant man physically—portly, nearsighted—and knows there's only one way to woo an attractive younger woman into bed. With secrets. So he told her that his boss, Xin Zhu, had an important source within the CIA."

Milo waited, but Drummond didn't continue. "And that's it?"

"Sadly, she didn't sleep with him. Her controller asked her to give it a try, but she has her limits. Can't blame her, though. It might have been a test. That was my friend's guess, and it would have been

mine, too, if it hadn't been for Marko Dzubenko. But," he said, sighing a cloud of white, "Marko does exist, and I see it all entirely differently. I believe it."

"That's a lot of loose tongues," Milo pointed out. "Both Zhu and
his secretary."

"People are flawed."

"What do we have on Xin Zhu?"

"It's tough getting information out of the Guoanbu. He's a
colonel—we do know that. Late fifties. There was a verified residence in Germany during the early eighties. No wife we know of, but
rumors—unverified, so far—of one son. Last mention of his name
was in '96, when the State Council approved a consolidation plan
that recalled a lot of their Western undercover agents, the ones living
as businessmen and academics and journalists. He was against it, but
Jia Chunwang, the minister of state security, gave him a semipublic
rebuke. After that, Zhu essentially disappears from the records. His
office is a marginal outpost of the Sixth Bureau, and our girl on the
inside can't even tell us the scope of its purpose. Were it not for Marko
Dzubenko, we'd just assume Zhu's department dealt with regional
politics."

"I still don't buy it," Milo said. "You've got Xin Zhu. By all appearances he's politically dead in the water. He's a heavy drinker
with a weakness for women. Not only that, but he's sharing extremely classified information with a nobody—a Ukrainian lieutenant who ends up defecting soon afterward. He's also got a loose-lipped,
horny secretary. How does a man with all these flaws end up a
colonel, and a colonel running a mole in our department?"

"You're not the only one to ask that," Drummond said after a
moment. "The Tourist who first met with Dzubenko brought that
up. Which brings us to another theory, one that I'm starting to
warm to. It's that Zhu has reached the end of his rope. After the
humiliation of the midnineties, he's grown bitter. The mole, then,
isn't his. It's the brainchild of one of his competitors, and he's sabo-
taging it to block that person's career."

"That would make the drunkenness an act. As well as the secretary's indiscretions—which would mean that he knows the girl works for us."

"Or not," said Drummond. "There's no way to know. Marko certainly wouldn't know the difference. In any case, what's indisputable is that this Chinese colonel shared information he couldn't have unless he had some kind of connection to Tourism. Do you know what the biggest threat to Tourism is?"

"Other than a mole?"

Drummond shook his head. "Don't get me wrong. A mole would be a terrible blow. Still, we could reorganize and regroup. Myrrh is a radical decision, but it's the safest. Bring everyone back, hand out new names and go-codes, replace staff. The crucial thing for us is to keep it quiet. I've already assured Ascot that we've discounted Marko's story, so if he gets wind that we really are hunting a mole, he'll shut us down in a heartbeat." He stared at Milo significantly. "Everything we do from here on out is under the radar."

"Understood."

Drummond chewed the inside of his mouth again. "While a mole would hurt, Tourism could survive. That's not our biggest threat. The biggest threat to Tourism is knowledge of its existence."

"Which the Chinese have. So does a Ukrainian lieutenant."

"They're not the only ones. The French have an inkling of it, and so do the Brits. There are sites on the Internet that speculate about us, too. Which is as it should be. Right now, Tourism is a myth. It's a fable that people either consider poppycock or believe in. The believers are terrified that we might exist, because a myth is far more frightening than reality."

He finally stepped off the porch, and Milo followed him to the car. He moved slowly, and Milo had to measure his steps to avoid bumping into him.

"What do you think would happen if someone popped up with real evidence of our existence? Don't strain yourself—I'll tell you. An investigation would be launched. An official one. Senators and representatives would start asking questions. They would wonder just how much we cost—and that answer, as we both know, is embarrassing.

We would go from being a frightening story spies tell each other at night to being just another overpriced Company department whose failures start making the newspapers on a regular basis. We would become a joke, just as all the known departments already are. People—American citizens—would start blogging about us and protesting our existence. *Tell us what our tax dollars are doing*, they would say. And what excuses would we have for our epic budget and the way we have to rob art museums in order to fund ourselves in the crunch times? Please."

He stopped, and even in the darkness Milo could see his boss's face was as red as his hands.

"We'd be finished before we got a chance to defend ourselves. Not that we even have a defense."

They stood in silence broken by the high grass tinkling in the wind and the dull rumble of the Lincoln. Milo felt that he should say something, but he had nothing to say. At this point Drummond seemed to just be thinking aloud, musing over the immediate and more distant future.

"I'll contact you about Dzubenko's other stories," he said finally. "I'll have you and some other Tourist check their veracity. Who knows? Maybe we'll find out we have a Ukrainian mole, and the Ukrainians are positioning us to run up against the Chinese."

"Or maybe there's no mole at all."

"Maybe," said Drummond. "Your cover still computers?"

"Dropped that a while ago—couldn't sustain a conversation. Expat insurance."

"You can't talk computers but you can talk actuarial tables?"

"If forced."

Drummond grunted amusement but said nothing. When they reached the car, Milo unconsciously opened the door for his boss. Drummond got in and looked up at him. "We're running things differently now. It's not the old Tourism anymore."

"I appreciate that, sir."

"Maybe you do, maybe you don't. Anyway, I don't believe in lying to my employees. If I want something from you, I'll tell you directly. If I don't want you to know something, I'll just tell you it's above your clearance. What's important is that you won't have to do a lot of second-guessing with me—I'm an obvious man."

He'd said it earnestly, so Milo said, "That means you're either an idealist—"

"—or a fool," Drummond finished. "Yeah. I've heard it all already. And this thing with the girl, the Moldovan. Not my idea of good foreign policy, but it really was necessary."

"I'm sure it was," said Milo.

"I doubt you are. But it's like any new administration. Before you can move forward you have to take care of the screwups of the previous administration."

"Maybe you want to tell me why it had to be done."

"Sorry," said Drummond. "That's above your clearance."

Milo shut the door, then came around the other side and got in beside him. The man behind the wheel began driving along the pocked field toward the main road.

"I'm glad I met you face-to-face," Drummond told him. "Turns out you're smarter than your file made you out to be."

"That's very reassuring to hear, sir."

10

Two days later, Milo broke into a white sedan parked on a secluded street in the northern Milan suburbs, a car that was perfect in its dull inconspicuousness. Some chipped paint on the left flank, a hair-line crack down the rear windshield, and just old enough to be un-threatening, but still new enough to play nicely with his magic key ring. With a full tank of gas.

Earlier that day, he had bought an aerosol can of polyurethane from a vast OBI store, and after picking up the car he drove to an address on the Crocetta side of Viale Fulvio Testi, a tall apartment block beside an Esso station. He walked around one side and squat-ted by the whitewashed wall. He uncapped the can and spray-painted MARIANS JAZZROOM. While wet, it was visible, though once it dried someone would have to look hard to find it.

He tossed the can into a wastebasket and drove north. It was 6:00 P.M., Tuesday.

By eight, he was in a hotel in Melide, Switzerland, just south of Lugano, to rest up before the final stage of the Bührle job. He flipped through television channels, pausing on CNN, where the forty-third president of the United States had been cornered in Dar es Salaam, Tanzania. In answer to a reporter's question, Bush said, "The Kosovars are now independent."

Drummond's discussions had obviously gone well.

He wondered idly what Radovan thought of all of this, and suspected he and many of his friends couldn't help but succumb to a measure of nationalism now that Kosovo, the birthplace of Serbian Orthodoxy, was at stake, but it didn't matter now. Their fight was dead, and Milo had twenty million dollars to collect.

At one o'clock in the morning, he cleaned the room and put his few spare clothes and toiletries into the hotel's Dumpster. Before returning the room key, he swallowed two Dexedrine.

At his rented garage in the northern Lugano suburbs, he lit his first Davidoff of the day. He considered the canvases. Degas's *Count Lepic and His Daughters*, Monet's *Poppy Field at Vétheuil*, van Gogh's *Blooming Chestnut Branches*, and Cézanne's *Boy in the Red Waistcoat*.

The decision wasn't about which paintings Milo thought should live or die; the decision was about which paintings meant more to the museum. All four were masterpieces of similar financial value, but there was a difference. Two portrayed nature scenes, while the other two portrayed people. Museum curators and insurance adjusters know that the public's interest lies with faces; that's just human nature. Therefore he would give them nature, so that they would act in the hope of saving the faces.

Using gloves, he loaded the sedan with the Monet and van Gogh, then went back inside to examine the remaining two. The boy in the waistcoat looked, at a certain angle, petrified as Milo again took out his Zippo. Necessary, he told himself. Allowing the paintings to survive would only leave him open to risk, leave one more clue for the police to track down. He thought of Adriana and the risk he'd taken letting her survive, and wondered suddenly about Yevgeny's words. For the old man, killing a girl was a practical necessity, but at the mention of stealing art he'd reached something like a moral core. *It's the social contract you've broken, Milo.* What kind of man cared more about paintings than a girl's life?

Nearly two hours later, a little before five, he parked around the corner from the E. G. Bührle, in front of the Psychiatrische Universitätsklinik Zürich. He wiped down the inside of the car, then tossed the keys down by the gas pedal and shut the door. He walked west down Flühgasse to the Tiefenbrunnen commuter train stop and on the way found a pay phone out of the reach of street cameras. Still in gloves, he pulled up the name and number Drummond had texted him, and dialed.

After seven rings, a groggy, irritated voice said, "Ja?"

"Is this Jochem Hirsch?"

"Ja, ja."

"Wake up, Jochem. I took the paintings from the Bührle museum."

Silence. Then he asked, "How did you get this number?"

"Listen to me. If you go to the psychiatric clinic just down the street from the museum, you'll find a white car with Italian plates. Inside it are the Monet and van Gogh."

"Wait, are you—"

"This is a show of goodwill, Jochem. Two for free. You've had a week and a half to learn that you can't find the paintings on your own, so you know that this is the only way. You'll have to pay for the Degas and Cézanne. Twenty million in U.S. dollars."

"Twenty million? I don't—"

"It's a deal, Jochem. They're worth far more than that."

Jochem Hirsch thought through his options, while in the background a woman's voice said, "Wer ist da?"

"Shh," was his reply.

When he spoke again, it was to state the obvious. "Twenty million is still more than you'd get for them. You know that. They're too famous—no one would pay that much for the risk."

"I'm not interested in selling them, Jochem. If you don't pay the money in the next twenty-four hours, then I'll burn the two remaining paintings. Run that by the investors and see what they think. You have a pen?"

"Wait a minute," he said, and Milo heard him grunting, moving around his bedroom. "Yes."

Milo recited the IBAN code he'd given to Drummond. "For your sake, I suggest you don't share this with the press. Say the paintings were discovered by accident, by a passerby, whatever. Otherwise, half the museums you insure will start having trouble."

"That's very considerate of you," said Jochem Hirsch.

"Twenty-four hours, understand? I won't call again; you won't hear a thing. But if the money doesn't reach the account, then the Degas and Cézanne will be ash."

He hung up.

The train brought him to the center of town, where he got some breakfast. He was famished, and as he ate he read a copy of *Kurier* someone had left behind. It was on the front page, which was surprising. There she was, a posed photograph, probably from the high school. Smiling as if nothing bad could ever happen to her.

Of course it was on the front page, he realized as he finished his meal. The Germans, embarrassed retrospectively, would have remembered that they had seen this potentially dangerous man talking to the very girl who'd gone missing. Evidence of foul play was all over it. Yet all *Kurier* said was that she had been seen leaving the school but had not appeared on the other side of the block, where her father had been waiting. There was nothing about Sebastian Hall or Gerald Stanley.

The Germans, he imagined, had checked in with the Company administrator that had put them onto him. Alan Drummond would have asked them to please keep it quiet.

His food settled heavily in his stomach, and as he laid down Swiss francs for the bill he took out his cell phone and typed out a message.

Check acct tomorrow this time. Will be offline until Saturday.

He sent the message, then turned off his phone, lest it receive an immediate reply, and removed the battery. On the way to the Hauptbahnhof, he picked up a copy of *Le Figaro* because he saw a photo of the dejected parents, Andrei and Rada Stanescu, dazed by photographers' lights. The French newspaper had printed a translation of Rada's public plea, which had been broadcast on German television:

I want to speak to the person who took Adriana. You know who you are. You can put right the wrong you have done to her, and to my husband and myself, by placing her somewhere safe now. You don't have to put yourself at risk by going to a police station or a post office. You can put her in a church, or somewhere with a pay phone and money so she can call us. We'll pick her up. That's all you have to do to end this.

Milo popped two more Dexedrine, wiped some ash off his sleeve, and boarded the eleven thirty train to Paris.

11

By Friday, his anxiety had nothing to do with Adriana Stanescu, a possible mole in Tourism, the art extortion that was now complete (AP reported that a clinic employee had noticed the two paintings in the backseat of an abandoned car), nor even the fact that Alan Drummond would be fuming because he'd gone offline. Those were nothing beside this interminable wait in the Manhattan rain while students with knapsacks and cell phones passed him in pairs and solo. Those old worries meant nothing compared to this.

For the first time in months, he knew exactly why he was here. "Here" was the grounds of Columbia University, across from the high, majestic columns of the Avery Architectural and Fine Arts Library on a drizzling but unseasonably warm afternoon. The trench coat he'd picked up at Macy's that morning kept his body dry, but he was still shivering. He had resisted the urge for more Dexedrine; a clouded head was the last thing he wanted.

One thing that might have helped him now was self-righteousness, an emotion common to men who've been rejected by their wives. In some men it leads to harassing calls or intrusions at four in the morning, or even haunting a loved one's place of work, as Milo was doing now. Self-righteousness had never been part of Milo Weaver's repertoire, though, and if Tina came out now and told him to leave, he would do so without argument—he felt sure of this. Self-righteousness is born of the conviction that you deserve something from someone; Milo, on the other hand, didn't believe anyone owed him a thing.

His crime had been secrecy.

Among other things, he had hidden the identities of his parents—his real parents—from her. Yevgeny Aleksandrovich Primakov and Ellen Perkins. One a Soviet spy Milo briefly lived with in Moscow during his teenaged years; the other, his mother, a 1979 suicide in a German prison, someone described, alternately, as a Marxist terror-ist, a mentally disturbed nomad, or—as he thought of her—a ghost.

Milo's lies (or, generously: omissions) might have been bearable had he confessed them on his own, but he hadn't. Tina had learned the truth from strangers, and the humiliation had been too much for her.

Therefore, the fault was his, and reconciliation was something he did not deserve. He hadn't needed a marriage counselor to tell him that.

Yet when, a little after five thirty, he spotted her trotting down those few front steps, phone to her ear, he had to stop himself from rushing forward to kidnap her. That was his Tourist side, demand-ing what he desired. He followed her around the corner to the car, where she hung up and got behind the wheel. He broke into a jog and appeared at her window. She was starting the engine, not look-ing at him, so he tapped the glass by her head. She turned and let out an involuntary shout.

Neither moved. The engine rumbled, and she stared at him, her green eyes comically widened in shock, her soft lips separated, one hand over her heart as if pledging allegiance. He wondered if he looked different to her, if the last three months had altered his fea-tures. He knew he'd lost weight, and in a rush of vanity he hoped it made him more attractive. He hoped—and the thought later struck him as ludicrous—that the man she saw through her window aroused her desire. The woman he saw aroused his.

She didn't open the door, just rolled down the window—she wasn't giving in yet. "Oh, shit. *Milo.*"

"Hey."

"Well, what," she said. "You're in town?"

"Not really. Just a few hours. To see you." When she didn't answer, he thought that maybe he was taking too much control, being too forceful, so he added, "If that's all right with you."

"Well. Sure."

"Are you picking up Stef?"

"Mom's in town—she's taking care of that." She paused. "Were you wanting to see her?"

There was nothing he wanted more than to see his daughter, that single spark of Technicolor in his grayscale existence, but he shook his head. "Probably not a good idea. I have to leave again pretty quickly. I don't want to upset her."

He hoped she noticed how considerate he was being now. Not like last year when he'd demanded that they disappear with him.

He said, "Look, I don't want to keep you."

"Get in." She pressed a button to unlock the doors. "I can drop you off on the way."

He ran around to the passenger side before she could change her mind.

In the old days, he always drove. This was her seat, and behind them Stephanie would sit, asking inopportune questions. He realized that he had seldom watched her drive, and was impressed by how smoothly she pulled out of her parallel parking situation. She seemed to be doing just fine without him.

"How's Little Miss?"

"She's all right," Tina began, then shook her head. "Not entirely. She's been cracking her knuckles."

"Who'd she pick that up from?"

"She doesn't even know she's doing it. It's a nervous tic."

Six-year-olds weren't supposed to have nervous tics, Milo thought as he felt the desire for a pill. "She feels anxiety in the house," he said.

"Because you're not there? Maybe. The counselor says it's common in divorced families."

"We're not divorced."

"Maybe it's something else. She's been having nightmares."

"Oh."

Tina nodded at the road. "Did you hear about that kid in Germany? Adriana Something? Just another kidnapped girl, but it's all over the news here. She had a nightmare about it last night. About being kidnapped."

Milo really wanted that Dexedrine.

"She'll get over it. Besides, it's being replaced with Olympic fever," she said to the road. "They've been talking it up at school, learning about the Greeks and Beijing. Stef's crazy for the javelin throw—it's really fired her imagination. Dana Pounds is her hero."

"Dana Pounds?"

"One of our javelin throwers—or whatever you call them. Stef's anxious about her upcoming trials." She grinned. "Patrick keeps threatening to take us."

"To Beijing?" he said, terrified of the image that provoked.

"That's what he says," she said, shrugging into a turn, "but you know him. When you've got him in front of you, he'll do anything. Once he's out the door, he's really out the door."

He said nothing at first, because he didn't want to speak too quickly, too unthinkingly. He reassessed his terror. Though Patrick, Stephanie's biological father, was hardly an ideal role model, the fact was that Milo couldn't take her to the Olympics. Patrick was her only chance. And the Chinese themselves? The mole? According to Dzubenko, they knew about Milo Weaver's family and could easily pick them out of a crowd of thousands, but that didn't mean they would be in danger. Families were neutral ground in their trade. "I hope he follows through," he admitted finally. "It's something she'd never forget. Hell, you'd never forget it. You should call his bluff, let him catch you boning up on Mandarin."

She laughed. "I just might do that."

"Yevgeny said he's come by a few times. Is that right?"

She nodded at the traffic ahead. "I think he does it just to see Stef. He's nuts about her. Says she reminds him of his daughters. When they were little, at least."

"And you? You like him?"

"He's very . . . *European*, isn't he?"

"I suppose so."

"And he's crazy about you. Reminds me of Tom, always making excuses for your shortcomings."

He scratched at an itch on the back of his head. She seemed to be turning the conversation in a bleak direction. "Does he need to?"

"Sometimes, yeah. Sometimes I get pretty pissed off." She shook her head. "I don't want to get into that argument again, okay?"

"Okay."

"We've been through all of it," she continued, as if she actually did want to get into it again. "I still get angry sometimes, but it's not because I don't understand. I get it. You made it clear with Dr. Ray. You'd been living all your life with this secret side, and it never really occurred to you to share it with me."

"Yeah," he said. "Something like that."

"And that's the problem, isn't it?"

He didn't understand, so she explained. "You didn't make a conscious decision to keep it a secret; the idea of sharing it simply never entered your mind." She took a breath. "*That* makes it worse. It means that it's hardwired into you. It's something that'll never change."

"People can change. Remember? Dr. Ray said that, too."

"Before you suddenly decided to return to the field without even running it by me? Or before she told you that you weren't taking our sessions seriously enough?"

Suddenly, this transatlantic visit felt like a mistake. It was as if she were looking for reasons to reject him, milking them out of whatever new facts she had discovered. The truth, though, was that Milo still didn't understand. "You need more time?" he asked.

"Time for what?" She glanced at him. "You're working in Europe again. If we give the marriage another try, then what kind of marriage are we talking about? I'm still not interested in moving, you know. I like my job. I like the life I've got here. Stephanie's in a great school."

He rubbed his face. Despite the many times he'd planned and played this conversation in his head, she was irritating him. "Why do I have to have all the answers? Why can't we just play it by ear?"

"Because we have a *child*, Milo."

All the air seemed to leave the car.

She gave him a quick look. "What did you think would happen here? Did you think we'd fall in love all over again and you'd return to your . . . I don't know. Do you even have a home?"

He didn't answer. It was out of his hands now.

"Maybe you think we can have some kind of satisfying long-distance relationship. But tell me: Could we really depend on you showing up for birthdays and holidays? You're not working a nine-to-five." She stopped at a light. "Unless you're quitting. Is that it?"

"Not yet," he managed.

Silence followed, and after they'd gotten moving again she spoke more softly. "I've had a lot of time to think about things, and one thing I couldn't understand was myself. Why didn't I go with you back in July? My husband comes to me, tells me his life is in danger, and the only way we can all stay together is if we leave the country. You made it very clear, Milo. An idiot could have understood."

He waited.

"I couldn't understand why my 'no' had come so easily. There were plenty of practical reasons, but those weren't enough. It was my unconscious making the decisions, and my unconscious knew that, even without all the melodrama, there was something wrong in the marriage. Maybe I'd never really trusted you in the first place. Maybe my love had its limits. I don't know, and I still don't. All I know is that if we got back together it couldn't stay the way it was. It would take work. We'd have to work together to figure out what was wrong and then see if we can fix it. Not that one-sided therapy we were doing before, but real, engaged therapy we're both committed to."

She knew how to make him feel as if he'd lost control of a debate; all she had to do was use that word of hers, "unconscious." It made her into the adult, standing alongside Dr. Ray; it made him into the child. And as if he were indeed a child, a swift fantasy took hold, a shallow reasoning: She was confused. She was confusing herself.

Their marriage had gone so well for six years, and now that a few problems had appeared she'd lost faith. Patrick—yes, her ex was obviously deluding her. So Milo would take control. He would get her to pull over and then overpower her. He would move her to a place where he had control, where he would have the time and means to convince her of her bad logic, because that's all it was—bad logic. It left out love, and any logic that ignored love was flawed from the outset.

Then the fantasy left, as quickly as it had lumbered into his head, and he knew that this had been the problem all along—he'd been thinking like a Tourist. For Tourists, everything is possible; contradictions are minor inconveniences. Tourists, like children, believe the world is theirs. He hadn't been like this before. The job had infantilized him.

She said, "I asked him. Yevgeny. I asked him if you could just leave your job and come back. Just like you, he said, *Not yet.* He said you needed more time." She waited for him to dispute that. He didn't. "Remember what I told you before? When we met, you were a field agent, but if you'd stayed one I wouldn't have married you. I'm not the kind of wife who can take long absences, or worry that my husband won't make it home at all. So, you know what I told Yevgeny? I told him that when you quit running around the world, when you finally fall back on the name you were born with, then you should come and see me. Did he tell you that?"

"No," Milo said.

"Well, he should have. You wouldn't have wasted a trip."

12

She pulled up outside the Franklin Avenue A-train station in Brooklyn, from which he could ride to Howard Beach and take the AirTrain to JFK. For a full minute they sat in that awkward silence of farewell. He sat hating Yevgeny for offering him the unrealistic hope that is the lifeblood of the desperate.

Then, perhaps taking pity, Tina tugged on his sleeve, muttering, "Come here." She pulled him close and kissed him hard on the mouth. She tasted of chewing gum. Though he knew that it was pity, he would take it in lieu of anything else. They lingered for a moment; then she pulled back. "I mean what I said. You get your life straight, come back home, and I'm willing to give it a try. But *here*, you understand? Not in some other country with fake names. And we *work* on it with Dr. Ray."

"I understand."

"I hope you do, mister."

He grinned. She had offered him a plan. "Give Stef my love."

"You sure about that?"

"Maybe you're right," he admitted. "I'll give it to her myself when I can stay more than a few hours."

A brief smile joined them; then Tina jolted. "Oh! Take this." She popped open the glove compartment and fished out the iPod he'd given her months before, with headphones and a car-lighter charger.

"No. It's yours."

"Please," she insisted. "I never listen to the damned thing, and a few weeks ago I dropped it. Broke it. Pat got it fixed, but . . . look, all your music got wiped."

"After Pat touched it?"

"Ha ha. He filled it before giving it back, but I still don't listen. So, please, take it back. He filled it with seventies crap—you'd like it. Besides, I can't really imagine you running around the world without it."

He held it in his hand. "Thanks. I mean it. And don't give up on the Olympics. The more I think of it, the better the idea sounds. Tell Pat to get those tickets before they sell out."

"I'll do that," she said and let him kiss her again. Once he was standing on the wet sidewalk, she lowered the window. "One last thing."

"Yeah?"

"Cut out the smoking, will you? You taste like an ashtray." She winked and raised the window as she drove away.

He boarded a slow train, not worrying about the time. In the cool cloud of his hope—the better hope that she had offered him—he wasn't in a hurry to do anything. There was always a chance, even for louts like himself. He would catch an outbound flight with his Tourist passport, and even hope that Drummond was keeping watch, and that this unscheduled visit with his wife would provoke his anger, and perhaps lead to a quick dismissal.

It would weaken Adriana Stanescu's position with his father, but for the moment he didn't care. He'd regained that lack of empathy that Tourism drills into you.

Who knew? Maybe by morning he'd be free.

When switching trains at Howard Beach, he gave the rest of his Davidoffs to a beggar, and at JFK he purchased a ticket to Paris with his Sebastian Hall credit card. He joined the line at the security check. In front of and behind him anxious travelers sighed and grunted as they removed their shoes and unpacked their laptops and undid their belts. Milo followed suit, though he carried no luggage.

Off to the left, propped against a thick column, a television was tuned to CNN. An urban night scene: A familiar-looking building was billowing smoke. He read the rolling newsfeed at the bottom of the screen. It was the U.S. embassy in Belgrade on the previous night. Protesters had broken in and set it ablaze.

As the line brought him nearer, he heard the commentator explain that the riot was in reaction to President Bush's validation of Kosovo's independence in Dar es Salaam. There was a sign: КОСОВО JE СРБJA. KOSOVO JE SRBIJA—Kosovo is Serbia. One protester had turned up dead in the building, overcome by the smoke of the fire he'd been setting. Milo hoped that Radovan and his mother were all right.

He passed through the metal detector and received his shoes and disassembled phone (which got an extrasuspicious examination from the X-ray operator), then continued into the international terminal, where he had a coffee to brighten himself up. He put the phone back together, but no one called, so he scrolled through the iPod's playlist. It wasn't a random selection of the seventies as Tina had thought, but the entire David Bowie discography, from his self-titled 1967 release until 2003's curiously titled *Reality*. Not knowing where to begin, he put it on shuffle and soon found himself whispering, "Modern love . . ."

Not until he was at the gate itself did he begin to think something was wrong. It came to him via two faces. One man, he thought, was French . . . or Albanian. The conflicting nationalities seemed to find a shared home in his features as he looked back at Milo with a forced nonchalance. Then the woman—she was standing by a column, talking on a cell phone, gazing at the window near where Milo was sitting. Her face seemed entirely American to him. Neither carried any luggage.

Only two faces, but they did not belong. He saw that in the way they interacted with their surroundings, as if they had no interest in the plane that taxied to the gate. The verification came a half hour later, as he stood in line with the other passengers, shuffling to where the flight attendants checked passports and tickets. Milo's attendant ran his ticket through the scanner, which gave back a disappointed tone. She tried it again with the same result, then directed him to the desk, where he was told that, unfortunately, the plane was overbooked. There was another flight leaving in two hours. Would he like to wait for it?

Milo considered protesting, but seeing the man and woman waiting among the now empty seats, he really didn't care. That's what hope can do to you.

"Sure," he said. "I can wait a couple hours."

Her smile showed that she appreciated his understanding.

As she worked on his new itinerary, he glanced back to see the woman lean down to speak to the man. Her jacket fell open to reveal the grip of a pistol in a shoulder holster. The man twisted in his seat to stare directly at Milo. He stood up. The ruse was over.

Milo thought, *Drummond must really be pissed.*

"Don't worry about the reservation," he told the clerk. "I'll take care of it later."

She was baffled. "What?"

He was already heading toward the couple, who met him half-way. The woman spoke.

"Come with us, please, Mr. Hall."

The French-Albanian grunted his agreement, then followed him while the woman led the way through a locked door by a shop full of NYC caps and T-shirts and into the secret back corridors of JFK.

Unlike many of the guests these corridors were built for, he wasn't pushed through with a hood over his head, and for that he was grateful. They took so many turns that, when they finally deposited him in a windowless room with an aluminum prison toilet in the corner, he had no idea where he was. They left him to think over his flaws. There were so many, he didn't know where to begin. So he thought about Tina, but that inevitably drew him back to his flaws, and Dr. Ray, on whom the marriage now depended. The truth, which Tina had no way of knowing, was that their sessions would never truly work until Milo quit being so dishonest.

His dishonesty didn't take the form of outright lies but of silence, and it was something Dr. Ray sometimes noted, saying, "Milo? Would you like to add something to that?" Milo would usually answer, "No, I think Tina covered it pretty well," even when she hadn't.

A case in point was Tina's description of how they had met and fallen in love more than six years ago. The story had all the elements of high melodrama. Tina, eight months pregnant and single, in Venice for a last vacation. She meets an older man, a gentleman, who it turns out has stolen millions of dollars from the U.S. government. He brings her along to a meeting that goes disastrously wrong. Milo and Angela Yates, his partner, are there to arrest the man, and a teenaged girl is thrown off a high balcony to her death. Shots fired— Milo is hit twice—and the stress brings on Tina's labor.

The convergence of all these events made the story absolutely unbelievable, but Milo had no argument with Tina's retelling of those facts. They happened. It was during the mundane part of the story, the epilogue, that their versions differed. Tina woke in her Italian hospital room to find Milo asleep in a chair beside her bed and saw on the television that two planes had hit the World Trade Center. Milo woke up, and they watched together, and then . . .

"The event, it joined us in a way that nothing else could. Two strangers. We'd just been through a terrible moment together, and then we were witness to something even worse, grander. It tied us together forever. I know that sounds corny, but it's true. We fell in love at that moment."

"Milo? Anything to add?"

"What could I possibly add to that?" he'd said, though he'd been thinking the same thing he thought every time she retold that story: *That's the most ludicrous thing I've ever heard.*

Milo stared at the bare walls and felt desire. Not for Tina, or even escape, but for that pack of cigarettes he'd optimistically ditched at Howard Beach.

13

A pair of suits arrived, ignored his request for dinner, and led him out. More hidden corridors, then he was taken outside to where the whine of planes soaked the cold, wet air. A black Ford Explorer awaited them, and he climbed into the back. The two men joined him on either side, and another put the SUV into gear and began to drive.

Questions are only useful when the answers will lead somewhere. In this case, there was no point. He'd jumped the Tourist train, and now he was going to pay for it.

They stopped near one of the domestic terminals, and Drummond climbed into the passenger seat, wearing a disheveled tux. Milo wondered if he'd been dragged from the opera, but it was two in the morning. He didn't bother looking at Milo, just pointed at the windshield, and the driver got going again.

"You seriously fucked up, Hall."

Milo didn't answer; he was serene.

"Did you think we wouldn't know? That we wouldn't figure it out?"

Milo cleared his throat; his hunger had subsided. "Did you get the money?"

A pause, then he said, "Yes, we got it. Kudos on a fine job there." Another pause, longer this time, and when Drummond spoke again he turned to face Milo. "Who do you think you are? Don't let your job title go to your head. I knew where you were as soon as you sent that last message from Zürich. We watched you hop the train to Paris, where you lifted a passport, then wander around Charles de Gaulle waiting for your plane. They're called video cameras. You used the passport of a Monsieur Claude Girard—he looked enough like you for it to work. JFK? Simple stuff. You were followed all the way to Columbia."

"I didn't know seeing your family was a crime."

That was greeted by the rumble of engines and wheels humming across tarmac. Beyond the driver the colored lights of airplanes taxied endlessly in the blackness.

A queer grin filled Drummond's face. "When I found out who you were meeting, I called off the tail. I'm not an ogre. An employee feels the need to take a day to see his wife, that's not a problem. You'd finished your work, and the next assignment hadn't been sent yet. Sure, I was pissed off that you did it behind my back, but you guys are paranoid. It's to be expected. No. Visiting your wife wasn't a problem. This," he said, lifting a gray folder from his lap. "*This* is the problem. Adriana Stanescu."

"Oh."

"Who were you working with? Who was holding her?"

Milo looked at the guard to his right, who had a military buzz cut and a wide, clean-shaven jawline. Neither he nor the one to his left carried a gun, which made this somehow less tragic. The doors just beyond them were unlocked. Though he had no plans to make a break for it, he charted possible escape routes, figuring where he had to land blows, and in what order, to get out of here—and in which direction, then, to run, but this geometry of escape was only academic, a way of distracting him from the question.

"Well?"

"Some guys. From the Bührle job."

"Their names?"

"It doesn't matter."

"It does to me."

So Milo gave him two names—the German, Stefan, and the Italian, Giuseppe—then changed the subject. "Where did you find her?"

"You don't know?"

"I didn't have time to find a safe house, so it was up to those two. Where was it?"

"France. In the mountains."

"Which ones?"

"It doesn't matter."

It does to me, Milo wanted to say, but Drummond was right. The details were beside the point. He should have known from the start that, once the frustrations of temporary parenthood kicked in, Yevgeny Primakov would cut and run. Let the girl go, and let Milo face the consequences. Perhaps he'd decided that, son or not, Milo's occasional intel wasn't worth the trouble.

Milo was struck by another *How did I end up here?* moment, because even in his business it was a strange thing for your own father to cheat you.

He considered giving up the old man's name. It would end his obligations, making his job so much easier. He could give more, too: *Yevgeny Primakov, my father, is running a shadow agency within the United Nations.* That would certainly ruin Yevgeny's day.

Milo wasn't ready for that level of vindictiveness, though. Not yet. Nor was he ready to be turned into a triple agent, informing on Yevgeny, which was the least Drummond would demand.

"Will you put her back?" Milo asked.

"What?"

"Adriana. I failed that test, but there's no need to make her pay for it. Drop her off somewhere in Berlin and let it go."

They had reached the end of the tarmac, far past the airport buildings, and the driver turned the Explorer in a long arc and headed back again. Drummond's grin had returned, and he said to the driver, "Do you hear this guy?"

He rocked his head in a kind of answer.

To Milo, he said, "Test? What are you talking about?"

"Enough, Alan. There was no reason to kill that girl, not unless you had a Tourist you couldn't trust. Not unless you wanted a last test before you put him on to more serious work."

"Ha *ha.*" The laugh sputtered forcibly out, and Drummond had to wipe spittle from his lips. "Christ, the ego on this man! You think I'd kill a teenager just to find out if you were loyal? Do you really think that?"

Milo just stared.

"Jesus, Weaver," he said, mistakenly letting his real name slip out. "The whole world really does revolve around you, doesn't it?" He shook his head. "No. I knew it would be tough on you, sure, but we wanted her killed for the most excellent of reasons."

"What's the most excellent of reasons, then?"

Drummond considered him a moment, then shrugged. "The future of our relationship with German intelligence, if you must know. With her alive, we remain out in the cold. With her death, we're in."

The geometry of escape left him, replaced by some weird algebra of cause and effect. "I don't get it."

"Because there's no need for you to get it. I'm not here to connect the dots for you. Just know that what you did put the entire transatlantic relationship in jeopardy."

"So you're going to kill her anyway?"

"You haven't been reading the papers," said Drummond. "Adriana Stanescu's body was found only hours ago—late Thursday night, I mean. All of Europe is in mourning, or so the newspapers would have you believe. Me, I kind of doubt most of Europe gives a damn about a Moldovan girl, but I'm like that. I suspect most people, particularly in that racist backwater across the ocean."

It was too much to keep straight; he couldn't chart the repercussions of everything he'd just heard. So he said the first thing that came to mind. "Who did it?"

"That's something we'd all like to know."

They pulled up to one of the terminals—he'd lost track of which was which—and parked beside a tall figure illuminated briefly in the headlights. Hat, long overcoat. Drummond said, "Time to meet your babysitter," and then the men on either side of Milo got out of the Explorer. The one on his right left the door open so the tall figure could climb in beside him. "I think you know Mr. Einner?"

He had last seen James Einner the previous July in Geneva. Milo had attacked him in his hotel bathroom, bound him in duct tape, and wrapped him in a shower curtain. Hatred or anger hadn't motivated his actions, just expediency. In fact, he liked James Einner.

"James," he said, smiling.

In James Einner's memories, however, the humiliation of that July incident colored everything, and when Milo stuck out a hand to shake, Einner planted a swift fist into the center of Milo's face, knocking him back against the far door. Shock, then pain, filled Milo's features.

Mildly, Drummond said, "Now, James."

Einner raised both his hands, his long fingers dancing merrily and his bright blue eyes twinkling. "All done, sir."

The pain poured into Milo's nose now. His eyes were awash in tears, and he tasted blood. "You fucka," said Milo. "You bwoke my nose."

Einner took a silk handkerchief out of his pocket and handed it over, still smiling.

"Meet your babysitter, Sebastian. He'll be your partner while you vet Marko Dzubenko's tales. Unlike me, Einner doesn't have a soft spot for old farts like you. He'll cut your throat at the first sign of disloyalty. Isn't that right, James?"

"You've got that right, sir."

With the handkerchief pressed to his leaking nose, Milo looked back and forth between these two men, and to the driver, who was trying hard not to laugh. As he tilted his head back to avoid too much mess, he was consumed by hatred. Not for Drummond, or even James Einner, but again for Yevgeny Primakov, who had abandoned his parental responsibilities as soon as they had become inconvenient. Yevgeny's abandonment was nothing new, but that made it no less appalling.

14

They were sitting seven rows apart in coach, another sign of Tourism's budget constraints, and James Einner looked comfortable in his pin-striped, and not very cheap, Tom Ford suit (a ludicrous expense since most Tourists tossed their clothes after a couple of wearings), while Milo was stuffed into an ill-fitting and starchy Italian suit. Correctly predicting that the clothes Milo had picked up back in Zürich wouldn't be presentable by the time he left JFK—blood spatter didn't sit well with any country's passport control—Drummond had brought him the suit, as well as a wheeled Baggallini tote full of necessities: the official "Tourism kit" most Tourists soon realized was too cumbersome for the life.

Once they had boarded this American Airlines flight to London, Milo plugged himself into his iPod, pressed a complimentary napkin to his nostrils, and tilted his head back as far as it would go. He closed his eyes and listened to David Bowie, circa 1972:

News guy wept and told us,
Earth was really dying

He wasn't angry about the punch—he'd deserved it. Last year's fight with Einner had been particularly humiliating for the younger man, who'd been dragged off a toilet in the middle of a bowel movement, then wrapped in a shower curtain, pants around his ankles, stained with his own shit.

The real shock was that he was still here. Drummond hadn't released him from Tourism; the morning hadn't found him free of all this. Now he even had a chaperone to make sure he didn't step out of line.

Somewhere over the Atlantic, they met by the bathrooms. Einner said, "If you're waiting for me to apologize, then forget it."

Milo gave him a generous smile and looked at the dried blood on the napkin; the flow was finished. "I'm just wondering why I'm still employed. Drummond doesn't trust me."

Einner rocked his head from side to side, then made room for a stewardess to pass. He whispered, "You know how many Tourists we've got in Europe right now?"

Back when he'd been in administration, twelve had been the default number, but there'd been cutbacks. "Eight?"

"Five," said Einner. "Including you and me. We lost three in the last few months, and one of us five is laid up in a hospital in Stockholm."

"He told you all this?"

"This guy's not like Grainger. I know the old man was your friend, but he was a goddamned sphinx when it came to sharing information. And Mendel—you dealt with him, right?"

Milo nodded.

"You got a little more information from him, but it's like he was always leaving out the most important detail. Drummond, though . . ." He faded off a moment. "He's trying to make you a partner with him. I like it, this new Tourism."

"So what else has he told you?"

Einner wagged a finger. "You're not going to get me that easily. Just know that the situation has saved your ass. We can't afford to lose any more Tourists, not even ones as washed up as you."

"We."

"What?"

"You said *we* can't afford to lose Tourists. Drummond really does have you thinking you're partners. It's fantastic."

Einner waved off his cynicism and wandered off. Milo envied his belief in the new Tourism, the Tourism of "we."

Because of air traffic, they had to float for a half hour over Heathrow before finally descending at nine Saturday night. Milo hadn't been able to sleep at all, so when they finally approached the gate, he was flagging, and Einner looked noticeably young and alert among the tired passengers shuffling off the plane. They continued separately down the labyrinth of corridors to the crowded border control, where, after twenty minutes' wait, an overly polite official said, "You have an accident, sir?"

"Excuse me?"

He tapped the side of his nose.

"Back in America. I'll survive."

"Then please enjoy yourself, Mr. Hall. And try not to have any accidents here."

He felt itchy and clammy in his starched suit as he moved through the throng of real-world tourists, but it was another rule of Tourism that, when traveling, one should look as much like a businessman as possible, like someone who has come to invest in the host nation, who has money to blow, who has no patience for customs delays and might easily take his gold card elsewhere. As young and old tourists flushed in the face of hard questions from British customs, Milo passed unmolested, pulling the Baggallini behind him.

In preparation for the next day, he perused the stores in Terminal 3 and bought a T-shirt with a silhouette of London across it, white sports socks, and sunglasses. He took the escalator back down to the arrivals level and joined a twenty-minute taxi queue.

As he finally made his way into the redbrick metropolis, to Piccadilly and Mayfair, he considered his situation. His new boss looked upon him with suspicion, and James Einner, despite their past camaraderie, was here to threaten him each step of the way. Why should he put up with this? Why not ask the driver to turn back to Heathrow? He could dump his phone in a wastebasket and buy a ticket back to his family.

Adriana was gone—but only a fool could believe that it set him free of anything other than guilt, and it didn't even do that.

The reason he remained, like the reason Drummond hadn't fired him, was far more practical than the safety of a Moldovan girl: He wasn't sure he could survive the exit interview.

These extended interrogations went on for weeks as you spilled everything you had done and seen, accounted for all your absences and contacts, and made a general accounting of the money you'd spent. The Company didn't spend so much on Tourists just to have them walk away. It wanted to squeeze every dollar out of each Tourist before setting him free. Milo knew this because he'd once supervised the exit interviews himself. He knew how an interrogator sniffed out inconsistencies like a truffle dog burrowing under wet leaves.

And what if he did make it? What if he survived weeks of interrogation, and by some stroke of luck they didn't find a way to connect him to his father, his confessor, and charge him with treason? What then? Would Drummond really trust him to keep his mouth shut about his work? Tom Grainger would have—but Grainger had been an old friend. Drummond had only met Milo twice, once to congratulate him, once to reprimand him. There were limits to the new Tourism, but Milo had no idea where they lay.

Before entering the modern Cavendish Hotel, he found a Boots pharmacy. What he wanted was a pack of Davidoffs, but the only way to keep going was to hold on to the promise of a future. He'd decided on the flight to end his relationship with Dexedrine, and in the pharmacy asked the cashier for a box of Nicorette gum, the "fresh mint" flavor. He ripped open the box as he returned to the hotel. He chewed two, the rush of eight milligrams of nicotine bringing on hiccups at the front desk, and his desire for a cigarette ebbed. Predictably, though, it was nowhere near as good as the real thing.

15

He woke at six and checked his nose. It wasn't actually broken. He could breathe through it, but it was bruised a faint purple and slightly swollen, which would make his surveillance that much harder.

Beneath his suit and tie he wore the London T-shirt and a pocket held the white socks. He took the half-empty Sunday morning tube to Hampstead, then walked up to East Heath Road. Among the facades looking out over the park was an inconspicuous Georgian belonging to a man named Edward Ryan.

There were two London vignettes within Dzubenko's stories, and Milo had been assigned to verify one that focused on a man the newspapers commonly described as "xenophobic, racist, and nationalist," much like the political party he headed. Despite having been the subject of exposés by the *Guardian* and BBC's *Panorama* linking it and its leader to pro-Nazi movements, the party had gained 4.6 percent in the most recent round of local elections.

Drummond had briefed him in the Explorer at JFK while Einner, still beside him, listened. Assumedly, he had received his brief beforehand. Drummond first showed Milo a photograph of a trim, gray-tinted Englishman in a bowler. "Edward Ryan, national chairman of the Union of British Nationals. According to Marko, he's on the receiving end of Russian money funneled through the SSU. Essentially, Moscow's funding the revitalization of the UBN. Once the party gets a member into Parliament, Moscow can point to the growing racism in England. That in turn will energize the anger of British Muslims and lead to deeper divisions. That's long-term. In the meantime, Moscow and Kiev get inside information on the Labour Party, which the UBN regularly spies on."

Beside him, Einner said knowingly, "Why risk sending in your own people, when a bunch of xenophobes will do it for you?"

The question, of course, was how to verify that this was true. On that point, Drummond repeated Dzubenko's own suggestion. "On the second to last Sunday of each month, Ryan passes Labour Party information to the SSU's representative, who he thinks is a Ukrainian businessman sharing his interest in racial purity. You will shadow him, and if he meets the representative you'll ID him for me."

"The head of the party does this?" Milo asked doubtfully.

"Trust, Marko tells us, is in short supply in the UBN. He'd rather do it himself."

Ryan's Sunday itinerary was no secret. An adoring interviewer had, in December, spelled it out in order to show what a busy and important man the politician was. At eight o'clock, he went for a jog on the Heath. By ten thirty, he was in his front pew for the Anglican St. John-at-Hampstead's parish Eucharist, having walked the distance along busy Heath Street, where the occasional supporter (few and far between in an area full of liberals and Muslims and Jews) could shake his hand. When the interviewer asked how a man of his high principles could take part in the services of a church with a reputation for encouraging multicultural and interreligious cohesion, Ryan smiled and said, "My community is my community. The effort to clean white Britain must begin on our own streets."

Afterward, like any respectable family man, he returned home for tea and newspapers, then took his two sons, six and nine, to whatever Sunday activity had been decided upon that week.

Milo had been over the schedule the previous night, considering where Ryan might best hand over information. Each place, it seemed, was perfect. The expanse of Hampstead Heath was classic dead-letter drop territory. Pass-offs could be made all along Heath Street, and it was part of the nature of church that its members mingled and whispered to one another. Children's events, as Milo knew, divided instantly into children on one side and parents on another, and the parents quickly sank into lengthy chats. There were any number of ways for Ryan to pass on information, if he were going to pass on anything at all.

Milo found a spot in the park and pressed his phone to his ear, so that in his suit he looked like a churchgoer involved in early business. He drifted to some bushes and used the camera phone to zoom in on the front of the house. Tourism had long ago eschewed the high-end phones that were a magnet for thieves, instead making its own adjustments to mundane models, like increasing the camera range and resolution of this store-bought Nokia.

Just after eight, Ryan emerged in jogging pants and a sweatshirt. He walked briskly down the sidewalk, knees high, then crossed into the park and began his morning run. No security detail followed him.

The environment worked to Milo's advantage. Winter had stripped the concealing foliage of its leaves, and the Heath's naturally rolling terrain gave him numerous vantage points. While Ryan was in motion, the chance of a drop was unlikely; anything thrown on the ground could easily be intercepted by passersby. It was during the pauses—and despite Ryan's air of athleticism, there were plenty—that Milo brought the camera to his eye and zoomed in on the man's hands. Two stops at trees, where he leaned against the trunk and tugged his ankles up high behind himself, and three stops at benches. At the third one, he reached into a pocket in his running pants but only took out a pack of cigarettes, which went back into his pocket. While he smoked, Milo found a better position, then watched him deposit the butt into a trash can. At one point, Ryan ran into a friend, also jogging. They shook hands, the friend still bouncing in his springy shoes, and talked for a couple of minutes. Milo took photographs of the entire encounter.

Ryan returned home by nine thirty. Milo found a trash can, in which he dropped his jacket and tie, and slipped on his sunglasses, so that when Ryan left for church he was a slightly different man.

Ryan reemerged in a charcoal suit, joined by a thin, birdlike wife and his two cleaned and pressed sons. Heath Street was waking up, the stores just opening. While in most of London blue laws kept Sunday shop hours to a minimum, tourist areas like Hampstead were exempt, and the mixed population raised their blinds in preparation for the rush of Sunday shoppers arriving from quieter neighborhoods.

The Ryans paused three times along that walk, and Milo photographed each encounter. The first was with an old woman heading in the same direction. Mrs. Ryan approached her and helped her cross the street. Then, after a moment's consultation, the whole family remained with the woman, keeping to her shuffling pace. Next, a heavy white-haired man shook Ryan's hand in both of his, grinning madly, his pink cheeks glowing. Ryan made a joke, which caused the man to erupt in fits of laughter, then patted his shoulder to send him on his way. The third encounter occurred outside a halal butcher's, when a bald younger man stopped Ryan, shook his hand, and whispered something close to the side of his face. Ryan smiled broadly but didn't laugh. As they talked, a bearded man in a taqiyah opened the butcher shop's front door, and both men stopped their conversation to stare at him. Then the bald man left, and the family continued with the old woman past the Hampstead tube station to Church Row, where more Georgian houses led down to the crowd of parishioners entering St. John-at-Hampstead.

Though there were plenty of ideal aspects to passing messages in a church, the Ryans sat, without fail, in the front pew, a location that precluded any secret conversations. The only chances were just before services, or just after, as they greeted their fellow worshippers. From across the street, Milo shot pictures of Ryan's various handshakes, then headed back to Heath Street until services ended. He took advantage of the opening shops to buy a pair of jeans, a jacket, and some sneakers, which he carried in a bright red shopping bag. As he hurried back to the church, he noticed a Hyundai parked halfway down Church Row, with a man in his fifties sitting behind the wheel. He glanced at the face and kept moving toward the church.

There was something familiar about it, but he couldn't place it at first. It only came to him as he was taking shots of the parishioners again. The surprise, when it came, nearly made him drop the phone.

He looked up, but the Hyundai was gone. The driver had been one of the two in Berlin, the "Germans" who'd been shadowing him.

16

The existence of his shadow put a pall over the rest of the day's surveillance. Had the Germans tracked him to London? Unlikely. More likely, they hadn't been Germans in the first place, and it only proved that the file on him was more correct than Drummond knew: Milo wasn't so clever after all.

He felt tense and exhausted by 4:00 P.M., when Ryan returned home for the evening. Still, he'd gotten his photographs, and in a pub, over a tepid plate of steak and kidney pie, he sent them to one of the phone numbers Drummond had given him—an analysis unit that had probably been pieced together from friends in the "war on drugs."

By then, he had played and replayed his shadow's face in his head, going over the previous months' jobs, searching for some connection. Tourism, as Drummond had pointed out, is only as secure as its anonymity. The same is true for Tourists themselves. Their only real safety lies in their lack of identity, and when that disappears the world becomes far more dangerous.

Not just dangerous, but . . .

He stared at his plate, realizing that his shadow's existence proved something larger than his own stupidity. He called Drummond. The voice mail answered. He said, "It's no longer a theory," then hung up. Within five minutes, his phone was ringing.

"What's with the elusive messages, Hall? Is he or isn't he selling secrets?"

"No sign yet. I mean the larger story. It's not a theory."

Drummond cleared his throat. "Some explanation, please."

Milo tried. It was all about his shadow. Berlin, and now London. "Only the department knows my day-to-day location—correct?"

"Correct."

"Well, if you really don't have someone shadowing me—you don't, do you?"

Drummond verified this with a grunt.

"Then someone inside the department is leaking my location, and has been doing so at least since Berlin."

"Is the guy Chinese?"

"Don't be simple, Alan. I just don't see another way to explain it."

He mused over that, humming. "Well, if you see him again . . ."

"I know. I will."

The image analysts texted their reports on Ryan's acquaintances. None raised any red flags, though one—the old woman the whole family helped to church—was unidentifiable. It was possible that Dzubenko had been mistaken about the day that information was transferred, or that the meeting time had been changed since his defection. Milo needed to be sure, though, so he returned to Hampstead Heath as the sun hung low, preparing to disappear, and rain began to fall. He checked the sodden ground along Ryan's path and examined the two trees against which he'd stretched, but it was while he was crouched in the wet grass under the second of the three benches that he found it, and finding it surprised him almost as much as the German had.

It was a small USB flash drive, cleverly encased in two inches of wood, stuck with adhesive to the underside of the bench. A casual observer wouldn't have noticed anything, and in the failing light Milo nearly missed it, too, but he was depending more on his hands than his eyes, and when he caught the edge of the wood he pulled and felt it break off easily into his palm.

He took out his phone, which contained a Company-installed standard USB port. As a light shower began, he copied the contents of the flash drive—three Word documents—then replaced it. He was soaking wet by the time he squatted among high shrubs farther down the incline.

The documents were encoded and unreadable, so Milo sent them to the analysts with a note for Drummond: *From subject—no recipient yet.* He pocketed the phone and made sure his view of the bench was unobstructed and clear (a lamppost illuminated the area), then checked the time. It was seven o'clock, cold and pouring rain, and he had no idea how long it would take for the drive to be picked up. It would be, he suspected, a very long night.

He was wrong. At a little after eight, a tall, elegant figure crossed the Heath, heading toward the bench. Milo brought the phone to his eye, zooming in. The figure paused by the bench and looked around. Milo lowered the phone and stood. "What the hell are you doing?"

Einner shook his head and walked down to him. "You must be freezing your ass off."

"Get out of here."

"Drummond thought you could use some help. You hadn't moved for nearly an hour—he wanted to find out if you were dead."

"He could've called."

Einner didn't answer. They both knew that Drummond just wanted to make sure Milo hadn't abandoned his phone and walked.

"Did it pan out?" Milo asked.

"I found you, didn't I?"

"I mean your angle. Did Marko's story check out?"

"Yeah. And I assume that you sitting in the rain means yours is checking out, too."

"Just waiting for the pickup."

Einner grinned, then turned to look at the empty bench up the hill. He pointed at the nearby lamppost. "See that?"

"The lamp?"

"Yeah. Look at the top of it."

When his eyes adjusted to the glare, he could make out three inconspicuous cameras atop the pole. He exhaled. "I think I see where you're going with this."

"Sure you do," Einner said and took out his phone. After a moment, he said, "Can I get a visual on a surveillance camera? Exactly, baby. Just see where I am and there should be three to choose from. I need a bench."

As he waited for the reply he shrugged at Milo.

"How's it coming in? Great. Listen, we're going to need IDs on anyone who sits there or fools around with it. Particularly the latter." He covered the mouthpiece and said to Milo, "Underneath?"

"Yeah."

"You heard it? That's what we're looking for. And you'll be reporting it directly to Hall. You have the number? Thanks, you're a doll." Einner hung up and opened his arms. "Come praise your betters."

Milo patted his pockets and came up with Nicorette, feeling inept next to this tech-savvy young man.

Einner said, "Let's go find some girls."

17

They left the park separately and took the tube back into town. Appearing in public together would have broken any number of Tourism rules, so they settled for an indoor party. Milo picked up a new suit, and, even though Einner had said he would bring "something fun," Milo bought a bottle of Finlandia vodka and another of some very dry Noilly Prat vermouth. He had just showered and dressed again when there was a knock at his door. Einner swept past him and examined the room, then sniffed the steam in the bathroom.

"Where's the party favors?" asked Milo.

"Am I not enough?" Einner stripped off his coat, which was dry despite the rain outside—he was probably staying in the same hotel. "You just take care of the drinks, old man."

"Vodka martini?"

"I'd kill you for one."

Milo mixed them up in glasses in the bathroom, and when he emerged found Einner by the window, the blinds pulled, leaning over the breakfast table. With a credit card he was cutting up sixteen lines of cocaine.

Einner looked up, squinting. "The nose? Will it work?"

"I'll give it my best shot."

They sat across from each other at the table and toasted their survival. Einner made a face after his first sip. "Ouch."

"More vermouth?"

"An olive might help."

"They were out."

Einner took another sip, then handed over a rolled ten-pound note. "Try that on."

Milo stuck to the one swollen nostril with an open passageway, then passed back the note. He wiped his sore nose unconsciously and drank and watched Einner inhale two lines as if this were his morning routine.

"When was the last time you did blow?"

Milo's memory seemed to be both slow and quick. "Christ, six years ago? No, seven."

"Aha! Back when you were the great Charles Alexander."

They'd had this talk before. Milo said, "He was never as good as people would have you think. It's a myth, just like the Black Book. It keeps Tourists on their toes."

They did two more lines. Milo mixed more drinks. As he came out of the bathroom, his phone vibrated for his attention. It was a message from the analysts:

Package picked up. Pavlo Romanenko, third secretary political section, Ukrainian embassy, London.

"My lead checked out."

"Two for two," Einner said, then refused Milo's offer of a Nicorette and nodded at the four remaining lines. "Ready?"

"I should take a break."

"What you should do is quit wiping your nose."

He hadn't realized he was doing it. They both laughed; then Einner settled and said, very seriously, "You really think we're in trouble?"

"With a mole?" Milo frowned at his glass. "Maybe. It's looking like it."

Silence followed. Einner then related the story of two Iranians he'd killed a few months ago in Rome. "Direct from Tehran to make local al Qaeda contacts. Typical setup. One, the nervous moneyman. The other a Revolutionary Guard to do the heavy lifting and keep

Moneybags in line. I took out the tough one first—the guy hung around his hotel window too much—then went in for the soft target. It turned out I was wrong. Moneybags was as frothing as his guard. Nearly killed me with his hands," Einner said, raising his own in a pair of claws. "Before I shot him, he asked if I knew why, in the end, his people would win. *No, Mohammed. Tell me.* His people, he said, still had belief on their side. We, on the other hand, had nothing."

"How'd you answer that?" Milo asked, curious despite himself.

"How do you think? I killed him." Einner finished his drink. "I wasn't about to lecture him on the Black Book."

Milo left to refill their drinks in the bathroom, wondering about the point of that story. When he returned, Einner was stretched out on the bed, stomach down, his chin resting on the backs of his hands. He took the martini with thanks.

"So why'd you come back?" Einner asked. "You were out of the Company. Grainger was dead, and you'd spent time in the pokey for his murder. You still came back."

"Maybe I wanted a last fling with adventure. Some fun."

That provoked a shake of the head. "No, man. You're the least happy Tourist we've got."

"Maybe I realized I'm no good at anything else."

Einner seemed to believe that, then he didn't. "You're not that good. Not anymore."

"To be honest, I don't know. It was probably a mistake. You heard Drummond. I don't care what reasons he comes up with, I'll never regret not killing that girl."

"She's dead anyway."

"Not by my hand."

Einner sighed loudly. "Sounds like Mohammed was wrong—you, at least, have run head-on into your beliefs."

Milo felt anxiety slipping through his buzz. "Maybe. But any department that orders a hit like that doesn't deserve to stay around."

"You just wander into the spy business yesterday?"

"Come on, James. Even you've got limits, right? If you'd been given that assignment—don't tell me you'd actually do it."

Einner thought a moment but didn't answer. He raised himself from the bed, grabbed his martini, and lifted it. "To knowing what to do, and when." They both drank; then Einner asked, "Did you ever figure it out?"

"Figure what out?"

"Last we talked, I was stewing in my own shit, and you were off to figure out who was assassinating Sudanese mullahs."

"Yeah. That's right."

"It really was Grainger?"

Milo nodded. "But the orders came from Senator Nathan Irwin. He's the one who ordered Angela killed, then Grainger, once he'd become a liability."

"Fucking senators," Einner muttered, and Milo realized that he'd already known all this. Perhaps Drummond had shared. He just wanted to know what Milo knew. Finally, Einner said, "This man must be on your shit list."

There was no need to answer that.

Einner cleared this throat. "Let's finish up this stuff."

They took turns, then wiped the remnants onto their gums. Milo refilled their drinks, but when he came out again there were eight more white lines on the table. Einner was in one of the chairs, wiping his nose. "I'm close to the Book, Milo."

"It's Sebastian. And I don't believe you."

"Why not? You found a copy of it. In Spain, you said."

"I was lying, James. There's no such thing as the Black Book of Tourism."

Einner rocked his head from side to side, digesting that. "We'll see. Anyway, I've found clues. I think it's in Bern."

"What clues?"

"You think I'd tell you? An unbeliever?"

According to the legend that all Tourists learned at one point or another, twenty-one copies of the Black Book of Tourism had been hidden by a retired Tourist in secret spots throughout the world. The myth of Tourism's Bible fed into each Tourist's desire for a single guide to show him the path to survival and sanity and perhaps even morality in a profession that encouraged none of these things. Until last August, it had only been a myth.

Milo, driven by some undeniable desire while in prison, had sat down and written it himself. Not long—maybe thirty pages—but it summed up what he thought such a book should say. He'd later copied it out by hand into twenty-one children's schoolbooks and, over the first month of his return to Tourism, spread them throughout Europe and Russia. Then, over time, he'd slowly left clues to their whereabouts.

So when Einner said that he was closing in on a copy in Bern, Milo could chart the clues that had brought him so far. A name engraved on the rear of a tombstone outside Malmö, Sweden. An address included in the records of that name, of a nonexistent patient in the Centre Hospitalier Universitaire, a Toulouse teaching hospital. On one of the exterior walls of that address in the north of Milan, the hardly visible polyurethane words MARIANS JAZZROOM. Einner was nearly there. Milo wondered, with a tinge of despair, just what he would make of his collected wisdom.

Einner was in the toilet when the knock on the door came. It was 11:00 P.M.

"Get that, will you?" Einner called, as if this were his room. "And don't ever say I don't take care of you!"

Through the peephole, Milo saw a wide-angled view of two women with faux-fur coats, short skirts, and tiny purses. They not only dressed the same but looked the same, and when he opened the door he realized they were twins.

With a rough working-class accent, one said, "James 'ere?"

"Be right out!" he called over the flushing toilet. "Make them some drinks, Sebastian!"

Milo invited them in and scooped up his phone. They peered around the room as if they'd never been in a hotel before, which he seriously doubted. One alighted on the lines of cocaine. "My kinda party, innit."

"I'll be back with the ice," Milo said. They were already sitting down at the table, tightening the ten-pound note, when he closed

the door behind himself. On his way down the corridor to the stairwell he heard Einner saying, "Where the fuck?"

Milo kept on until he had reached the hotel bar. He was suddenly
ill, and for some inexplicable reason kept imagining James Einner
with his throat cut. He drank gimlets to wash away the image. When
he returned two hours later, the room was empty, but it stank.

18

The phone woke him at six. "Yeah?"

"Riverrun, past Eve."

"And Adam's."

Drummond cleared his throat. "Looks like it's verified."

"Bad news."

Milo heard papers shuffling through the line—if he was calling from New York, it was 1:00 A.M. there. "You're going to Warsaw for the next one. It'll take a little more time."

"Okay."

"How's Einner treating you?"

"We're old friends. But you knew that, of course."

"Are you?" he said, then sighed. "Listen, I've gotten some word from a friend in Germany."

"Friend? This have to do with—"

"It has to do with you, Hall. Your ethnic radar might not be so bad. Someone in German intelligence was looking for you, but I'm assured that it's being taken care of."

"Why were they looking for me?"

"It doesn't matter. You should be clear now. If you do see them again, let me know. Got it?"

"Sure. That's good news."

"Good?"

"If the Germans are shadowing me, then a Chinese mole is no more likely than it was the day before yesterday."

"It means we're still deciding, Hall, which means you're still vetting."

He popped aspirin, a multivitamin, and two Nicorette—he'd left the Dexedrine in the hotel trash—then checked out. He tipped the doorman who found him a taxi, and nearly dozed on the ride to the airport, half dreaming of James Einner and his two friends.

Milo hadn't slept with a woman since October, and that had been a clumsy, desperate attempt with his wife. A part of him wondered if he'd made a mistake sidestepping a night of mindless sex, if only because it carried no investment. Simplicity: just an easy trajectory toward orgasm. Unlike that last attempt in October, it might have been fun.

Fun.

You're the least happy Tourist we've got.

His phone shivered on the M4, and he read the Warsaw instructions.

He was just in time to catch an eight twenty British Airways flight, and when he touched down at Frederic Chopin Airport a little before noon, he was nearly sick with hunger. The official guarding this Schengen entry point gave his Sebastian Hall passport a little more of an examination than he was used to, but in the end it was all the same. "Business or tourism?"

The answer rolled off his tongue without thought.

He picked up a bottle of Coke and a cheese sandwich, which he gobbled down before reaching the Avis rental counter. As he took the long, traffic-jammed road toward town, he drank the Coke too fast and it burned the back of his throat. At least it woke him up.

He'd last been to Warsaw in 2000, during that earlier time when he was known as Charles Alexander. Despite what James Einner and others believed, back then he was more anxiety and suicidal bluster than efficiency and purpose. Back then he took whatever drugs could keep him going—pills, powders, and the occasional syringe. He'd felt as if it were someone else's body he was abusing.

Then he remembered why he'd come to Warsaw in 2000 and understood why he had walked out of his room the previous night. He felt childishly proud, knowing that Dr. Ray, the marriage counselor, would be impressed by his self-knowledge.

He'd come to buy information from a Lebanese traitor in the Bristol Hotel. The Israeli occupation of southern Lebanon had just ended, and in the inevitable internal shake-up that followed, this man feared for his position. So he was preparing for retirement by selling pieces of his extensive library of secrets to the Americans, the British, and the Israelis.

The purchase had gone smoothly, and at the end of it the door to the suite's second room burst open and two Polish prostitutes danced in with bottles of champagne. The Lebanese grinned—he'd arranged a party to celebrate their newfound cooperation.

Milo hadn't resisted, and it had been fun in its peculiar way, but it had been only as pleasurable as it could be for someone so disconnected from himself. Early the next year, though, he learned that, six months after their meeting, the Lebanese traitor had been found on a cannabis farm at the northern end of the Beqaa Valley, his throat cut and his tongue removed. Last night, he realized, that image had been triggered by the women, and he had somehow imagined that if he stayed Einner would end up mutilated.

How do you like that, Dr. Ray?

He came gradually into town, the open fields and sooty buildings slowly replaced by modern, postwar architecture. It was after two by the time he checked into the immense Marriott tower—he had no desire to revisit the Bristol—and while he knew he should immediately begin working on Dzubenko's Warsaw story, he decided to take the rest of the day off. He had a vodka martini in the hotel's Panorama bar, then lifted a complimentary *Tribune* and headed out to CDQ, an arty bar where he could drink in peace to the strains of what the pretty bartender told him was Charlotte Gainsbourg's latest album, *5:55*. Serge Gainsbourg's daughter was an inspired coincidence, because until last year he'd listened incessantly to the father's songbook, which had been a sure way to find a better mood. With everything that had gone bad, though, even his musical salvation had been contaminated, and he hadn't listened to it since. Yet here he was, among the young art crowd of Warsaw, gazing at skinny girls and ugly paintings, listening to the daughter of the man who had once been able to bestow upon him so much joy. He ordered another drink and found a corner with enough light to read the *Tribune*.

The first article that caught his eye extensively quoted Reuters about the discovery of Adriana Stanescu's body on a road that led to Marseille. The details, Milo noticed, were sketchy, and the press releases by the Berlin police suggested that Adriana had been captured and killed by human traffickers with Russian connections. He stuck more Nicorette in his mouth and tried to chew away the shakes.

Then, three pages in, he saw a photograph of Senator Nathan Irwin, Republican from Minnesota.

There was nothing truly notable in the senator's appearance here—he was pictured with a group of other senators looking into the real estate slump that had been causing problems for the last few months—but seeing his smug face did Milo no good. He ordered another martini and considered how much more empty life had become because of this man. Thomas Grainger hadn't only been his boss and friend; he'd been Stephanie's godfather, who would sometimes show up at the apartment unexpectedly with gifts and a ruddy smile.

Though theirs had been a long-distance friendship, he'd had a particularly warm connection to Angela Yates. She'd attended his wedding, and their history stretched back to when both of them were young, enthusiastic recruits for the Central Intelligence Agency. She'd even been on hand during that disastrous morning in Venice, when Milo and Tina first met. The day Stephanie was born. September 11, 2001. Angela and Tom had touched so many important moments in his life, and because of Nathan Irwin they were both dead.

In truth, there were only two survivors from last year's mess— Irwin and Milo himself. They had never met, but each knew the other existed.

Kill the little voices.

It was his mother again, whom he'd only known as an occasional visitor in his childhood. Until he was nine she would visit in the night, fearful of capture as she and her German Marxist comrades spread fear throughout Europe. She came to her son like a ghost, whispering urgent lessons that he was too young to understand and would later seldom follow.

Listen to the Bigger Voice. It's the only one that will ever be straight with you.

What did the Bigger Voice say now?

It was only later, after he had lost track of his martinis, that he succumbed to that voice and went to look for a Telekomunikacja Polska phone booth. His anger had returned. He had spent too long thinking drunkenly of injustice, and when he shoved in the zloty coins the pad of his thumb hurt. He dialed just as forcefully. It only rang twice before the old man answered with a hesitant, "Da?"

In Russian, Milo said, "You couldn't stick to our deal, could you?"

"I was wondering when you would call. It's not like you think. She got away."

"How hard is it to hold on to a kid?" Milo demanded. "You lose a kid, it's because you want to lose her."

"She got away."

"Bastard. She got away, then you tracked her down and killed her."

"You're drunk, Milo."

"Yes. And you and I are done."

"Listen to me," he said. "I did track her down, but she was already dead."

"Then who killed her?"

"Your people, I'd wager."

"They don't know who did it."

"Is that what they told you?"

Milo considered some replies, but they were all too crude and childish—he didn't want to be childish with Yevgeny. So he hung up.

He got another drink but was out of Nicorette and had to bum cigarettes off a table of pretty girls with extravagant mascara and matching platinum blond hair. They were talking politics. After an initial wave of curiosity, they soon realized that he was just another drunk American and sent him packing.

"Go to Iraq," the sexiest one told him, and the others laughed.

He was in bed by eleven, unconscionably drunk, the television on and the spinning room stinking of the cigarettes he'd bought on the way back to the hotel. He briefly flipped to BBC World News, which was full of Fidel Castro's retirement, and the unanimous election by the Cuban National Assembly of his younger brother, Raúl. The phrase "end of an era" was repeated endlessly. The results of the previous night's Academy Awards distracted him from those heavier issues.

But they're all the little voices, his mother said.

After he drifted to sleep briefly his eyelids rose as, on the screen, a tall BBC reporter Milo recognized walked through a park alongside a Chinese man. It was Zhang Yesui, the Chinese ambassador to the UN. Though he moved and spoke with that bland diplomatic nonaggression that to outsiders looks like weakness, his words were pointed. "After learning of the pre-independence discussions between Kosovo and certain current members of the Security Council, it falls on us to suggest that these members should drop their unilateral positions in regard to other nations."

"I believe you're talking about the United States," said the reporter.

"I am. The current policy of intruding on sovereign nations is counterproductive to global peace. We've seen it in Iraq and Kosovo and the Sudan."

"The Sudan?"

Milo blinked, rubbing his eyes.

"It has come to our attention that certain elements within the American government had a hand in last year's unrest, which killed nearly a hundred innocent civilians. China, along with the United Nations as a whole, considers stability in that region paramount, and it hurts us to find that another member has been undermining our efforts for peace."

Surprisingly, there was no follow-up question to that accusation, but more surprising was the fact that it had been made at all. Milo watched for a while longer, waiting for some reference to the ambassador's statement, but it had slipped away, as if it had never been made.

He considered calling Drummond, but Drummond would already be dealing with the fallout. It would be one additional piece of evidence for Marko Dzubenko's story, and certain politicians—Nathan Irwin, in particular—would be calling him up, demanding answers. For the moment, Milo was grateful he no longer worked in administration.

The worry slipped away as the fatigue caught up to him, and he flipped to a thriller dubbed into Polish and lowered the volume.

He snored so loudly that he sometimes woke himself, and when, a little after three, his door opened quietly and three visitors entered, they exchanged silent smirks over the noise. In the light of the silent television now playing soft-core pornography, they took positions around him.

One grabbed his feet; the other put him in a headlock. As Milo snapped awake they raised him briefly from the bed and slammed him down again. He tried to claw at the one holding his head but was too confused to do a thing. He felt the sharp prick of a needle in his arm.

He continued to struggle, weakening, until his arms first lost energy and then his legs. They were shadows, these men, and behind them the bright television displayed blurred bodies, bare white breasts with smeared pink nipples.

They were wrapping him now, and panic shuddered through him weakly as he imagined plastic, but it was just the bedsheets. He was so tired. He could hardly keep his eyes open. A blur of a man with a bruised eye and what might have been a mustache leaned over him and spoke in heavily accented English. "Don't worry. We're not going to kill you yet."

Milo blinked at him, his vision going fast, his tongue heavy. "You're German?"

"Yes, I am."

"Thought so." He tried to add something else, but his tongue would no longer cooperate.

Part Two

The CLOTHES of the
KIND of PEOPLE
we HATE

THREE DAYS EARLIER

FRIDAY, FEBRUARY 22

TO WEDNESDAY, MARCH 12, 2008

1

Hasad al-Akir nodded politely at the fat old woman. As this night was like all other nights, she didn't even acknowledge him as she lumbered past the counter to the wall of refrigerated glass doors in the back. There were plenty of customers he conversed with, whose names and backgrounds he knew, customers who even addressed him as *Herr* al-Akir and asked how his family was. Not this one. Despite her appearing every working evening punctually at seven and buying the same bottle of Rheinland Riesling and a Snickers candy bar, their conversation never broke from the same routine.

Guten Abend.

Her answer: an indecipherable grunt.

That will be ten euro sixty.

No reply, no smile, nothing to suggest a man was even standing in front of her. Only the exact-change deposit on the counter, sometimes a ten-euro bill with fifty and ten cents, sometimes a precollected pile of coins, but always exact. Then she'd pocket the candy bar, grab the bottle by the neck, and ignore his farewell as she shuffled her enormous weight out the door.

Tonight, though, would be different.

Ekhard Junker, his sweets distributor, had raised the price of their Snickers bars five cents. So tonight, after six months, she would put down too little money with those plump, gnawed fingers, and

Hasad would have the pleasure of informing her that she'd paid too little.

This, at least, would be something.

He had lived in Munich since the mideighties, arriving with a wave of Turkish laborers that came to do those jobs the West Germans considered beneath them. Construction, mining, recycling collection, staffing convenience stores. For a long time, Hasad had regretted his decision to leave Ankara. The Bavarians were a petty, closed race of pale bigots. The money he sent back to his parents and wife couldn't be ignored, though, so he stuck it out, finally sending for his family in 1992. By that time, Germans from the East were taking over previously Turkish jobs—nothing was beneath those *Ossis*—and many of his friends talked seriously about returning home. Not Hasad. Unlike his friends, he hadn't pissed away his earnings on liquor and nightclubs. He'd saved, and began scouring the *Süddeutsche Zeitung* for property. He was going to run his own business.

When he finally settled on this store in Pullach, an industrial suburb south of Munich, the building had been empty a year. The owner, a clever Bavarian who'd decided he was too good for the service industry, tried to squeeze as much as possible out of Hasad, but he clearly didn't know what he was in for, because the art of negotiation is a Turk's birthright.

It wasn't all anise and cinnamon, though. After two years, in late 2001, chilly tall men from the German foreign intelligence service, the BND, whose headquarters was just up the street, began visiting. They checked and rechecked his immigration papers, the deeds to his business, and his financial spreadsheets. They asked about his friends, sometimes flashing photographs of dour-looking Arabs, wondering if he, or someone he knew, might be under the sway of radical Muslim clerics.

Over the years, as his business blossomed (he'd opened a second location on the eastern edge of Munich last year, run by his son, Ahmed), their visits became less frequent, their expressions steadily more apologetic. "Just the way it is," one of them, a soft-spoken German Muslim, admitted. "When you're this close to the center of operations, you've got to expect it."

In the last half year, though, they'd left him alone. Either they were finally convinced of his loyalty or they no longer cared. For that same amount of time, he'd nightly faced this obese, mute woman who was now trudging back to him, the chilled Riesling in one hand, a Snickers bar in the other. He gave her the same nightly smile of welcome, and as usual she ignored it.

In all honesty, she annoyed him more than those tough guys from the intelligence service ever had. Looking into her weary, grouchy face, cheeks covered in downy hair that made her almost mannish, he couldn't imagine that she'd ever been attractive in youth. Add to that a personality of indistinct grunts and a genetic inability to smile—no. He couldn't imagine that any man had ever loved this woman. She had a haircut like a young boy's, trimmed around the ears, and unplucked, shabby eyebrows. She was the type who drank her white wine and chewed her candy and fingernails in a dusty house full of cats and cat hair, whose only enjoyment came from insipid German soap operas.

She placed the wine and candy on the counter and reached into her cheap, plastic-looking purse for the money.

"Guten Abend," Hasad said, smiling as he typed the items into the register.

Her grunt, as ever, said nothing as she plopped down a small pile of coins. Hasad counted the money, fingers dancing. She reached for her supplies, and he cleared his throat, raising a warning hand.

"Moment, Frau. As you can see," he said, pointing at the register's display, "the price is ten sixty-*five*. It's the Snickers. It's more expensive now."

She raised her heavy-lidded eyes to the display, then turned to him. "When did this happen?"

Her voice, surprisingly, was high and melodic. He had to fight the urge to shout, *Success!* Instead he said, "This morning, the distributor raised his price. I have no choice but to do the same."

"Oh." She nodded, perhaps confused, then went back to her purse.

As prescient as he'd been so far, Hasad couldn't have predicted what followed.

The front doors slid electrically open as a young, broad-chested man in a suit jogged in, out of breath. Hasad recognized him from those old question-and-answer sessions. One of the ruder interrogators, who wore his authority with about as much humility as an Ankara cop—which is to say, with no humility at all.

Instinctively, Hasad raised his hands, but the man didn't even notice him. He instead went to the *woman*.

"Director Schwartz. Sorry to bother you, but there's a situation."

Unlike this damp-faced visitor, Frau Schwartz—no, *Director* Schwartz—wasn't in a rush. She was rooting around for Hasad's five cents. "What kind of situation?" she said into her purse.

"Gap."

She looked up at the man, who was a head taller, and blinked. Hasad would later reflect that she seemed angry, though at the moment he was too busy dealing with his shock. The obese alcoholic with all the cats was the boss of these tough young men.

She said, "You have five cents?"

The man colored and groped in his pockets.

She turned to Hasad with an apologetic smile. Were it not for the strange, unnerving way that expression twisted her features, he would've been elated. "I'm sorry, Herr al-Akir. I have to run. But this gentleman will pay the balance." She grabbed her wine and Snickers and walked directly out to the parking lot, where she climbed into the rear of a waiting BMW.

There was a sudden clap as the man banged a five-cent coin on the counter. At that moment, the car roared off, and he stared, aghast. They had left without him.

Hasad didn't even notice the money. He was consumed by a single thought: *She knew my name.*

"Well?" said the man. "My receipt?"

2

As the BMW turned back onto Heilmannstrasse, Erika Schwartz stared at the small, mustached man sitting next to her in the back-seat. "Well?"

Oskar Leintz had a printed page in his lap that was almost destroyed by nervous folding and unfolding. "She's dead."

"When?"

"Body was found a half hour ago."

"In Gap?"

"Outside. On the way to the airport. The French agent is dead, too."

"Press?"

"Too late. They're already running with it."

While Oskar and Gerhardt, the driver, showed their papers to the guards manning the reinforced concrete gate, she took out her cell phone, and by the time they reached the modern building known as the Situation and Information Center, she had finished with Inspector Hans Kuhn of the Berlin Kriminalpolizei. "I don't get it," he kept repeating. "It makes no sense."

"Of course it makes sense," she snapped. Despite their long-standing friendship, the Berlin detective's mawkish helplessness could be irritating. "We just don't know the logic behind it yet."

"But a girl. Fifteen years old . . ."

"That only limits the possibilities, Hans, which is good for us."

The call had come that morning. Adriana Stanescu had found a way out of her captors' small mountain cabin north of Gap, France, in the Hautes-Alpes département. She'd stumbled into town and chanced upon a farm couple who gave her their phone. Her call home was a particular surprise for Inspector Kuhn, who, as a veteran Berlin cop, had given up hope. For a week there had been no ransom calls, and so he'd gone with the textbook, which told him there was no hope. Adriana Stanescu's kidnapper was a sexual predator, and by now she'd been shipped off somewhere, neutralized by drugs and violence, or she was dead. He'd only stayed with the Stanescus be-cause of the publicity. If he dropped the case of an immigrant's ab-ducted child, the press would crucify him.

So he was there, with the Stanescus, when Adriana called. Re-markably, the girl was levelheaded enough to give a quick chronology: Kidnapped in Berlin by a man who pretended to be her father's co-worker: late thirties, dark hair. Transferred to a white van—Mercedes, she thought—and taken to France by three men, German, Spanish, and Russian. Held in the mountains. She'd escaped through a broken window.

He'd told the farmers to take her to the Gap police station, then asked Erika to liaise with the French Direction de la Surveillance du Territoire—DST—to fly her to Berlin.

"Who's going to cover the costs?" Erika had asked.

"We can do that, if necessary."

"It might be," she told him, looking for an excuse not to be in-volved. "You know, the Gap police can take her to the airport with-out having their hands held. Why the production?"

"It just feels wrong," Kuhn had explained, clearly frustrated that this was the best answer he could offer. She understood, though. Ac-cording to Adriana's story, there had been no rape, no attempt at rape, just three men keeping watch over her in France. Yet none of the men, according to her, were French. Nor were they Moldovan.

Why?

So Erika had done as he asked and called her DST contact and received the promise that by morning Adriana would be back home, with an escort.

It had kept her busy all day, distracted from more important business, and she had looked forward to nothing more than her nightly Riesling and Snickers. Now, this.

Because she moved so slowly, Oskar led the way up the steps, through the metal detectors and down the long corridor to Schwartz's office in the back. He had turned on the lights and powered up her computer by the time she arrived, still clutching the wine and candy. She settled behind her desk and cleared away the day's excess papers. Most were printouts of desperate e-mails from Belgrade worrying about the safety of their embassy. In light of the smoldering shell that was left of the American embassy from the previous night's riot, they wanted to close down, but she had advised against it. The Serbs, despite history, had no problems with today's Germany; it was America they hated, the way a poor child envies and hates a rich cousin who has taken something from him. Their hatred masked a long-standing love. Toward today's Germans they felt nothing, and so there was nothing to worry about. The embassy had not been pleased with her explanation.

She looked through her top drawer, pushing around loose pens and paper clips and rubber bands before she gave up and ordered Oskar to find a bottle opener and a glass. "Two, if you want some."

"No, thank you."

"As you like."

Once he was gone, she unwrapped her Snickers and checked the Reuters feed on her browser. A DST agent, Louise Dupont, had been found dead in her car from an accident. The fool hadn't been wearing her seat belt. Much farther down the road, Adriana Stanescu's body had been found by French police in the woods.

She pulled up the file on Andrei and Rada Stanescu, which had been updated over the last days as their faces had graced more and more periodicals. A taxi driver and a factory worker. They had arrived in Germany legally two years ago, a move facilitated by Andrei's brother, Mihai, a baker who spent his spare time volunteering for the German branch of Caritas, the Catholic organization that worked for human rights and against poverty around the world. Caritas had recently been putting pressure on the EU to loosen its immigration policies, and she imagined that was why Mihai volunteered. According to a file she pulled up, Adriana's uncle had been twice arrested in the last six years for helping easterners slip illegally into Germany. That, certainly, would merit further examination.

She got details of the girl's murder from a phone call to Paris and Adrien Lambert, a French contact in the DGSE, Direction Générale de la Sécurité Extérieure. Though Lambert's agency was not specifically responsible for the Stanescu case, he had already assembled the information in his Boulevard Mortier office, expecting her call. Stanescu's neck had been broken by hand. The killer knew his way around a neck, he said, and had completed the task with one movement. Gap police had found the mountain cabin in which Adriana had been held. Forensics was working the place over, but it had been cleaned professionally, and they held out little hope. The cabin was owned by François Leclerc, a plumber from Grenoble who was on vacation in Florida with his family. He had no idea who would have been using his place.

"And you believe that?" Erika asked as Oskar returned with a plastic cup and a corkscrew and proceeded to open the bottle.

"More than I believe you," said Lambert, "when you tell me you don't know anything about this."

"Believe it, Adrian. We're all wandering in the dark."

After hanging up, she sipped the wine Oskar had poured, took a bite of her Snickers, and peered through her assistant as if he weren't there. She ran through what she did know. An immigrant girl kidnapped, no ransom requested. In a country with Germany's racial tensions the kidnapping wasn't unthinkable, nor was the lack of ransom. It *was* unthinkable that, for a whole week, the girl had not been harmed or killed.

So the crime was neither sexually nor racially motivated. The girl had escaped by her own means, and someone felt her death was so important that this person was willing to take out a French civil servant as well.

Or was that a coincidence? Had Louise Dupont had an accident, died, and then the girl, with the kind of ill luck you only find in Greek myths, had run into a local psychopath? She doubted it, but the facts did not rule it out, so it remained.

If not, then one of the three men holding her had done it. The German, the Spaniard, or the Russian. Why, though, had they let her live unmolested for a whole week? Did that suggest the involvement of another party? She couldn't be sure of anything.

She drew back.

Perhaps it had nothing to do with the Stanescus at all. What if Adriana had, say, witnessed a murder, and the killers took her to keep her quiet? There would have been an argument about what to do with her, a schism among criminals. She's let go by one of them, while another tracks her down and silences her.

Then what about the unknown man, late thirties, dark hair, who first captured Adriana, before these other three took her over?

Unnerved by the small eyes fixed blindly on him for so long, Oskar said, "You're doing it again."

A pause, eyes wide. "Doing what?"

"That stare. You're freaking me out."

She blinked finally, smiled, then looked at her desk. "Sorry, Oskar. I promise to work on my manners. In the meantime, would you please ask Gerhardt to go see Herr al-Akir? He can bring someone to drive my car back and . . ." She gazed at Oskar. "And we'll need another bottle of Riesling. This is going to take all night."

She returned to the beginning. She called Hans Kuhn again to ask about police cameras in the area of the Lina-Morgenstern High School, where Adriana had disappeared.

"You think that didn't occur to me over the last week, Erika?"

"I'm just asking a question."

He sighed. "We had some protests last year. The Turks thought we were targeting them, so the order came down to remove a bunch of cameras. We kept one at the corner of Mehringdamm and

Gneisenaustrasse, but some kids screwed with it a month ago. The city won't repair them until the next budget comes through."

"Those are busy streets. There had to be some witnesses."

"Four thirty in the afternoon—it was so busy that no one noticed. Besides, they don't trust us pigs."

"I see," she said. "Thank you, Hans."

Oskar returned with her car keys and a second Riesling and asked if she wanted him to stay around. She didn't. His company would just distract her, and he clearly wanted to get home to his girlfriend, a Swede he'd recently become infatuated with.

Once he was gone, she began her reading. It was a technique she'd not so much learned as fallen into decades ago when her gaze had been focused across that opaque border into the ironically named German Democratic Republic. She'd had to learn what was happening there not by direct observation but by inference. Crop reports, crime statistics, train schedules, export flows, and the sometimes panicked messages sent by lonely informers marooned on that side of the Curtain. In such a situation, little can be taken at face value, and Erika had learned to gather her intelligence from the cracks between the questionable facts that reached her desk. She learned to let her mind drift from the central subject in slow outward circles, making dubious connections along the way that would be held up against other dubious connections to gradually create a jigsaw picture that could be rearranged, pieces dropped out or repainted, until, eventually, enough pieces remained that the larger picture could be gleaned.

She didn't need to hear what the office wits said to agree that she'd stumbled on this technique as a way to make her life a little easier. She'd been a big woman since the seventies, an obese one since the fall of the Wall, and as her desk life slowly grew to encompass her entire life, her body continued to grow until reading was the only feasible technique left to her.

After finishing the files directly related to the case, she took her initial, small leaps outward. She remembered, first of all, that a recent World Bank report had placed Moldova, Europe's poorest country, at the top of the immigrant remittances list, a dubious honor for any country that received more than 36 percent of its gross domestic product from those who had emigrated and sent cash back to their families. This fact made humans Moldova's most valuable export.

Did the Stanescus send money back home? She made a note to check on it.

These days, the Moldovan mafia spent much of its time stealing German cars to sell back home, and trafficking women westward, which was far more profitable. While there was no reason to connect the Stanescus to these criminals, she didn't want her sense of propriety to limit the broadness of her survey, so in addition to the BND files on the subject she tracked down recent articles in *Der Spiegel*, *Stern*, and *Bunte*, refamiliarizing herself with that tiny, troubled country.

Much of its history she already knew. Stalin had carved the area known as Bessarabia out of Romania in 1940, then absorbed it into the Soviet Union as the Moldavian Soviet Socialist Republic. For the rest of his rule, deportations were commonplace, sending Bessarabians to the Urals, Kazakhstan, and Siberia. In the late forties, due largely to the Soviet quota system, a famine spread through the country, and in the fifties the deported and dead were replaced with ethnic Russians and Ukrainians. To help suppress the desire to rejoin Romania, Soviet scientists talked up the independence of the Moldovan language, which, unlike Romanian, was still being written in Cyrillic. This reminded Erika of Serbs and Croats who for political reasons insisted their languages were utterly different—while to the rest of the world they sounded pretty much the same.

After its 1991 independence, and despite protests from the government based in Chisinau, Russian troops remained in the breakaway region of Transnistria, just across the Dniester River, to "protect" its population of imported Russians. This self-proclaimed Pridnestrovian Moldavian Republic fought a brief 1992 civil war to gain autonomy. Its sovereignty was only recognized by itself; the international community still considered it a region of Moldova, though a lawless one run by criminals with a GDP of drugs, guns, and flesh.

The Stanescus were not from Transnistria, though; they were from the north of the country.

She returned to Mihai, the uncle. In 2002 he'd been arrested on the Austrian border, driving a truck with a Moldovan family—husband, wife, and two children—hidden in the rear. A prosecutor in the case pushed for kicking him out of the country, but by then Mihai was a full-fledged German citizen. Six months in Moabit Prison and a ten-thousand-euro fine was the best he could manage.

One would have thought that this would end Mihai's smuggling activities, but he was picked up again in 2005 with a young couple entering Germany from the Czech Republic. Again, they were Moldovan, and in the case that followed it turned out that they'd only paid him seven hundred euros—a sum that only covered the gas and bribes along the way. The defense made a talking point of this, and the judge became convinced that he had committed his crime solely out of conviction, not for profit. He was let off with a twelve-thousand-euro fine and no jail time.

She would have preferred that he was a profiteering smuggler who sent his cargo on for slave labor or prostitution—that kind of man could be understood and dealt with—but Mihai Stanescu was the worst type. He was a believer, and this was an age in which believers were to be feared.

With a sinking feeling, she realized that reading alone would not solve anything. She would have to talk with the Stanescus.

She made the call, and a young-sounding woman answered in a groggy singsong, "Hejsan."

"Oskar, please." When he came on, she apologized for waking them, then gave the bad news. "I'll need you to be my driver tomorrow."

"But it's Saturday."

"Yes, Oskar. It is."

"Where?"

"Berlin."

He sighed loudly. With a five-hour drive ahead of him, his entire weekend was shot.

"If you want," she said, "you can bring along your little Swede. Maybe she'd enjoy a road trip."

Oskar hung up.

3

She knew the rumors would begin in the morning. Oskar wouldn't spread them, but the janitors would eagerly discuss the two empty bottles of Riesling in her wastebasket, because even the janitors had clearance to judge. By the time the bulk of the staff returned on Monday the rumors would grow to a level of truth that would have to be investigated, so that those above her—and besides Teddy Wartmüller, her direct superior, they were innumerable—could decide whether to graduate the rumors to a higher level or demote them. Not even demotion would make them vanish; instead, all rumors were filed away in case of future need.

So, if only to limit potential dissemination, she collected the bottles and plastic cup and slipped them into an overnight bag she kept in the closet and rolled it out past the night guards to the parking lot. It was two in the morning, and she drove very carefully out the gate, past Herr al-Akir's closed store, through the thickly wooded Perlacher Forest, and on to home.

She spent Saturday morning sleeping off the wine in her bilevel, on a gentle green lane of secluded houses populated by successful businessmen, other BND administrators, and a few foreigners from the European Patent Office. Along the street, security cameras mounted on streetlamps made sure they slept easily.

When she woke at noon, she instinctively took a plastic bowl out of the cabinet and searched for the bag of cat food—for Herr al-Akir had been partially right. Erika Schwartz had owned a single tabby, but a week earlier she had discovered his corpse by the back door. Even now, a week later, she would get halfway through the ritual of feeding Grendel before realizing she'd thrown away the cat food, and then remembering why.

She'd been suspicious because the cat's body looked twisted by poison, but the BND forensics section explained that it had been twisted by cancer, not foul play. Despite the fact that she didn't mix with her neighbors enough for them to build a grudge, she still maintained her suspicions.

Oskar picked her up at two with his Volkswagen, and during the drive up the A9 she used his BlackBerry—she still hadn't succumbed to those ubiquitous beasts—to continue her online reading. Sometimes Oskar cut in, and she was obliged to fill him in on the little she had. "No, it's not a pedophile ring. She wouldn't have escaped in the first place. Even if she had, I don't see how they could have tracked her unless they had a foothold with the French police."

"It's not impossible."

"No," she said quietly. "I suppose it's not. We'll have to keep it in mind."

He smiled, pleased to have added something to the cloud of possibilities. So she decided to dampen his enthusiasm, just a little. "We'll meet later on at the hotel. First, you'll drop me off at Hans's place, then go on to Gneisenaustrasse."

He blinked. "Gneisenaustrasse?"

"Look for cameras. The police camera isn't working, but there are bound to be shops with some kind of security."

"Wonderful."

"Don't be down, Oskar. You've got a lifetime with the Swede ahead of you."

He dropped her off at Hans Kuhn's apartment over in Pankow, and she declined Kuhn's offer of a drink. She wanted to know about the Stanescus. "What were your impressions?"

"Simple," he said, sipping on a whiskey that dampened the ends of his white mustache. "Decent enough, very earnest. I was there when the child called. Their hearts were on their sleeves. I'm sure they're not involved."

"And the uncle?"

"Mihai?" He rocked his head. "The brains of the family. Tough, too. But he's a German citizen; he knows the lay of the land. The parents have that vague confusion all new immigrants have."

"Maybe I should talk to them now," she said, feeling impatient.

"They just received their daughter's body."

"Then they're emotional. It'll make an interrogation easier."

"Interrogation? Christ, Erika. Give them a break. Talk to them tomorrow, after they get back from church."

"Churchgoers?"

"Bulgarian Orthodox on Krausenstrasse. There aren't any Moldovan churches here, and the closest Romanian church is in Nuremburg, so they make do."

"It's late, anyway."

Hans Kuhn raised his glass. "And you're being rude. Now, have a drink."

Four whiskeys and a dish of Mecklenburg cod later, Erika was ready to leave. It wasn't the alcohol or the overdone fish that soured her but the awkward emotional scene Kuhn put her through. Teary-eyed, he said, "I was sure she was dead. Convinced. I'd had a week for it to settle in. Then she wasn't. God's own miracle!" He raised his glass while his tongue rooted around in his mouth. "Then, once more. Dead. So much worse. Why couldn't she have just died in the first place?" Later: "I hate my job."

His guilt flickered into fits of anger, and he made unwise predictions about what he would do to the men who had kidnapped her, once he had them. That's when she knew it was time to leave. She called a taxi, which took her to the Berlin Plaza Hotel in Kurfürstendamm, and, before checking in, bought a Snickers from a nearby convenience store. She ordered a bottle of Pinot Blanc from room service.

She had finished the Snickers and was halfway through the wine when Oskar knocked on her door. She had spent the preceding hour avoiding all thoughts of the case by using her deductive skills on a television crime series starring a handsome cop and a dog that had a kilometer more charm and brains than his master. To her embarrassment, she still had no idea who the killer was.

She unlocked the door and paused to examine the bright red bruise around Oskar's left eye, which seemed to reset all his features, making him look a few years younger. It was a curious effect. Coagulated blood marked a split in his eyebrow.

"You going to invite me in?" he said testily, then waved a shopping bag, heavy with a box that, through the thin plastic, she could see was a new Sony video camera. "This should at least entitle me to a free drink."

She drenched a washcloth in hot water and set to cleaning off his face with the rough hand of an inexperienced caregiver. He winced and finally took it from her. He got up, one hand clutching the plastic cup of room-temperature wine, the other pressing the cloth to his brow. She took out the contents of his bag—one new video camera ("which I expect to be reimbursed for") and a single mini DV cassette marked in quick black handwriting, *15-2-08, 16-21.*

"It wasn't easy," he said. "I should get a commendation."

"I'll buy you your own bottle next time. Now, talk."

Funnily enough, it was a camera store, Drescher Foto, which sold a sketchy mix of antique and new video, 16mm and still cameras stacked alluringly in the window. "They all pointed to the side, so you could see how pretty they were. Except one, up high in the corner. It pointed out to the street, and a little red light on it glowed. The owner had set up his own security system."

"Very nice," she said as she tipped the bottle for examination; it was empty. "Want me to call down for another?"

"Please."

After she'd made the call, she settled back on the bed while he took a seat at the desk, which looked out over Berlin's busy nightlife; shouts and car engines rose up to them.

"Of course," he said, "Drescher Foto was closed. So I checked the list of names for the apartments overhead."

"Let me guess: There was a Drescher residing in the building."

"You should be a detective, Frau Schwartz."

"Was he happy to meet you?"

"I wouldn't say that."

Herr Drescher turned out to be a recluse, dividing his time between his shop and a filthy apartment stacked to the ceiling with mini DV cassettes and four televisions for watching the world pass by his store. Paranoid, perhaps, because at first he wouldn't let Oskar come up. "I told him where I was from, and that seemed to cause more trouble than it solved. I had to finally threaten him with a search warrant—which, given what's probably on some of those cassettes, worried him more than anything else."

"I can imagine."

After a conversation stalled by long silences and evasions, Herr Drescher finally admitted to having the tape from that day. Oskar asked if, when he heard about the missing girl, he had considered showing the tape to the authorities. All he would say was, "It's none of my business. I keep to myself."

Looking around the apartment, full of dirty plates balanced precariously on columns of cassettes, Oskar had no reason to doubt it.

"So we sat down and looked at it together. As you'll see, the quality's excellent, and it's all time-coded. Better than that, there's a perfect view of the entrance to the courtyard."

"And?"

He got up and started unboxing the video camera. "And I'll see if I can hook this thing up to the television."

As he settled on the floor and took out the camera and instructions and the pages of obligatory, multilingual warnings, she said, "So when did he hit you?"

"Drescher?"

"Yes, Drescher."

He touched his brow, grinning. "The light in his stairwell doesn't work. I would have told you immediately, but you might not have let me in."

"You tripped and fell."

"I'd like to see how well you negotiate those stairs."

It took about fifteen minutes—Oskar, despite his boyish love of modern technology, wasn't adept at using it—and during that time room service delivered another bottle of Pinot Blanc with two wine-glasses. The young girl who brought it up seemed amused at first by the scene in front of her: wine for two, an enormous old woman, and a scrawny, mustached man in his thirties sitting on the floor. Then she noticed the video camera and the man's swollen eye, and her amusement seemed to turn to disgust; she was gone before Erika could dig out a tip.

Oskar had cued up the tape back at Drescher's, at 16:13. The camera didn't shoot straight across Gneisenaustrasse but at an angle, so that it could take in the store's front door. From that angle the foreground included the sidewalk, parked cars, and the swish of traffic speeding past bare trees lining the median. The background was dominated by the apartment building and its wide courtyard entrance.

"There he is," said Oskar, pointing to a black BMW turning into the courtyard.

She squinted at the hazy image, then reached for her reading glasses. "Did you get a license number?"

"It's clearer on the way out."

He fast-forwarded to 16:27, when a man emerged from the courtyard, checked his watch, and tried to look inconspicuous. He kept his head slumped between his shoulders, so that his face was hard to make out, but Erika guessed he was in his late thirties or early forties, 180 to 190 centimeters tall, dark-haired. Not heavy. Just like half Europe's male population.

Erika was momentarily shaken when the man seemed to look directly at the camera, at her, and she said, "Does he see the camera?"

"I noticed that, too," Oskar said as he took a sip of wine. "I don't think so. I think he's looking at this car." He touched, in the foreground, the dark blue, almost black, front hood of some unknown make of automobile.

Between then and 16:37, the man disappeared from view again before reappearing and looking to his right, taking note of something and disappearing again. Among assorted people passing on the street, Erika spotted Adriana Stanescu. After all the photos that had been pasted across Europe over the last week, she didn't need to see her in close-up to know. Tall for her age, almost swaggering with the public confidence that consumes pretty teenaged girls. She briefly considered telling Oskar that, many, many years ago, she had been as pretty as this Moldovan girl, then wondered why she would consider it, particularly when Oskar wouldn't believe her.

As she passed the courtyard, the man stepped out again and spoke to her. She didn't stop immediately, but with the man's second statement she paused and turned to him. Then he—and this struck her as remarkable—took a card out of his pocket and showed it to her. Business card? Driver's license? Then she remembered—he'd pretended to be her father's co-worker, which would require some ID. Even then Adriana hesitated, and Erika dug her chewed nails into her palms, muttering, "Good girl. You're no one's fool."

History had already written this story, though, which made it all the more difficult to watch. The man stepped aside to let her in first and then followed.

"It's fast," said Oskar, finishing his glass.

It was. Three minutes later, at 16:45, the BMW rolled slowly out to the street. One driver, no visible passengers. It turned right and left the frame.

"Just a sec," said Oskar.

The BMW reappeared on their side of the street, heading in the opposite direction toward Mehringdamm. Then it was gone.

"Watch this," said Oskar.

"Watch what?" she asked, a sudden depression filling her.

Then she saw it: The blue car in the foreground, an Opel with Berlin plates, pulled out into the traffic and drove in the same direction.

"Oh," she said.

They went through the tape two more times, Oskar making note of the most crucial time code: 16:39, when the man's face was most visible. At that moment he was speaking with Adriana, his head raised to show what an open, friendly person he was.

At 16:46, as he headed toward Mehringdamm, they got a clear shot of the BMW's tags, which Oskar noted along with the Opel's tags at the tail end of 16:47.

By the time she called the Berlin office for an all-night courier, it was nearly one, and she was finally feeling a buzz from the wine and the realization that they were very close to something important. The courier brought an envelope, in which they put the cassette and a note asking the Pullach office to use its face-recognition software to identify the man talking to the girl at 16:39. She doubted they would come up with anything—the software was notoriously buggy—but at least they could clean up the image.

The courier sealed the envelope in their presence and predicted that it would arrive by seven in the morning. He, too, seemed to note Oskar's black eye, the empty wine bottles and glasses, and the video camera, but he was too well trained to show his emotions.

4

Erika knew surprisingly little about the Orthodox Church, most of her understanding coming from a single conversation she'd had in the eighties with a Romanian informer who had come to Vienna to discuss the terms of his employment. He'd been a professor of sociology, or whatever Nicolae Ceaușescu's communist regime chose to call that field of study, and he was trying to explain why his price was so high: The Romanian mind was too conspiratorial for him to be able to do anything safely.

Her job that day had been to keep his fee as low as possible—the West German economy was raging, but pressure from the Greens was throwing all future BND budgets into question.

The professor had been a talker; she could hardly get a word in at all. A stream of sociocultural lessons poured from his mouth. On the subject of the conspiratorial Romanian mind, he started with the obvious variable: the Securitate, the regime's feared secret police, which, according to rumors Erika didn't believe, employed in some fashion a quarter of the population. When he saw this didn't sway her, he turned to religion and democracy.

He said, "Democracy functions in Protestant nations. It barely functions in Catholic nations. It doesn't function at all in Orthodox nations."

It was a troubling statement, as West Germany's boisterous ally on the other side of the Atlantic based its entire Cold War philosophy on the notion that all nations and cultures could, and should, embrace democracy.

"It's about independent thinking," the professor explained. "How God's word is interpreted. You Protestants, you believe that all it really takes is a Bible to work through who God is and what He wants. The Catholics read on their own, but they require a pope to help them through the difficult parts. They can't absolve themselves of sin; the Church has to do that for them."

"And Orthodoxy?"

He smiled. "An Orthodox church represents the link between the earthly and the spiritual. The dividing line is at the front of the church, at the iconostasis. Medieval images of Christ and the saints gaze out, as if heaven is on the other side of the screen, and the Holy peer through. Judging. Then it happens. The priest steps behind the screen into the sanctuary. After a little while, he steps out again to share what he's learned. You see?"

Erika, worried over the time and money already devoted to this questionable source, said, "No. I don't see."

"Where does truth come from?" he asked rhetorically. "For Protestants, it comes from self-examination. For Catholics, from assisted examination. For Orthodox Christians, a man of importance steps behind a screen, talks to God in secret, and comes out to tell you what God wants. It works the same way with politics. Politics for us is a dark, smoky room where a few important people come to an agreement. Afterward, they step out into the morning light and tell the masses that, say, they now live in a communist country. Or that they live in a capitalist one—it doesn't matter. What matters is that my people will never believe that they've taken history into their own hands. That's not reality for them. In our reality, democracy will always be an illusion."

Erika nodded at this, if only to be polite, then realized she still didn't have her answer. "And this is why you want double what we offered?"

"My dear, in a world where all important things are run by men behind closed doors, those outside would kill their own mothers to gain the favor of those on the inside. They will turn in anyone who smells vaguely off and even those who smell of roses. You see, I don't have to work for you to risk my life; all I have to do is take the train back to Bucharest. You're not only paying for my cooperation; you're paying for my return."

Nearly a quarter of a century later, Erika tried to align that assessment with the St. Tsar Boris the Converter Bulgarian Orthodox Church in the southeastern district of Neukölln, just below Kreuzberg. She stood in the back, the heavy smell of incense filling the gloomy air as the liturgy was almost hummed by a white-bearded man with a black cap and robes. The worshippers seemed to focus more on their hands, clutched in prayer, and most of them stood, which made her feel better hidden.

She had spotted the Stanescus early on. They were near the front with Adriana's uncle, Mihai. Other pale-faced worshippers had embraced them in their time of need, and despite herself she felt a brief warmth at the thought that here it didn't matter that the Stanescus weren't Bulgarian; they were just grieving parents, which anyone could understand.

Then she cut the distracting thought from her head and stepped forward to get a better look. She wasn't sure what she expected to find here inside the church, but she'd been in her particular line of work for so long that there was always the possibility she'd recognize a person of interest. None of these faces were part of her extensive memories, so she left.

She stepped out into the cool morning light and joined Hans Kuhn, who was waiting by the car. Inside it, Oskar tapped the wheel to the rhythm of a hip-hop CD he'd brought along.

By the time the worshippers began to spill out onto the sidewalk, she and Kuhn had gone through two coffees apiece from a sausage vendor, and she had eaten two käsewurst. She sent Kuhn ahead so she could finish wiping greasy cheese off her chin.

He returned with all three Stanescus. Andrei and Rada were small people who seemed smaller the nearer they were to Erika's large frame. Both were in black, as was Mihai, the only one with dry eyes. It was Mihai who spoke first.

"Leave them alone, all right? Can't you see they've been through enough?"

As if he'd said nothing, Erika introduced herself to the parents and offered a hand that would have taken rudeness to refuse; Andrei and Rada were not rude. Mihai, however, ignored her hand and went on. "They received their daughter's body yesterday. My niece! Have some respect."

"We have new information," she told them and produced a printed-out image from the videocassette that Pullach had cleaned up and e-mailed that morning. "Do you recognize this man?"

Mihai grabbed the photo first, full of energy. Then he shook his head and passed it to Andrei, muttering something in Moldovan. Neither the mother nor father recognized him either.

"I think this is the man who took Adriana," she explained.

Rada Stanescu began to cry, and her husband held her closer, an arm around her shoulders. "We answer your questions. Later, yes? Please." Andrei had a pleading quality to his voice, and Erika remembered again why she hated going into the field.

"I understand," she said, then turned to Mihai. "Perhaps you can spare a few minutes?"

He wasn't as accommodating as his relatives, but as he watched his brother and sister-in-law walk away, he shrugged. "You can always take me down to the station if I refuse, yes?"

"I'm not a cop."

"Then I don't have to answer a thing."

"In which case, I'd be very curious why you wouldn't."

Mihai blinked rapidly, perhaps a sign of an upcoming lie, perhaps not. "You know what I do for a living?"

"You're a baker, and you help people move here."

He smiled. "Yes, and no. It seems I spend most of my time answering police questions about the people I help. If pressed, I would have to say my main occupation is answering questions."

"Then you're experienced," Erika said and opened a hand toward the car; Oskar was already starting it up. "Shall I occupy you a few minutes?"

Despite his attitude, Erika liked Mihai Stanescu. He was abrupt, to the point, a quality Erika herself was often accused of. He, like his brother, was a small man, but heavier and with an excess of dark hair that grew too quickly on his face and spilled out under his neck when he took off his tie in the Kreuzberg coffee shop they settled on. Erika ordered espresso, but wished she hadn't when Mihai ordered Trendelburger Feuergeist—"fire ghost," an aptly named clear liquor she felt she could use right now. When she stared at his shot glass too long, he raised an eyebrow. "You are paying for this, right?"

"Absolutely."

"Good." He swallowed it all in one go, then said, "Who's the bastard?"

She glanced at Hans Kuhn near the doorway—she'd asked him to stay back. "You didn't meet Inspector Kuhn before?"

"Not him." He tapped the table with a stubby finger. "The one in the picture. The one who took my niece."

"I don't know yet."

"How sure are you about him?"

"We have him on video talking to her just before she disappeared."

His cheeks and forehead flushed; then he waved to the waiter for another Feuergeist.

"So?" said Erika.

"You're the one with the questions, right?"

"You know what questions I have."

That seemed to throw him. He leaned back and took her in with his eyes, then leaned forward again. "You want to know if I have any suspicions."

"Yes."

"If I did, I'd tell you."

"Then tell me about Adriana. Why her?"

"How should I know?"

"Because you do," she said. She'd been sure of it from the moment he started protecting her parents; he had the guilt of knowledge all over him. "Adriana Stanescu. Fifteen. Moldovan, like you. None of that is exceptional, but there was something special about her. It's why she was taken. You tell me what makes her special."

The second Feuergeist went down slower than the first as he considered his answer. He set down the half-empty shot glass. "I have my own demands."

"Of course you do."

"Silence. What I tell you—it's not for the public. Can you promise me this? It's only to help you do your job, nothing else. Because this is one case I'd like to see you solve."

If his information proved valuable, the truth was that its public dissemination wouldn't be her choice. The decision would move up to the second floor, and her opinion would be relegated to one of many blabbering voices that could be—and usually was—ignored. "I can promise this," she lied.

He drank the rest of his Feuergeist to steel himself, then began to speak.

It didn't take long, and when he was finished he didn't wait for her to end the conversation. He simply stood and walked out past Hans Kuhn, who waited for some sign from Erika. She gave none. She couldn't move from her seat, could only stare ahead into the empty distance, thinking what a truly miserable world she lived in. She flagged down the waiter and ordered a double shot of Feuergeist. Sometimes the world hardly seemed worth saving at all.

5

She and Oskar were on the A9 again, heading back to Munich, the winter sun setting off to their right. She'd told Mihai's story once, a quick summation, and Oskar's foot had weakened noticeably, so that now they were crawling in the passing lane. She suggested he speed up or move, so he switched to the right lane and even used his signal, which was in her memory unprecedented.

"Tell me again," he said.

She took a breath, the Feuergeist making a small fire in her gut. "Adriana came to Germany four years ago, two years before she arrived with her parents. She was eleven at the time. Mihai wanted me to understand, so he described the poor little village they came from, that it's riddled with despair and alcoholics and for a teenager it's a curse of nothingness. He attributed Adriana's stupidity to optimism, and I suppose that's right. A modeling agency came to town. They said they were from Hamburg, but there's no telling. They were looking for new talent, fresh faces. They told the girls that if they were chosen to work for them, there would be an official contract, and the company would take care of the passport and visa paperwork. Adriana didn't tell her parents—she knew what they would say. They, unlike her, were patriots. They had no desire to leave or see their daughter leave Moldova. So she went with a girlfriend to the audition, in a rented warehouse on the edge of town. Two days later, she returned to find out she was one of five or so girls who'd been chosen. Her girlfriend, Mihai explained, was sick with jealousy."

They passed a sign for a gas station, and Erika asked him to pull over. As soon as he'd parked, she was out the door, lumbering toward the station's clean, modern store. Oskar considered following, but instead stared through the windshield at the barren fields beyond the highway. What was most unbearable about these stories was that they always began the same way—a modeling agency, a scout for secretarial work, a company finding nannies for rich Western children—and very soon you knew where they would end up. Yet despite the repetition, no one ever learned.

She returned with a bottle of cheap white wine with a screw top, but no Snickers—he suspected the story had killed her appetite. She settled into her seat, gasping for air, and said, "Sorry—did you want something?"

"No. Nothing."

"Good."

He merged onto the highway but returned to the passing lane. His foot was working better, and he wanted to get back to Munich as soon as possible.

"Where was I?" she said.

"She'd gotten the modeling job."

"Yes," Erika said as she unscrewed the wine, the cap's aluminum seam popping. "All the successful contestants sat for photographs, gave their names and addresses, and then the agency left town. A week later, they returned with fresh passports and told the girls they had five hours to collect their stuff and get to a bus in the center of town.

"There were other girls already on the bus, girls from nearby villages. By the time they reached the border with Romania, there were probably a total of thirty or forty. Though Adriana couldn't have known this part, you and I and Mihai all know that their long border stop was for bribes. They crossed Romania, stopped again, crossed Hungary. They reached the Austrian border."

She took a long draft from the wine bottle. Oskar waited.

"You know, we like to think we're better than those easterners, but all it takes is a little money. Money is the great equalizer, don't you think?"

"I suppose it is."

After another sip, she said, "They arrived in Hamburg two days later. They were herded off the bus into a warehouse in the more dangerous part of St. Pauli, gave up their passports, and were told that a lot of money had been invested in them. As soon as they paid it back, they would be free to start their modeling careers. Then, one by one, they were raped."

She took another swallow and spoke to the road ahead.

"There was a man and a woman who worked together, looking over the girls and making notes on a clipboard. They were deciding which girls would go where. Adriana was shipped to a whorehouse outside Berlin. This, according to Mihai, was a sign that they liked her looks. The occasional government functionary made it to their establishment and would pay well for an eleven-year-old as pretty as she was. Not so fast."

Though on this stretch of the A9 there was no speed limit, Oskar hadn't realized he had slowly accelerated to something far above any safe speed. He let off the gas and glanced at her. "Sorry," he said, then noticed she was already halfway through her bottle. "Maybe you should slow down, too."

Erika followed his gaze. She wedged the bottle between her thighs and rested her hands on her knees. "One of the worst curses for anyone in our profession is imagination. We should all be born without it."

"Go on."

"Is there any need?" she asked. "You know what happened next. Five to ten men a night, and if they paid enough—and most did—they could do with her what they liked. Adriana was checked after each visit, because a bruise would cost the visitor extra. Adriana made a lot of money for them. But then . . ." Unconsciously, she removed the bottle from between her thighs and held it near her lips. "She was lucky, wasn't she? She had an uncle who had been in Germany for years, a man who was familiar with the criminal classes.

He got a call from his brother, that Adriana had gone missing. He'd
learned from her jealous girlfriend that she was modeling in Germany. And while Andrei was too much of a villager to understand a
thing, Mihai immediately understood. He did his homework. Among
the immigrants he helped out, some had contact with the flesh road.
They tracked her to Hamburg, and then to Berlin. And then . . ."
She paused again, ignoring the bottle. "I didn't ask him why he didn't
just call the police. I think I know why, but it would have been good
to hear it directly from him."

"He doesn't trust cops."

"Yes, but that's not it. It's his brother. Adriana's father is a dunce,
and if the police raided the place and sent her back to Moldova with
an escort, then he would learn what had happened to his daughter.
Mihai wanted his brother to remain in blissful ignorance. He still
wants it—that's why he demanded silence from me. It's why he took
matters into his own hands four years ago. He approached the men
who ran the Berlin house and made them an offer. If they gave up
this one girl, then he would give them the use of his bakery to laun-
der money. They thought he was crazy and suggested a counteroffer.
They would give him the girl if he gave them his shop. He would
continue to run it, but for a salary, and all profits would be deposited
into their bank."

These were the details she'd skipped on her initial telling, and
Oskar waited impatiently for Mihai's reply. "Well?"

"What could he do? He signed the ownership papers over to
them, then took Adriana back to Berlin. He nursed her until she was
fit enough, then smuggled her back into Moldova. It was a secret between them—her parents would continue to believe she'd been pur-
suing a modeling career."

Oskar considered that, but however he looked at it, it still made
no sense. "Andrei didn't suspect? No one's that stupid."

"I said the same thing. Mihai thinks Andrei suspected but was
too horrified to ever ask the question. But he did change. A month
after her return, he called to ask if Mihai could help them get papers
to move to Germany. He wanted to do it, he said, for Adriana, be-

cause if she could run away to go to Germany, then leaving was very important to her."

"The man lives with blinders."

"Don't we all," said Erika. "When I asked Mihai for names, he seemed very nervous—it was the first time during our talk that he was. But he gave me one. Rainer Volker, the man who owned his bakery. Ring a bell?"

"No. He doesn't own it anymore?"

"He's dead now, so he doesn't own a thing," she said wistfully as she gazed at the gray sky ahead of them. "His name didn't ring a bell with me either, but when we got into the car, I remembered him from a piece in the *Hamburger Abendblatt*. Last month—first week of January, I think. Rainer Volker was found shot to death down by the Elbe. You know what the article said he was?"

"I don't know."

"A philanthropist."

6

Radovan Panić had been home less than a week, making arrangements for his mother's cancer treatments in Vienna, when he learned from a friend in a smoky Novi Beograd café that the parliament of Kosovo, the Serbian province they had fought a humiliating war to keep, was holding a vote on independence that coming Sunday. Radovan, distracted by the details of the Zürich heist and finding a visa for his mother, had stayed away from newspapers.

The result was a foregone conclusion, because the Serb-dominated northern region of Kososvo was too much of a minority to hold any sway. Had there been a public referendum, they might have all boarded buses to offset the vote, but since it was a parliament vote the only idea anyone had was to send buses of Kalashnikovs.

As Sunday grew nearer, his more optimistic friends pointed out that the results didn't matter. Kosovo had already declared independence before, in 1990, and only Albania had recognized it. This time around, no one would, because Article 10 of the UN Security Council's Resolution 1244, which had ended the Kosovo War, gave Kosovo "substantial autonomy" within Serbia, which negated the possibility of real independence.

"That's historical record," said one, clutching his cigarette in a fist. "Internationally recognized. Go ahead and let them play their game. They'll end up with egg on their faces."

The optimists weren't worried. The others—and they were far more numerous—included friends and most of the politicians he heard on television. The world, they reminded him, had long ago singled out Serbs for eternal punishment. They adored the Muslims in Kosovo because they had been fooled by their crying women and those alleged mass graves. The Americans, who after 9/11 should know better, would once again let their stupid political correctness get the better of them.

Radovan preferred optimism. With a mother being slowly eaten by cancer, it was the one stance that could give him some measure of peace. However, he was also a career criminal who knew the world didn't always bow to your optimism. The result of the vote that chilly Sunday one week ago was no surprise to anyone. What followed was.

Afghanistan was the first to recognize the Republic of Kosovo. Then Costa Rica and, of course, Albania. There were jokes, because sovereignty is only as strong as the nations that agree with it. Then France said yes. The French president was of Hungarian stock, and Hungarians hated Serbs more than most, so perhaps it was an anomaly. Breaths were held. Turkey—more Muslims, so what else could you expect? Then, in Dar es Salaam, George W. Bush, that ignorant cowboy, said, "The Kosovars are now independent."

Exhale.

By then Radovan had settled most everything with his mother's Austrian visa and had a final appointment for the following Monday. So, with her blessing, he took to the streets with his friends and shouted and raised his fists. They cursed the UN and the USA and sang Orthodox hymns and war songs. Each night, exhausted and pleased with themselves, they got drunk and told their Kosovo stories. Some had been there for the fighting, and Radovan drank in their tales of burning villages and Muslim terrorists and tracking down soldiers who had gone MIA. Others were amateur historians— most Serbs these days were amateur historians—who could recite a litany of dates that tied the region more tightly to the Serbian breast. The 1389 battle against the Ottomans on Kosovo Polje— Kosovo Field, or the field of the black birds—figured heavily in any discussion, so that any Serb could, and would, proclaim that they had been fighting for Kosovo for the past six hundred years, ever since that first gloriously lost battle.

When a crowd is convinced it has been truly wronged, little can stop it from smashing windows and pulling up sidewalks. When the injustice reaches back into medieval times, and the humiliation has lasted six centuries, then the anger is buoyed by religious fervor. You break glass not only for yourself but for all who have come before you, and when, on Thursday night, one of your comrades, a functionary with the Radical Party, suggests a visit to the American embassy, there is no choice but to go.

All Radovan's ancestors hung behind him, watching with pleasure as he went to give a history lesson to the monolith nation that thought history was something you only read about in books. History, his lesson would say, was the blood that kept you alive. History separated you from the beasts. This was tonight's lesson.

It was beautiful. The ease of their entry was breathtaking, for the marines guarding the unassuming building on Kneza Miloša drew back like troublemakers hoping that in the rear of the room the teacher wouldn't notice them. Then the windows were shattered, drunk professors scaling the facade, legs flailing at the sills as they slid inside. They ran cheering through the narrow, dark corridors of the empty building, banging against locked doors that likely held the darkest secrets of the American empire, and when they couldn't get them open someone—Dejan? Viktor?—decided the best way was to burn it down. If there are no students, then what use is the schoolhouse? Perhaps in the morning, when the students see the pile of ashes, they just might understand.

By the next day, though, no one understood, and their own policemen collected them in the streets and knocked down apartment doors looking for the professors of history. One died in the embassy fire, consumed by smoke, but Radovan didn't know that one. Some Bosnian rounded up with him said the dead man was a martyr, but with a crushing hangover accentuated by the cold morning light, Radovan couldn't be sure of anything.

Now, the Sunday after the vote, he was still here: a group cell in the Belgrade District Prison on Bačvanska ulica.

Occasionally, policemen arrived to take away this or that prisoner for questioning. The ones who returned said they were asking who had organized the attacks on the Croatian and American embassies, as well as the attempted attacks on the Turkish and British embassies, but the pressure depended on which interrogator you got. Some didn't care for those mysteries and just sat discussing minor offenses, like the trashed McDonald's and other stores along Terazije.

So far, no one had asked him a single question, and he wanted out. He'd grown sick of the stink. He'd watched the testosterone overflow and fights break out. Some skinheads had smuggled in a couple of knives, and two Bosnians had been cut already. More importantly, tomorrow he was expected at the Austrian embassy, and at this rate he wouldn't get questioned until the middle of the week. So when one of the skinheads was returned to the cell, grinning, Radovan flagged his escort. "Tell Pavle Đorđević that Radovan Panić has information for him."

He'd seen Pavle Đorđević in the unheated entrance when he and ten others were dragged in to join the crowd of young men that now numbered about two hundred. He'd known Pavle in high school, though to call them friends would have been a stretch. He'd punched Pavle's face when both were fourteen, and the policeman's long nose still made a slight detour halfway down to his lips. But it was the only name he knew.

The cop pretended to ignore his request, and after he left some of the Bosnians began to hassle him—who was he planning to give up? He stood his ground and told them that a well-known Novi Beograd gangster was his boss. It was enough for them to give him breathing room.

Hours later, around six thirty, he was led to an interview room, where Pavle sat smoking a Marlboro and scratching his broken nose. He ignored Radovan's attempts at reminiscing and pocketed his cigarettes when Radovan made a move for them. He spoke as if he'd been awake for a week straight. "I don't have time for your bullshit, Radovan. Get to the point."

"I've got information. Let's make a deal."

"What kind of information?"

"The good kind. The kind that gets you a promotion. You agree to let me go, and it's yours."

"You're going to tell me who organized the burning of the American embassy?" Pavle grinned. "That information won't get me promoted. It might just get me a bullet in the head."

"It's got nothing to do with that. Nothing to do with Belgrade. No one gets in trouble except some foreigners." He paused. "In particular, an American."

Pavle exhaled smoke, then after a moment placed his Marlboros back on the table. Radovan took one and waited for Pavle to light it. "Go on," said the cop.

"Do we have a deal? I've got to get out. Family business."

"If it's as good as you say, then sure."

"It is, Pavle. Believe me."

7

The request came in the form of a morning e-mail with a red priority flag, asking her to please come to Conference Room S on the second floor for a 10:00 A.M. meeting. It had been sent by Teddy Wartmüller's secretary.

The second floor was a rarity for Erika. She kept to her office on the ground floor, and when the directors of the various departments wanted to talk, they came to her. There had always been a silent understanding in this, since the second floor was where they stocked the French wines and the ten-year-old single malts for serious intelligence bureaucrats poring over policy dictates and making serious decisions. Such important people required their meals be delivered and their drinks poured; it was a place Erika Schwartz did not belong.

She'd been invited not merely to the second floor but to the most esteemed and contentious of the conference rooms. Each department had been tapped to pay for S's renovation more than two years ago. They paid for the Spanish leather upholstery, the Italian cabinets, and the long conference table made of Finnish oak and fitted out with its own laptops and cameras for conference calls displayed on an enormous plasma television at the end of the room; at the other end, windows with electric blinds surveyed the grounds. The inevitable argument over funding this monstrosity had finally uncovered the true purpose of S, which was to impress the Americans. This, of course, was before the CIA's Afghan heroin scandal shut down most of their joint operations, but construction had continued anyway. Since the room's completion last year, not a single American had entered Conference Room S, nor had Erika.

The irony was deeper, because Room S was only a stopgap before the entire building moved to the new headquarters in Berlin, which, according to recent estimates, would be finished by 2011. Even though the move was still at least three years off, the arguments and deals over who would get corner offices had been going on ever since Gerhard Schröder's security cabinet decided five years ago to centralize the BND in Berlin. This, too, was a debate Erika had been left out of.

As she prepared for the trip upstairs, her suspicions running in various unproven directions but self-consciously dwelling on those two empty wine bottles from Friday night, Oskar wandered in, his eye looking only a little better. "Any word on the face recognition?" she asked.

He shook his head. "I can call down."

"Don't rush them." She used the edge of the desk to pull herself up, then took a few steps forward. Her feet were sore from the weekend, and she wondered miserably if she was going to have to buy a cane. That, really, would be the end.

She went alone to the elevator, and on the second floor young assistants with folders sped past her to their important duties. Room S, on her right, was locked, but through the blinds she saw four people positioned around a hectare of oak. The laptops were packed away.

Her heart sank. Standing around the head of the table, sipping coffee from a china cup, Brigit Deutsch and Franz Teufel were laughing at one of Teddy Wartmüller's bad jokes, while Berndt Hesse, the one friendly but unexpected face in the room, sat nursing his cup as if no one were there. She knocked, and Berndt looked up and said something to Brigit, who pressed a button on the table to unlock the door.

"Erika!" Wartmüller announced as she came in. His cheeks were unusually red today, belying a long-lost youth that had been crushed by his rigorous climb to the top of Berlin's intelligence apparatus. Not that his wild ways had disappeared entirely, though—the world of rumor had a special corner for stories of Theodor Wartmüller's sexual escapades. A devout bachelor since a late-seventies divorce, he'd over the years let slip innuendoes about key parties, exotic clubs, and boys, though no one ever knew if they were true or only to embarrass guests.

"Please," said Wartmüller, waving his hands around. "Sit down and I'll have Jan bring some croissants."

"Just coffee, please," she said as she shut the door and gradually made it to a seat on Berndt's side—he gave her a clandestine wink.

Wartmüller pressed another button and ordered a fresh round of coffees, then clapped his hands together. "We're all here, then."

Brigit and Franz took seats on either side of Wartmüller like, Erika thought, synchronized dancers. They were his twin acolytes—Wartmüller always kept two young apprentices to play off one another—and between them, in the middle of the table, was a single yellow file. Yellow—a departmental work order.

Jan, an elegantly attired Pole who'd come with Room S, arrived carrying a tray. He collected the empty cups and replaced them with steaming coffees, then left. With a twinkle in her eye, Brigit went to a cabinet at the end of the room. She took out an untouched bottle of Asbach brandy and said, "I'm going to spice mine up. Anyone else?"

A trick, Erika thought. She covered her cup with a hand, wondering if they'd actually gone over security footage just to find out how much she was drinking. Had things really become that petty? "Straight for me, thanks," she said.

Brigit, unfazed, cracked open the bottle and poured a healthy dose into her own cup.

"Now that *that's* out of the way," Wartmüller said, giving Brigit a mock glare, "we can get to it. Erika has had a busy weekend."

Talking as if she weren't in the room was another Wartmüller technique, a very effective one.

"Perhaps she can tell us what she's been up to?"

She saw no reason to lie, so she didn't. As she talked, though, another part of her wondered how they'd learned about her activities—from their faces, none of what she said was news. She was confident enough of Oskar's loyalty not to question it now, but perhaps poor, emotional Hans Kuhn had been cornered.

Then again, she had nothing to hide, so perhaps their source didn't matter.

"Would you call this investigation a personal favor for your friend the policeman?" Wartmüller asked.

Berndt cut in, speaking his first words. "Favor or not, I think this falls under your jurisdiction."

Erika appreciated the interruption. Back in West Germany, during that other time, she and Berndt had been confidantes of a sort. Once foreign policy had been reassessed after '89 and each was forced to find new specialties, they had kept up contact. She remained in intelligence, while he moved on—she couldn't quite call it *up*—into politics.

She said, "As Berndt points out, it did seem to fall within our scope. Yes, Inspector Kuhn called me because of our friendship, but I took it on because I considered it our responsibility. That's why I felt free to use our resources."

Wartmüller grinned. "Oskar Leintz—he's one of our resources. Looks to me like you've been getting the poor boy into trouble."

"He had an accident on some stairs."

"I'll bet."

As this seemed to be his cue, Franz reached for the yellow file and pushed. It slid down the long table toward Erika but stopped halfway. Berndt had to get up and reach out to drag it the rest of the way. Because they worked as two sides of the same person, Brigit did the speaking for Franz. "This is part of your investigation?"

Inside the file was a still from the Berlin video. The man, clear from the excellent image reconstruction, had heavy, tired eyes but otherwise looked fit. Handsome in an entirely anonymous way as he talked to Adriana. She turned it over and scanned the next page, important details leaping out at her. The BMW the kidnapper had driven had been reported stolen and subsequently found, abandoned and clean, in the Tempelhof parking lot. The Opel driven by the kidnapper's possible shadow had been rented by an American, whose name they had no record of. Then she saw that the face-recognition software had found a name: Milo Weaver. American. Last known employer: Central Intelligence Agency.

Despite the elegant surroundings, she said, "Scheisse."

"Indeed," Brigit said into her spiked coffee.

His point made, Wartmüller returned to the second person. "I'm beginning to wonder if you're objective enough for this job, Erika. You do seem obsessed with the Americans."

There was a time, and it wasn't so long ago, when the intelligence she offered on the Americans could be taken at face value. No longer. That had ended with Afghanistan, poppy fields, and processed heroin making it all the way to Hamburg.

She'd discovered the trail in late 2005, more luck than detective work, while tracking suspected terrorists who turned out to be simple drug barons. Yet the foil-wrapped bricks they brought into the EU had begun life in fields of Taliban prisoners guarded by the U.S. Army. The bricks were sold on to packagers and then distributors in Europe. All run by the CIA to fund things that its masters in Congress chose not to pay for, or didn't know existed.

She'd brought the information to Wartmüller immediately, and his initial reaction had been the same as hers: disbelief, followed by outrage. She'd even been impressed that a man like him could still feel outrage. He praised her work and told her she would be a crucial part of the nasty job they were going to pull on the cretins at Langley.

A week passed, then two, and she finally got another appointment with him—his schedule had suddenly become full. The outrage was gone, replaced by the stoic pragmatism that she'd expected in the first place. Yes, they were all outraged, he explained, but it had been decided that the greater good needed to be served. In this case, the greater good constituted the reams of excellent intelligence the CIA shared with them as it battled terror around the world. "It's a matter of keeping your head, Erika."

Maybe Erika had been at fault—two years later she still couldn't be sure. In her own estimation, she had kept her head, even as she arranged a slim package of evidence and, in a London pub, handed it off to a representative of Senator Harlan Pleasance, a Republican who was running a committee investigating CIA finances. Pleasance, she knew, was eager for the national spotlight and would squeeze the maximum use out of it. Which was what he did. The story spread like a pandemic, and in the face of protests Berlin had no choice but to condemn the CIA and sever many of its joint operations. Which was why Room S had never been used for its intended purpose.

Wartmüller figured it out, of course. Though no physical evidence could convict her of leaking classified information, she was the only possible source. Evidence has only a slight advantage over rumor, and Wartmüller had spread the story around the intelligence community: Watch out for Erika Schwartz. She's corrosively anti-American.

Now here she was again. She had a CIA employee on tape kidnapping a Moldovan girl who had spent an unimaginable period suffering nightly multiple rapes in a foreign land that later became her home.

"I've talked to Dieter," Wartmüller told her. "He's happy to take over the case."

Dieter Reich was one year away from retirement, with an undistinguished history that had earned him a basement office. "Sir, I don't think Dieter can—"

"It's done," said Brigit, and Franz nodded to remove all doubt.

She looked at Berndt, who seemed to be avoiding her face. "Well, Berndt? Is there a reason you're here to witness this?"

He swallowed and stared at his hands, still clutching his coffee cup. "I'm the one who brought the order, Erika. It's direct from Berlin. No one wants you mixing with the Americans anymore. They wouldn't stand for it."

"They? The CIA, you mean?" It came out louder than she had planned, and she felt sweat collecting on the back of her neck. "Well?"

"Yes," he said while the others just stared. "We can't afford to piss off the Americans any more than we already have."

"And Reich?"

"Their suggestion," he said, an involuntary twitch playing around his left eye. "They feel like he's someone they can work with."

8

She spent the rest of the morning in her office, researching Milo Weaver, once of the Central Intelligence Agency. As of last year, according to what information they had, he had been dismissed from his supervisory position in a New York office (the purpose of which was murky) under suspicion of financial misconduct. For this, he'd spent a month and a half in prison until his name was, also according to the file, cleared. Since then, Milo Weaver had been unemployed, living in Newark, New Jersey. He was separated from his wife and daughter, who lived in Brooklyn.

None of this was familiar, but she still felt a pang of something like familiarity. Had she met this man before? She didn't know the face, though something in those heavy eyes nagged at her. The name? Milo was not so uncommon in the East, but this man was a westerner . . .

There was only one record of him being in Europe recently— Budapest. She found this not from his file but by cross-referencing reports from various European sources. In December, Johann Thüringer, a German journalist who made occasional reports to the military's intelligence office, the ZNBw, from his home base in Hungary, reported that a stringer for the Associated Press, Milo Weaver, had arrived looking for Henry Gray, another journalist, American, who had disappeared. Interesting, but of little use to her now.

At noon, the BND operator forwarded a call to her. It was Andrei Stanescu, Adriana's father. He'd said so little in Berlin that at first she didn't recognize his soupy accent, but she did recognize the desperation in the gasps between his labored German words. "What I like to know is the name, please. The name of this man what kill Adriana."

She lied. She said that they still didn't have anything on the man. When he asked why his face wasn't in the world's newspapers, as his daughter's face had once been, she began to stutter. Literally. She couldn't quite get the lies out in a convincing manner. So she pushed responsibility away entirely. "I'm sorry, Mr. Stanescu, but I'm no longer heading the investigation. You'll have to take that up with Mr. Dieter Reich."

After getting rid of the Moldovan, she called on Oskar, who had been sipping coffee in the break room, chatting up the girls from the second floor for information. "Anything?" she asked.

"Wall of silence."

"I want to know where Milo Weaver has been during the last few months, and where he is now. Can you do that?"

Oskar had the energy of youth and the temerity to think all doors were open to him. In this case, he would have to reach the basement-level room that tapped into U.S. satellite communication, which kept real-time track of border stations across the world and the passports that crossed them. "Sure," he said, "but Teddy will know. An hour, maybe two—but he'll know. Is it really worth it?"

"How do you mean?"

He frowned at her desk, perhaps wondering if he was overstepping some line.

"Go ahead," she told him.

"Why not just let it go? It's barely even our jurisdiction. Let Dieter have it."

She considered that, because it was a good point. Erika had enough to deal with. Why fight for a case no one wanted her on? Perhaps it was this, finding out it had to do with the Americans. She was living up to the role they had all imposed on her, of the slavering anti-American.

No. It was Adriana. It was knowing all she'd been through.

"The way I see it," she said, "I can either do my job, or I can retire. I'm not quite decrepit yet."

The answer didn't seem to satisfy him, but he shrugged. "Well, in an hour or two he'll know."

"By then," she told him, "I'll be back on the case."

Her self-confidence was more than delusion. Before her fall from grace, Erika had devoted numerous hours to investigations directed at members of the BND itself. Occasionally, when rumors became too prevalent, she was called in to assess their factual basis—a position that had earned her no new friends. Twice her investigations had ended in dismissals, once in jail time, and once in suicide—yet in that last case her research finally cleared the man in question.

In 1998, Dieter Reich had ended up under her microscope, and now, ten years later, she pulled up that file—or the copy she had kept for her personal records—and refreshed her memory.

BND minders had noticed weekend purchases on Reich's credit card in Aalsmeer, just south of Amsterdam. There were dinners and clothes and, most importantly, hotel rooms with double beds. Reich had been married for fifteen years, and during those weekends his wife, a Czech named Dana, had remained at home.

That he was having an affair was not the issue. The issue was that he had not reported his mistress's name for vetting. So Erika took care of it herself.

Haqikah Badawi was a thirty-year-old Egyptian graduate student of economics at the University of Amsterdam. She had met Reich during one of his trips to Brussels in 1996, when she was interning with the EU public affairs office, and by the next year he was visiting her whenever he could come up with a work-related cover to fool his wife.

Badawi came from a respectable and progressive Cairo family that had made its money in that indefinable industry called import/export. Her student friends, though politically active, showed no real sign of radicalism, and she wrote occasional articles for the weekly *European Voice*, where a friend was associate editor. Bright, erudite, and attractive—the only question, which Reich himself was psychologically unable to ask, was why she opened her legs to an unexceptional German bureaucrat who was twenty-five years her senior.

It took three weeks and a hated trip into the field for Erika to realize that the impossible had happened: This Egyptian girl was in love with Dieter Reich. Though no real explanations could answer this paradox, from their conversation she inferred that Reich reminded her of a beloved uncle back in Cairo. Erika returned to Pullach bewildered but satisfied that while Reich should be reprimanded for his secrecy, nothing should be done to get in the way of his liaisons.

However, the damage had been done. Two weeks later Badawi herself broke off the affair, explaining that she'd realized (Erika got this from an intercepted e-mail) that there was something infantilizing about her role in the relationship, and she didn't want to live through her thirties pining over a father figure. It was time for her to grow up.

Erika didn't know if Reich knew about her visit, or suspected (as she did) that her conversation with Badawi was the catalyst for her to reconsider their relationship. Reich showed no sign of animosity in the office, even as his life shrank suddenly, his international affair dead. As far as she knew, he and his wife were getting along wonderfully.

There was no joy in this, but in the present situation it felt necessary. The Americans had suggested Reich because they knew he would cut off his own hand before doing anything to risk his pension. Berlin also knew this but was too scared to dispute the suggestion. So she would have a talk with Dieter Reich. He would continue to head the case—she didn't care who got credit—but he would allow her to assist. If he refused . . .

It was all here in the Badawi file, because what Reich could never have predicted was that on September 11, 2001, the world would change, dragging a variety of ambivalent people into the extremes. Badawi had been one such convert who, like Erika, felt the Americans had too much of a hand in things that didn't concern them. Badawi, however, lacking any real power to effect change, returned to Cairo just after the 2003 invasion of Iraq and became a member of al-Gama'a al-Islamiyya, considered a terrorist group by the Egyptian government, the European Union, and the United States—which since 1993 had held its blind leader, Omar Abdel-Rahman, in a federal prison. There was no telling what pieces of German intelligence had crossed their pillow and made it eventually to ears in Egypt.

By one, when Oskar returned from the basement, she had settled on her plan of attack. He closed the door behind himself, and she noticed a folded sheet of paper in his hand, and that, below his puffy eye, his cheeks were very red. "Did one of the secretaries slap you again?"

Oskar leaned so that the edge of the desk cut into the meat of his palms, the paper held tight between two fingers. "Three things. One: Milo Weaver—or, at least, his passport—wasn't in Europe when Adriana was kidnapped. As far as we can tell, his passport hasn't left America since last summer."

It wasn't entirely unexpected, but it was still disappointing. "What about Budapest?"

"No record of it," he said with a dismissive wave of his free hand. Then he grinned the way he did when he hoped he might shatter Erika's cool exterior. "It doesn't matter."

"I can see you're burning to put me in my place. Number two?"

"Milo Weaver hasn't been in Europe recently. But Sebastian Hall—he's been around for months."

"Who?"

He unfolded the page to display a police sketch of a man who looked for all the world like Milo Weaver.

"That's . . . ?"

"Exactly. As Sebastian Hall, Milo Weaver robbed the Bührle Museum a few weeks ago."

"The Bührle? How did this come in?"

"Face popped up on the Interpol list fifteen minutes ago, and I was downstairs to see it. Sebastian Hall, American. Seems he made the mistake of adding a Serb to his crew."

"No need to be racist, Oskar."

"Sorry," he said through a smile. "But I thought you might like to know the third thing."

"I think I would."

"Mr. Hall just arrived in Warsaw, from London, an hour ago. Another couple hours, and we'll have the hotel and room number."

Erika blinked at him. It was excellent work, but Oskar was too easily charmed by his successes. "You're going there, of course."

"Of course," he said. "As soon as my boss is put back on the case."

"Right." She groaned to her feet. "Give me a minute."

Once she reached Dieter Reich's dusty basement office, it only took seven minutes—more time had been spent getting there. She made her case concisely. All it took was a suspicion of helping the enemy for not only this case but his career to slip from his hands. An early dismissal, and then his entire pension would be called into question. "It would certainly be hard on Dana. The loss of money, of course, but the details of the affair—it would crush her, I imagine."

By the time she returned to her office, she desired nothing more than a long bath to wash off the dirt, and Oskar misinterpreted her expression as failure. "Ask the motor pool for something reliable," she told him. "Dieter will okay it."

"How did you do it?"

She took a long time to settle back into her chair. "I put on the clothes of the kind of people we hate." She stared a moment at her desk, then peered up at him. "The trouble is, they fit rather well."

9

Despite the fact that, at thirty-two now, Oskar Leintz had been only fourteen when the German Democratic Republic ceased to exist, he would remain, for the rest of his life, an *Ossi* living in the West. It was a fact he was never able to forget, particularly when he traveled back to Leipzig for family gatherings. His parents still considered Munich a foreign city.

He sometimes wondered if this in-betweenness, or this lingering outsider status, was why Erika Schwartz had plucked him out of the training center in 2000 as her personal assistant. When he asked, she joked, "You looked like you could lift things, which is really all I need. Someone who can lift things."

Things like you? he'd wanted to ask, but at that point he still had no idea how good she was. Her name had come up among the other students, no more than rumors about an obese, caustic woman who could take a stack of files and ferret out a mole and turn him into a triple agent, all without leaving her desk. It took a while before he finally believed the rumors.

At various points during their eight years, he had wondered if accepting the position had been career suicide. Others even mentioned it to him. Franz Teufel, probably acting for Wartmüller, approached him after the CIA heroin scandal—a liaison position had opened up in Berlin, and perhaps Oskar was interested? When he said he wasn't, Franz gave him an opaque lesson on the biorhythms of bureaucratic careers. "They max out, lose their internal drive, and after a while simply collapse. Schwartz has had her time, Oskar. There's no need to be on hand to witness the collapse."

Was it loyalty, misplaced or not, that compelled him to remain Erika Schwartz's manservant?

Perhaps, but more than that Oskar tended to believe that he had chosen the right side, and that in the end, despite evidence to the contrary, Erika's camp would be victorious. Whatever that meant.

He signed out a gray Mercedes and was on the road by three. Though the drive would take as much as twelve hours, flying was impossible, both because of what would be done with Milo Weaver and because Weaver's fate had to be kept from their superiors. As he drove, he made two calls. Following Erika's suggestion, he contacted Heinrich and Gustav, two Leipzigers he'd known from the BND academy, both of whom had been useful for other under-the-radar operations. They promised to meet him at an OMV station along the E51, and when he arrived they were waiting with thick jackets, sunglasses, and cheerful smiles.

The first leg took five hours, heading north toward Potsdam, then turning east. After nine, they stopped in Frankfurt an der Oder and ate rushed meals of ready-made sandwiches and jogged around a bit to stretch their legs, then continued into Poland, taking turns at the wheel so everyone could nap in the back. That last dismal stretch after Łódź was the worst, and just before Warsaw they topped off the gas tank and verified that all the lights were working—a Polish cop pulling them over for a broken blinker would have been a disaster. Then they continued into town and parked as close to the Marriott as possible.

As they took the stairs up to Weaver's room, Oskar had to talk himself down. Over the last hour his adrenaline had begun to kick at him as he remembered that video clip. This man, the girl, and the report of a professionally broken neck. Then the footage he'd seen over the previous week of the miserable parents making their inept televised plea, and later seeing them in the flesh outside the Bulgarian church. These memories coalesced into a hatred that surprised him, and he had to whisper to himself to make sure he didn't kill this CIA man.

Before entering, he measured 30 mg of liquid flurazepam hydrochloride into a syringe. Gustav found the switch to turn off the hall lamps, while Heinrich used a homemade skeleton keycard on the lock. They entered slowly, and in the light from the television the two helpers nearly laughed at the sound of Weaver's snoring, but Oskar didn't. He took in the form on the bed, half dressed, stinking of alcohol and cigarettes, his nose swollen from what must have been a fist. Then he noticed the soft-core pornography. He shut the door.

When they struggled with him, Oskar considered making a mistake. It was a thought that came and left quickly, but while it remained he felt some comfort in it. Pull the plunger on the syringe to add a little air, and then let God decide whether or not the bubble should kill this killer of children. When Erika cornered him about it later, he could admit his mistake and point out that it had been dark in the room.

Afterward, as the American weakened and the agents began to wrap him in his sheets, Oskar settled beside him on the bed. "Don't worry. We're not going to kill you yet."

"You're German?" Weaver muttered, his voice slurred.

"Yes, I am."

Weaver said something short and utterly indecipherable before losing consciousness completely.

As the men finished their job, Oskar collected the items on the bedside table. A keyless ring, sunglasses, a wallet and passport full of the name Sebastian Hall, an iPod, and a cheap-looking Nokia, which he was careful to disassemble before they went anywhere.

10

When Milo woke hours later, the world would not remain still long enough for him to focus in the darkness. A high whining noise enveloped him. He was folded up in a cramped fetal position, arms behind him, and in pain from some ungodly mix of hangover and whatever he'd been injected with. No matter what he did he couldn't stretch out, the world wouldn't stop shaking, and that high whine wouldn't stop. That's when he knew: He was in the trunk of a car.

He choked for breath as it all came back, that brief consciousness and the three Germans, lit by a television with naked women rolling across the screen.

Panic is best dealt with by locating yourself, with as much specificity as possible, in both geography and time. It was at least morning, he knew, because dim light bled through the seams of the trunk. Though he stank of other things, there was no urine smell—his bladder hadn't yet emptied. So he doubted it was afternoon.

Geography: He was on a highway, and, given the number of times the car shifted, changing lanes, it was a busy enough road. He guessed that he was on the E30, the highway leading westward from Warsaw.

When had he been taken? Bed by eleven, and then—how long did Polish television play porn? Until three or four, he guessed. He'd been taken at the latest by four. Sunrise was around six thirty, so they'd been traveling for at least two and a half hours, probably more. They were in Germany or the Czech Republic by now.

He could be wrong—they might have driven east—but the man with the bruised eye and the mustache had admitted to being German, and so he supposed they were taking him to Germany. If he was wrong, it didn't matter. All he wanted was to control the panic.

Yet even though he'd given himself a place in time and space, his blood-sapped, frigid hands still twitched, because he couldn't shake the thought from his head: *This is how she felt. This is how she felt when I kidnapped her.*

Later, when the trunk opened, gray light and cold air spilled in. It was an overcast day, the sky visible only straight up; to the left and right were the sides of big rigs the car had parked between. He was in his coat—someone had dressed him—and around the coat was a white sheet. He blinked up at the mustached man looking down at him, chewing gum, and felt an urge for some Nicorette. Or Dexedrine.

"I'm an American citizen," he said in his most American voice. "You can't just push me around."

"Of course not," said the German. He peered over the top of the car and behind himself, then settled on the bumper. Milo, folded into the trunk, considered ways he might kick the man, but none would work. "You want water?"

"I want some answers."

"And water?"

He was cool, this German, so Milo nodded. "I'm parched. Some aspirin, too, if you've got it."

He did. One of his partners, a huge man, appeared and held Milo's head at an angle so he could swallow some bottled water; then the mustached one slipped two paracetamol between his lips. More water. When it was done, Milo's chin was drenched and cold.

It was a roadside stop, and they were hidden between trucks to avoid easy detection. The one who'd lifted his head lit a cigarette, and in the distance Milo saw the third one—a small, wiry guy—

standing at the end of the trucks watching the road. They were waiting for something.

"Food?" asked the mustached one.

"I'll just throw it up."

"Probably right."

"You want to tell me why I'm here?"

"I don't think so," he said, then stood but didn't walk away.

"I've got to pee."

"You are a big boy. You can hold it."

"Any Nicorette?"

"Excuse me?"

"I've been using nicotine gum, but I'm out. Any chance you have any?"

The man frowned, thinking this over, then shook his head. "We'll get you some cigarettes."

"I'd prefer not to start again."

"You think that matters at a moment like this?" he asked, his expression suggesting he was truly curious about it.

"Forget it," said Milo. "Why don't you shut the door and let me get some sleep?"

The man smiled at that, then closed the trunk. Milo regretted his joke.

Less than five minutes later it opened again, and behind the mustached man, between the trucks, a small van had pulled in backward, its rear doors open to reveal a wheeled hospital cot locked into place. The EU license was German—he'd been right about their direction. "Time to get up, Mr. Weaver."

"Mr. What?"

The man stared at him, and Milo grinned.

"Now I get it—you've got the wrong guy! My name is Hall. Sebastian Hall. Listen," he said, not really believing this would work, "I don't know who you are. Just cut me loose. I won't say a thing, and you can go find this Weaver character. I mean, you don't want the wrong person, do you?"

The man's morose expression didn't change. "Milo Weaver, Sebastian Hall—it's all the same to me."

His two friends helped Milo sit up, then lifted and moved him to the cot. There was nothing smooth about the transfer—this wasn't their regular occupation—and Milo's head bumped against the door frame as they tried to climb inside with him. He said, "Slowly now, fellas." Neither answered.

Now that they were taking them off, he could see that his ankles had been bound by PlastiCuffs, which they cut with Swiss Army knives as they strapped his legs into the cot. Then they pushed him into a sitting position and undid his hands, the blood rushing coldly back into them. They tingled and hurt. The men pushed him flat again and stretched more straps tightly across his chest and around his wrists.

The whole process took about three minutes, and the mustached man joined him in the back of the van as the others closed and locked the windowless doors from the outside. There wasn't much space, so the man settled on the floor beside Milo as the van started up and began to roll. Soon they were back on the highway.

"You going to tell me anything?" asked Milo.

"No. And I've got another syringe in my pocket in case you insist on talking the whole way."

11

When, at three that afternoon, she heard the knock on her door, Erika was reading up on the international sex trade. Once she'd decided on what to do with Milo Weaver, she made sure to cease her in-office investigation of him, because every site and document she looked at was logged in the central database. However, instead of returning to what she was supposed to be working on—namely, the backgrounds of two Iranian nationals applying for asylum—she found herself drawn to the industry that had set Adriana Stanescu's life moving along its particularly atrocious path.

It was bleak. Part of the reason sexual slavery continues unabated is that imagining it is so abhorrent to most people that they choose instead to ignore it. Imagining the travails of someone like Adriana led to upset stomachs. Law-abiding citizens preferred the knowable crimes of murder and robbery to the unknowable of slavery. This silence on the issue only encouraged the industry to thrive.

So it was almost a relief when Thomas Haas interrupted her. The young analyst from the basement-level surveillance center had been at Pullach nearly a year and was one of the few with whom she chose to exchange words. "Good afternoon, Thomas."

He wasn't smiling. "Frau Schwartz, we've spotted a van at your house."

"A van?" She let herself appear concerned. "Markings?"

"Toledo Electrik GmbH."

"Oh!" She smiled and touched her breast. "You had me scared. No, that's nothing. There's a problem with the circuit breaker—it keeps switching off in the middle of my shows. I gave Toledo a set of keys."

"Would you like someone to check on it? To be sure."

"No, I'll call the electrician," she said, picking up her office phone. "Thanks."

Once he was gone, she called the number of a throwaway cell phone she'd bought the previous night and left inside her house. Oskar answered on the third ring. "Toledo Electrik."

"Yes, this is Erika Schwartz. Do you have someone at my house right now?"

"Schwartz . . . here it is," he said and rattled off her address.

"That's it."

"Should take an hour or so. We're mailing the bill, right?"

"Exactly. It looks like it won't be a problem?"

"No problems yet, ma'am. We'll let you know if anything comes up."

"Thank you."

The rear doors opened to reveal a woody bilevel, and when he was brought out he saw that they were surrounded by gangly birches and broad elms, stripped of leaves, creating a black web through which he could just make out other houses that made him think of American planned communities. Large homes set far back behind tended lawns, clean automobiles in the driveways. He could only see these things when he looked hard, though, which meant that anyone looking in would simply see four men getting out of a van with—he now saw—the markings of an electrical repair company. From their perspective, the man in the center of the group would be walking with his hands clasped behind his back; the new set of PlastiCuffs would not be visible at all.

There were no guns involved, just a light, almost comforting, hand on his back, while the little man with the mustache hummed some song. He was clearly the boss, and it was he who unlocked the front door, typed the security code into the alarm, and pocketed a cell phone sitting on a fragile-looking end table beside the door. "Come in," he said. "We'll soon have you out of those restraints."

It was all so polite that Milo began to sweat profusely.

They went downstairs, where the man turned on some lights and found, beside a spare bathroom, a heavy security door with a keypad. He typed the code with a flat hand, fingers covering the pad so it was impossible to tell the combination, then pulled open the door to reveal stairs heading deeper into the earth.

A couple of decades ago, he would have called it a fallout shelter. Times had changed, though, and these were now referred to as panic rooms, but the function was the same. A secure place where one could survive for days or weeks with no need of the outside world. Along the walls were shelves of provisions—canned food, soap, bottles of water. A refrigerator beside an electrical generator. A propane stove. There was a television/VCR combination, a radio, and a shelf of books. Two small monitors, now black, were assumedly connected to CCTV cameras observing the grounds. Two lounge chairs, one sofa, and a dining table. Against the stone wall in the back of the room, a single cot with fresh bedding. On the concrete floor beside it were two rolls of duct tape.

The mustached man gazed at cans of soup while the other two removed Milo's cuffs and took his coat. "You needed to urinate?" he asked.

"Desperately."

The man nodded in the direction of a small door, and the other two led Milo to it. Inside was a spotless toilet, but no sink. It was a small space, but both his guards squeezed in behind him, peering over his shoulder, hands on his back as he relieved himself. He pulled the chain to flush, then raised his hands. "Can I wash?"

Neither answered. They pulled him out and led him to one of the chairs. The mustached man, still reading the cans, said, "Are you hungry perhaps?"

"Could use some coffee."

"Yes. So could I. Heinrich? *Willst du auch einen?*"

The block of muscle looked up from Milo. "Ja, danke."

The mustached man turned to the wiry one. "Dann also für alle?"

The wiry one nodded and trotted upstairs.

Their exchange, figuring out how many coffees were needed, struck Milo as amusing. Nothing else did. He was in a secure basement from which he would never escape unless they let him leave. He was here for as long as they wanted, and in here they could do anything they desired. No one would hear a thing.

Heinrich took the chair across from Milo as a phone began to ring. The mustached man took out the cell phone he'd taken from the foyer and said, "Toledo Elektrik."

A conversation followed. He got the name Schwartz, that something would take about an hour, and that a bill would be mailed. And *Frau*—ma'am—he was talking to a woman.

He pocketed the phone again and said to Heinrich, "In Ordnung."

Heinrich looked relieved, though the mustached one didn't seem concerned either way. He held Milo's coat folded over his arm and paced the room slowly, peering at everything as if he'd never been here before. Perhaps he hadn't. His free hand searched Milo's coat pockets, coming up with receipts and lint. He stuck the receipts in his pants pocket and tossed the coat on the bed. "You should make yourself comfortable," he said. "It'll be some hours before things get started."

"What, exactly, is going to get started?"

"Conversations."

"When your boss gets home from work?"

The man stared at him.

"This is his house, isn't it? Or *her* house. Your boss's."

"All that matters to you is that this is the easy part. Have some coffee, something to eat. Get over that headache . . . does it still hurt?"

"A little."

"Heinrich."

Heinrich half-rose from his chair and, with a large flat hand, struck Milo across the temple. It felt like a wooden board and rekindled the pain that had, until then, been subsiding. He cradled his head in his hands and stopped himself from shouting an obscenity. "What was that for?"

"For nothing," the man said as he passed behind Milo. "I'm not a big believer in the carrot and stick. It's fine for mules, but for people? No. Much too predictable, and anything that predictable can be manipulated. The unpredictable stick—that's much more useful because there is no clear answer to it."

Milo raised his head, half of it pulsing sorely, and could feel his damaged nose dripping blood onto his lips. "I think I understand," he said.

"Good." The mustached man sat on the sofa, just beyond Heinrich. He used a remote control to turn on the television against the wall. "My boss, as you say, isn't entirely comfortable with modern digital technology. So we have this." He pressed PLAY, and the embedded VCR began to whir, flickering grainy images on the screen, the buzz of static, then voices. News items. A German newscaster. The image of a girl, Adriana Stanescu. A camera ranging over mountains, then a mountain road, the scene of a wreck, a path into the forest. Then again. Another newscaster—Spanish—and more of the same. And more: childhood shots of Adriana, swimming with her parents, a young birthday. Now Dutch. Then Italian. French. Moldovan. British. German. American. Polish.

It went on, in languages he couldn't even identify, with scenes of the mother breaking down on camera, screaming, her stoic husband hollow-eyed behind her. The occasional angry person-on-the-street giving an opinion. It lasted for over an hour until it faded to black and the mustached man pressed STOP and then REWIND. As it whirred loudly, he said, "Heinrich," and another board struck Milo's temple.

"Jesus! Cut it out!"

He started to rise, but Heinrich pushed him down again. The mustached man retrieved one of the rolls of duct tape and tossed it smoothly to Heinrich, who began to strap Milo in the chair.

There was nothing to be done. This had all been planned ahead of time—the hard hand, the video, and even his eventual outburst. They knew what they were doing.

The VCR clicked loudly. Then they all looked up as their missing member trotted down the stairs holding a tray with large, steaming coffee cups. Milo wondered why it had taken so long to make them, then realized it hadn't. The man simply knew he wasn't to interrupt the videotape.

"Excellent!" The mustached one got to his feet. "What kind?"

The wiry one began passing out cups. "There was a bag of Starbucks grounds. Ethiopian."

"Starbucks?" He seemed confused. "How about that? You know their coffee, Mr. Weaver?"

"Intimately."

"Delicious," he said and sipped from his cup, then leaned back. "Too hot for me. Heinrich?"

Heinrich was holding two cups—one for him, one for Milo. "Very hot," he said, then looked over at the mustached man. Heinrich seemed to interpret his superior's silence as an order. He poured a little of the steaming coffee onto Milo's chest. It burned straight through his shirt, but he didn't shout out this time, only grunted. Heinrich set down the cup and began to drink from his own.

The mustached man took his coffee to the stairs. "I think Mr. Weaver would like some more television."

The one who'd brought the coffees used the remote to start the VCR playing again. Newscaster. Adriana. Barren trees.

"Let's make sure we remember every image on that tape, yes? There'll be a quiz later."

The man with the remote laughed lightly, and Heinrich smiled. The mustached man left them alone as Adriana's mother wept uncontrollably on-screen.

None of this, really, was a surprise. Just as he tried to keep himself grounded, his interrogators would only be interested in keeping him off balance, and for the next five minutes he felt himself slipping. Then the man with the mustache made his first mistake. As a Dutch newscaster with dour features discussed Adriana's murder, he quietly came down the stairs, holding a crumpled slip of paper that had come from Milo's pockets. It wasn't a receipt. Heinrich paused the video.

"Excuse me," he said as he unfolded the paper. It was hotel stationery. "I was just curious—who wrote this?"

Honestly, Milo said, "I've never seen it before."

Heinrich's open hand crashed against the side of his face. Milo took a labored breath.

"I'm telling the truth."

"I know," the man said, then brought the paper over for him to read.

The world was too blurry for him to read a thing. "Closer, please."

The man obliged, and he could now see that it was from the Cavendish, London. Below the name, in sweeping letters, he read:

Tourism, like Virginia,
is for lovers.
Turn that frown upside down, man.

It was followed by a smiley face.

Despite himself, Milo began to laugh. James Einner had a wonderfully idiotic sense of humor.

"Well?" said the man.

"I wish I knew," he said. "It's kind of lovely, isn't it?"

Heinrich struck him again, but he hardly felt it.

"Who's it from?"

"A secret admirer, I guess."

12

She made sure to follow her routine and visit Herr al-Akir's shop for her Riesling and Snickers. She'd noticed a change in his demeanor the previous evening, and it had taken her a moment to realize that it was the result of Friday's irregularity. That idiot who had run in to collect her, foolishly calling her Director Schwartz. That was the only explanation for the heavy stare that flickered away nervously when she turned to meet it. Tonight was the same. The *Guten Abend*, then nervous silence as she trudged to the back to collect her wine. She placed her ten sixty-five on the counter and watched him tap at the register. "Herr al-Akir," she said, "did the gentleman give you the five cents last week?"

He blinked three times, then nodded. "Yes. Your account is settled." He handed over her receipt.

"Is there anything wrong?"

He shook his head eagerly. "Everything is very fine."

"Perhaps you have a question for me."

He seemed stunned by the suggestion. "No. No questions."

She tried for a smile, even though she knew the effect her smiles had on strangers. "Good evening to you, then."

Back in the car, she put Herr al-Akir out of her mind and focused on the road. It had been a quiet day. She had waited for a visitor from the second floor—not Wartmüller himself, of course, but

perhaps some intermediary—to wonder to her face how she'd gotten
Dieter Reich to keep her on the Stanescu case. But no one said a thing
to her; in fact, she got the pleasant feeling that the second floor had
been abandoned.

Though they'd exchanged no significant words since that three
o'clock phone call, she had seen Oskar at the office. He came in after
four looking exhausted and worked on his computer, filing nondescript vetting reports and running some of Erika's errands. They
had decided beforehand that nothing about Milo Weaver would pass
between them in the office, no matter how safe they considered themselves. Which was why he stayed behind briefly when she left at
seven thirty. While Erika visited Herr al-Akir, Oskar drove his own
car into the Perlacher Forest and waited for her to pick him up.

He looked frigid by the side of the road, his Volkswagen parked
out of sight, and once inside he fooled with the heater until it blew
loudly. "You took your time," he said.

"Had to pick up my Riesling."

"I think you have a drinking problem, Erika."

"How's he doing?"

"Watching videos."

"Nothing broken, I hope," she said, because she had noticed the
underlying hatred in Oskar once he had learned of Adriana Stanescu's past. He was looking for someone to blame, and Milo Weaver
was as good as anyone.

"Not yet. But we've still got time."

He knew something was happening when Heinrich, after receiving
a call, got up and turned off the television. Milo had watched and listened to Adriana Stanescu's multilingual story for, he estimated, four
hours. Four hours duct-taped to a chair facing the video loop. Even
now, with the television black, he kept seeing the grainy family photos, the stunned father and screaming mother, and the bare branches
that led to her final resting spot in the mountains of France.

Of course, with repetition everything dulls, and the panic he'd
felt during the first and second viewing had waned so that by this

fourth (or was it fifth?) viewing he was more interested in his ability to predict the actual phrases and emotional outbursts. A memory game; a distraction.

The mustached man descended the stairs first, looking cold and perhaps ill. In his hand was a bottle of white wine. Then, much more slowly, a breathtakingly heavy woman followed him down. She gripped the wooden rail, making no effort to hurry herself, until she finally reached the concrete floor and looked around to get everything in focus. Her salt-and-pepper hair, thick and untidy, was chopped into a pageboy cut. When she got Milo into focus she started forward again and settled on the sofa, legs splayed, breathing heavily. "Mr. Weaver," she said, producing something like a smile that could easily have been a sneer. Her accent was thick. "Welcome to Germany."

The mustached man, no longer the authority in the room, began to open the wine bottle, using the Swiss Army knife that had been used to remove Milo's cuffs.

The woman he assumed was Frau Schwartz said, "Heinrich, perhaps Mr. Weaver would like something to drink."

"My name is Hall."

"Perhaps Mr. Hall would like something to drink."

Milo gestured with his chin at the coffee stains down his shirt. "I think I've had enough, Ms. Schwartz."

"Someone made a mess," she observed. "Maybe we can get your hands free—it would be easier that way."

"Yes," said the mustached man, leaving the bottle. He clicked the corkscrew back into place and worked open a blade. He began to cut through the duct tape.

"Heinrich," she said, nodding at the open bottle. "Why don't you bring us two glasses from the kitchen?"

Heinrich headed up the stairs.

"Don't cut him, Oskar," she said, and Milo finally had a name for the mustached man.

For a while Schwartz just watched him, while Oskar worked on the duct tape. She produced that plastic smile again. "Mr. Weaver—no, please. Let me use that name. I am Erika Schwartz—that's my real name, too. Have you some knowledge of me?"

Now that he had the first name, he recalled a fragment of biography from his previous life in administration. An antagonistic BND director who, to the Company's delight, was being slowly sidelined within German intelligence. "No. I sell insurance for a living—are you in the business, too?"

She placed her swollen hands together, as if praying. "Let's step back a moment. Milo Weaver, thirty-seven years old. Employee of the Central Intelligence Agency." She held up a hand when Milo started to protest. "Until last year, you were in administration, and your records were semipublic. So we know some things about you. You have an apartment in Newark, New Jersey. You have a family—a wife, Tina, and a daughter named Stephanie—who live in Brooklyn. But you haven't seen them much recently because you've been traveling in Europe under the name Sebastian Hall. Except for one known instance, in December, when, under your real name, you went to Budapest."

Budapest? Then Milo got it. She was slipping in a piece of fiction to see if he would refute it, thus proving that the rest of her story was true. She really was good. "I don't know who this guy is, but yes, I've been traveling in Europe. It's called establishing a client base, Miss Schwartz. It's what you do when you want to sell health insurance to expats."

"Of course. And in Budapest, you were a journalist for the Associated Press. You can go through all the stories you like, Mr. Weaver, but I do know who you are. So what's the point? You could waste time—that's always possible. You could live in the hope that if you stretch out your silence your people will finally come to collect you, or they'll pressure my people to let you go. But listen to me, Mr. Weaver, because this is important: No one knows you're here. Your people don't know. My people don't know. No one would imagine that I know anything about your whereabouts. They won't even ask me. So this can last a few hours, a few days, or even months." When she paused, her breaths came out loudly, as if speaking so long had been an exertion. "It's all the same to me. But it won't be the same to you."

As Heinrich returned with two glasses, Milo wondered again about Budapest. Was she really making it up? Heinrich filled the glasses with what Milo could now see was Riesling and gave one to Schwartz. She sipped it and made a pleasant expression. "It's really very good. From Pfalz. Go ahead."

Milo accepted the second glass. She was right. It was cold and crisp and soothed his sore throat. He drank slowly, watching Oskar, Heinrich, and Erika Schwartz. The third man was somewhere behind him.

Schwartz said, "I'm not unreasonable. You should know that. Though I believe you killed Adriana Stanescu, the method of her death is less interesting to me than the reason for it."

"I've done a lot of questionable things in my life," Milo told her, "but I never killed any girl."

"You did kidnap her. Of that there's no doubt."

"You're crazy."

"Oskar, can you please show Mr. Weaver to Mr. Weaver?"

Oskar went to the television. He ejected the tape, then found another unlabeled one among a short stack and slipped it in.

There it was. With a date and a time code and—there—Milo himself, waiting for her. Looking at the camera, or—no. He was looking at the blue Opel tailing him. The Opel was in the fore-ground, while Milo . . .

She was tall and full of life, and seeing it from the outside filled him with self-disgust. There he was, the cretin who stepped out and said *Entschuldigung*, then showed off his fake ID. Then led her to her doom.

When Oskar stopped the tape, Milo was out of breath. He could hardly manage the words "That's not me."

"No?" she said, unfazed. "Oskar?"

Oskar reached into his jacket and removed a standard 10 by 15 cm photograph and held it up for Milo to examine. Milo in the doorway to that courtyard, talking animatedly with Adriana Stanescu. The image was cleaned up; it was undeniable.

Oskar waited until he'd had an eyeful, then put it away.

"Photoshop," Milo said, his breath back now. "Special effects. I don't know why, but you're trying to frame me."

"You've been busy. The week before kidnapping her, you robbed an art museum in Zürich. That, of course, is how we came across your work name."

The gears turned in Milo's head. Radovan Panić, who had lifted his passport. Goddamned Radovan and his family-centered morality.

"So we know who you are. We know of at least two of the crimes you've committed. We know you work for the CIA—or, at least, you did work for them until last summer, when you spent a couple of months in jail. I won't even ask about that—that's how unobtrusive I am. I only want to learn about Adriana Stanescu. I want to know why you were ordered to kill her."

He slumped and looked at the glass in his hand. He could dig it into Oskar's little eye, but by that point Heinrich would be on top of him, beating him senseless. Then it would all begin again, this time strapped into that cot.

Time—that was what he needed. Time to think through it all. Anything would do, just as long as it bought him another hour.

He said, "No one ordered a thing."

"You did it for the fun of it?"

"I have a problem. I killed her for my own pleasure, but it didn't feel like I thought it would feel. It was . . ." He dropped his glass, the shattering sound making everyone jump, then began to weep quietly into his hands.

Schwartz grunted, then smiled. She gripped the arms of her chair and pushed herself to her feet. "Oskar, let's go upstairs. Mr. Weaver needs more time for reflection."

Oskar stood up, but Milo didn't drop his act. Once they were at the stairs again, Schwartz turned back. "Heinrich, Gustav—could you help Mr. Weaver with his thinking?"

"Jawohl," said Heinrich, getting up to switch the videotapes back again. Milo heard the springs make an awkward noise as Gustav rose from the cot.

13

"What do you think?" Erika asked once they reached the second floor. The climb had winded her, so Oskar helped her to a sofa near the window. Neither of them turned on a lamp, and they sat in darkness.

"He's a professional liar."

"Well, that's obvious, Oskar. He knows he's not fooling us with that sad pervert act. We know too much. Did you see his face? The surveillance video threw him."

"Do you have anything to eat?" he asked.

"Chicken in the refrigerator. Bread on top. Make two, will you?"

As Oskar made chicken sandwiches in the semidarkness of the kitchen, she stared into the middle distance, a few feet short of a Tawaraya Sōtatsu print of Japanese demons. She'd always hated the painting, but it had been a gift from the Japanese embassy, and it was important to display her few gifts. At this moment, she even appreciated having the Sōtatsu, because such an abysmal work couldn't distract her from the problem of how to approach Milo Weaver.

Annoyingly, she again felt that vague familiarity. It was in his facial features, and in his resolute obstinancy. But from where? She wasted time on this, going back over the past twenty years, but she was sure: She'd never met this man before. So she set it aside and returned to the problem.

It was a classic interrogation conundrum: How much does the subject know of what you know? Is it better to feign more knowledge or less? Is it better to share more or less?

That Weaver came from an allied agency made it no easier. At some point she would let him go, and there would be repercussions. Though she wasn't particularly concerned for her own position—she was, after all, already on the way out—there was no reason for this escapade to end Oskar's career. There was also Wartmüller himself. A political animal, yes, but essentially a good man. She didn't think her actions would taint him directly, but in Teddy's eyes the future of their relationship with the Americans was of paramount concern. Sitting in front of the Sōtatsu, with an American in her basement, she could admit that, despite her apprehensions, it might be true.

Milo Weaver's attempts to obfuscate had told her one crucial thing: He was working for someone. Either he was still a CIA asset, or he was an ex-Company man working with organized crime. Either way, he was protecting an organization of some sort by taking the blame upon himself.

But was he really, though? That head-in-the-hands routine had been just that: a routine. No one really could have believed it. So perhaps by confessing so poorly he was in fact professing the truth— that he, in fact, was a lone murderer—and supposed his obvious act would throw them off.

No. She didn't get the sense that this man thought so far ahead, or so deeply.

Or—and this was the problem with thinking too hard about anything truly unknowable—was this all part of his act? Was Adriana perhaps beside the point, a diversion while he protected something else?

Now the one detail she felt she had learned from this initial interview dissolved before her.

Erika was no novice when it came to interrogations, and she knew that the question of his allegiance had to be answered, even if the answer was wrong. Interrogations are fluid, but they exist in time, moving steadily forward. When they stall, rot sets in. Decision is the only way to keep them moving forward. Either Weaver still worked for the CIA, or he didn't. If he didn't, then he had gone private, and under different names had expanded his self-employment to include art heists, kidnapping, and murder.

If he did still work for the CIA?

In that case, she asked herself, what kind of agent would be involved in such a spectrum of illegal activity? What kind of Renaissance man was dropped off the Company books and sent to travel around Europe with no known home base? There really was only one answer, but it was difficult to swallow.

She'd heard the rumors ever since the early seventies, when she began in the business, and a quarter of her country lived under a different name and regime. There had been a spate of disappearances: East German agents who had set up shop in Bonn, West Berlin, and Hamburg. One moment they were living their lives in full view of the Federal Republic's surveillance men, then they weren't. They were usually agents of known interest to the Americans, and when Erika tried to find out their fates she was always frustrated by the cleanest crime scenes she had ever come across. She discussed the phenomenon with her boss; his later career was annihilated by an uncovered Nazi past, but at that time he was held in high respect. He took a cursory glance at her notes and muttered, "Tourists."

"They weren't tourists, sir."

"They certainly weren't, Erika," he said, then lit his pipe and proceeded to tell her of the legend that had spread during the decade following the fall of Berlin, of a secret sect of American agents that required none of the comforts of normal humans. No steady identity, no home, no moral center beyond the virtue of work. "What Hitler could have done with men like these," she remembered him saying.

They were called Tourists because they were as connected to the world as a tourist is to the countries he visits—which is to say, they were not connected at all. They appeared and then disappeared. While her boss described these men—and the occasional woman—in awed tones, Erika found herself disappointed by his gullibility.

"Don't be absurd. It's called disinformation. It's the open secret that makes you fear them."

"I used to think that, too," he said, then told a story. Berlin, August 1961. On the twelfth, a Saturday, he and his colleague found a dead American along the border with a Minox and handwritten notes. The camera contained photos of an outdoor garden party, with, among other guests, DDR president—or, as he was officially called, chairman of the council of state—Walter Ulbricht. The notes said that they were gathered to sign an order to close the border and construct a wall. "So we knew it hours before it happened. We took it to our CIA friends that night, but they were more interested in the corpse of their agent."

"Why?"

"Because they had no idea who he was. Since no one could identify him, we decided not to act on the information. It might have been another Bolshevik trick. By midnight, when they closed down the border, we realized it wasn't. The little quirks of history are fascinating, aren't they?"

"How does this connect to Tourists?"

"Well, we didn't know what to do with the body. The Americans were still claiming it wasn't theirs. It certainly wasn't ours. So we started showing his photo around. Next thing we knew, we had five more names. Two from the Russians, one from the Brits, another American name, and a German name. Then, a surprise—the CIA's London station chief, of all people, showed up and demanded the body. Swept the thing away, and every time we requested information about it, we were asked, *Who are you talking about?* The man who took the body was Frank Wisner, the rumored founder of the Department of Tourism."

"That proves nothing."

"Of course it doesn't. If it did, then they wouldn't be doing their job. It's funny, though—each of this man's assumed identities had a price on its head. The Russians wanted both names for murder, the Brits wanted theirs for forgery, and we wanted ours for industrial sabotage. A wide range of talents for a single man."

Thirty-five years later, that conversation came back to her as she considered the range of crimes that could be attributed to this one person.

Either Weaver no longer worked for the CIA, or he did. If he did, then he looked and smelled much like a fabled Tourist. Which was why, only minutes later, Erika nearly died.

They were eating dry chicken sandwiches in the darkness when she asked what they'd found on Weaver when they picked him up. "A phone, but clean," said Oskar. "No phone numbers in the memory. It's nothing special."

"You expected secret gadgets, maybe?"

He shrugged, then wiped a crumb from his chin. "There was a bag. Clothes, mostly. Pills—Dramamine, things for the bowels, pain relievers, that sort of thing. A key ring."

"Keys?"

He shook his head. "It's got a car remote on it, but no actual keys. An iPod, but all that's on it is music. David Bowie, actually. The man seems obsessed."

"Pockets?"

"Receipts. From London, mostly. A couple Polish ones. And a personal note written on hotel stationery."

"Love letter?"

Oskar reached into his pocket and handed over the note. "I don't think he knew it was there. He seemed surprised when I showed him. He laughed."

She turned the slip so that it caught the streetlight from outside. She read, then read it again and felt the blood rush into her cheeks. "What does he say about it?"

"He says it's kind of lovely."

She read it a third time, then folded it and recited it from memory: "*Tourism, like Virginia, is for lovers. Turn that frown upside down, man.*" She shook her head, unable to control the wild, involuntary grin, and then swallowed. She wasn't paying attention, though, and a rough wedge of chicken lodged in her esophagus.

"What?" said Oskar.

She waved her hands, pointed at her throat, and tried in vain to speak. Oskar rushed over. She felt the oxygen leaving her body, her arms going cold. Oskar got behind her and pushed her up, grunting, then wrapped his arms around her layers of fat and jerked his fist into her stomach, or thereabouts, several times. A slimy piece of chicken shot out of her mouth and landed on the rug. She gasped as Oskar came around to check on her.

"Thank you," she managed.

"You're all right?"

"Do you believe in fate, Oskar?"

"No."

His pragmatism was coming along just fine. "Good. Let's find out what kind of Tourist our friend is."

14

When Erika Schwartz finally returned with Oskar, Milo was feeling disgusted with himself. She'd given him what he'd aimed for—time, an extra hour to think over his predicament. Yet he'd come up with nothing, and found himself dwelling on the irony of his situation: At a time when the Department of Tourism was worried about a Chinese mole, it was because of Adriana Stanescu that he'd been captured.

That's because you serve them, the little voices. You're a fool.

Schwartz settled across from Milo. Her cheeks and forehead were red, and he wondered if stairs really were that hard on her. What kind of health was she in? Might a few well-placed words bring on a heart attack? Oskar, too, seemed flustered. Perhaps they'd been arguing—another thing that might work to his advantage.

She said, "I will act based upon my suppositions, while my suppositions will be based on my limited knowledge. Does that seem reasonable to you?"

"Sure."

Schwartz opened her plump hands. "For the moment, we'll set aside the events in Zürich. Let's stay with Adriana. My supposition is that you were asked to kill her. Maybe you were asked to kidnap her, and then the order was changed—the distinction doesn't matter right now. What does matter is that, like any hired gun, this was probably all you knew. The name of the victim, perhaps the method of disposal. Simple facts, from which you could improvise as you wished, so long as the orders were followed."

Milo stared at her, a blank slate. Then: "This is crazy. When my embassy finds out—"

"Please," she said, raising a hand. "As I've made clear, what interests me is the why of her murder. Not the how. The who, I hope, will become clear once I know the why." She blinked, as if confused. "I did make that clear, yes?"

Milo didn't answer, but Oskar said, "I believe you did, Erika."

"Good." She crossed her hands in her lap and then, noticing crumbs, flicked them away. "So what I'm realizing now is that you, Mr. Weaver, won't be as much help to me as I'd hoped. You're a killer, which means it's not your purview to know the why of your orders. I also doubt you know anything about the girl you killed. Which is why I'm going to tell you about her." She smiled. "Don't get me wrong—I don't think anyone as versatile as yourself will have his heart softened by a story or two. I just think it's a good thing for humans to know the full measure of their actions. Does that sound pompous?"

"Certainly not," said Oskar.

Something upstairs had convinced her to try this new angle. Maybe it was guesswork, or just the acute senses of an experienced interrogator, but she had decided to tell Milo the one thing that he had been desperate to know: the story behind Adriana Stanescu. So he said, "It sounds very reasonable."

"Excellent," said Erika. "It took some digging, but I had help from Adriana's uncle, Mihai. He, you have to understand, isn't like us. He doesn't have the apathy—is that the right word?" Milo didn't answer, so she went on. "Mihai doesn't have the apathy that we from intelligence are full of—the apathy toward individuals that our job requires. No, Mihai Stanescu is sentimental to the extreme, particularly when it comes to his dead niece. He doesn't understand—as you and I do—that good little girls and boys must sometimes disappear when important things require it. Because, really, Milo—despite all the claptrap from priests and politicians about the value of the little children, the fact is that the world doesn't change when they die. The value of the dollar remains the same. Your *American Idol* doesn't lose ratings. The stores remain fully stocked. And children disappear all the time."

Though he held on to his stolid expression, Milo wondered where she was going with this. It wasn't just a story.

She said, "Take, for instance, the so-called tragedy of sexual trafficking. Thousands of women and children—and let's not soften the blow with vagaries; they're sometimes as young as six months— disappear every week and end up in whorehouses, sold as sexual slaves, or videotaped for Internet sites. They are abused, raped, tortured and sometimes killed for the pleasure of a certain demographic. Does this change the value of the euro?" She shook her head, and her discomforting smile reappeared. "Certainly it does not. People like you and me, we understand this."

What could she read in Milo Weaver's face? Very little. Either he truly was a pro—she'd decided to set aside the term "Tourist" for now—or he had no idea where her monologue was heading next. Perhaps he really didn't know Adriana's past.

"A case in point. Of one such girl who went through what the media would certainly call a tragedy if they caught wind of it. But, really, Stalin aside, tragedy is when thousands of people are killed, and when their deaths bring down financial institutions—*that's* tragedy. This is more . . . I don't know. A blip in the moral universe? Something like that, though for people like us, there really is no moral universe, is there?"

Milo looked like he was going to answer, but didn't. Oskar stared at the side of his head. Heinrich and Gustav were mesmerized by her speech; she almost expected them to start taking notes.

"Ah, well, the story," she said. "It began in Moldova, as you'd expect. At that time Adriana was only eleven."

Milo listened. Despite himself, he paid attention to every word, every digression, and, worse, all the physical details. Erika Schwartz described the design on the scarf Adriana wore when she boarded the bus headed west, and though he knew this was a detail she probably couldn't know, it remained with him anyway, all the way through to the warehouse in St. Pauli where the initial rapes occurred, to the Berlin apartment where she was used many times a night. The scarf was decorated with flowers shaped into paisleys. She had not used the mawkish word "tears," but she didn't need to. He knew that a paisley looked like the drop of salty water that forms at the corner of a child's eye, and the image just wouldn't leave him.

Because in the end Milo Weaver wasn't outside the moral universe, no matter how well the Company had trained him. Once, when he had been a younger Tourist, he had lived without empathy. That had held him in good stead for the first seven years, from 1994 until 2001. He had stayed alive because of it. But once he'd left to build a home, he couldn't escape the continual reminders that his universe had become imbued with morality—bathing his infant daughter's fat, squirming body, later walking her to school and listening to her rambling stories, making curry for his wife, vacuuming on the weekends. Simply taking out the trash every other day had reinforced a moral responsibility that he'd had to learn bit by bit. It hadn't been a smooth transition; he'd screwed it up many times during those first years, but even his wife's patience had taught him new lessons.

By the time Owen Mendel asked him to return to Tourism, he was too far gone. Tourism is for the young, the unmarked. Tourism is for the fatherless and childless. Milo was no longer any of these things, which was why he knew he was doomed, eventually, to failure.

Yet he was also aware. He knew why Erika Schwartz was telling her story, and why she was telling it in the way she was. She knew that he had a child. She knew how to get at him.

Knowing hardly helped, though. As he realized the full breadth of Adriana Stanescu's cursed life, the air kept leaving his body, and his stomach seemed to collapse upon itself. He even felt paisley-shaped saltwater building up, but he willed his eyes dry and said nothing. That was important. He focused his emotions elsewhere, on the traffickers. When he felt his eyes dampening, in his head he beat these faceless creatures senseless. But their very facelessness lessened the effect. So he drew from his memory one Roman Ugrimov, a Russian businessman who had once killed his own underaged lover, pregnant with his child, in order to prove a point. There, then, was someone real, someone he knew. So he went at the old man with his bare hands and crushed him slowly, as he never had in reality.

Was that enough? No, because Adriana's story was bigger than a few lecherous individuals. She hadn't been snuffed out by people as much as she had been cursed, from the moment of birth, by secret organizations. Her misery had been predestined.

He almost gave up. A large part of him wanted to throw up his hands and tell Schwartz everything she asked for, then return in disgrace to New York. It was another way of quitting Tourism. He could confess his weakness to Drummond and wait for the pink slip. Then the exit interviews. The discovery of his treasonous relationship with his father. The quiet bullet in the back of the head.

When she finished, Erika Schwartz offered another of her disturbing smiles and clapped her fat hands together like a child. "She was saved! Really, Mihai was a saint, or at least that's what the media would call him if they got hold of the story. But you and I know better, don't we? He was a chump. He gave up his own business for the life of a stupid little girl who shouldn't have gotten on that bus in the first place."

He wanted to shout *Enough!* but didn't. Instead, he stared at her blue eyes and tried to keep his throat open and clear. He managed a single, brief sentence. "It's a terrible story."

Erika watched him, admiring his coldness while hating it. Was this Tourist a lover, or not? "Terrible in its own way," she said, "but if your name isn't Stanescu, what difference does it make?"

He blinked his red-rimmed eyes, which were the only outward sign that the story was having a real effect. Then he cleared his throat. "I suppose you're right. It happens every day. At least she was rescued."

"Exactly," she said, "but you know easterners—they don't learn. You have to pound even the simplest lessons into their heads. Her parents, though they didn't know the whole story, knew that she wanted to go to Germany. So they applied for a visa. And, finally, Adriana was in the West. Like every other kid, she went to school and made friends. She was foolish enough to think she had a life ahead of her. She thought that the past could remain past. Then, well, you came along. Didn't you?"

He considered his answer. "Does anyone here have a cigarette?"

"Sounds like someone's giving up," said Oskar.

"Gustav," said Erika, and the small man took out his pack, lit one, and handed it to Weaver. He didn't seem to like the taste at first, but by the third drag was inhaling heavily.

He finally said, "I'm my own man, Miss Schwartz. Yes, I used to work for the Company, but that was a while ago, and I certainly wasn't ever a secret agent—or whatever you think I am. You people are obviously convinced I'm something I'm not. I was just an analyst—I read magazines, mostly. It was the financial stuff that got me in trouble. They drummed me out, which was fine with me, but the pension plan was terrible. So I went into insurance—that's something everyone needs, right? Well, not as many people as you'd think. Expats seem to think they'll live forever. Or maybe they didn't trust me. I'm starting to wonder about that. Can people see in your face that you're a murderer? I mean, is it marked on there?"

It was disappointing. Would withholding the cigarette have made a difference? Probably not. It had just given Weaver a moment to reweave his idiotic story. She stood and gazed down at him. "Why don't you watch some television? Heinrich, Gustav—please make sure he doesn't doze."

They nodded their assent, and she walked slowly up the stairs, Oskar behind her, impatient. No one said a thing, least of all Milo Weaver. She was starting to despair about her whole plan. Then she heard Rada Stanescu weeping on the television. It gave her hope.

15

Erika slept upstairs in her bedroom, while Oskar took a downstairs guest bedroom. Heinrich and Gustav took turns on the cot, allowing Milo to stretch out on the sofa, but even though they had cut off the sound the video loop of Adriana Stanescu's media coverage greeted him whenever he opened his eyes.

In the morning, drinking coffee in the kitchen, Erika mused over whether or not to have another talk with Weaver before work. She decided against it. As she told Oskar, "This man will expect a morning chat—and I'll lay odds that over the night he's come up with something clever, some piece of information he'll share with me. Something about our operations, maybe. Some information that looks like a favor. When I follow up on it, it will alert his people. So I won't even go downstairs. I don't want to be tempted."

"What do we do with him?"

"Show him videos until I get back. I want him to remember every frame."

Once Oskar had passed on the order to Heinrich and Gustav, Erika drove him back to his car in the Perlacher Forest, and they arrived at work fifteen minutes apart.

Everything she did felt like busywork. Even her noon conference call felt like busywork, and that included Berndt Hesse and the minister of the interior, Wolfgang Schäuble. They discussed two topics: Sunday's news that Fidel Castro had retired from power, and the minister's conviction that the controversial *Jyllands-Posten* Muhammad cartoons should be reprinted by German newspapers—an issue that couldn't raise Erika beyond a dull ambivalence.

The one thing that provoked emotion was the BND operator telling her that Andrei Stanescu was on the line for her. She told the operator to please tell him she was out, and to refer him in the future to Dieter Reich. Again, the stutter hit her, and the operator said, "Could you please repeat that last bit?"

She had sent Oskar off to wait in the forest and was preparing to leave when she heard a voice. "Erika? Want to take a walk?"

She looked up from her desk, surprised to find Teddy Wartmüller filling the doorway. Surprised he had condescended to visit her office instead of summoning her to his. He was looking as elegant as ever, a black overcoat hiding his long frame, but he was tired, too. "Right now?"

"I'd appreciate it. I'm off to a black tie dinner in an hour."

"Black tie?"

"American consulate, and they don't appreciate lateness. Grab your coat. I'm dying for a cigarette."

He waited patiently, watching her close the folder she'd been browsing and then work her way into a standing position.

He peered around the office. "Oskar not in?"

"Interviewing some new applicants."

"Anything promising?"

She shrugged as she slipped into the vast quilted coat that hid her own frame. "Too early to know."

"That's how it always is," he said pointlessly, then stepped aside so that she could leave the office first. As they continued down the long corridor, he remained behind her, which gave her the unsettling sense that she was being shadowed. He said, "This should only take a few minutes."

"It's no problem at all."

They nodded at the front-door guards hovering around the metal detectors and crossed the empty lane to a small park on the edge of the grounds lit in the early evening darkness by lamp poles amid the trees. By the time they arrived, Erika was out of breath, and he suggested they share a nearby bench. She was very aware of her own weight when the bench creaked and sagged and Wartmüller had to take the far end lest he slide into her.

"So," she said.

"Yes," Wartmüller answered, then peered across the shadowy grounds. He licked his teeth and took out his Marlboros. "It was a nice trick, cornering Dieter like that, but I don't think that's the way we should be running things here."

"No?"

"No. And I'd like you to give back the American."

"American?"

He lit a cigarette, taking his time. "Milo Weaver."

"Oh, Milo Weaver," she said. "I don't know where he is."

Wartmüller pursed his lips and gave a disappointed *tsk-tsk*. "Please, Erika. He's in your basement. Oskar is probably tending to him now. I certainly hope he's not damaging the man—he's not, is he?"

Erika didn't answer. Had she let something slip? Perhaps all it had taken was a bit of suspicion and a review of the neighborhood security tapes—the excuse for the van had probably been weak. Perhaps Weaver had been visible from the road when they transferred him into the house. Or maybe Gustav had stupidly stepped outside for a smoke. "Listen, Theodor. If I did have Milo Weaver, I wouldn't keep him in my house. I'd use one of our nice, secure cells."

He continued to smoke, staring into the distance. "You want to play it this way, fine. Don't admit a thing. Remember that I'm a friend. I'm not interested in undermining your career. I simply want the man set free—no paperwork on this at all. I've also received assurances that the Americans won't seek retribution. Just make sure he's in one piece, okay?"

She stared hard at the side of his face. "The Americans talked to you about him? Are they the ones who say I have him?"

"Do you really think there's anything you can do without the Americans knowing, Erika? If they really want to know? We have a staff of six thousand. The CIA? At least twenty thousand. Not to mention their technology: A satellite can follow you home and take pictures of your house, while the infrared watches you go to bed."

"That's ludicrous, and you know it."

He flicked away his cigarette. "Don't ask me how they know. To someone my age, it's all magic. Just know that they know, and please give them back their man. None of us can afford their wrath just now."

Erika watched him head back to the building. She breathed in the cold. She wasn't prone to cursing, but at that moment a stream spewed from her. Then she got up and put all her frustration into stamping out Wartmüller's smoldering cigarette.

She bought her wine and Snickers from Herr al-Akir, making no effort to ease his anxiety, then picked up Oskar. He began with his complaints, but she cut him off and explained the situation.

"I don't believe it," he said. "So fast?"

"We made a mistake. We were stupid."

"How long do we have?"

"Until tomorrow afternoon, I'd guess. Any longer and they'll send GSG 9 to knock down my door. Probably burn down the house while they're at it."

"So can we do it my way now?"

"We beat him, and he'll just tell more stories."

"If we don't, he won't say a thing."

He was taped into the chair again when Erika Schwartz descended the stairs holding wine and two glasses, but something was different. She moved faster, and there was an air of confusion about her, or panic. She began from the beginning again, with the simple questions. Why did you kill Adriana Stanescu? Who do you work for?

It had been a long day with these two men who sometimes took random pops at him as he watched the Stanescu story over and over, but it had also given him time to think. The truth was that he and Erika Schwartz were seeking the same answers. They were both disgusted by what the Department of Tourism had done, and both needed to know what could possibly justify it. Milo had received a vague answer from Drummond, but it wasn't enough, and it wouldn't be enough for Schwartz either, so he didn't bother telling her.

His silence now seemed to upset Schwartz. A look of despair overcame her, and she turned to Oskar. "I don't know. Maybe you're right," she said, then got up and settled on the sofa. "Go ahead."

Oskar stood. "Gustav, why don't you give Mr. Weaver a cigarette?"

While Gustav lit one, Heinrich tugged at Milo's dirty shirt-sleeves until his forearms were exposed, and Milo closed his eyes. He'd known it might come to this, but he'd expected a longer wait.

Gustav had done this before. He blew on the cherry before each touch and knew how much pressure to use so that the burn went deep but the cigarette didn't go out. He was an expert of sorts.

Milo screamed a few times, but worse than the pain was the stink. The sulfurous smell of his hair melting, then the flesh, like charcoal. His stomach convulsed, but there wasn't enough food in him to follow through on the action. Then he screamed again.

In their business, no one wasted time or energy pretending something didn't hurt. Facts were facts, and denying the truth of pain was a wasteful show of braggadocio. Their business had no time for braggarts.

"Talk," Oskar said after five burns, as he used a paper towel to roughly mop up the blood lest it stain the furniture.

Oskar was blurry through his tears; Schwartz, beyond him, was reclining. He couldn't focus enough to see her expression. "Who's doing it?"

"Excuse me?" said Schwartz.

"This. Who's making you rush this? You were doing well before. You were taking your time. You even had me convinced you had all the time in the world. But it's changed, hasn't it? Someone's telling you to get rid of me."

"Gustav," she said. "I think Mr. Weaver could use another smoke."

Milo stiffened, though his face went slack, waiting for the pain. Gustav blew on the end of the cigarette while Heinrich again held the arm still, and when he placed another burn among the red and black spots Milo screamed freely. It was all so damned professional.

Oskar waved a wisp of smoke from his face and leaned closer. "Talk."

From the sofa, Schwartz explained, "Mr. Weaver, we may be rushed, but we have all night. Gustav has a carton of cigarettes in his bag."

Milo stared at his taped knees. He heard Gustav blow on the cigarette behind him, but when he looked up the man was stepping back, sticking the cigarette between his lips.

Milo said, "It was for you."

"Me?" said Schwartz.

"The plural you. German intelligence. I don't know what department, just German intelligence. Adriana was killed so that the Company's relationship with German intelligence could continue."

While Oskar stared doubtfully, Erika Schwartz squinted at him. "What does that *mean*, Mr. Weaver?"

"No one defined it for me. Now that you've told me her background, I can make some guesses. I think you can, too."

He could tell from her face that she was already ahead of him.

"It's why I asked you," he said. "Who told you to get rid of me?"

She wasn't listening. He knew what she was thinking, because he'd had a whole day to think it over. She was thinking that a girl with a history like Adriana's meant nothing to an organization. Not to the CIA, not to the BND, not even to the human traffickers who'd already gotten their money's worth out of her. Adriana Stanescu only meant something to an individual, or a few individuals. The kinds of individuals who took trips to questionable clubs to find gratification in the sweat and allure of anonymous, illicit sex.

"Erika," he said, and even he was surprised by the softness in his own voice. "Tell me who your boss is. Tell me who wants us to stop talking to each other."

She didn't answer. Instead, she got to her feet and walked to the stairs and ascended without a word. Her three men seemed confused by the sudden lack of direction, and Gustav settled on the cot to finish his cigarette. Heinrich sat on the vacated sofa but didn't look at Milo. Oskar remained standing, staring at the empty stairwell. Then he followed her up, carrying the wine and glasses she had forgotten.

16

In the morning, she asked Oskar to stay behind. She would call within the hour with instructions, and in the meantime Weaver should be allowed to rest. The videos had ended last night, and they had even dined together in the panic room. She had let him shower in the house itself with Heinrich as company. Though no more information was exchanged, Weaver spent dinner asking questions before realizing that she would not answer. Primarily, he wanted to know Theodor Wartmüller's identity.

When she arrived at the Pullach office she rolled slowly through the parking lot. There—his bright red MINI. She took her time hobbling to the building and emptied her pockets into a small plastic basket before walking through the metal detector. It blipped, and with the guards' magic wand they discovered a ballpoint pen that had slipped through a hole in her pocket to settle in the lining of her quilted coat. When one offered her back the metal items she'd removed, she asked to keep the basket for a little while. With a wry grin, the guard told her that that was fine.

She placed the basket on her desk and, without sitting, called up to the second floor. Wartmüller was in, she was told, but on another line. She asked if he would please call her as soon as he had time.

As she waited she found herself unable to do a thing. She turned on her computer and stared at the blue start-up screen but still didn't sit. When her desktop appeared, she didn't even bother checking her e-mail, only gazed at the artistic flower photo that was the background to her daily work. Her phone rang.

"Erika? I heard you wanted to talk to me."

"Outside, if you don't mind."

"Now?"

"If that's at all possible."

He considered it. "Not too long, though. I've got a conference call with Berlin soon."

"Then you could probably use a cigarette."

"Probably right, Erika."

She returned to the front-door guards, who expected her to hand over the plastic basket, but she hadn't brought it. All she did was stop a few feet short of them and turn around to face the corridor. When Wartmüller appeared, tapping the filter end of a cigarette against his knuckle, they shifted, suspecting now that they were in serious trouble.

"Hello, Erika."

"Theodor." She turned to the guards and pointed at the metal detector. "Is this still on?"

They nodded—of course it was on. Regulations required it to be on.

"Good," she said and walked through it. The light above her head flickered green. Wartmüller continued around it. "You saw that, sir?"

"Sure," said Wartmüller, frowning. "You really are an oddball, aren't you?"

She smiled and continued through the door he held open.

As they crossed the road, heading to the park, Wartmüller began to talk about the party at the consulate. There had been an American musician there, over on a Fulbright grant to research Swabian folk music. So that's what he played. "Unbelievable! I mean, none of us would listen to that stuff for money, but can you imagine being forced to listen to it sung with one of those flat midwestern accents? Jesus, what were they thinking? Next time I'm getting you an invitation. You'll only believe it if you see it with your own eyes."

It was the friendliness that grated on her. That catty camaraderie was Wartmüller's best weapon. It had the nasty effect of making everyone feel like a partner in this man's worldly ways. It made her feel a partner in everything he did, and only now did she fully understand what that meant.

He lit a Marlboro as she settled on the same bench from yesterday, then sat beside her. "So," he said.

"You want him quiet," she said.

"Excuse me?"

"You want Milo Weaver sent away so he won't fill in the blanks of Adriana Stanescu's murder. You want . . . yes," she said and nearly smiled, then stopped herself. It had come to her before, but now she felt sure. "Blackmail, I suppose. That's really what provokes these things."

"It must be too early for you, Erika. You're not making sense."

"You have a history," she told him. "An open history. The rumor mill is full of Theodor Wartmüller's sexual adventures. Not all of them are legal, are they?"

He grinned around his cigarette. "Please, Erika! You're embarrassing me!"

"There was a place in Berlin. Very expensive. You could go there and be assured of confidentiality. You weren't the only one—no. Politicians and directors, businessmen. Actors, maybe. A who's-who of the sexually deviant rich."

He exhaled smoke and knotted his brows. "That's what the dance with the metal detector was about, wasn't it? You wanted me to know you're not wired."

"Exactly."

He thought about that, going through his options.

She said, "There was a girl at the club. You were being blackmailed with photos of her and you, yes?"

He didn't answer.

"So you asked your friends in the CIA to get rid of her." She paused. "Of course you would do that. You couldn't kill her yourself, and if you'd asked one of us to do it—even Franz or Brigit—we would ask why. And we both know how rumors get around the office."

"Yes," he said distantly. "We do." He took a long drag.

"Theodor," she said. She made her voice as soft as she could manage. "I just want to understand."

He flicked away some ash, but the movement was clumsy, and the whole cigarette tumbled to the ground. He sighed. "This hasn't been going on so long. Just since December."

"Of course it hasn't," she said, though she wasn't entirely sure what he meant.

He patted his jacket and came up with his crumpled pack. He took his time lighting another one. "A letter. To my home. A package, really. It contained a letter and photographs. It asked for money to be transferred to an offshore account. The photos were stills from a video—that was obvious. Me and a girl in bed. The light was poor, but it was clear enough who I was, and who she was. She was very young—too young. That was obvious, too. I could still remember that night, and I knew that on the video it would look like . . ." He took another drag. "It would look like I was forcing myself on her."

"Like you were raping her."

"Something like that."

"And the girl was Adriana Stanescu."

Wartmüller stared at the ashy end of his cigarette. "I didn't know her name. This was a private club. Berlin. I wasn't the only customer. It was—at least, it was supposed to be—extremely confidential. Like you said. It had a reputation for this. I believed, as did the other customers, that I had no reason to worry." He shook his head. "For that price, confidentiality should have been assured."

Erika looked past him to where a figure moved along the edge of the park. An old woman with a tiny dog. What was an old woman with a dog doing on the grounds? She said, "When was this?"

"December. I told you."

"No. The night with the girl."

He exhaled. "Four years ago? Something like that."

"And who sent the extortion letter?"

"That was the question, wasn't it? I had our lab go over the envelope, but I wasn't about to show the letter or the photos."

"Of course."

"Mailed from Berlin. No recognizable prints. Address from a

laser printer—nothing to tell from that. So I went back to the club myself. The thing had been shut down. I backtracked and found out who had been running the club back then."

"Rainer Volker."

Wartmüller halted in midsmoke. "You are good, aren't you?"

"Was he the one?"

"Before I got a chance to talk to him, I got a call from one of my American contacts."

"Who?"

When he exhaled, smoke drifted from his nostrils. "Owen Mendel. Turns out they had been watching Volker. They learned what he was up to, that he was blackmailing me. It wasn't their business, really, but Mendel understood that I couldn't take care of it through BND channels. He offered an exchange of services."

"An exchange?"

"He makes my problem go away, and in return I lobby for a little more cooperation with the Americans. The cooperation that was lost, mind you, because of your obsession with Afghan heroin."

The woman and dog had left Erika's field of vision, but then a young couple began to cross the park in the opposite direction. That's when she knew—it was Brigit, suspicious Brigit, keeping an eye on her mentor with some of the extra staff.

Wartmüller continued, "The Americans knew that Volker was blackmailing me, and they even knew the name of the girl in the photos—Adriana Stanescu. All this trouble, over a Moldovan!" He shook his head. "Very quietly, they took care of Volker."

"Killed him."

"Yes. But quietly. I thought it was done. Just to be sure, I did a search on this girl, this Moldovan. Somehow she'd gotten a visa and was living up in Berlin. I started to think. Soon, we'll all be up in Berlin. It was too easy to imagine—me on the street every day, my photo appearing in the newspaper. Really, there were a hundred ways for this girl to look up one day, raise her finger, and point. For her to start screaming." He rubbed his face, which despite the cold was damp. "It began to drive me crazy. I called Mendel, but it turned out that he'd left the Company and I was passed on to some other guy.

Alan Drummond. We talked turkey, as they say. After conferring with his people, he promised to get rid of my anxiety if he could start seeing some results from my side." Wartmüller paused. "I told him thank you very much."

"Did he?"

Wartmüller cupped his ear. "Eh?"

"Did he see results from your side?"

He shrugged. "Hamburg, primarily. You know about that operation. But there were some other things in Cologne and Nuremberg. Rwanda, too."

Erika considered whether or not to say it aloud, because both of them knew it already, but her anger got the better of her. "That's treason."

"Is it?"

"Unless you got clearance to pass on that information. Did you?"

He pursed his lips, then changed position, and it struck her that Wartmüller had passed through the emotional stages very quickly and come out the other side. "Listen, Erika. I've been in this game as long as you have. You're good—we both know that. You've connected the dots and ended up with me. Really, though, what do you have? Suppositions. Rumors, at best. Trust me: You'll find nothing else. I've made sure of that."

Now he was doing it, giving voice to the fact that both of them already knew. She had an American spy's single line—*It was for you . . . German intelligence*—the tragic history of an immigrant girl, and the involvement of a secret department across the ocean that would never open up its files for her perusal. She had nothing, but she wasn't about to admit that. The best she could do was fan his anxiety. "The photos of you came from a videotape, which is still out there."

He shook his head. "The Americans destroyed it."

"That's not what I hear."

He wasn't going to take the bait, not yet. "You lie like a politician, Erika. It's a beautiful thing to watch." He stood and squashed his cigarette beneath his heel and looked down on her. "I've got that conference call."

She didn't bother watching him walk away. Instead, she took out her cell phone and called Oskar. "It's your mother," she told him. "Send your friend home immediately."

"Is that all?"

"Just do it, and I'll be in touch."

"Of course you will," Oskar muttered. He sounded very disappointed.

17

It was a simple enough transfer, but even Milo, eye-strained from two days of television and sore down his burned arm, could see that they were worried. Oskar led the way while Heinrich followed; Gustav had left earlier. They didn't blindfold him or bind his wrists, just walked with him out Erika Schwartz's back door and down the woody incline of her yard to a dried creek bed that separated properties. They followed it to the left—north, Milo thought, then wasn't sure—and passed the occasional high security fence and signs warning trespassers away from the homes of important people.

"No cameras?" Milo asked after a while.

Oskar rocked his head while, behind, Heinrich stumbled in the undergrowth. "Here, no. At each end, where the roads are, yes. We'll have to be careful there."

"You could have just taken me out the way you brought me in."

"Unfortunately, this is the only way to assure your safety."

"I didn't know you cared."

Oskar stopped and looked back at him, hard. He didn't need to say a thing. They went on.

They reached a residential road where a quaint stone arch spanned the creek, and Oskar pointed out the cameras. There were three— one on the stones, two in the trees—so they remained in the woods and continued fifty yards up the road. They waited until a white van with the insignia of a Karlsfeld plumbing company pulled up to the side of the road. Gustav was behind the wheel. Heinrich took the passenger seat; Oskar joined Milo in the rear.

The drive took about an hour and a half, and during that time Oskar slowly relaxed. He never warmed to Milo, but neither did he seem to view him as a tactical enemy. The distinction was important. Then his phone rang, and he answered it, grunted a few times, and handed it to Milo. "It's for you."

"Hello?"

"Theodor Wartmüller," Erika said. "He's the one who ordered your release."

"Thanks," Milo said, then waited. Only silence followed, and in that silence he realized he knew the name Wartmüller, but wasn't sure where from. "Do you have it covered?" he asked.

"Excuse me?"

"Have you got the whole story?"

"Enough of it."

"You have evidence?"

More silence followed. No, she didn't have the evidence to arrest the man.

"If I can, I'll help."

"Why?"

"You know why. You know I didn't hurt her."

"I don't know anything, Mr. Weaver."

"Was it blackmail?"

"Of course."

Then Milo hesitated, because he finally remembered why he knew that name. "When?"

"What?"

"When was the blackmail?"

"Do I get the sense you know something?"

"I need details if I'm going to help you."

"December."

Milo felt a wave of acid climb into the back of his throat. He swallowed it down. "Anything else you want to tell me?"

She sighed, and Milo thought he heard wind—she was outside,

away from ears. "I don't think I need to tell you anything. You can ask your own people."

"I'll do that. And I'll find a way to pass on anything that looks useful."

"Let's hope I don't need anything from you."

"Let's hope," said Milo. "One last thing."

"Yes?"

"Budapest. You told me I'd been in Budapest, but I hadn't. Were you making that up?"

She sounded surprised. "We have it through a source. You were there, all right. Not just a writer—you also claimed to be a doctor and a film producer."

"Why?"

"You don't know?"

"Please. It's important."

"You were looking for an American journalist named Henry Gray. He'd just come out of a coma and had disappeared. You apparently plagued his girlfriend, who's also a journalist."

"Does she have a name?"

"Zsuzsanna Papp, I think. Hungarian. Works for *Blikk*."

"Did I find this Henry Gray?"

"Not as far as we know. All we know is that you were there some days, asking around, then disappeared." She paused. "Is someone out there using your name?"

"Thanks, Erika. I'll be in touch if I can help."

He returned the phone to Oskar, who grinned oddly as he hung it up. It was no more comforting than his boss's smiles. In English, he said, "So Mr. Weaver is going to help us. Excuse me if I'm not filled with the hope."

When they finally stopped a little before noon, they were in the center of Innsbruck, across the Austrian border. "The train station is a block that way," Oskar said, pointing, then handed over Milo's wallet, disassembled phone, key ring, and iPod, along with two hundred euros in small bills "to get you closer to home." He made no move to shake hands, so Milo didn't either, but when he passed the cab he waved to Gustav and Heinrich. Gustav, confused, waved back with a smile.

The Innsbruck Hauptbahnhof was stocked with stores and cafés. After looking over the departures schedule, he bought a fresh gauze bandage for his forearm, a bottle of orange juice, and a large sandwich of cold cuts, which he ate outside, staring at the Friday lunch crowds and the gray traffic pushing through Südtiroler Platz. Once he was finished eating and had wrapped his arm in the bathroom, he put his phone together again, powered it up, and went to a café to wait. As soon as he sat down, the phone vibrated for his attention. A message: *Myrrh, myrrh.*

Never in his career had the universal return code been sent. It meant that Dzubenko's various stories had checked out, a Chinese mole was assumed, and the entire department was closing down.

If there was a surprise in all this, it was only that he didn't give a damn anymore.

Things could change so quickly—a department could panic and call back all its agents, and one of its agents could hear a single name, Theodor Wartmüller, and decide that the department itself no longer deserved to exist. *Let it go down in flames,* he thought.

Still, he followed procedure, if only because it was second nature. He didn't call in, because Schwartz could easily have wired his phone to send her any numbers he dialed, and no one called him, because his reappearance might simply mean that another agency had control of the phone. He also avoided pay phones, since he couldn't be sure that Schwartz hadn't warned the Austrians of his arrival. He wanted to trust her, but that wasn't really an option.

He ordered a caffè latte and settled in for the long wait, which turned out to last four hours. During that time, he drank coffee and wandered the claustrophobic streets around the train station, peering into windows selling liquor, chocolates, and aids for sexual gratification. He plugged into his iPod and found himself listening to Bowie's *Low*, that desperate-sounding voice saying, "Oh, but I'm always crashing in the same car."

It was around three when, on his way back to the station, he saw

James Einner walking briskly toward him. There was a smile in his eyes, but nowhere else, and as they passed one another he only said, "Check the window," and continued on. Three doors down, on a windowsill, he spotted a cheap Nokia; it was already ringing.

"Lovely to hear from you," Milo said into it as he continued back to the station.

"You being watched?"

"Doubtful, but with this many cameras around they don't need to leave their laptops. Where am I going?"

"Vienna, then Dulles. I'll be on the plane with you. You see the recall message?"

"Why the panic?"

There was a pause. "We'll talk about it in Vienna. The Eurotel at the airport. I'm bringing the drinks," he said and hung up.

Milo bought a first-class ticket to Vienna's Westbahnhof and dozed briefly as the landscape turned black. Occasionally, his forearm throbbed, but he didn't feel like checking for infection, and during a particularly stinging session he noticed a dark-skinned man—midthirties, long sideburns, fit, glum—enter the car and move slowly along, touching seat backs as if counting them. As he approached Milo's seat toward the rear, he glanced briefly into Milo's eyes and dropped a gray Siemens onto the empty seat beside him. Milo stared at the phone, then glanced back, but the man was already exiting the car.

It was common enough in his line of work to gradually collect cheap phones, but it didn't usually happen so quickly. Milo left the phone where it was and peered out at the night, the train gradually overtaking the lights of a distant city. Then the phone rang a monotone *beep-beep*, and he answered it but said nothing.

"Misha, it's me."

"You're here?"

"The front of the train. You met Francisco?"

"He's charming. How did you find me?"

"You think your boss is the only one who keeps track of your phone? Really, Misha."

He sounded very pleased with himself, so Milo hung up. He

kept the phone on his knee and noticed that they had finally passed the town—no lights were visible at all. He waited until the phone had rung seven times before picking up again.

"You're angry," said Yevgeny.

"Think so?"

"Listen, son. I take full responsibility for Adriana."

"I'll give you that."

"But what I said before was true. It was my fault, but not my intention. She got away, and someone else killed her. One of your Tourists, I'd guess."

Milo knew he was right. "It doesn't matter anymore, Yevgeny. I'm done with you. I'm done with all of this."

The old man didn't answer immediately. He was likely considering what technique would best keep hold of his precious source. "Okay," he said finally. "You're done with me. I've failed you. Let me redeem myself. You know I can help. What's your new project?"

Involuntarily, laughter shook through Milo's frame; his arm throbbed. He had to set the phone down until he had control of himself. He lifted it to his ear. "Sorry, Yevgeny. Your tenacity is hilarious. I'm not going to tell you what I'm doing now."

"Fine," he said in a tone that Milo remembered from his teenaged years—abrupt, insulted. "Don't tell me a thing. Still, because of Adriana, I do owe you, and I intend to repay that debt."

The old man was serious—that, too, was a tone he knew. Various favors crossed his mind—*find me a new job* was high on the list—but then he remembered his father's particular range of knowledge and networks. "Okay. Here's something. Find me everything you can on a Chinese colonel in the Guoanbu, Xin Zhu. I'll need it as soon as possible."

Yevgeny sighed, the barely satisfied exhale when he had finally gotten his way. "I can do that without a problem. It would help to know what exactly I'm looking for."

"You're looking for everything," Milo said, then hung up again and placed the phone on the empty seat. Within five minutes, the dark man had worked his way back through the car; the phone left with him.

18

By eight thirty he was in Vienna, boarding a taxi on Europaplatz, outside the Westbahnhof. He hadn't seen the dark man again, nor his father, and guessed they had disembarked earlier.

At Vienna International, he used a Sebastian Hall MasterCard to buy a ticket for the next flight to Washington, which wouldn't leave until 10:50 A.M. He walked over to the arcade of airport stores, passing cafeterias and newsstands and a music store to reach the pharmacy at the far end, where he used Erika Schwartz's money to buy two boxes of Nicorette. He chewed so vigorously that it provoked hiccups again. He picked up a fresh change of underwear, socks, a new shirt, a toothbrush, toothpaste, and antiperspirant. He was still hiccupping when he reached the curb.

Though he saw James Einner follow him out to the shuttle that would take him to the Eurotel, he made no sign of recognition. Einner let his bus go without boarding.

The room was bleakly cheap and small but functional. He took a shower and dressed in his dirty clothes. He left his four-day beard untouched, but in the mirror noticed among the chestnut tones several white hairs. It was all so disappointing.

Einner made no jokes when he arrived, and that was also disappointing. He marched past Milo and placed a bottle of Cabernet

Sauvignon on the desk. He pulled back the curtains enough to look down on the parking lot.

"Anyone behind me?" Milo asked.

Einner shook his head, then shut the curtains.

"How'd you get me out?"

"Ask Drummond. I assume he's got a German contact."

"Why Myrrh?"

Einner looked around as if confused, then picked up the bottle. He took a corkscrew from the room's minibar and began working on it. "Get the glasses."

Milo unwrapped a pair of plastic cups from the bathroom. They drank.

"Well?"

Einner finished his wine and refilled the glass, then shook his head. "Politics. It's always politics."

"Who?"

"Nathan Irwin."

"I sure hope you brought some blow."

Everything, Einner explained, had gone to shit three days before, on Monday, when the Chinese representative to the UN made direct reference to what had happened the previous year in the Sudan. "*That* operation."

Milo recalled his last voluntary television memory, in Warsaw. "I saw it on the BBC."

"So did Irwin, and if anyone can smell an approaching scandal, it's a senator. He knew his career could be on the chopping block. He cornered Drummond. Demanded to know how it had gotten out. Drummond had to admit to the mole investigation."

"I bet he didn't take that well."

"You'd win that bet. He's upset enough that the Chinese know about the Sudanese operation, but apparently that's not the only pie Irwin had his finger in. So he's taken over the department. Drummond's now his errand boy. Irwin recalled everyone to New York to be debriefed and given new legends and go-codes."

"What about you?"

"Drummond thought you might need someone to hold your hand."

They drank until late, Einner running down for another bottle, but Milo never mentioned that he wouldn't be boarding the plane in the morning. There was no point to it. Einner was there to hold Milo's hand; he was there to make sure Milo made it back home safely.

When, after midnight, Einner left for his own room, Milo considered just leaving right then. He knew Einner, though, knew he was a good Tourist who could probably track him down before he got out of Austria. So he let him hold his hand all the way to the gate, where they sat separately, waiting for the flight attendants to announce boarding. Milo stood with his boarding pass in hand and gave Einner a nod to go first. He hung around the rear of the line until Einner had disappeared down the jet bridge to the plane; then he walked back out through security. He first found an ATM and withdrew the machine's limit of five hundred euros, then walked to the Hertz rental counter. As he waited for the keys, his phone rang.

"Where the hell are you?"

"Sorry, James. I've got something to do before heading home."

He didn't sound angry, just amused. "And you couldn't've asked me along?"

"You wouldn't've let me go."

"You know who I've got to call now, right?"

"Go ahead. I'll leave the phone on for a half hour. Tell him I'll be expecting his call."

Einner hung up. By the time the phone rang again, Milo had reached the A4 that led, with a name change, all the way to Budapest. Drummond said, "What the hell's going on, Hall?"

"You tell me."

"Tell you what?"

"There should be something in the files. Back in December, someone used my name in Budapest. My real name."

"So?"

"You're still new, Alan. Maybe you don't realize what a no-no that is. Someone uses my real name, then other people can track it to my family. It's simply not done."

"Then come on back," said Drummond. "We'll figure out who did it."

"Not during a freeze, we won't. And later, I won't have a chance."

"Why not?"

Milo pulled into the slow lane behind a big rig. "Theodor Wartmüller."

"What?"

"It was you, Alan. It was you the whole way."

"You're making no sense, Hall. What did the Krauts do to you?"

"I didn't remember at first," Milo said, "but then it came to me. Theodor Wartmüller. In December, one of my first jobs was to mail a package to him. I didn't know what was inside, but now I do. Photographs of him with Adriana Stanescu, in bed. It was us. We're the ones who blackmailed him, and then we swooped in to save him in exchange for favors."

Drummond made some grunting noises, and Milo realized that it was after three in the morning there. "Can we talk this through later?"

"There's no point, Alan. We set up Wartmüller by setting up the girl. Then we killed her."

"Hold on a minute," Drummond said, and Milo heard movement on the other side and a muffled voice, perhaps female. Walking. He was leaving his wife to find some privacy. A door closed; then he came back on. "It wasn't my watch, Hall. You know that. Mendel set it up. I told you before—I've had to spend all my time cleaning up his mess. From what I gather, we monitored the whorehouse for some time and collected pictures of various German politicos before letting the police shut down the operation. Then Mendel used you to send those photos, which were to get us back in with the BND. Really," he said, "no one even told me this when I took over the department. I didn't know a thing about it until Wartmüller called me directly, asking us to get rid of Stanescu. Had to backtrack to figure out what he was even talking about, and I made my decision."

"It was the wrong decision."

"I don't like it either, but we got plenty in return."

He merged into the eastward flow of traffic, which was lighter than the westward flow. "Just tell me, then. Who actually pulled the trigger?"

"I'm sure you'll figure it out on your own."

"It was us, yes?"

"Yes, Milo. It was us. Wartmüller learned of your failure, so I had to send someone else. Someone with a little more loyalty."

"Someone with fewer scruples."

"A Tourist."

"Einner?"

Drummond didn't answer.

"This is why I won't have time later to find out who was using my name in Budapest. Because I'm finished. I quit."

"You're not serious."

"I really am, Alan. Find your mole on your own, and enjoy working for Senator Irwin. I hear he gives a brutal Christmas party."

Milo switched off his phone, then steered with his knee as he took it apart. He was careful about it, because he didn't want to have a wreck. He didn't want anything to go wrong—he'd had enough of that.

19

When, just over the Hungarian border, he tried to withdraw forints from an ATM, the machine told him the transaction had been denied. He'd expected this, which was why he'd taken out euros in the airport, but he'd hoped that Drummond would drag his feet. The truth was that he actually liked the man and believed his excuses. Drummond had arrived in a department already so morally twisted that he'd had no choice but to follow suit until old cases were settled. Milo had hoped that Drummond might empathize enough to let him keep his cards a little longer. He was wrong.

Despite what Schwartz had learned from her source, Milo had last been to Budapest four years ago, in 2004, under his real name. He'd brought Tina and two-year-old Stephanie for a vacation. It was Tina's first visit to the land that once lay behind the Iron Curtain, and she was taken by the imperial architecture rising through the bright late-summer light. She'd puzzled over the language—*gyógyszertár*, the Hungarian word for pharmacy, had particularly stunned her—but fell in love with the grandiose bridges crossing the Danube.

As he came gradually into town, open fields were replaced by huge shopping centers—IKEA and Tesco—where, despite his money situation, he stopped to pick up a cheap change of clothes, losing sixty euros all at once. The stores were soon replaced by sooty Habsburg buildings that, under the winter sky, held less charm than they'd had in the summer of 2004. It was still light when he crossed the Danube from Buda to Pest and checked into the Ibis Budapest Centrum's tiny, nondescript room. He would have chosen an upscale hotel along the water, but his money wouldn't last long. Besides, he was alone now, and wanted to maintain as low a profile as possible.

He visited one of the many café-bars along Ráday utca, which had been renovated to better accommodate the increase in prosperous customers, then ordered an aperitif of Unicum, that mysterious herbal liqueur Hungarians pretend has medicinal qualities. In the rear of the bar were three computers with Internet access.

Very quickly, he tracked down a biography of Henry Gray posted on a blog with the dubious name "Random Looks Inside the Inside" that focused on news items backing up its conspiratorial worldview. Additional information came from a more professional source—the American Society of Journalists and Authors—and a personal essay from 2005 penned by Gray himself. He even found a Budapest address for him, on Vadász utca.

Gray was a Virginia native who in his teens began traveling on student exchanges—Germany, Yugoslavia—and had quickly been bitten by the travel bug. By the time he was twenty-five, he had turned to freelance journalism and packed a suitcase. Thinking, no doubt, of Hemingway and Henry Miller, he flew to Paris, where he failed to find any regular work. This was in the early nineties, when the Balkans were exploding, so he packed again and headed for Belgrade, but the climate for Western journalists wasn't favorable. After the Serb secret police, the UDBA, kicked in his door and held him for an hour in the local militia station, Gray fled north to the relative tranquility of Budapest, where he could report on the entire region from a safe distance.

His reputation was built largely upon one piece, reprinted in many major newspapers, on the airbase in Taszár, Hungary, unimaginatively named Camp Freedom. There, the U.S. military trained three thousand Free Iraqi Forces, which they hoped would make their upcoming invasion look like natives returning to reclaim their birthright, rather than Western imperialism. Like the name of the camp, it was a failed exercise in optimism.

Many of the other clippings he came across, besides mundane pieces on trade deals in Central Europe and the Balkans, were less impressive: "The 9/11 Conspiracy—What the Commission Doesn't Want You to Know" and "One World Government—Does It Represent You?"

Yes, there were mainstream articles attributed to Gray, but they drowned in the mass of his conspiracy pieces littering the Net. He took on bottled water companies, which had, assisted by the American government, convinced the world that they should be paying for what nature considered a free resource. He speculated on the Bilderberg Group, an annual secretive meeting of influential business-people and politicians that, according to him and some similarly minded people, were working steadily toward the implementation of a world government. Gray had no doubt that the CIA was behind 9/11, a proposition that Milo, despite his ambivalence about his soon-to-be-ex-employer, found unbelievable. Not because someone at Langley couldn't have dreamed it up—some were paid solely for their ability to dream up the unthinkable—but it was unimaginable that the Company could have pulled off such an enormous ruse without getting caught; its track record wasn't encouraging.

In the end, the picture he gained of Henry Gray was of a paranoid, rootless investigator into conspiracies, who hoped that they might someday explain away the dissatisfaction of his own life. People like that were a dime a dozen. Which raised the question: Why did someone using Milo's name want to find him?

Even with such opinions, Gray would have friends in Budapest, because expat circles, particularly journalistic ones, are tiny. Milo gathered a list of British, Canadian, and American stringers based in Budapest, with addresses and phone numbers.

Though Schwartz had said Gray had been in a coma, Milo found very little to back this up beyond a brief mention in a sidebar of the August 8 edition of the *Budapest Sun*: "Local journalist Henry L. Gray is in serious condition in Péterfy Sándor Hospital after a fall."

Of Gray's girlfriend, Zsuzsanna Papp, there was little. He found some of her Hungarian-language articles for the tabloid *Blikk*. These, as far as he could tell, covered the tensions between the nationalist Fidesz party and the socialist MSZP party, which now held shaky power.

Then he ran across Pestiside.hu, a satirical English-language news outlet on all things Hungarian, which spent as much time ridiculing the Hungarian character as it did the expats that filled its capital. February 28, 2008, yesterday: "Journo-Stripper Ends Humiliating Sideline; Quits Journalism."

Fans of Zsuzsa Papp's biting *Blikk* commentaries on political targets such as right-wing nut job Viktor Orbán and fey communist liar Ferenc Gyurcsány will soon have to discover their political opinions unaided. According to *Blikk* management, Papp has left the paper in order to pursue her first love, undressing in front of drunk English hooligans at the 4Play Club. Who ever said there was no such thing as journalistic integrity in Hungary? Not us.

20

In the morning, he took a bus to Oktogon Square, where he mixed with Saturday pedestrians around the gray Central European inter-section. They leaned against the wind, smoking or hurrying to the next warm café. Milo faced the winds along the boulevard that marked a Pest-side circular route cut in half by the Danube, then turned right onto Szondi utca. Szondi was less kept up than the boulevard, and years of soot lodged in its crevices, but the buildings had an undeni-able charm.

Number 10, one block in, was hidden by scaffolding swathed in black plastic netting to avoid tools falling on pedestrians' heads. It wasn't the only building undergoing renovation, and when he looked he saw these occasional black masks all the way down the street. He checked the buzzers and pressed the one with PARKHALL stamped on it. After a moment, a weary "Igen?" sounded over the speaker.

"Mr. Terry Parkhall?"

"Yeah?"

"Sorry to bother you. My name's Sebastian Hall, and I'm look-ing into the disappearance of an associate of yours. Henry Gray. You think you could spare a minute?"

"You press?"

"No."

There was a moment of static. "Then what are you?"

"A private investigator. Gray's aunt, Sybil Erikson, hired me."

"I didn't know he had an aunt."

"A lot of us have them, Mr. Parkhall."

The heavy front door buzzed, so Milo pushed it open as Parkhall said, "Third floor. Take your time; I'm not dressed yet."

The stairwell was a mess of dust and chunks of concrete and loose steel pipes left behind by construction workers out for the weekend. He mounted the stairs and tested the railing, but it wouldn't hold a child if it came to it, so he continued up with his hands clasped behind his back.

He'd settled on the cover story during his walk here. Originally he'd thought that introducing himself as a new freelance journalist would do the trick, but on reflection realized that this would take too long—inevitably the way to greet a newcomer is to take him out and get him roaring drunk, not to answer questions about a missing colleague. Nor would honesty work—this man might have met the previous Milo Weaver, and wouldn't believe that he had been fooled before. So a private investigator came to mind, and an aunt that would take days for Parkhall to realize didn't exist.

There were two doors on the third floor, both with barred steel gates on the outside, but only one of these was open, so he stepped up to it and rapped on the wooden door. "Mr. Parkhall?"

From behind him, a male voice. "Wrong way."

He turned to see a tall, thin man in a robe and pajama pants standing behind the bars opposite, rubbing his disheveled hair. He went to Parkhall as the door he'd knocked on was unlocked and an old woman peered out. "Mi van?"

"Nincs," Parkhall said with a wave of his long fingers. "Bocsánat, Edit."

As Parkhall unlocked his gate, Edit locked her own door, filling the stairwell with the echo of locks being turned. They shook hands, but Parkhall didn't let him in that easily. "You have some kind of ID?"

"I left my investigator's license in the hotel. Passport do?"

Parkhall shrugged, then examined the Hall passport to his satisfaction. Milo followed him into a large living room decked out in

IKEA and a muted television playing BBC News. The place had been nicely renovated from what must have been a ubiquitous chopped-up communist apartment. Parkhall grabbed a coffee and two pills from the coffee table and swallowed them. "Hangover. You've had Unicum?"

"Sure. It's not bad."

"Just remember moderation, or you're in for a world of hurt."

"I'll make a note of it."

"Coffee?"

"No, thanks. I've had enough already."

Parkhall flopped onto his couch. "Go ahead. Sit down."

Milo kept his coat on and took a chair. "This should just take a few minutes. I mean, I have the background already. Gray was in the hospital before he vanished, wasn't he?"

Parkhall nodded.

"How did he end up in a coma?"

"You don't know?"

"I've got conflicting reports. I'd rather hear what you, as a journalist, have to say."

Parkhall shrugged. "According to him, an intruder in his apartment threw him off his terrace. Back in August."

That was unexpected. "Did the police find the intruder?"

"You'll have to ask them. As far as I know, they didn't."

"I'm visiting them next," he lied.

"So why ask me?"

"It's good to cover your bases."

A smile slipped into Parkhall's face. "Particularly with Hungarians."

"What about Gray? Did he have any idea who did it? Or was it just a random break-in?"

Parkhall considered him a moment, then stood up with his mug. "Sure you don't want some coffee? I'm getting a refill."

"Twist my arm. Thanks. Black."

Milo followed him to the kitchen doorway. "What about Gray?"

Parkhall was filling the cups from a French press, and when he turned his expression was pained. "Henry has a lot of ideas—theories.

He's that kind of journalist. A theory about everything. Conspiracy theories."

"I saw a few things he wrote," Milo admitted. "Kind of weird. To me, at least."

"To the rest of us, too," Parkhall said as he handed over a cup and they returned to the living room. "Honestly, the guy was a bit of a joke with us. That tsunami that wiped out Indonesia a few years ago? We were out drinking, and I joked that I'd heard of a document proving the CIA was behind it. Weather experiments. Everyone laughed except Henry—I mean, he really *bought* the story!"

"Unbelievable."

"Yeah. So if you asked him who tossed him off his terrace, there's only one possible answer, and it's the one he spouted about as soon as he woke from his coma. The CIA had tried to kill him."

"He told you this?"

"Called me after he woke up. Thought I would write something for the *Times* on it. Pure delusion."

Milo set down his coffee. "Any reason the CIA would want him dead?"

"It's called hubris, Mr. Hall, and Henry has it in spades. According to him, he received a letter that would have blown the CIA apart. The CIA knew he had it, so they decided to liquidate him. The guy really should be writing thrillers."

Milo shared a polite laugh over that, then drew a serious face. "Any idea what was in this letter?"

"God's own mystery. Disappeared when he was tossed off his terrace. When I asked what was in it, he said he couldn't tell me. Know why?"

"Why?"

"He didn't want them coming after me, too. Shocking!"

"But then he disappeared, didn't he?" Milo said, trying to stay on topic. "Isn't anyone worried about him?"

"Ah, hell," Parkhall muttered. "I mean, the boys like him all right, but . . ." He frowned, thinking through his words. "But life hasn't gotten much worse with him gone, if you know what I mean. No, we're not worried, because we know he's just holing up somewhere, maybe in Prague, maybe Belgrade, with a bottle of vodka, waiting for the heat to blow over. An extended bender, probably. We've all had them."

Milo nodded agreeably. "Listen, I heard something—maybe just a rumor—that just after he disappeared someone else came looking for him. A man."

"Milo Weaver," Parkhall said with some enthusiasm. "Nice guy. Works for AP, you know."

"AP?"

"Associated Press."

"Right, of course. I have a feeling I've met the guy before, but I'm not sure—can you describe him?"

"Sure. Blond. Tall. What else? Blue eyes—vivid blue. Jesus. Sounds like I'm describing a girl I'm hot for, doesn't it?"

"Exactly," Milo said. While it wasn't much of a description, it was a start. "Speaking of girls, didn't Gray have one? A Hungarian girlfriend?"

"Zsuzsa!" Parkhall exclaimed, sitting up. "If you believe him, they did sleep together, but 'girlfriend' is a stretch. Now, *she* was worried about him. Spent a while poking around. Zsuzsa's all right, but she got obsessed to the point that she lost her job."

"That's a shame."

"Maybe. But she takes her clothes off now for much better money." He paused. "If you want to know about Henry, she's the one to talk to. When you see her you'll understand why none of us could believe he actually got her in bed. Me, maybe. But Henry?"

"That good, huh?"

"Better. Listen," Parkhall said, straightening. "If I can get rid of this damned headache, maybe you and I should go see her. She's dancing tonight at the 4Play. If you go alone, she'll think you're just some pervert . . . or from the Company. Which is the same difference."

"Thanks," Milo said. "That would be really kind of you."

21

On the surface, Milo and Henry Gray were not so different. To an outside observer, Milo realized with despair, they might just look the same. Both viewed the world with a paranoid eye, were prone to sudden disappearances, and chose to leave their friends in the dark in order to protect them—this was what Milo had done to his wife. In the hours leading up to his eight thirty rendezvous with Parkhall, though, he concentrated on their differences.

While Gray puzzled over Masonic symbols to back up his conspiratorial premises, Milo looked at facts to find the connection, if any, between them, and *then* built up his theories. This distinction, though small, was crucial: For someone like Gray, Occam's Razor did not exist, for his logic was already corrupted by assumptions. Milo's, hopefully, began with as few assumptions as possible.

So he examined the facts at hand by breaking into Gray's dusty Vadász utca apartment. He browsed Gray's extensive collection of books (nonfiction with a small shelf of international thrillers), the elaborately renovated kitchen (which suggested a budding chef), the unopened box of twenty condoms in the bedside drawer (Gray lived in hope), and an enormous plasma television.

He called the closest major hospital, the Péterfy Sándor Kórház, and like his namesake claimed to be an American doctor interested in Henry Gray's medical records. After being passed to someone who spoke English, he was told that Gray and all of his records had been forwarded to the Szent János Kórház last year. He took the number 6 tram across the Danube to Buda and visited the St. János grounds, but the doctors were gone, and the few nurses who spoke to him were too busy to help. They told him to come back on Monday.

So he returned to Pest and drank caffè lattes at the Peppers! restaurant in the Marriott, overlooking the quay against the steely Danube.

Again, the facts: In August, while Milo was in a prison in up- state New York, Gray received a letter that contained something that could do damage to the CIA. Soon afterward, someone tossed him off his terrace and stole the letter. It was a curious method of dis- posal, but he supposed the agent in question—there was nothing yet to prove it was a Tourist—thought it would look like suicide.

Gray proved more resilient than expected. By December, he not only woke up but was soon able to walk out of the hospital and dis- appear.

You don't begin with assumptions; you begin with facts. A para- noid journalist's delusions are proven right when someone tries to kill him. What does he do when he's finally able to walk?

He runs.

Then, days later, someone calling himself Milo Weaver came looking for Henry Gray.

Presumably, this was the same man who had tried to kill Gray. Once Gray woke, he returned to Budapest to finish the job.

Why would he use Milo's name? It made no sense.

Milo was back at Oktogon Square by eight twenty, in front of the Burger King. Parkhall was fifteen minutes late but made no apolo- gies, instead explaining that being late to meetings was an obligation of life in Budapest.

First, they went around the corner to Ferenc Liszt Square, where, between a statue of the famous composer and the music academy, restaurants and cafés faced off, vying for business. They went to the upscale Menza, a restaurant with orange-toned retro decor, where Parkhall introduced him to a table of four friends.

Milo wasn't comfortable advertising his presence with such a large group, but soon realized that the entire table was drunk. They'd spent the day in the Rudas bathhouse, then moved through three bars until, famished, they had ended up here. None of them were lively enough to investigate Sebastian Hall's credentials, or even rouse themselves at the mention of the 4Play Club and the chance to see Zsuzsa Papp naked. So Milo turned the conversation to Henry Gray.

The other journalists, it turned out, felt much the same way Parkhall did about Gray. The Canadian, Russell, referred to him condescendingly as "a gifted amateur." Johann, the German, questioned the word "gifted." There was an English stringer, Will, and an Irish radio reporter, Cowall, who was apparently between jobs—according to Parkhall, he'd come to Budapest "to find himself." Only Cowall felt sympathy for Henry Gray, but his day of drinking had deepened his sour mood.

"We make fun of him, yeah? We all get a good laugh out of his crazy ideas. But what happens? You can come up with any explanation you like, but the fact is someone *did* toss him off his terrace, and expected the fall to kill him. It nearly did. Whether it was the CIA or the Hungarian mafia or the Russians or just some lunatic—it doesn't really matter. Someone was after him." He paused, staring sickly at his plate of goulash. "Goes to show. Even paranoid people get it right now and then. It's the law of averages."

"Christ," said Russell. "If I'd known you'd be such a downer I wouldn't have invited you out."

"Oh, well," Cowall said halfheartedly, then stood and walked out of the restaurant without looking back.

"He didn't pay for his goulash," Will said, unbelieving.

"I'll cover it," Milo said.

"Don't worry about it," said Johann, his German accent very faint. "Cowall, I mean. He's no good with his alcohol. Besides, his opinions don't mean much—he's a devout member of the Church of the SubGenius."

"Spent too much time in college," said Parkhall. "Like he never left."

Milo ate Cowall's heavy goulash, hoping to dull the drinking he would do at the club, and probed for more theories about Gray's whereabouts. No one knew, nor did they particularly care. They were too exhausted to feel anything. He paid Cowall's portion of the bill, calling it Company expenses, and he and Parkhall jumped a tram farther down the boulevard to the 4Play.

"Well, hello, hello," Parkhall said to the large bald doorman.

Throughout his life, Milo had found himself in a surprising number of strip clubs. They were ideal for money laundering, their profits constant because men all over the world are willing to pay for a glimpse of bare female skin. His first visit, to a Moscow club, had been Yevgeny's eighteenth birthday present—and each one since took him back to that June night in 1988 when he'd felt little arousal, mostly just shame and a childish love.

It was, like many of the stores and vacation dachas his father took him to, a KGB-only place. Inevitably, the best-looking dancers worked there, and Yevgeny was dismayed by the look on his face. "Why the attitude, Milo? Come on. This is your day." But his father's encouragement and the steady stream of mixed drinks made no dent in his misery as he looked over these beautiful girls from all over the Russian Empire who had, he imagined, run into some kind of trouble that had left them with no alternative than to take off their clothes for lascivious secret policemen. Lust was overcome by sympathy and pity.

He fixated on one, a morose-looking brunette his father told him was Siberian, and felt an absurd desire to take her away and save her. Misinterpreting his interest, Yevgeny called her over and ordered a private dance in one of the back rooms, promising a tip if she sent him back a man.

How did Yevgeny know that his eighteen-year-old son was still a virgin? He worked for the KGB, and those people knew everything. Or maybe he was just old enough to know that the most secretive, bitter teenagers were still unfamiliar with that one thing that makes life most interesting.

He could still smell the acrid smoke and lubricant from that velvet-curtained room, where she showed him everything and then began to unbutton his pants. He knew what he had to do—he had to tell her to stop, to talk with her about her family, about what had brought her to this terrible end, and help her find a way out—but he could not move. Afterward, when she collected the tip from Yevgeny, he overheard her say in her harsh Novosibirsk accent, "Sweet kid you got there." Milo felt his heart cease beating.

Zsuzsa Papp, though, evoked none of those missionary feelings. When she came over to kiss Parkhall's cheeks, she walked like someone who'd been to prep schools all her life. Confidence and entitlement and, with the kiss, a vague whiff of solicitude toward her inferiors. Somehow she filled out her floor-walking costume—a black miniskirt, red silk blouse, and platform shoes—without looking like a whore.

"Come to unwind, Terry?"

"Absolutely. And to bring someone who wants to meet you. Sebastian Hall."

She settled her condescending eyes on Milo. Below them, high cheekbones showed a faint flush. "A fan?"

"Soon to be, I'm sure," Milo said as he shook her limp hand. "I'm a private investigator. Looking for your friend, Henry Gray."

The flush in her cheeks neither expanded nor contracted. "Someone's hired you?" Her tone suggested that this was unlikely.

"An aunt," Parkhall informed her. "What's the name?"

"Sybil Erikson. From Vermont."

A smile fixed itself to her face as she said, "Just a second," and led Parkhall a few feet away. As they talked, Parkhall became flustered, making excuses for Milo's presence. Then Zsuzsa returned wearing the same smile. "Why don't you buy a private show? Otherwise we stay out here, and I'll have to look like I'm chatting you up."

A private dance, it turned out, cost fifty euros, or fourteen thousand forints, for fourteen minutes. She led him by the hand around tables and the main stage to a booth sectioned off by a heavy curtain, and he felt as if it were twenty years ago. There was a single plush chair, which she told him to sit in, and she took a moment to catch the rhythm of the ballad from the main room. She began to dance.

"Listen," he said, raising his hands. "You don't need to do this. I just want to talk."

Without breaking her movements, she said, "You gay?"

"No."

"Well, you paid for it," she said as she slipped out of her blouse like a candy bar losing its wrapper. "I never cheat anyone."

She was left in a black lacy bra and the miniskirt, and then she unwound the skirt to reveal a very small black thong. He could only think of one way to make her stop, and unlike twenty years ago he now had the courage to speak.

"I lied," he said.

"What?"

"The story about me being a private investigator. It's not true."

She lowered her arms so they half-covered her bra. Smile gone. "What's your name again? Sebastian?"

"No. It's Milo Weaver."

She cocked her head, as if he'd tapped her cheek. "Milo Weaver?"

"A couple months ago someone came here claiming to be me. I'd like to know who he was."

Zsuzsa waited, staring with big eyes, giving no sign she knew anything about any of this.

He said, "You're probably confused—I would be, too. And I can't give you much more than my word. This guy who was pretending to be me—he was looking for your friend Henry. I think he's the same guy that tried to kill him back in August. I think he'd come back to finish the job."

Her face twisted, and she stepped back.

Milo started to get up—"Want to sit?"—but his movement provoked her to raise her arms in a defensive motion, so he settled back down.

"James Einner?"

He blinked at her. "What?"

"The man who tried to kill Henry. Before he attacked Henry, he said his name was James Einner. Who is he?"

"I don't know," Milo lied.

"But you know who he works for."

"I have suspicions."

"CIA?"

"Very likely."

"So do you. You did. You used to work for the CIA."

"That's true."

She breathed through her nose so loudly that he could hear it over the music. "It's about the letter, isn't it?"

"I think so. But I don't know what was in the letter. I don't even know who sent it."

She said, "Thomas Grainger."

Milo stared hard. "*Grainger* sent Henry a letter?"

"You know this man."

Milo tried to get the facts straight, the timetable. By the time he was in jail in August, when Gray received the letter, Grainger had been dead for weeks. "He was a friend. He's dead now."

"I know."

"You know?"

"The letter said that if Henry received it, it meant that he was dead."

Milo wasn't looking at her; instead, he was staring at his own knees, assembling and reassembling the known facts, which were still too few. Then her platform shoes stepped into his field of vision. She said, "Is Henry dead? Did that man kill him?"

Milo looked up, and Zsuzsa's mascara was bleeding at the corner of her eye. "I don't know. You haven't heard from him?"

She shook her head.

"Where did he go? How could he just disappear? He'd have to have resources."

"He told me nothing. He wanted to protect me. He just told me he would go away for a while, and that I should only answer questions from Milo Weaver."

"From me?"

"Or that other guy. I don't know the difference anymore."

"Why me? I don't get it."

"The *letter*," she said as if he were dense. "Thomas Grainger's letter said that Henry could only trust Milo Weaver, because Milo Weaver was already looking into it."

"It?"

"The story he told Henry. About the CIA and the Sudan and Tourists."

Milo stared hard at her. "That's what the letter was about?"

"Henry said we would be like Woodward and Bernstein. Or maybe I said that. We were going to write the story together."

Milo considered just how much she'd been through in the last half year. Her boyfriend was tossed off a terrace, put in a coma, then revived only to disappear immediately afterward. During those few days before he vanished, he must have talked endlessly about CIA conspiracies, China, and assassinations in the Sudan. And Tourists. Because of her obsessive search for him, she'd lost her newspaper job and now spent evenings stripping. At least it was safer than international intrigues. Until now. A new Milo Weaver had stormed her safe haven.

Her tears had disappeared, and she'd fixed the mascara smear without him noticing. She was looking at a clock on the wall. "Your fourteen minutes are up."

"I'll buy fourteen more."

"No way. I don't even know who you are."

"Anything I can say to convince you?"

"Nothing," she said. Without making a show of it, she unclipped her bra and slipped out of it, standing over him so that he was watching her breasts from below. She bent slightly to remove her thong, gingerly unhooking it over her heels, then stood straight, hands on her hips, staring down at him, showing off the geometric perfection of her sculpted pubic hair. It was, he reflected later, the pose in which she might feel most powerful when dealing with a man. It worked, because a trembling weakness slithered through him.

"You paid for it," she said, then collected her discarded clothes and walked naked out through the curtain.

22

He found Parkhall up against the stage, grinning wildly at a pair of blondes gyrating across one another like Greek wrestlers, sharing a bottle of baby oil. To Milo, he said, "Fantastic, isn't she?"

"Which one?"

"Zsuzsa, you idiot. My God. How a loser like Henry Gray got on with her . . . it's a mystery for the ages."

"I'm heading out," Milo said, but he didn't leave. Parkhall convinced him to buy a ludicrously priced bottle of Törley champagne, which they shared with a girl named Agí, who turned out to have an in-depth knowledge of European economics. Parkhall went into interview mode, as if she were a government finance minister, and Milo had a suspicion that Agí was going to show up in one of his *Times* pieces as a "parliament member speaking under condition of anonymity."

The champagne went down weakly, so Milo ordered a gimlet. A gaggle of loud English hooligans in the front got on his nerves, and the sight of so much flesh left him with a vague but lasting impression of skin covered in fingerprints, like overused shot glasses.

The American-run 4Play Club, he learned from Parkhall, marketed itself to non-Hungarians for the simple reason that Hungarians wouldn't pay as much for what they had to offer. There were other clubs in town, but most were dark and potentially dangerous fleshpots run by the Russian mafia, where you would receive an outrageous bill, and then big men would walk you all the way to the cash machine. The majority of the customers were young Englishmen, part of the weekend vacationer boom made possible by cut-rate European airlines. Since it was often cheaper to fly to and get loaded in Eastern Europe than to spend a weekend drinking at London pubs, some cities had become flooded with these kids bursting with beer and itching for fights. They had done so much damage to Prague that laws had been passed to keep them out. Now the hooligans had discovered Budapest.

James Einner, he thought. Of course they'd sent James to get rid of Henry Gray. He was the only living Tourist, besides Milo, who knew anything about the Sudanese operation.

James had only been following orders, just as Milo had only been following orders when he mailed a package to Theodor Wartmüller that resulted in the death of Adriana Stanescu. When James returned in December to finish the job, he'd remembered the letter—*only trust Milo Weaver*—and used that name. Knowing all this did nothing to curb Milo's anger. He drank and watched the endless parade of flesh and, though he would soon leave it, hated everything to do with his lousy business.

At twelve thirty, Zsuzsa appeared onstage to the unbridled joy of the MC, who referred to her as a "shining example of Hungary's national product" before mixing in Bow Wow Wow's "I Want Candy." The English boys seemed to agree.

He watched the entire performance, about halfway through realizing he was hypnotized by it. She moved to the off-beats rather than the drums, and it created the illusion of a movie that's gone slightly out of sync. By the time she was down to her heels and thong, his eyes were red and tired, and he closed them. As he faded, an unexpected memory came to him: his and Tina's first visit with Dr. Bipasha Ray, back in September.

It had been during a downpour, and he'd had to run from the train, coat over his head, to make it on time. Tina's car was parked outside the therapist's Long Island residence, and when the doctor opened her door Milo saw Tina sitting dry and composed on the couch, watching him closely. Examining him. He wasn't sure why until he looked into Dr. Ray's face.

He didn't know what he had expected. Some elderly Indian specialist, perhaps, or some awkward social outcast. Bipasha Ray, who was actually Bengali, looked like a Bollywood film star, breathtakingly gorgeous. Rounded chin, blue eyes between her impossibly dark lashes, a summer dress. Her toenails—later, they would refer to her as "the barefoot therapist"—were painted bright red. He shook her hand and came inside, apologizing for dripping on the hardwood floor, and for the rest of the visit felt as if Tina were inspecting his every interaction with her.

The next day when they met for lunch, Tina seemed almost outraged by Dr. Ray's beauty. "I wonder how many marriages she's ended. I mean, couples come in, their relationship fragile, and I'll lay odds half the men fall in love with her by the third session."

"Erotic transference?" he'd asked and wondered if he might have a problem with that. He never did. How could he? The therapist's beauty, and Tina's close, continual watch, kept him guarded at all times. He didn't have the time or energy to fall in love with Dr. Ray.

A change in music woke him, and he drowsily paid his tab, realizing that Parkhall had put all his drinks on it. He reached the door before Parkhall caught up with him. "Hey, man. Where you going?"

"Hotel. I'm beat."

"Well, you did something right. Zsuzsa wants a word with you."

Milo didn't feel up to that mix of seduction and scorn. "She can find me at the Ibis."

Parkhall looped an arm over his shoulder. "You don't get it, do you? She wants a word with you in the *private* booth. You lucky cunt."

It took another fifty euros—he was nearly broke now—but soon he was in the same place where they'd talked before, and Zsuzsa was already waiting. She was dressed for home, the makeup cleaned off, her hair up, and a fur-lined coat hanging from the back of the chair, where she sat. "All right, Mr. Weaver," she said, her arms crossed tightly. "Now you."

"Now me what?"

"The clothes. Off with them."

"For this I pay fifty euros?"

He did as she asked, thinking of mothers who tell their children to always leave the house wearing clean underwear. He paused when he was down to his T-shirt and underwear, but she flicked a long, painted nail and waited until he was completely naked. He felt cold, and wondered how the girls took to the iffy heating here, if they complained, or if the exertion of dancing made it bearable. He thought of a lot of things to avoid speculating on how he looked.

"Why is your arm bandaged?"

"I burned myself cooking."

"Okay," she said. "Put them back on."

"What was that?" he asked as he stepped into his underwear.

"Checking for a gun. Or a wire."

"You've got to be kidding."

"I don't know who you are, Mr. Weaver. I do remember your name from that letter, and I remember a man who used your name. But you? Maybe you're James Einner."

Milo had gotten one leg into his pants. "If you don't trust me, then why are we here?"

"One thing I've learned is that I'll never find Henry on my own."

Milo buttoned his shirt.

"When I was dancing, it occurred to me that I'm going to have to trust someone. Why not you? I like your face."

"Thanks."

"Your body's a joke, but your face is almost believable."

"Oh," he said.

"This is hard for me," she said philosophically. "I'm shaking. See?"

She showed a slender hand, but in the dim light it looked perfectly still.

"And I lied."

"You lied?"

"Yes," she said. "I don't trust you at all."

"Then why—"

She raised her hand in a silencing motion. "*He* said to trust you. He called me. Just now, just after I danced."

"Who's he?"

"Who do you think, Mr. Weaver? Henry."

He stared at her. "You've been in contact with him all this time?"

She shook her head but didn't say anything. Briefly, she focused on some point between them, thinking. She said, "I was starting to believe he was dead—and then he calls."

"Now? Why now?"

She snapped out of it and shrugged. "It's a coincidence, isn't it? The other time you showed up just after he'd woken. Now, he calls the same night you're here. Remarkable."

Remarkable, yes, but Milo didn't believe in a coincidence like this. James Einner had arrived in town because he had learned that Gray had woken. That was cause and effect. It was explainable. But Henry calling while Milo was in town? "What did Henry say?"

"He said he's done."

"Done with what?"

"His work. It's done."

"The story? He's done with that?"

"I don't know. I didn't ask. I'm just happy he's alive." She didn't sound happy, though.

"It's good news."

She looked at him, the corner of her lip rising slightly. "Don't patronize me."

"Sorry. But it is good news, for us both."

"What do you have planned?"

"I just want to talk to him."

"And then?"

"And then leave. I've got a family I want to return to."

She smiled and said, "That's charming."

"Now you're patronizing me," Milo said as he kneeled to tie his shoes. "Can I meet him?"

She considered that. Henry had told her to trust him, but Zsuzsa was the one with the power now, and she seemed to be toying with it, estimating its weight. "I'd like to see him first."

"Why don't we go together?"

She shook her head, then grabbed her coat. "Tomorrow at Moskva tér. You know where it is?"

Milo had passed through Moscow Square on his way to St. John's Hospital. "Yes."

"Go there at two o'clock, and he'll come to you."

"How will he find me?"

"Unlike me, he knows what the real Milo Weaver looks like."

It was a kind of answer. Milo stood. "Thank you."

With awkward formality, he shook her hand and thanked her again. He gave her a few minutes so she wouldn't suspect he was following, then left the club by keeping close to the wall, far from Parkhall, who was laughing uncontrollably with two girls, both his hands occupied under the table.

23

He woke with a mild hangover and a sore arm but left the hotel quickly. He was down to less than a hundred euros, which he changed into forints and used to buy breakfast from a bakery on Batthany Square, on the Buda side of the river. He considered writing an e-mail to Alan Drummond, to assure him that he would return soon, and to ask for a meeting with James Einner, but decided against it. He could think of no reason for putting Drummond's mind at ease. Then, as he was finishing his coffee, he noticed, out on the street, a man in his fifties, thinning on top, wearing a heavy overcoat and smoking beside a closed travel agent's office with sunbleached posters of Egypt and Rome.

With the Gray meeting just a few hours away, it was easy to forget that there were more things going on. The shadows from Berlin and London, whom he'd never identified. Perhaps they were working for the Chinese, perhaps for the Germans. Or maybe Drummond was a liar, and they were working for him. Whoever they were, he didn't want them around when he met with Gray.

He paid his tab and descended into the subway without looking back. He took a train to Deák Ferenc tér, then switched to the Millennium Railway—the world's second-oldest subway—that took him back to Oktogon. Again, he joined the crowds on that busy square and worked his way around to Szondi, but continued past number 10, keeping an eye on the scaffoldings with the curtains of plastic netting. It was Sunday, and the construction workers were still gone. There—on the right side of the street was a particularly messy site, with loose steel bars that had yet to be pieced together. He parted the netting and went inside, grabbing a heavy, meter-length of pipe, and stepped into the cavernous, dirty foyer. He waited.

He didn't know how long it would take, but he was willing to wait as long as necessary. In the end, it took a half hour. During that time, two residents left the building, and each time he took out his battery-less cell phone and spoke German into it, pretending to be an investor wondering where his workers were. Then, a little after twelve thirty, his shadow entered the building.

There was a moment—less than a second—when he had to examine the face from his squatting position. He didn't want to brutalize some innocent Hungarian. In that moment the shadow, too, recognized him. Milo was prepared, the pipe already drawn back, and as soon as he registered the heavy jowls and deep-set eyes, he put all his effort into the swing. The hollow end of the pipe made a faint whistling sound as it arced along the low path, just below the knee. A muted thump and crunch as the shin cracked.

There was no dramatic pause. Milo followed through with his swing, only briefly slowing on impact; then gravity took over, dropping the man to the ground, the tails of his trench coat catching on the pipe as the screaming began, filling the old Habsburg entryway.

At first, there was nothing intelligible from the screams, and Milo straightened and held the pipe like a shotgun aimed at the man's head. He waited. Certainly some residents would be waking to the sound, suddenly interrupting their lunches, but he ignored that. He stared at the man's twisted, screaming face.

He knew, of course, that this was just a man hired for a job. A simple job that Milo himself had done many times. Milo felt nothing. This was just collateral damage.

He squatted again as the screams became more intelligible. *Oh Jesus fuck, my leg! My leg!* American. The man held on to his shin, as blood spilled between his fingers. Milo got close to his bucking face and shouted, "Who do you work for?"

"Jesus Fucking H. Christ!"

"Who do you work for?"

The curses continued, and Milo dropped the pipe and grabbed the lapels of the trench coat and dragged the man deeper into the foyer, close to the stairs. A long trail of blood streaked the dirty tiles. He worried the man was going to pass out, so he slapped him twice, hard, and repeated the question. He didn't get an answer, but the shouting ceased as the man fumbled with his wet, flopping shin and moaned softly.

It had been a mistake. He could see that now. He went back for the pipe, then squatted by his head. "Listen to me. Are you listening?"

Finally, the man registered him with his eyes. He didn't answer, but the eyes were enough. Milo held up the pipe. "I'm going to brain you unless you tell me who you're working for."

"Global. Security."

Global Security was one of the smaller security firms that had received government contracts to ease the military strain in Iraq and Afghanistan. Hired guns, which told him nothing. "Who hired you to follow me?"

"How should I know?" the man shouted. His face was wet with tears.

A woman's voice shouted from above: "Mi történik legyöz ott?" Milo dropped the pipe, and as the clattering noise filled the building he started going through the man's pockets. The man didn't fight back. Finally, he found the cell phone and began running through the call logs. "What's his name?"

"I told you, I don't know!"

"Your boss. What's the name of your boss?"

"Cy!"

There it was—cy—three calls in the last two days. Milo called the number and waited until a male voice with a southern accent said, "You lose him again, Raleigh?"

"No, he didn't lose me," said Milo. "He's right here."

"Shit," said Cy.

"Listen, I've broken Raleigh's leg, but he's not telling me what I need to know. Maybe you can. Otherwise, I'm going to kill him."

"What do you want to know?"

"Who's hired you to keep tabs on me?"

"You know I can't tell you that."

Milo picked up the pipe and swung it against Raleigh's broken leg. As the echoes of his screams started to fade, Milo returned to the phone. "You'll tell me now, Cy. Otherwise, Raleigh dies right here. Then, over the next week, members of your family start disappearing. At the end of the week, I come for you."

The boss made a sighing sound. "Don't you think that's overkill?"

"You've caught me in a very poor mood."

"Fuck," said Cy.

"Én hívja a rendőrséget!" called the upstairs voice.

A half hour later, Milo was back in Buda, joining the crowded, steep subway escalator up to Moscow Square as he chewed Nicorette. Faces passed him heading down into the earth, a whole range of faces, all the varieties of Caucasian. His anger had left, and with it the adrenaline shakes. Now all he felt was a stoic animosity. Why hadn't he figured it out before? Who would give a damn about where Milo Weaver was at any time? Not the Chinese, and not the Germans. Alan Drummond didn't need to track him all over the place. There was only one person who cared about what Milo was up to. Senator Nathan Irwin. He lived in fear that Milo would sit up one day and present the evidence that tied the senator to last year's Sudanese debacle. Irwin, like any careful politician, was covering his ass.

For the rest of today at least, Irwin would have to depend on guesswork.

Moscow Square had the intense feel of a transportation hub. Teenagers met in small groups, others walked quickly to buses and trams, and small, dark men in leather jackets sold things from rickety tables and from beneath their jackets. There was something seedy about this open, triangular space, and the smell of fried food and the incessant traffic around its border just added to that feeling. The one blessing was an unseasonable warmth in the air, a premature spring day.

He browsed a magazine stand and walked the circumference of the square, stolidly ignoring vendors who approached with cell phones, Easter trinkets, shoes, and books. For the benefit of blue-clad Hungarian policemen, he kept moving. On one side, traffic jammed the roads leading around old buildings with billboards for McDonald's, Raiffeisenbank, and Nespresso, with an enormous George Clooney taking a pleasing sip. The other side rose precipitously to Castle Hill, where tourists boarded squat electric buses to take them all the way up into that rarefied district.

A little before two, he chose a spot near the steps leading up to the castle road, stuck his hands in his pockets, and let his slack face be seen from as many angles as possible. No one seemed to notice him, or care. Everyone was heading somewhere or selling something.

Henry Gray approached from behind, trotting down the steps in a light, airy manner that was decidedly not Hungarian. "Sorry I'm late," he said without any sign that this was a potentially life-threatening rendezvous; it threw Milo. He stuck out a hand, and Gray took it casually, a single pump before releasing.

He was in his midthirties: narrow face, dark sideburns, thinning on top. His green eyes looked as if they had been put on with CGI. Three- or four-day beard. He looked like a hundred other young expats.

"And you are?" Milo asked to be sure.

"Henry Gray. And you're Milo Weaver. You look just like your photographs."

"My photographs?"

"Yeah," he said as he pointed across the square and began to walk, "but your nose wasn't so fucked up."

24

Milo walked with him along a crowded crosswalk to a small, busy side street that led to a mall—Mammut Mall, with its signature woolly mammoth logo. "I used to go to the pubs when I first came. Sörözős. Dark, gloomy places. After a while they just tire you out. Then the cafés. The bonus there is all the pretty girls, and nowadays the coffee is actually good. But that's tiring, too—there's always some social aspect to it. Now, it's easiest to just go to the mall for a drink." Gray smiled, as if he hadn't had a chance to speak with an American in a while. "Moved all the way to Central Europe, just to become a suburbanite!"

They took escalators to the third floor, then crossed a glassed-in bridge over another street to enter the modern half of the mall, where overpriced restaurants tempted shoppers. Gray headed directly to Leroy's, the darkest of the bunch, full of smoking women and their overdressed hangers-on. Gray ordered a mojito, so Milo ordered the same, and as they waited Milo cut into another monologue about the virtues of shopping malls. "Why'd you disappear, Henry?"

"Disappear?"

"From the hospital. You didn't even tell Zsuzsa where you were."

Gray considered that, then smiled when the waitress returned with two tall drinks stuffed with fresh mint, lime, and long brown straws. He took a sip and said, "What do you think? You think that when I woke up I'd just go back to my life like everything was fine? This guy, he meant to kill me."

"You mean James Einner."

"You know who he is?"

"I can probably find out."

"Good. Good." Another sip. "Anyway, James Einner messed up. I knew that. And sooner or later he was bound to find out that I'd woken up. What was I going to do? What would you do?"

"I'm not sure."

"Me, I'm a journalist. If I can't track stories, I don't want to keep living. It's the only thing I know how to do. The only thing I want to do."

"So what did you do?"

Gray wrapped his lips around the straw and arched his brows. "You don't know already?"

"All I know is, you got a letter from an old friend of mine, Thomas Grainger. Then this other guy, James Einner, tried to kill you. When you woke from your coma, you disappeared, and someone showed up looking for you, pretending to be me. Maybe it was Einner, maybe not. Then, yesterday, you called Zsuzsa while I was at the club, looking for you. How did you know I was there?"

"That was a coincidence. I didn't know you were there. Not for sure."

"So what triggered the call?"

"I told her. I was done. I'd finished my story."

"And you told her to trust me."

"Of course I did. The letter said to trust you."

"The one from Thomas Grainger."

"Exactly," Gray said, then smiled. "I see what you're thinking. If some other guy showed up pretending to be you, how could I be so stupid as to sit with you now?"

"No, I wasn't thinking that, but it's a good point."

"I'm not entirely gullible," he said with satisfaction. "First, the photograph—I know you are who you say you are. Of course, there's always the possibility that maybe Grainger didn't know you as well as he thought he did, right?"

"Sure."

"That's why I've got backup."

"Right now?"

He nodded, then glanced around. There were enough people in the restaurant and just outside in the mall itself that his backup could be anywhere. "They're good at hiding," he said.

"Who?"

"The Chinese."

It felt like the kind of non sequitur a conspiracy theorist like Gray would make; then it didn't. "Why the Chinese?"

"Because that's who I went to, all right?"

"After you woke up?"

"When your own country is trying to kill you, it's not called treason. It's called survival."

"That sounds reasonable."

Gray looked like he didn't believe Milo, but it didn't matter anymore; he had backup, after all. "I woke in that hospital, and I knew that as soon as James Einner figured out I was alive, I was dead. Days, weeks, whatever. In the end, dead. I couldn't go to the Hungarians, because they would just hand me to the CIA. And what did I have? Nothing, except a story. Einner might have stolen the letter, but he couldn't take this," he said, tapping his skull.

"After months in a coma, you remembered it all?"

"Not all. Fragments. Zsuzsa remembered more than I did. We worked together on it before I left."

"Before you disappeared."

"Yes."

"So by the time you disappeared you had something of value to give the Chinese."

"Exactly." Gray chewed the end of his straw. "I got the hell out of the hospital and went to Benczúr utca. I went to the front desk of the embassy and asked for political asylum. I was passed on to someone who took down my story."

Milo followed the brown straw from Gray's pursed, damp lips down to the forest in his glass. Gray had gone to the *Chinese*—what were the odds? Milo said, "You gave them the whole story right away?"

"Pieces. The important pieces—the Sudan, the Tiger, the mullah. I wanted their protection for the rest. I told them I'd be staying at the Marco Polo—it's a hostel in town. Took them two days, then I got a call. They wanted to meet me, but not at the embassy. They gave me some address out in Budakalász. That's north of here. I took the tram and then walked a while. They picked me up on the way and drove me someplace completely different."

"They were careful."

"Of course they were. I was important to them."

Milo noticed pride in Gray's voice. "Where did you go?"

"South. Budaörs, off the M1. There was a fat guy there. Chinese— they were all Chinese. We talked."

"Name?" Milo said through a suddenly dry mouth.

"He told me to call him Rick. It was a joke—he wanted me to know that the Chinese people really could pronounce the letter *r*." He grinned—clearly, Gray liked Rick. "Knowing his real name wouldn't do either of us any good. It didn't matter to me—I was just afraid for my life. Rick wanted to help me. I would tell him all I knew about this story—everything I could remember from the letter—and he would help me do the research in safety. This was crucial. Only by publishing the story would I be safe."

Milo didn't answer. He rested his chin on his knuckles, trying to digest the sequence. Gray told the Chinese about the Sudan. Why? Because Milo's own friend, Tom Grainger, had written a letter. That letter would have stayed with Gray were it not for James Einner and his botched murder—and it wouldn't have been sent in the first place had Nathan Irwin not ordered Grainger's execution.

Where, really, did the blame lie?

As if reading his mind, Gray said, "I'm not going to make apologies, you know. It's you people who put me in this situation."

"I'm not asking for apologies," said Milo. "Go on."

"Well, that's what we did. I wrote down everything I remembered from the letter, and he worked with me to remember what I'd forgotten. He had some interrogation techniques—no waterboarding, nothing like that, just mind tricks, free association. When I remembered something, he would leave and go to verify details along the way. When I had trouble, he'd prod me with things he knew—secret things—to see if they brought up more information."

"Until you had reconstructed the whole letter."

"Yes. And he was angry. Rick was. He didn't know about the operation in the Sudan, and I could see how pissed off it made him. People say the Chinese are inscrutable, but that's bullshit. They're as hot-tempered as the rest of us."

"Did he say anything? That he was going to take revenge?"

"You're not listening. *I'm* his revenge. My story—it's going to bust open the Department of Tourism. Expose it. Rick says that for a department like that, the only real threat is exposure. We don't even need to show people how bad it is, just that it exists. Then the politicians and journalists will do the rest of the work. Pick it apart until there's nothing left of it. But we have to prove it exists."

It was eerie how perfectly that echoed Drummond's own fears. "So how do you prove it exists?"

"Elbow grease. Work. They hooked up the safe house with broadband, and I got to work. Wasn't easy—it's taken two months. Rick came back from his trips with new information to help out."

"What kind?"

"Financial records, biographies of some of the players. Thomas Grainger, for instance. I learned all about him. Angela Yates, your friend who was killed. You."

"What did you learn about me?"

He grinned. "Wouldn't you like to know?"

"Yes," Milo said without smiling. "I would."

Gray's smile disappeared. "The usual. Family, the job—that you used to be one of those Tourists but had moved into administration—and that you were the one guy who had been interested in uncovering what happened in the Sudan. That it cost you your family, and your freedom. In some ways, of the two of us I'm the one who got off light."

Milo leaned back, not liking the easy way Gray placed them both in the same category. He hated that this man knew so much about him. "How far have you come?"

"Far enough. I've already written the first two articles on the department. I e-mailed one to the *New York Times* this morning."

That surprised Milo; then it didn't. It was why Gray was willing to meet him now. He'd already unleashed the Chinese revenge. E-mail was notoriously insecure, of course. By now it would have been flagged and a Company representative would be sitting with the editor-in-chief, ready to make a deal. "They won't print it."

"Then I'll try the *Washington Post*. And I'll keep trying until I've got a sympathetic ear." He had the earnest tone of a true believer. "The evidence is there—the fiscal black holes that pay for the department, the links between Senator Nathan Irwin and the oil lobby wanting to push the Chinese out of Africa. It was international—you know that, right? They had help from French oil. It wasn't just an American plot; it was a Western plot. This is as big as stories come, Milo, and I'm not going to let it go."

25

The waitress returned, and Gray ordered another round. Milo hardly noticed. He was working his way through everything, feeling paralyzed by the slow buildup of revelations. Rick was, he felt sure, Xin Zhu, the Chinese spymaster. Before following that to its logical conclusion, though, he felt he had to deal with the remarkable coincidence of their meeting now. "Last night, when you called Zsuzsa, did you clear it with Rick?"

"Of course I did. We'd had a ton of progress over the last week, and I was writing like mad. I was exhausted. I wanted to see her again."

"What kind of progress?"

"Well, we learned what happened to you, for instance."

"What happened to me?"

"You survived, didn't you? Grainger's letter told us you were investigating, but we weren't sure if you were one of the casualties or not. Everyone wanted your ass, after all. You got out of prison and went to live in New Jersey—we knew that—but then you disappeared, and we didn't know until this week that you really were still alive."

"How'd you figure that out?"

"Ask Rick. He came in with the information."

Milo nodded at this. "So you had all the information you needed, and you wanted to see your girlfriend."

"But Rick wanted to be cautious. Last night he finally told me it was safe to call."

"And me? Did he know I was around?"

"What do you think?" said Gray. "Yeah. He said you might be around. And that I shouldn't worry about you."

Milo thought a moment, then said, "They're done with you. You do realize that, right? You're on your own now."

Gray shook his head. "I might look like I'm alone and helpless, but trust me—they've got my back. They want this story out as much as I do."

Milo turned to gaze at the crowds in the mall. "They're not there."

"These guys are much better than you think."

Milo stared at him, at the confidence he was working hard to sustain. Gray hadn't asked the most important question, which was whether or not Milo was working for Tourism again. Either it hadn't occurred to him, or it had, and he was too terrified to ask. That's how people worked. They avoided the things that most terrified them, even if knowing could save their lives.

Milo changed tactics. "Why do you think your friend Rick wants to expose the Department of Tourism?"

Gray blinked at his denseness. "Why do you think? To ruin it. To finish it off, so it won't keep blustering into China's business."

"Rick's a smart guy," said Milo. "He knows that as soon as you get rid of Tourism, another department will take its place. There's always clandestine funds available. He gets rid of Tourism, and he loses the one secret he has on the Company. That's not how a spy works. When you get hold of intelligence, you keep it and use it. You only give it up if you're forced to do so."

The lesson was lost on Gray. He raised a hand and patted the air. "Rick's no more complicated than the rest of us, Milo. He was angry about the Sudan. An angry man isn't going to fool around with intelligence games."

Milo doubted that. What Gray couldn't really know in his bones was that espionage rarely, if ever, provoked wild emotions from men like Rick. Xin Zhu and Alan Drummond and Nathan Irwin—and even Milo himself for a while—worked from behind desks, and, to them, losses and gains were extended mathematical equations. Variables represented trade alliances, corporate influence, nuclear programs, spheres of influence, and the occasional human being. No one could get so upset over math.

"What kind of man is Rick?"

"Physically? Fat, but he carries his weight well."

"Personality? Is he a joker?"

"Oh, the *R* joke." Gray shook his head. "That was his single one-liner during the past two months. This guy doesn't laugh. Doesn't drink or smoke. He's like an angry priest."

"What about women?"

"Never came up, not really. But I get the sense that if he has one it's a little wife back in Beijing he would never think of cheating on."

Just the kind of man you'd trust, thought Milo. While Marko's drunk, womanizing Xin Zhu was tailor-made for him. Milo wiped his mouth to suppress a smile of admiration.

Not just admiration but awe, because he'd followed everything through to its logical conclusion. Zhu had played this brilliantly.

Henry Gray had been used from the start. Thomas Grainger had tried to use him, posthumously, to reveal an operation he had grown disgusted with (disgust was one of the few emotions administrators knew intimately), and then Xin Zhu had used him to collect enough intelligence about Tourism so that he could pretend to have a mole working in it.

Because there was no mole in Tourism, and there never had been.

He couldn't help it; the smile flowered on his face. Gray leaned forward and said, "What?"

No mole.

Now, everything fell into place beautifully.

It began with a story written by Grainger. The letter would have remained in his lawyer's office if he'd remained alive. The Company had killed him, though, and so it was sent to Henry Gray. The Company tried to clean up the mess as it too often did—by killing—but there was a mistake. Gray survived, and so did the story of the Sudanese operation run through the Department of Tourism. Again, the

Company was at fault, for its attempted murder led Gray straight into the hands of Xin Zhu, a Chinese spymaster who kept Gray around to help with the investigation.

At the beginning, this had probably been the entire plan: Help a journalist humiliate the Company as payback for its reckless interference in Africa.

Then, during one of Xin Zhu's absences he found himself in Kiev, liaising with the SSU, and learned of one Marko Dzubenko, a blustering lieutenant planning to defect. With the kind of creativity that's rare among administrators, he asked the SSU to please not arrest Dzubenko—some sort of deal would have had to be struck. *Bring him to the next embassy party, will you?* In person, pretending to be a drunk blowhard, he gave Dzubenko a story he couldn't help but use later to buy himself a new life in America.

It was beautiful because it was so clean. In the end Zhu did so little. He helped an American journalist work on a story. He told a lie to a defector. Later, when he decided Tourism needed another kick, he passed along the request for the Chinese ambassador to the UN to deliver a single sentence about the Sudan, then refuse to go into details. Zhu knew that there had been a senator working behind the scenes, and any senator would panic at the possibility that the Chinese held a scandal in their hands.

It was beautiful, too, in that its minimalism reflected the minimalism of the original operation in the Sudan. Kill one man and make it look as if the Chinese committed the murder. Zhu's plan was even more beautiful because no one needed to be killed, or even hurt, whereas last year's plot had killed one man initially, resulting in riots in the Sudan that had killed more than eighty; then more died just to keep it quiet. Milo was stunned by the audacity of Xin Zhu's ingeniousness.

"What is it?" Gray insisted.

"Where's the house?"

"What?"

"Where's the safe house? I want to see it."

Gray considered that, staring past Milo at the diners and shoppers, probably looking for his backup. "Why?"

"Because I'd love to meet Rick," he said. He really did want to meet Xin Zhu but knew it wouldn't happen. Not today, at least.

"This might all sound like a joke to you, but you won't be safe there."

"Henry, really. I'd love to meet him. Hell, I might even offer him my services."

"Why are you jerking my chain?"

"I'm jerking nothing."

Gray considered that, then shrugged and stood up. "I'm not going to be responsible for what they do to you."

"You're officially exempt from responsibility."

Milo paid the bill, then followed Gray back out to the street, where he waved down a taxi. Gray negotiated with the driver while Milo went back and forth over his realizations, checking them off one after the other. He was sure of this.

When Gray turned to look at the cars behind them, Milo said, "They're not there, are they?"

"What you don't know could fill the Vatican."

To reach Budaörs, the taxi driver took the same highway Milo had used to reach Budapest, then exited near the IKEA and ended up in a town of small, clay-tiled houses with muddy yards and new cars. To their left a fallow field opened up, and then a right placed them on a gravel street of new houses, with foreign cars and reinforced concrete gates. They stopped at number 16, and Milo paid the taxi bill with the last of his forints.

"Your last chance," Gray said as he used a key on the gate.

"No cars," Milo noted.

"They like public transport. More democratic."

"Of course."

Gray rang the bell on the front door, then used another key. No one waited for them, and the first room they entered was stripped down to its bare walls and hardwood floor. Gray stopped, shocked, then ran to the other rooms, finally shouting, "Mother*fucker*! They took my computer!"

Involuntarily, Milo started to laugh. Xin Zhu had only been interested in sending a message, and Milo was there to receive it:

We know who you are and what you did. We can touch you whenever we like.

He took the pieces of his phone out of his pocket and put it back together, walking slowly through the empty rooms. He found Gray coming out of a bathroom, wiping vomit from his lips. He started to say something to Milo but changed his mind.

Milo's phone rang. He took it to the kitchen.

"Riverrun, past Eve."

"And Adam's," said Milo.

"You're in some serious shit," said Drummond. "Irwin's on the warpath for you."

"I bet he is."

"Get yourself back home."

"I'll need my credit cards."

"They'll be working in an hour, okay?"

"One more thing," said Milo. "You can unfreeze the department. There's no mole."

"What?"

Milo gave him the short version, and though he was doubtful, Drummond said, "What kind of bastard dreams up such a thing?"

"Don't talk that way about the man I love," Milo said, then hung up.

26

By the time he landed at JFK, it was Tuesday morning. He drove a rental into midtown and, knowing the lot beside 101 West Thirty-first would be full of employees' cars, parked in a public lot on West Twenty-ninth and walked over to the Avenue of the Americas, then up the busy sidewalk to Thirty-first. Cameras positioned along the streets surrounding the Department of Tourism's headquarters tracked his progress, and when he reached the entrance to the inconspicuous brick tower two doormen were already waiting.

In the old days, he would have known these huge men who acted as Tourism's first barrier against intrusion, and called them by name, but these two had come along after his dismissal, and they were as mute and humorless as their predecessors. There was one familiar face, though—Gloria Martinez, who worked the front desk. She was pretty but stern; this had never stopped Milo from flirting with her in an unending game of proposal and rejection.

The last time she'd seen him, Milo was being beaten to the ground by three doormen in this cold lobby. Now, the look on her face suggested she had assumed him dead, and she showed the maximum emotion her position would allow: "Good to see you again, sir."

"Ms. Martinez, you are, as ever, a sight for sore eyes."

When he stopped to be photographed by the computer and

stated his name for the microphone, Gloria Martinez didn't even blink when he said, "Sebastian Hall." She had only ever known him as Milo.

In the elevator the doormen patted him down, then used a key to access the twenty-second floor. The ride was silent, and Milo watched their stony faces in the mirrored walls.

When the doors opened, he involuntarily caught his breath. This, for six years, had been his daily destination, his nine-to-five. A quietly productive floor of cubicles and computers and busy Travel Agents combing through the intelligence sent in by a whole world of Tourists. Now, though, the most striking thing about the Department of Tourism was its emptiness. The maze of cubicles was still here, but they were empty. In a few, kneeling in mock prayer, technicians fooled with computer cables, tagging and logging hard drives, but they were like sweepers cleaning up after a parade, not even raising their heads to acknowledge the visitors heading to the offices along the far wall.

On the left and right, windows watched over the midpoints of skyscrapers under slate clouds, and ahead of them, through open blinds, was the office Grainger had used when running the department. It had been taken over by Owen Mendel, then the surprisingly young Alan Drummond, and now, behind the large desk, sat a prematurely white-haired man with reading glasses—fifty-five, Milo remembered. It was a familiar face from CNN talk shows and the occasional C-SPAN sleeper. He was a man not used to having to work through such volumes of paperwork, not used to having to lead a mole hunt. Senator Nathan Irwin.

Milo hoped that, for their first meeting, he wouldn't snap and murder the senator.

Then again, he wasn't sure what he hoped.

Irwin wasn't alone in the office. Drummond was leaning back in a chair used for visitors, and two young men in suits stood around, slouched. One muttered into a cell phone and watched the visitors approach, then turned and said something to Irwin, who took off his glasses. All the men watched them enter.

"Thanks, guys," Drummond said as he got to his feet, and the two doormen withdrew.

Irwin remained seated, so Drummond made introductions. "Nathan, this is Sebastian Hall."

Irwin blinked at him, then shook his head. "You mean—"

"Yes," Drummond cut in, "but for security we stick to work names."

"Of course," said Irwin. He finally pushed himself up and stretched a large hand across his desk—actually, Grainger's desk. The department had decided to keep the oak monstrosity after his death.

Milo stepped forward and shook the senator's cool hand.

"This," Drummond continued, "is Max Grzybowski, the senator's chief of staff."

The blond young man stuck out a hand, smiling goofily. "Pleased to meet you."

The one with the phone kept whispering into it but raised a hand and offered a salutary smile.

"He's Jim Pearson, legislative director," said Drummond, and Milo waved casually back. "They're Senator Irwin's personal assistants, and they've been given the same clearance as the senator."

The senator nodded agreeably, then pointed at Milo. "I've been looking forward to meeting you, er, Hall. Have time for a drink?"

"That's up to Mr. Drummond, sir. I'm due for some debriefing, I think."

"It's up to me now," Irwin said before Drummond could answer, "and I want us to chat before your debriefing. Max, can you take care of it?"

After months on the road, there was something freakishly civilized about what followed. Max took out a BlackBerry. "Four o'clock all right?"

Milo shrugged.

Max said to Irwin, "That way you can still make dinner at six with the Joshipuras. Stout—it's a bar up on Thirty-third."

Jim Pearson finally ended his call. "Would you like me on hand?"

Everyone looked at Irwin, who shook his head. "Let's keep this off the record, shall we, Hall?"

"I'm a big fan of off the record, sir."

"Four at Stout should work," Max told them both. "Minimal clientele."

"You sound like a regular," said Milo.

"Max is a regular of all the world's better drinking establishments," Irwin informed him, then settled back down. "Now, though, I'd like to hear a little more about your theory."

"My theory?"

"Your theory that there is no mole in Tourism."

There were no spare chairs, so Milo remained standing. "Sure. But first you have to get your mind around one thing that's almost nonexistent in our line of work."

"What's that?" asked Irwin, and Drummond leaned forward expectantly.

"A sense of humor, sir."

He took them through it all—Grainger's letter, the failed attempt on Gray's life, Gray's approach to the Chinese, and Xin Zhu's priming of Marko Dzubenko.

"It sounds to me," Irwin said once he'd finished, "like you're fond of this Chinaman."

"He found a way to throw us into complete disarray and make us fear for our existence—all without harming a single person. We could learn a lot from his way of thinking."

"Alan, what do you think?"

"About Xin Zhu?" Drummond asked, frowning.

"About the theory."

Drummond mused on this, tilting his head from side to side. "It holds water. The strange thing, to me, was always that Marko Dzubenko and the Chinese ambassador referred to only one operation. We had to assume the Chinese had wider knowledge but preferred to only let this one out in order to pressure us. It was poker, and we had to assume they weren't bluffing."

"So now you've decided they were."

"The Budapest safe house," Milo cut in. "That's what settled it for me. After helping him for months, they cut Gray off completely in the space of an afternoon. Took all his research with them. They're not interested in him blowing our secrets."

"Now that's something I don't quite get," said Irwin. "Why wouldn't they want to blow our secrets?"

"Because right now Xin Zhu owns that secret. He's got the upper hand. All this was just to inform us of that fact."

"Why now?" asked Jim Pearson, leaning against the blinds.

Milo blinked at him. "What?"

"Why did they decide to let go of Henry Gray at this moment, rather than later? We'd just started the vetting process. If they'd waited another week, we might have completely gutted the department. It would have really damaged us."

"It was me."

"The world revolving around you again?" asked Drummond, smiling.

"Zhu learned I was in Budapest looking for Gray. It was convenient. He even told Gray that I was looking for him, and said he should meet me. He was never interested in ruining us."

Irwin nodded slowly as it all became clear. "Jesus. The sons of bitches! I'm starting to share your admiration, Hall." Then he turned to Max Grzybowski. "Make sure no one ever knows I said that."

"Will do, Captain," Max said, grinning.

"Let's not all fall in love with Zhu," Drummond said, shifting in his chair. "The fact is that his game cost five lives."

"Who?" asked Milo.

"Recalling Tourists is never foolproof. You pull agents out in the middle of an operation, and some don't make it. A couple of them were being watched and tried to hurry home too fast. One had to break out of jail to get back; he made it as far as the train yards before the dogs got him. The other two are just dead—no explanation yet."

Everyone remained silent a moment, thinking about those deaths in far corners of the world.

"So don't tell me Xin Zhu is some intelligence saint," Drummond said.

Everyone in the room noticed the disgust in his voice, but Milo was the only one impressed by it.

27

Drummond walked him back to the elevator, and as they waited for it he muttered under his breath, lips unmoving, about the mess Irwin had been causing. "He's comprehensive. It's great when you're going through a federal budget, but not now. I have no idea when we'll be online again."

"But it's done now. Irwin can head back to Congress, and you can get back to work."

"He's demanding to oversee the reassignments. His assistants are advising him that if something blows up just after he's left, he'll get blamed for it. He's already entered the swamp, and he wants to make sure he doesn't track anything back onto the Senate floor."

Milo glanced back. Irwin and his assistants were huddled together over their game plan. The technicians were far away.

Drummond said, "The Germans didn't hurt you much, did they?"

"Just my pride. How did you know where I was?"

"When?"

"When I was at Erika Schwartz's house. They took apart my phone, but you figured out where I was and got to her through Theodor Wartmüller. How?"

Drummond shrugged. "I guess I can share—you've got a tracker in your left shoulder."

"No, I don't."

"You do," he insisted. "Since October all Tourists have one. Phone trackers are too easy to bust, or lose. You got yours in training, one of the hundred immunization shots."

"No one told me?"

"We don't tell anyone."

Milo began to reflect on this fact, that every move he'd made had been easily tracked by Drummond on his computer. "Wait. That means you knew where I was after I kidnapped Adriana. You *knew* I didn't take her body out into the countryside."

Drummond stared back at him but said nothing. There was a kind of sadness in his face.

"You didn't expect me to kill her, did you?"

Finally, Drummond said, "Don't give yourself a headache. No, I didn't want her dead, but we had to get rid of her. That's why I chose you, the only Tourist with a child. I knew that, given a whole week, you'd find some other solution."

"You could have told me that."

"Maybe, but I wanted you to hide it from me. If I couldn't figure it out, then no one else could, either."

Milo couldn't speak.

"And you came through—almost. What really went wrong?"

"I overestimated my friends. Then you had her killed anyway."

"You were her last chance."

Silence fell between them, and Milo hit the elevator button again. He didn't know if he believed any of this, or if he just didn't want to.

"You're not really quitting, are you?"

"You'll get my resignation letter by tonight."

"Jesus, Weaver. I need you here."

The elevator opened, and Milo stepped inside. There was a pleading quality to Drummond's voice that worried him, but he'd been through this so many times in his head that it was as if the resignation had already been filed. There were so many arguments he could make, but only one mattered: "We set up the girl. Then we killed her."

"And because of that, we now have an open invitation at BND headquarters. They built an overpriced meeting room—Conference Room S—solely for meetings with us. After a year it's finally being used. That's no small thing."

"Yet not big enough."

Milo watched the despair grow on Drummond's face as the doors slid shut. Beyond, one of the senator's aides—Jim Pearson—was standing at the blinds, watching them.

By the time he was out on the street again, having nodded to the doormen and winked at Gloria, he felt something like freedom. Not freedom exactly, because he knew he would have to work to make it safely through the extensive exit interviews, but he was certainly lighter. It was the release from obligation, a rare and wonderful feeling.

He wanted to call Tina, and even stopped at a pay phone, but changed his mind. Better to go to her later, when he knew he could stay. He stuck a square of Nicorette into his mouth.

Stout was mostly empty, partly because the after-work revelers had moved farther uptown, partly because most of its remaining clientele hadn't gotten out of work yet. He settled at the extremely long, woody bar and ordered a vodka martini. It was delicious, and he thought over all the vodka martinis he'd had over the last three months, in Moscow, Paris, Podgorica, London, Zürich, Budapest, Berlin, Rome . . .

While the drink's name made most people think of Italy, the only place he'd ever had a really good one—big, ice cold, and very strong—was in Manhattan. Though Stout's version wasn't nearly as good as, say, the Underbar of the W Hotel on Union Square, it was still leagues ahead of any Florentine café's, and he gave the bartender—a blonde with a slight harelip—earnest thanks.

The other customers—five in all—were scattered at the tables behind him. One woman with a man, a pair of men, and a man on his own. The male pair, he decided, was Irwin's contingent, and he was proved right when one of them made a call from his cell, hung up, and seconds later Irwin walked in alone. He went straight to the bar without looking around, settled next to Milo, and summoned the bartender with a snap of his fingers. She hid her annoyance admirably and delivered his Scotch on the rocks with a smile, then moved to the far end of the bar.

"So, Weaver," Irwin said after taking his first sip. The way he said the name made Milo think of a high school principal beginning yet another session with the class troublemaker. "You do, I believe, know me?"

"I don't think we've ever met, sir."

"*Of* me, I should have said. You know *of* me."

"I think all politically aware Americans know of you, sir."

Irwin swirled his drink. "September twenty-eighth, October fifteenth, January seventh. Those dates ring any bells?"

"Afraid not."

"Those are three dates you accessed files related to me personally. Phone records, my home addresses, details on my foreign trips. You," he said, wagging a finger, then lowered it and began again. "You seem very interested in me, Milo."

"I got bored, Nathan."

The senator grinned.

"No, really," Milo insisted. "We both know why I should be interested in you. You had two of my friends killed. You tried to kill me. I'm not one to hold grudges, but that's a lot to bear. Then you had me followed. How is Raleigh, by the way?"

"Raleigh?"

"The shadow I nearly killed in Budapest."

Irwin's face went slack, and he wiped at the corners of his mouth, muttering, "So that's why Cy's not returning my calls," and took another drink. "I made a mistake last year. I didn't know Terence Fitzhugh would start doing things in my name."

Terence Fitzhugh had been Irwin's liaison with Tourism, his hand in the department. He, too, was dead. "I've seen the call records," said Milo.

"Oh. Right." Irwin considered that, then frowned, realizing his lie had been untenable. "And you're still bored?"

"I'm tired of blaming you. I'm tired of my own anger. I'm also sick of politicians who think they're patriots."

"You think I'm a patriot?" The idea seemed to please him.

"I think you believe you're a patriot."

"And you? Are you a patriot, Milo?"

"I wouldn't say that."

That seemed to kill the conversation. Both worked on their drinks and glanced at the bartender, who finally wandered over and had to be sent away again. Finally, Irwin said, "I actually liked Grainger. He was a likable guy."

"He was an excellent guy. There was a lot of blood when he died. I suppose you never looked at the pictures."

"I took a glance."

"Just to be sure?"

Irwin shrugged.

"Did you know Angela Yates?"

"Never met her."

"She was an excellent woman. A fantastic investigator."

"A lesbian, right?"

"Yes, Nathan. A lesbian."

Milo was doing it again, measuring distances. Geography, geometry, and time. How long would it take him to reach out, break the senator's neck, and get away before one of the two men at the table could pull a gun and stop him? He doubted he could do much more than bruise the senator's windpipe before he was stopped cold. That would have been enough for his mother, he suspected.

No, the math didn't add up, but it was comforting all the same.

Irwin said, "You know, politics is a funny thing. At first glance, there's something glamorous about it. Then you look harder, and you start to think that behind all the glamour, all there really is is a world of spreadsheets. Budgets and polls and itemized bills. That's true enough, but the real key to any political success is the ability to read people. If you can read another politician's real thoughts, then you've got something. I'm pretty good at reading politicians. People like you—simple citizens—they're a cinch. The fact is, you're not so good a Tourist that I can't see through you. You're not done with me at all."

"Talk to Drummond. He'll tell you I'm done."

"Will he?"

"I've quit."

Irwin raised his brows to show how interested he was. "Now, that's something."

"It certainly is."

"And how does that affect us?"

"It shows how uninterested I am. I no longer care about anything that happens in this world. I'd call it a tempest in a teacup if so many people didn't get killed."

"Tempest in a teacup?" Irwin grunted his amusement. "I'll have to tell that to the other guys on the committee."

"Tell them what you like. I just want you to know that we—you and me—we're finished. Here. Now."

"So you can go back to your lovely family? To Tina and Stephanie?"

Two and a half feet between his hand and the senator's neck. "Something like that."

Perhaps reading Milo's mind, Irwin leaned back. "Two things, Milo. First is that this doesn't make me feel any better. Why do you think you were even brought back into Tourism?"

"Shortages."

"Shortages, sure, but Mendel was my man, and I'm the one who made sure he brought you back in. Why do you think I did that?"

Milo went for his drink again. He didn't like where this was going. "So you could keep an eye on me."

"Very good. During Mendel's tenure I could find out where you were at any moment. Now that this kid's running things and sticking to procedure, I have to pay out of my own pocket for people to track you. Which brings me to the second thing." Irwin reached into his jacket and brought out a six-by-four color snapshot. He placed it on the damp bar. It was of Milo in Berlin, standing at a courtyard entrance, talking with a pretty Moldovan girl. "I believe they refer to this as the money shot."

Milo almost slipped off the bar stool, but didn't. Then he almost strangled the senator. But didn't.

"I've shelled out a lot on these private dicks, but with this I can finally call them off." He reached into his jacket again and took out another picture. "This one's the coup de grace."

It certainly was. Milo and Yevgeny Primakov inside the Berliner Dom, beneath a painting, discussing the future of Adriana Stanescu. He hadn't seen the shadows—they must have mixed with the Bavarians, just as Yevgeny had.

"Your father, yes?"

Milo didn't answer.

"You know, before taking over the department, I was largely ignorant of what it did. Of course, I knew the broad strokes, and sometimes I stepped in when I wanted to personally oversee an operation. Yes, yes—like the Sudanese one. Otherwise my only real function was making sure it received the funds it needed to keep working. My ignorance was protection—for myself, and for the department. No one likes to perjure himself on the floor of Congress. But for the last few days my clearance has shown me everything. Everything. It's like Pandora's box, the records of the Department of Tourism. Some of it makes even me queasy. Particularly this," he said, shaking the photograph before slipping it back into his jacket. "I see a man talking with his father; then the image shifts completely when I read the file. I learn that immediately afterward you kidnapped that girl and then went out of your way not to kill her. The sequence of events becomes clear, and it occurs to me that you not only didn't do your job, but you brought in a foreign national—a representative of the United Nations, no less—to help thwart your orders." He paused. "You shared all the details of your job with your father and asked for his help. Yes?"

Still Milo didn't answer.

"I think we understand each other," said Irwin. He lifted his Scotch to his lips.

The senator wasn't gloating, not quite. He was just trying to make himself understood. If Milo ever made an attempt to get back at him, the senator would quickly make him Europe's most wanted man. If that wasn't enough, he would have Milo arrested for treason.

That was how a senator protected himself in today's world. It proved that Nathan Irwin was still a terrified man, and no matter what he said, the surveillance would continue for a good long time, even after he'd washed his hands of Tourism.

28

Despite the worries that had plagued him, Milo survived his time in that blank cell on the nineteenth floor. Because of his short tenure as a Tourist, the exit interview lasted only five days, and John's questions were, particularly compared to their last session in July, when Milo had been accused of murdering Thomas Grainger, gentle. He could sense the open honesty in most of Milo's answers. When the story reached Berlin, though, John paused and backtracked and sniffed; something was wrong. He began to seek out individual hours. Six to eight in the evening on Wednesday the thirteenth. Nine in the morning on Friday. John seemed troubled by Milo's unprecedented Christian feelings, him heading to the Berliner Dom to seek out spiritual advice about a hit he wasn't sure he could go through with. Of course John was troubled; Milo's file stated his religious beliefs as "none." Finally, after John put it to him that all his hours, as a Tourist, were owned by the Company, and that therefore he required complete honesty, Milo said, "Well, I guess there's no reason to hide it anymore."

"To hide what?"

"Stefan Hassel. I knew him from the Bührle job. We met to set up the Adriana Stanescu kidnapping. Ask Drummond—he already knows."

"The kidnapping?"

"Yes."

Later, when they'd dealt in excruciating detail with his stay at Erika Schwartz's and his subsequent search for Henry Gray, John returned to Stefan Hassel. Milo had more stories ready.

On the last day, John became chatty. They'd worked together often during the previous years, when people needed to be brought down to these cells and interrogated, but the fraternity he showed was still surprising. The best he could figure was that Drummond or Irwin had told him he could relax.

"They're all gone now, you know."

"They?"

"The Tourists. New names, new covers, new go-codes. New phones, even. It's a relief. You ever had to oversee the interviews of thirty-eight people at once? It's a pain, I can tell you."

"I can imagine."

John even smiled—a rare event. "Okay. There's one last thing I want to go over. You told me before that you admired Xin Zhu because of the cleverness of his scheme."

"Yes—but not just because it was clever. There are a lot of clever people in the world. What I admire is the fact that no one was hurt, not directly. All he did was bruise some egos. Don't you admire it?"

"What I feel doesn't matter. We're talking about you."

"What you're asking is if I admire him so much that I might work for him in the future. That's what you're hinting at, isn't it?"

"Not necessarily. But . . . you might as well answer your own question."

"First I'll need to know what kind of health plan he offers."

"Ha ha, Milo. Good one."

Before he was released on Monday, he sat down beside a machine on a table in a locked closet. Though it looked a lot like an old sewing machine, John assured him that it was in fact magnetic in nature. He swiveled it out so that it pressed hard against the top of Milo's left shoulder, then typed a code into a keypad on the rear. There was no sound, no movement, nothing to tell Milo it had even been plugged in, but John swiveled it back into place and said, "Congratulations. You're no longer being tracked." They shook hands at the elevator, where John said, "I'd say don't be a stranger, but be a stranger," and when he boarded the doorman made that elusive statement comprehensible by informing him that he no longer had clearance to board this elevator ever again.

Milo wished Gloria Martinez all the joy in the world before stepping out onto the busy sidewalk. They'd returned all the items he'd given up three months ago upon his arrival—keys, phone, and a wallet with fifty-four dollars—as well as his iPod. No driver's license, no passport, no credit cards—all his Milo Weaver documents were in his Newark apartment.

He didn't go to New Jersey. Instead, he took the F train to Fifteenth Street–Prospect Park and then walked to Garfield Place. He reached the door by three, and though he had a key he didn't use it. He settled on the front steps and sipped some water he'd bought on the way, watching young professionals heading back home. He tried to listen to more Bowie, but the battery in his iPod was dead.

He thought what anyone thinks when one life has ended and another is about to begin. He wondered what shape the new life would take. Not the practicalities, but this other part, the part that lived on the third floor of the brownstone behind him. The part of his life that had provoked him to make dangerous phone calls on his way to commit art heists.

He hadn't forgotten anything, and Senator Irwin's threats were still on his mind, but all fears lose their malevolence over time. It can take decades, a few months, or in Milo's case just a few days. Milo had no interest in taking on the senator. He had what he wanted, and he wasn't going to do anything to risk losing that.

They arrived a little after six, and while Stephanie threw herself into him and began a lecture on the dangers of him sitting out in the cold—a regurgitation of one of her mother's speeches—Milo watched Tina for signs. She locked up the car and came around with a wary look. "Something wrong with your nose?"

"I'm accident-prone."

She nodded as she approached. "When's the flight out?"

"I got sick of airports."

She watched him run his fingers through Stephanie's hair. "You here to break our hearts?"

They ordered Thai takeout and ate in the living room without turning on the television once the whole evening. School was treating Stephanie roughly, it seemed, and later Tina said the teacher blamed her declining grades on their separation. "Half America's marriages are broken, and this is the best she can come up with?"

"Let's go meet with her this week. Together."

"Sounds like a plan," Tina answered.

That's when the reality of his return to family life hit Milo with the strength of one of Heinrich's blows. Plans for the future. Responsibilities. It wasn't freedom he'd been wanting all this time, just a different kind of obligation. Later, after Stephanie was in bed, he even said, "What about Dr. Ray?"

"She tells me she's kept our Wednesday slot open. You up for it?"

"Absolutely."

"You know?" she said after a moment.

"No, I don't."

"It's almost as if you never left."

She didn't mean it literally—she and Stephanie had, after all, spent half the evening catching him up on the things he'd missed—but in terms of the ease that filled the apartment his first night back, it felt to her as if it were a year ago, before things had begun to go wrong.

Saying all that made her self-conscious, so she pulled back again. "I know, it sounds corny. And really, it's probably just the initial glow. Tomorrow we'll be back to the same ol' same ol'."

After they made love in the wide bed that felt like a decadent luxury after months of hotels, and he had vaguely explained away the cigarette burns on his arm, Milo went to the kitchen, naked, and poured two Merlots to take back to the bedroom. On his way back, he noticed a thick manila envelope on the table beside the front door. Across it, in black marker, was MILO. He checked the door, but it was locked. He opened the envelope.

As they drank, Tina wiped a drop of wine from her breast and said, "What's wrong?"

"Nothing," he said, then thought better of it. Lies had ruined things, and he'd had enough of them. He went to get the envelope and showed it to her. "Seen this before?"

"No. Should I have?"

He rubbed his eyes; his father had placed the envelope while he and Tina were having sex. "It's from Yevgeny."

"Looks like work to me."

"Just something of interest."

"Well, don't wait for me."

"What?"

"You obviously want to dig into it right away."

"Am I that obvious?"

"Not often enough," she said, then kissed him.

He left her to sleep and went to the living room with his Merlot and a square of the Nicorette he was beginning to suspect had become his new addiction. He opened up the manila envelope and began to read about the life and times of Xin Zhu.

29

"Glad you made it, Milo," Dr. Bipasha Ray said, showing off a radiant smile he suspected was not entirely honest. They all shook hands, and despite the chilly damp outside Dr. Ray padded to her chair in bare, manicured feet. The pleasantries were dispensed with quickly, beginning with "How has it been between the two of you?" When they both agreed that the last two days had been like another honeymoon, she pursed her lips and said, "Very nice." She didn't have to point out that anyone in the world could last two lousy days.

"So, Milo. Anything you can say about where you've been these last few months? The few times Tina and I met, she didn't seem to know."

"I'd tell you, but I'd have to kill you," he said with a banal smile, but Dr. Ray didn't seem to find that funny. She was one of the few therapists the department had cleared for staff use, but she'd never had much patience for Company humor, particularly when it utilized the threat of death. "No, I just mean that all I can say is I was moving around a good bit. Working here and there."

"Working too much to call and check in with your family?"

Milo looked at Tina, who had no expression at all, then back at Dr. Ray. "No, actually. It's against the rules. It's not safe to call your family when you're working undercover. You place them and yourself in unnecessary danger." He decided against mentioning that he had tried to call a few times.

"Of course," Dr. Ray said, then brushed at the knee of her jeans. "Does that mean you were in real danger?"

"No, no. Just a figure of speech."

Dr. Ray nodded, smiling. "Milo, some months ago you were telling Tina that you thought these sessions weren't the way to take care of your marital problems. Could you expand on that?"

"I'm not sure I said that."

"You did, hon," said Tina. "I said I thought it was helping, and you said you didn't."

This was starting to feel like an ambush. "Okay, maybe I did say it."

"So, what did you mean by that?" asked Dr. Ray.

Milo rubbed his arms. The room was vaguely chilly, and he decided that if they wanted to ambush him, he would open himself up to it. He would, for the moment at least, trust that honesty was the path of rightness. He said, "What I meant was that I hadn't been entirely honest. During those sessions, I mean."

"What?" That was Tina.

"It's not so uncommon," Dr. Ray said generously. "What matters is that you've admitted it aloud, and we can move ahead in a more constructive manner."

Tina said, "Have you really been lying here?"

"Not lying. Just not always opening up completely."

"Tina, Milo may have good reasons for drawing the distinction."

"Yeah—to save his own ass."

"I'm not saving my ass, Tina."

She didn't believe him. Their drive here had been pleasant and light, and he wondered if she, in turn, had been dishonest with him, knowing that she and the good doctor would be setting him up. She said, "Just don't tell me you're protecting national secrets by lying in couples therapy. How much time has to pass before your life stops being classified, huh? It never occurs to you that by then it might be too late."

Where was this coming from?

"Tina, let Milo speak. Milo?"

In the silence that followed, he found himself fidgeting with the knee of his pants in some strange solidarity with Dr. Ray. He forced himself to stop, though he knew how it looked, how *he* looked—awkward and nervous, a man never to be trusted.

After the things he'd done, the places he'd been, what was this? A study belonging to a little Long Island psychologist. But *Christ*, it felt like one of those cells on the nineteenth floor, with John in a bad mood.

"For instance," he finally managed, groping for something that didn't include murder or kidnapping or robbery, "the story of how we fell in love. Back in September, at one of our first meetings, you went through it all right here. Remember?"

Tina nodded. "Of course I remember."

"It didn't happen like that. Not for me. I've never understood it—what does that even mean, falling in love while watching the Towers fall? I can't even comprehend it."

"It's what I felt. I'm not going to make apologies for my feelings, Milo."

"That's right, Tina. We should never apologize for our feelings. Milo, tell us more. We're listening."

He looked at each woman again, feeling the distance between him and them increasing, and thought that this was the exact opposite of what therapy was supposed to do. "It didn't start with love, that's what I'm trying to say. What I felt was desperation. My life had gone to hell, and I was desperate for something to hold on to. And there she was—Tina, I mean—going into labor right there on the street. I needed something, and Tina was there at the right time."

"Lovely."

"Tina, let him go on. Milo?"

"Well," he said, "when I woke up next to Tina's bed, and we were watching the Towers on TV, I was more confused than anything else. I didn't feel close to anybody. You were there, clutching onto me, but it was like I was alone in that hospital room."

"Alone. I see. I fell in love, and you just felt cold."

"Don't misunderstand me—love did come. It just took time. And Stephanie."

"Stephanie?" That was Dr. Ray, sounding as if he'd finally, after months, said something interesting. "What do you mean by that?"

"I don't mean my heart melted when I saw her, not quite. It just struck me that, for the first time in my life, I'd met someone who could do nothing wrong. That's how babies are. Nothing is their fault. If they cry or throw a fit or shit in your hands—everything they do wrong is your fault. That's not sentimentality—that's fact. To be honest, I was awed by this, that any human being could be utterly without guile and menace. It was new to me. It was a shock. I wanted to be near that innocence, to protect it."

Dr. Ray embarked on one of her favorite pastimes: rephrasing what her patients had said. "So you could say that you fell in love with your daughter before you fell in love with your wife."

"You could certainly say that."

"Tina? Anything to say?"

Tina was just staring at Milo, her expression betraying nothing.

"Tina?"

Tina raised both hands in the air, and when she brought them down again in an expression of impotence there were tears in her eyes.

"See?" she said. "This is what I'm talking about. Him falling in love with Stephanie—how come I never heard that before? Christ, Milo. How many times have I told that story? You could have stopped me years ago, before I made an ass of myself."

Dr. Ray said, "I don't think you've made an ass of yourself. Milo?"

"Of course she hasn't," he said.

"Let me tell you something," said Dr. Ray. "Tina, are you listening? I want both of you to hear it."

Tina said, "Sure."

Milo agreed with an "Okay."

"Though we haven't met as regularly as we all would have liked, I think I've gotten a sense of the dynamic between the two of you. You've probably noticed that I use the word 'listen' a lot. It's not because I'm some touchy-feely therapist. I say it because it's an issue here. You're not listening to each other. Wait, Milo," she said, raising a finger at him. "Yes, you're listening to each other's words, but you're not listening to the subtext."

Both Milo and Tina waited.

"For example, Milo—why do you think you lied about the circumstances of your meeting?"

"I wouldn't say I lied—"

"Omission is essentially the same thing."

"Okay," he said, ready to admit to anything. "I suppose I was afraid of hurting Tina's feelings."

"Why?"

"Yes," said Tina, "why?"

He had to think about that. "I don't want Tina feeling, I don't know, disconnected from me. From the idea of our marriage."

"And what's the idea of your marriage?"

"That. The story. The myth of how it began," he said, thinking suddenly of Tourism and how without its myth it would no longer be of any value. Was that really how he thought of his marriage? "No," he said aloud, feeling confused. "No, that's not it. What I mean is, whether or not that story is true for both of us, the marriage isn't affected, because it doesn't matter how we met. What matters is how we've lived together."

Tina blinked at him. Her eyes were wet. Dr. Ray was unmoved. "You still haven't answered my question: What's the idea of your marriage?"

"There is no idea of our marriage," he said finally. "It simply is."

He wasn't sure if this was what Dr. Ray was aiming at, but it was all he could manage when cornered.

Tina said, "Stephanie."

Both looked at her.

"That's Milo's idea of our marriage. It's Stephanie. That's what he thinks, isn't it?"

Dr. Ray shook her head. "I can't tell you what anyone's thinking. That's up to Milo to say. Milo?"

Now they were looking at him.

30

Tina stared at his features, waiting, because this felt like a moment of decision. Dr. Ray was good at this. She could take a seemingly happy relationship and with a few questions strip it down like a shitty old car to some lie right in its center. Or some misunderstanding.

She'd noticed this last year, right at the beginning, and more than Dr. Ray's animal sexiness this was what had frightened her, that she would discover the falseness of their marriage and show it to them proudly, wrecking their lives. Now she was trying it again, pushing them both into a corner where Tina had no choice but to ask the obvious question, and Milo had no choice but to answer.

His cheeks were coloring. He said, "It's an idiotic question."

"Is it?" Tina asked. Dr. Ray said nothing.

"Yeah." He was pissed off now. "How can anyone boil seven years down to a single idea? Of course Stephanie is one idea in our marriage, but do you really think there's only one? How about sex? That's one excellent idea in our marriage. And love?" He turned to Dr. Ray. "Our marriage is a hundred different ideas. I'm not going to name a single one."

"How about trust?" asked Dr. Ray.

"How about it?" he said ineptly.

"Of course a marriage is made of many different ideas, but they have their own biorhythms. Certain ideas come to the fore at certain times. If you listen to Tina, you'll hear that, for her, trust is very often the primary idea. Her lack of it, in particular. Tina—am I misrepresenting your feelings?"

She shook her head.

"Tina feels as if a large part of your life is a complete mystery to her."

"Which is why I've quit my job," said Milo.

"And that's an excellent step," the doctor said. "But what does that mean? Does it mean that, from this point on, she's going to start to get to know her husband? That's impossible if you still can't share your past with her. You may have quit your job, but that job still possesses the last fourteen years of your life. We are the result of our histories, Milo, not the result of our present."

This was really annoying Milo; she could see it in the edges of his heavy eyes, in the flushed cheeks, in the quick darting of his tongue. "So now I should open up the history books? That'll land me in jail and put Tina and Stephanie in serious danger."

"See what I mean?" Tina found herself saying. "Those national secrets again."

"They're a fact of life, Tina."

"And facts dictate the limits of our behavior," Dr. Ray said majestically. "But people have their own limits that facts cannot dictate. The question isn't what you can and cannot tell Tina, but how this makes Tina feel, and how well you can compensate for it."

"Wait a minute," Tina said, no longer worrying if she was going to sound stupid. "You said Stef and I would end up in danger, but you weren't in danger—you said that at the beginning of the session. If you weren't, then why would we be?"

He rubbed his face. "I was lying, Tina. Of course I was in danger. Those burns on my arm? Someone was using me as an ashtray. There's just no need for anyone to worry—I got out of it fine."

Ashtray? The word stuck in her head, and she had trouble seeing past it. "You hear him? Is there no way for you to be honest? Not even here?"

"Tina," said Dr. Ray, "he's trying to be honest here. This is real progress."

It didn't feel like progress to Tina, though, and she was starting to wonder if Milo coming back home was really what they both needed. That opening lie about danger had been a small one, as insignificant, really, as saying "Fine" when someone asks how you're doing, but it felt so much bigger. She pressed her hand deep into the sofa cushion. "Is it progress? Because I know how spies work. He's told me often enough. Cover. You go in somewhere with cover, and when the enemy realizes you're not that person, you have another cover prepared, just below it. You give that one easily. If they still don't believe it, you have a third one ready, but you really make them work for it, because otherwise they won't buy it. If you're really good, you've got another one beneath that, one so deep that it might as well be the real you. How many layers of cover do you have, Milo?"

He looked shocked by her outburst. Or appalled. "None."

"But you see? You see how he's got me screwed up? I even take it a step further sometimes and think that maybe his genius lies in the fact that the original cover, the first one I've peeled off and thrown away, that *that's* the real one. That I've long ago abandoned what really is Milo Weaver. That it's somewhere in the trash and I'll never find it again."

She was crying now, and she saw Dr. Ray's long, toned, lovely arm push a box of Kleenex across the coffee table to her. She took one but didn't use it, just balled it in her hand and squeezed it.

Dr. Ray said, "Are you listening, Milo? Because this is what your wife is saying to you. She's here because she wants to find the Milo she fell in love with. It doesn't have to be the Milo she thought she knew, just a Milo she believes in."

Milo wasn't listening to anyone.

Through her blurred vision Tina saw him sit up, stiff, staring ahead. Not at her, or at the therapist, but somewhere else, into the middle distance. Something had landed on him, had squashed him flat. Did he—and this thought made her feel suddenly very dependent—have an insight that would save their marriage? The magic bullet? Christ, it looked like it from his expression. It looked like he had something big. A breakthrough.

"Milo?"

Dr. Ray, while reaching a hand in Tina's direction, leaned toward Milo, frowning. "Milo, you with us?"

Then, unbelievably, Milo stood up. For the first time in known history, Dr. Ray looked confused.

"What is it, Milo?"

Tina wiped at her tears. "Milo? Hon? What is it?" She touched his arm, but he showed no sign of having felt it.

Then he sat down again, heavily, and reached for her hand. Squeezed it distractedly. To both of them, he said, "Sorry. I'm sorry. Something came to me."

"That's good," said Dr. Ray.

"What?" said Tina.

"It's not . . ." he began, then shook his head, leaning back. "It's about something else. Not about this."

Flatly, Tina said, "It's not about our marriage? Then what is it about?"

"It's—that stuff. All the stuff I'm not allowed to discuss."

"I *have* been vetted by your people," Dr. Ray reminded him. "What you say here stays here."

"Not this level of clearance," Milo said coldly. He ran a hand through his hair. "Maybe I should go."

"I think leaving now would be a serious mistake," said Dr. Ray.

He nodded obediently, but for the rest of the session was not even there. Tina wished he had left, so that she could have at least become emotional, but when faced with a man like this, a blank-faced automaton absorbed by something so far from the topic of discussion, how could she?

On the way to her car, he broke the silence, but not with anything constructive or even encouraging. "Can you drop me off at the train?"

"Drop yourself off, you self-centered shit," she said and got into the car. She didn't bother unlocking the passenger's side, just started it up and drove away.

31

The man, small and hairy and twitchy, was not German. This Hasad knew for a fact. He arrived driving an old taxi and entered the store with a soft worker's cap balled up in his fleshy fists covered in too much dark hair and rose on his toes and peered around the empty store before turning to offer Hasad a brief "Guten Abend." His accent was something eastern, like the Czechs who sometimes stopped by his store on their way to the BND headquarters on missions he was far too patriotic to ask about.

Like some of those Czechs, he dressed in an oversized trench coat, but the material was even worse than what the Czechs wore. Yet his shoes, Hasad noticed, were so well shined that they reflected the fluorescent lamps in the ceiling.

He walked to the rear of the store and began browsing slowly. Sometimes he picked up and examined a candy bar or a bag of chips, but always returned it to its spot.

At first, Hasad worried. The trench coat might have hidden a gun, though before worrying about his life Hasad calculated how much money was in the till. Then, when the man opened and closed his coat quickly three times to fan himself, he realized there were no weapons about the portly body.

He was sweating—that, too, could be seen from a distance. The hair on his head and the bits that emerged from his cheap sweater were glistening with it as he crouched to read the label on a packet of Holland Toast.

He was still going about his research when Frau—*Direktor*—Schwartz arrived. She nodded to Hasad as she charted her route to the back of the store and collected her Riesling. To his surprise, he saw that she was buying two, and when she turned back to look for her Snickers, she caught sight of the man, who said, "Erika Schwartz."

She froze. Hasad worried she would drop the bottles, but instead her grip tightened—he saw how her pink fingers whitened from the pressure. Then they relaxed and she said, "Grüss Gott, Herr Stanescu. I didn't know you were in Munich."

No answer. From his angle Hasad could see something wild in Herr Stanescu's eyes, as if he expected that her arrival would bring him great wealth. He was in one aisle while she was in the next, and they spoke over the potato chips. Then the man opened his mouth, but instead of speech a low animal moan came out and he began to weep.

She said, "You should probably go home, Herr Stanescu. We're doing all we can."

Stanescu—Hasad finally remembered. The girl from the newspapers, the girl killed by Russians. Then he recognized this man from the photographs—the poor girl's father, Andrei. He nearly fainted.

Through his sobs, Andrei Stanescu said, "I call him and I call him but he doesn't answer. Herr Reich isn't answering."

"I'm sorry, but I told you before—I'm not on the case anymore. Trust me, Herr Reich is working diligently on it."

"I need answers—can't you see? I am dying!"

"You should go home."

"Where is the man?"

"Herr Reich? He—"

"No!" he shouted, anger suddenly replacing that deep sadness. "The other man! In the picture! The one that kill her!"

"That was a mistake," she told him, and Hasad noticed that now only one bottle was in her hand, and she held it upside-down, like a club. He moved to the left and, below the counter, gripped a heavy nightstick he kept for emergencies. She said, "It happens sometimes.

Yes, he talked to your daughter, but he had nothing to do with her kidnapping."

"Don't tell me that!" shouted Andrei Stanescu. He marched toward the front of the store, toward Hasad, but only stared at Director Schwartz. As he rounded the end of the aisle, effectively blocking her exit, Hasad caught the heady stink of some brandy all over him.

"What are you doing?" Director Schwartz asked calmly.

"I'm sick!" he said. "I am sick of all . . . of *Germans*. Of you. You think I am a stupid immigrant what listens happy to all your lies. I'm not. No one cares about a little girl who is killed by the man in that picture. No one!"

"I assure you, Herr Stanescu—"

"Assure, assure! I'm sick of all that assure! I'm dying. You tell me now where is that Russian and I will take care of it myself."

"Herr Stanescu," she said, her voice firmer now, "you have to get him out of your head. He was a tourist, asking Adriana for directions. He's not even Russian."

That seemed to take some of the wind out of him; from behind, Hasad saw his shoulders sink. "Not Russian?"

"No," she said gently. "He's American."

"American?"

Hasad loosened his grip on the nightstick.

"But then who did it?" Stanescu asked, returning to his pitiful demeanor.

Director Schwartz blinked at him, then pursed her lips. "I'll tell you what. In the morning I'll sit down with Herr Reich and go through the case with him. Then I'll call you at home and tell you everything I've learned."

Andrei Stanescu, defeated, stared at the tiled floor. "I do not believe you."

"Of course you don't," she told him, "but I am being honest. Herr Reich took over the case because it was considered that important. If he's not answering your calls it's because he's busy tracking leads. Tomorrow, I will find out his progress and report it to you. But you have to go. Now. Do you understand?"

He shook his head; he understood nothing.

"In a couple of minutes men are going to come through that door, and if you're still here they'll arrest you. When you started yelling I pressed a panic switch," she said and opened her free hand to reveal a key ring with a button attached to it. "If you're gone when they arrive, I'll tell them that pressing it was an accident."

Stanescu raised his head.

"Do we have a deal?"

He nodded.

"Expect my call around ten. If I haven't called by eleven, you call me. Okay?"

Andrei Stanescu didn't nod again, just turned around. In his face Hasad saw not hope but the indistinct despair he knew from his own immigrant circles, often when jobs had been lost or residency applications turned down. He shuffled to the doors, which opened automatically for him, and slipped off into the night.

He hadn't, until then, realized that he'd been holding his breath. He met Director Schwartz's eyes as she picked up her second bottle from the shelf and brought both to the counter. "Well," she said.

"Should I call the police?" he asked.

She shook her head. "He's just grieving. There's no need to make his life any worse than it is."

"You handled that very well."

"Thank you, Herr al-Akir. But he was never dangerous."

He began to ring up the wines. "And the Snickers?"

"Not tonight. I might try to lose some weight."

"Good luck with that, Director Schwartz."

He took her money and watched her head for the doors before calling out, "And the men? Should I expect them soon?"

"Men?" she said, turning back.

"The ones you called."

"Oh!" She smiled, took out her key ring, and pointed it through the open doors. She pressed, and her Volvo winked in reply.

32

Heading down on the elevator, on his way to meet his wife for dinner, Alan Drummond felt an unfamiliar emotion that Wednesday afternoon: satisfaction. It wasn't the pleased satisfaction of someone who's just finished a particularly good meal or some fulfilling sexual act, but the satisfaction of someone who's spent too much time dissatisfied and has finally gone through a twenty-four-hour period largely free of disappointments.

Rebuilding the Department of Tourism had taken only four days. The technicians who had removed the computers and disassembled the cubicles had kept detailed records of where each had come from, and it was just a matter of repeating the procedure in reverse. There were glitches, of course. Human error. A couple of Travel Agents ended up with the wrong computers, but instead of bringing in the technicians again Drummond had them switch cubicles. By then the remaining thirty-eight Tourists had been redeployed, and while most were able to continue their previous assignments, seven had to abandon them and begin new ones. One, though, was less lucky. Her sudden disappearance was badly timed, and when she returned to Jakarta a welcoming committee was waiting for her at Soekarno-Hatta International; twelve hours later she was confirmed dead.

Though the number of Tourists was still dreadfully low, during the four days since their redeployment only that one had been lost, and they'd gained two more from the ranks of the Travel Agents, both of whom were now suffering through training at the Point. The memory of the Guoanbu's game still haunted him, particularly as he thought of those five Tourists—Stanley, Gupta, Mobuku, Martinez, and Yuan—who had been lost during the Myrrh recall. Among those who were left, though, significant work had been done, and not just the miserable work of keeping the department above water. Two terrorist cells—one Pakistani, one Saudi—had been infiltrated; three nuisances (Syrian, Moroccan, and Palestinian) had been liquidated; a Tourist had acquired choice intelligence about Hugo Chávez's government during the resolution of the Andean crisis between Ecuador, Colombia, and Venezuela; and one Tourist had even saved the lives of two French journalists in Najaf. That was positive work, progress, and it proved that Milo Weaver was a short-sighted fool. Despite his years in administration, Weaver had an incomprehensible misunderstanding of how compromise was necessary in order to do the good work.

The department had even survived Director Ascot, who had gotten wind of the mole hunt from God-Only-Knew-Who. Nathan Irwin dreamed up the lie to save them: "It's simple, Alan. You tell that bastard that since taking over you've grown disgusted by the lax security in the department, and the only way to deal with it was to bring everyone back to New York and give them new identities. You needed the fake mole hunt to justify the recall."

The fact that the lie worked beautifully had the ironic effect of making him and Irwin partners in crime. Ironic, because Irwin had savagely fought Drummond's appointment to head Tourism. That was politics for you.

By Friday, though, Irwin and his nosy staff would be out of his hair, and he would be free of the perpetual oversight.

Nothing was perfect; nothing had ever been. The new go-codes, for instance, were impossible to remember. Six-digit numbers. So each time he called a Tourist he had to pull out the abused list from his top drawer, which listed everything: work name, phone number, go-code, and reply code. If he wanted to call one while he was outside of the office, he had to hightail it back to the Avenue of the Americas, go up to the twenty-second floor, and unlock his office and then the damned drawer. Irwin and his aides insisted it was the only secure way to run things, and they were probably right, but it made Drummond's job that much more impossible.

Still, he'd survived—they'd all survived—and there was a certain satisfaction in that. He was starting to believe he could survive for a good long while in the Department of Tourism.

To celebrate his new lease on life, and to apologize for having missed a lunch date with his wife for a last-minute powwow with visitors from the Department of Defense, he'd reserved a table for two at Balthazar, Penelope's favorite restaurant. He and Penelope had a long, known history of blowing a significant amount of their income on expensive restaurants. He couldn't help it—seeing Penelope's joy when a goat cheese and caramelized onion tart was placed before her made it all worth it. For the truth, which was so rare in his circles that admitting to it publicly would have been social suicide, was that he loved his wife deeply and thanked God that his undeserving ass had ever been blessed with her.

Lost in these embarrassing thoughts, he settled into a black Ford in the basement garage. Jake was behind the wheel; Jake, who had just returned from a holiday in Miami with his family. Drummond asked about the weather down there, and how the family was doing, and when his phone rang and he saw it was Irwin he considered not taking it—but the man was still technically his boss. "Sorry, Jake. I have to take this."

"No worries, sir."

Drummond raised the separation window. "Hello, Nathan."

Nathan Irwin skipped the greetings. "What's this about Hang Seng Bank?"

"It's taken care of."

"One of their CEOs gets his laptop stolen, and the next thing we know HSBC is selling all its options?"

"What did you think they'd do with the information?"

"Sit on it. That's what I thought they'd do. I've got friends at Hang Seng, you know."

"No, I didn't know that. I also didn't know you were going through all our active case files."

"You expect me to just sit around on the twenty-second floor twiddling my thumbs? I want a sit-down with you on this Hang Seng deal. Try to salvage something from it."

"In the morning, Nathan. You know where to find me."

The senator hung up, leaving Drummond with a bad taste in his mouth.

Jake stopped beside the tower at 200 East Eighty-ninth Street, and Drummond collected his briefcase and climbed out, showing an open hand in farewell. As the Ford sped off, he nodded at the old doorman whose name he never remembered.

The doorman apparently knew who he was. "There's someone waiting for you, sir."

"Yes?"

He nodded at the long couch in the foyer, and Drummond suddenly lost his appetite. Milo Weaver got up to meet him. He wasn't smiling.

"You could've called beforehand," Drummond told him.

"Not sure that's a good idea."

"How did you find out where I live?"

"It's not a state secret, Alan."

Drummond frowned, then looked at the elevator. He wanted to ignore him and take that elevator straight up to the sixteenth floor, to Penelope, but Weaver had the wild-eyed look of someone who wouldn't be ignored. "So why the hell are you here?"

"Can we talk upstairs?"

"Absolutely not. I'm not having my wife get friendly with you."

"Right. Wife," Weaver said, as if he'd forgotten this important detail. He looked over Drummond's shoulder at the doorman, who had returned to the sidewalk but watched them carefully through the glass doors.

"The place isn't bugged, Milo."

Weaver nodded, then wiped at his nose, a move that covered his mouth as he spoke. "We were wrong, Alan. There is a mole, and he's been in place for a while."

"You're a fucking nut, Weaver."

Milo shook his head, his heavy eyes full of conviction. Drummond knew then that a quiet dinner with Penelope was now a vain hope. Maybe Weaver had been right all along—the world really did revolve around him.

Part Three

Is He STILL YOUR HERO?

WEDNESDAY, MARCH 12
TO THURSDAY, APRIL 3, 2008

1

The argument had come to Milo all at once in a voice that his mother would have known. Big. The bigger voice that would never lie to him.

It proved that, no matter what Tina or Bipasha Ray thought, he really had been listening to his wife.

I even take it a step further sometimes and think that maybe his genius lies in the fact that the original cover, the first one I've peeled off and thrown away, that that's *the real one. That I've long ago abandoned what really is Milo Weaver. That it's somewhere in the trash and I'll never find it again.*

How had the sequence of thoughts played out? He wasn't sure. "*Genius*"—that word had probably made him think of Xin Zhu, whom he still admired deeply. Zhu had been on his mind anyway, for over the last days elements from Yevgeny's file had come to him unbidden at unpredictable times. Like in the middle of couples therapy, at the mention of the word "genius." Tina had planted the seed: A genius gives you the real story with the first layer of cover, so that once you've discarded it, it's no longer viable.

Then he remembered her saying, *How much time has to pass before your life stops being classified, huh? It never occurs to you that by then it might be too late.*

Time. Too late.

The inverse: too early.

He recalled Marko Dzubenko and his drunken time with Xin Zhu. On the Chinese New Year, February 7.

But there was one thing this Zhu couldn't figure out, and it irritated him. This Weaver guy. He was the one who figured out what was going on, and as a result everyone wanted him. Homeland Security wanted him for murder. The Company wanted him dead so the story wouldn't get out. But this man, *Zhu said,* he lives the most charmed of lives. He survived. *That really confused him. He said Weaver spent a couple months in prison, and his marriage fell apart, but he did survive. Now, not only was he still living and breathing, he was even working for his old employer again. He wanted to know how he pulled off that trick.*

Then Henry Gray, on Sunday, March 2:

We'd had a ton of progress over the last week . . .

What kind of progress?

Well, we learned what happened to you, for instance.

What happened to me?

You survived, didn't you? Grainger's letter told us you were investigating, but we weren't sure if you were one of the casualties or not. Everyone wanted your ass, after all. You got out of prison and went to live in New Jersey—we knew that—but then you disappeared, and we didn't know until this week that you really were still alive.

How'd you figure that out?

Ask Rick. He came in with the information.

The timing was wrong. Xin Zhu already knew about Milo's return to Tourism, but he waited until that last week with Gray to let the journalist know what he had been aware of all along.

He remembered that part of Xin Zhu's technique was to become the kind of man you would like. For Gray, he was a serious and angry spy. For Dzubenko, he was a drunkard and a womanizer. What if he'd done the same to Milo? Because he did like Xin Zhu, a brilliant spymaster with an acute sense of humor, that quality so lacking in their business. What if Milo's Zhu wasn't the real one either?

None of this, though, would have come to him had he not read that carefully collated file that his father had broken into his apartment to leave for him. His father, it turned out, knew much more about Xin Zhu than Drummond did, and Milo had stayed up until four in the morning, reading about the fifty-seven-year-old man from Xianyang, near the ancient city of Xi'an, who had been swept up by the Cultural Revolution, then eaten by it as his middle-school education landed him in the Down to the Countryside Movement, which sucked up five years of his life, until 1974, farming wheat in Inner Mongolia. He survived, and upon his return went to work for the Central Investigation Division, moving on to the Guoanbu in the eighties. In 1982, he married Qi Wan (1960–1989), and that same year his only child—a son, Delun (1982–2007)—was born.

A two-year posting in Bonn followed, then under different names he spent three years in Moscow and two more each in Jerusalem and Tehran. He returned to Beijing in 1993 and set up shop within the Sixth Bureau, focusing on counterintelligence, which was where he remained to this day. His wife and son had died prematurely—no causes listed—but he had not remarried. There was one known mistress in Guangzhou. According to the file, he was a moderate drinker and smoked rarely, but when he did he preferred a Hamlet brand cigarillo, manufactured in Japan.

There had also been stories, and while sitting in Dr. Ray's office one had come to him, while Tina stared hard.

June 1987. According to source ESTER Zhu was asked by Beijing to acquire Soviet troop positions and battle plans in the Outer Manchuria region, which was accomplished within one week. Zhu's technique, as related to ESTER by another source, was to convince Lieutenant Colonel Konstantin Denisov, then based in Ulan Bator, that his wife, Valera, had discovered the identity of his mistress in Moscow. Denisov returned to Moscow immediately, and his second-in-command, Major Oleg Sergeyev—whose assistant, Lieutenant Feodor Bunin, was in the pay of the Guoanbu before his 1989 discovery and subsequent execution—took over. Bunin, now with complete access, passed the information on to his handlers.

"You're a fucking nut, Weaver."

"I'm afraid not, Alan."

Drummond submitted. He took Milo into the elevator and brought him up to the sixteenth floor, and into his life. There was a petite, rather sensual-looking blonde in the apartment, his wife, Penelope, who was unfazed by the surprise visitor. When Drummond introduced Milo and said, "Pen, we're going to have to use the office for a little bit. You mind bringing us some ice?" she grinned devilishly and replied, "How very fifties, dear."

Once they were settled in a room that was more like a lounge than an office, Drummond opened up a cabinet and started rattling off the names on the bottles. Milo stopped him at Smirnoff; then Penelope came in with a leather-skinned ice bucket. Milo couldn't help but smile. "This really is the fifties," he said to her.

"Golly shucks, it is," she said, winking.

"Thanks, hon," said Drummond.

Milo apologized again for the interruption and watched her close the door behind herself.

Drummond handed over a glass of iced vodka and said, "Great, isn't she?"

"Really is, Alan."

"Flirt with her any more, and I'll have you erased." He sat down with his Scotch, not smiling. "Now explain yourself."

Milo took a breath and began with the time discrepancy, but Drummond blew that off. "One minor detail? Gray probably got it wrong."

"It makes more sense if you step back and look at everything this way, imagining that Zhu does have a mole. Why, for instance, did he give up on his operation when I arrived in Budapest?"

"You said it yourself. He'd made his point."

"That's one way of looking at it. But let's say his sense of humor isn't as excellent as I believed. Guoanbu colonels don't waste all this time—and expense, remember—just to make a point. So what else could he get out of it? If there is a mole, then that means he completed his objectives and wanted Tourism back in operation so that the information he had would be useful."

"What information?"

"The information on how the department works." Milo opened his hands, but Drummond didn't speak, just stared, so he said, "Another curious fact: Zhu knew I was in Budapest. How did he know that? If he wasn't watching your computer tracking me, then he was hearing it through Global Security, the firm that had tracked me there—and they reported directly to Irwin."

Drummond frowned. "You're talking in circles, Milo. Besides, it makes no sense. You don't protect a mole by raising the specter of a mole. Not unless you're going to frame someone else to divert suspicion, which never happened. The fact is that we never suspected the existence of a mole in the department until Zhu started to play with us."

"Of course not. Because there's no mole in the department. There never was."

"Jesus Christ, Milo. Make some sense, okay?"

"The mole is on Nathan Irwin's staff."

All expression washed out of Drummond's face. He leaned back in his chair, shaking his head. "It's not going to work."

"What?"

"This. You're still after him, aren't you? Listen—you think that if you ruin Irwin it's going to make your marriage any better? I've got news for you—"

"No, Alan. You listen. And think. What's the one result of Xin Zhu's operation? What's the one lasting change?"

"It's made me into a permanent joke," Drummond said, then shook his head. "Okay, what's the one lasting change?"

"Irwin in control of the department."

Drummond shook his head. "But he's *not*. Not really. By Friday he and his staff are out of there."

"Which is long enough to get access to all the department's files."

That seemed to make Drummond uncomfortable. "Go on."

"From the beginning, the only operation we were sure Zhu knew about was the Sudanese operation. Right? He knew it inside and out."

"We've been through this—he knew it all from a letter that Thomas Grainger wrote."

Milo set aside his glass. "A beautiful coincidence. It's the one operation that Irwin's people were already familiar with, because Irwin himself ran it. Irwin told me that he knew next to nothing about what the department did before he took over. He stayed far away in order to protect himself. With one notable exception. The Sudan. His inner staff had to know about it."

"Okay," said Drummond, allowing him this one fact, "but by Friday he's out of the department. That's a lot of work for such a limited period of access."

"You're forgetting the other result of the entire game."

"What's that?"

"Myrrh. You recalled everyone—at Irwin's insistence—and he and his staff were around to oversee the redeployment. He knows the names and go-codes of every Tourist you have. If I'm right, so does Xin Zhu."

Drummond stared into his drink and thought through the implications.

"It does make sense, Alan. You just have to look at it. The timing. The details. I keep going over it, and I can't find anything to kill the theory."

Drummond finished his Scotch, refilled it, then opened a humidor full of cigars but didn't take any out. He shut it, then opened it again, a nervous gesture. "Let me get this straight. First you tell me, yes, we have one. Then we don't. Now, you're telling me we do?"

"Not we, Alan. Not you."

"Irwin. Right."

Milo waited.

Finally, Drummond looked at his hands. "Okay. I'm willing to treat it as a serious possibility. The question is, what do we do about it?"

"*We* don't do anything, Alan. I'm not in the department any-more, and I don't want to be. I'm bringing this to you, and I'll help look over some of the files, but I'm not taking part in any sting operation."

Drummond shrugged that off. "I'll bring in a couple of Tourists on the sly."

"How big is Irwin's staff? How many people are we talking about?"

"You met Grzybowski and Pearson—chief of staff and legislative director. There'll be a lot of interns, as well as staff at his district office, but I think there's only five more in the core D.C. group—I can get their names. Only those first two had direct access to the building and met with Tourists, but I'll lay odds Irwin's smuggling copies of files out of the twenty-second floor. In that case, all seven are possibilities."

"Seven," Milo said and sipped his vodka. "Not so many."

"Not so few, either. Not with the kind of hunch you're going on. If I round up seven congressional aides and put John on them, Irwin might just notice the disappearance of his entire staff. If I tell him one of them's a mole, he's going to ask for evidence. What do I do then? Bring *you* in?" He shook his head. "Besides, if you're wrong the department will lose its last ally. Even if you're right about it, Irwin will close us down before John's even put on his gloves." Drummond made a face, as if his Scotch had gone bad. "As much as it pains me, the only way might be to bring in some outside help. I know someone in the Bureau. Good guy, but—"

"But I'll bet he's interested in promotion," Milo said. "When competing agencies start going after each other, friendship goes out the window."

"Yeah," Drummond said into his glass.

"And if you choose another Company department, it'll run straight up to Ascot, or to the Committee on Homeland Security. Either way, the department is dead in the water."

"You almost sound like you give a damn, Milo."

"Almost."

Milo stuck out his glass, and, taking the hint, Drummond refilled it, saying, "We've gotten rid of everyone. If I make it a regular

Tourist case, Irwin will hear about it and the mole will disappear. There's just the two of us and whatever Tourists I can muster without anyone noticing."

"You bring the files," Milo said. "I'll help you work through them. Maybe we can narrow it down. But I'm not sticking around for the whole show."

"We can use the Bronx safe house."

"Good. I don't want to see you in public again. I think Irwin's goons are still following me."

The Scotch stopped halfway to Drummond's mouth. "What?"

"It's not important. We'll just have to be careful."

"Jesus."

Milo didn't share Drummond's anxiety; he wouldn't even later when he was heading home again, feeling the eyes of a young guy with glasses on the same subway car. The fact was that Milo had become the kind of dreaded creature that feels more comfortable evading surveillance and calculating the flow of information than discussing his feelings with a Long Island therapist while the eyes of his wife are on him.

He said, "If so, they saw me come here, but that's fine. I'm visiting my old employer, asking for help finding work. The important thing is that I know they're watching. Hopefully we'll find a way to use that to our advantage."

"Makes me wonder why you're bothering with this at all. Don't you have a marriage to suture back together?"

"Maybe I like you, Alan. Maybe I don't want to see you lose your job. Maybe—and this is sort of disturbing—maybe I really buy your line about making Tourism humane."

"That would make you the only one," Drummond said, then laughed despite himself. He took another sip of his Scotch. "You still like him, don't you?"

"Irwin?"

"No, Zhu."

Milo shrugged. "He's played this brilliantly."

Drummond's smile went away. "Before this is over, I'll lay odds you lose that hero worship."

"We'll call it a bet."

They both looked up at a knock on the door. "Yes?" Drummond called.

Penelope opened the door and knotted her arms. "Fellas, this fifties thing is getting pretty old. Is one of you going to cook me some dinner, or what?"

2

She began angry and, as hours passed and she kept getting recorded messages from his phone, moved steadily into the realm of worry. By the time she was giving Stephanie her bath, the worry was inching closer to panic. She showed none of these conflicting emotions to Stephanie, but children are antennas tuned to the frequency of hidden emotions. Stef knew something was up, and as she wiped shampoo from her eyes she said, "Where's Dad?"

"He had some work to do."

"But he doesn't have a job. He's *unemployed*."

"Don't you think he's trying to find a job?"

"This late?"

"Sure. Why not?"

"Then how come you keep trying to call him?"

Tina blinked at her. She was asking these questions with no particular malice, absentmindedly pushing a plastic power boat around the tub. "I want him to pick up some groceries," Tina lied.

"Why don't you go downstairs and buy stuff?"

"Because I'm giving you a bath."

"I can take my bath myself. I *am* six. I'm big enough."

"No, Little Miss. Not alone in the house you're not."

So it went, distracting Tina from her anger and worry, and once the water in the bath was draining and Stephanie was wrapped in a towel that stretched to her toes, they both heard the front door open, and Stephanie ran out in her towel shouting, "Dad! Dad!"

"Whoa," Tina heard him tell their daughter. "You're going to catch a cold."

As they had done many times during their life together, they temporarily set aside their conflict and focused on Stef. He apologized for missing bathtime, sounding earnest, but it was a sign of her trust issues that she even questioned that.

They finished the drying together, and Milo read a chapter of *Harry Potter and the Sorcerer's Stone* to Stephanie, while Tina took care of the dishes. She set aside a plate of chicken fingers and peas for Milo and placed it inside the microwave and left the door open—she had a feeling that if she didn't, he'd eat it cold. He sometimes became that absentminded when his mind was elsewhere. Once, when he'd been dealing with some particularly vexing problem at the office, he'd even left the house without shoes, not noticing until he'd reached the street.

"She asleep?" she asked when he came out.

"Not yet. She wants to Skype with some friend in Botswana. Did you know she had a friend in Botswana?"

"That's Unity Khama. It's a class project. We used to do pen pals, but these days they don't even know what a pen is."

He snorted a laugh and heated up the dinner.

"So I guess you've got some talking to do," she said.

"Can you wait a sec?"

He left as the microwave bleeped, and when he returned again he was carrying both of their coats. "Here," he said, handing hers over. "Put this on. We'll go upstairs."

"What about Stef?"

"I told her we'd be out a few minutes, and not to unlock the door for anyone. Come on. She'll be fine."

"Why can't we talk here?"

"Can you just indulge me?"

She wasn't entirely sure, but she was willing to try. Dr. Ray had said that mistrust breeds more mistrust, and that the danger of this was that it spiraled out of control, particularly when it remained locked inside you. So she said, "Milo, right now I'm not feeling very indulgent."

"I wouldn't either," he admitted, "but please."

She put on her coat and went back to check on Stephanie, who was talking via video link to Unity, a bright-eyed black girl in Gaborone. They were both laughing, so she left them to their jokes and withdrew.

When they left the apartment, Milo made a show of locking the door from the outside, then led her upstairs to the rooftop-access door, which took a heavy key. A cold evening breeze scattered their hair. She said, "Don't tell me you're afraid of bugs."

"Then I won't tell you. But I'm trying not to hide things from you anymore. You don't deserve it."

"I think I've heard that before."

"A few weeks ago, when I saw Yevgeny in Berlin, he told me that I didn't give people enough credit, least of all you. He was right. You don't deserve that. Come here," Milo said and led her to the edge of the roof. Beyond it rooftops led toward Prospect Park; to the left lights twinkled in the distance, heading toward Manhattan. Milo was pointing directly down, though, to the right, at Garfield Street. "See that Chevy? The blue one."

"Yeah?"

"The guy in it, he's following me. I can't be sure how long, but probably ever since I returned home."

"It's probably just a neighbor," she pointed out.

"Neighbors don't spend the night in their cars."

"Why's he following you?"

"I'm guessing he's working with some people who were following me in Europe. They're working for a senator."

The word "senator" didn't belong in that sentence. "Wh—" she began. "What senator?"

"Nathan Irwin, a Minnesota Republican."

"Fucking Republicans," she muttered.

"It's nothing to be worried about," he assured her. "I'm just trying to explain why we're talking up here. They probably didn't bug our apartment, but I'm not taking chances."

She looked at him, at the Chevy, and then back. The wind was making her eyes water, and she hoped he wasn't going to misinterpret it as weeping. She waited.

"About Dr. Ray's. I'm sorry, really sorry. But when we were talking my mind just switched into autopilot, and I realized something very important. About the department."

"The department you don't work for anymore."

"Yes. But I . . . look. I'm trying to tell you without actually telling you. Not because I'm trying to hide anything, but because it's not the kind of thing you should know. Maybe it wouldn't put you in danger, but maybe it would. I'm not willing to take the chance."

"Then try to make some kind of sense, Milo. Figure it out."

He seemed to accept the gentle scolding; he nodded. "I had to go talk to the new director about it, because if I'm right, then the department is in serious trouble. It could be destroyed."

She could see he was trying, and she appreciated that. "Didn't you tell me the other night that it didn't deserve to exist? What changed your mind?"

"It's easy to say that, but the department's made up of people. You start worrying about all the people who're going to lose their jobs, and some other people who are now in real danger."

"Are you talking about a mole?"

His face went slack, and she knew her stab in the dark had been right. A brief elation filled her, then slid away—did this mean she and Stephanie were in danger now? Milo said, "I'm trying not to lie to you."

"Go ahead. Lie."

"Then, no. Nothing like a mole. Nothing that serious."

She grinned, which gave him license to do the same. She said, "What does this mean?"

He ran his fingers through his hair and gazed across the rooftops. "It means I'm going to have to disappear for a few days. Through the weekend, maybe. But I'll certainly be back by next week."

"Can you at least call?"

"Sure."

"Some good-night calls for Stef might be appropriate. I think she'd appreciate it."

"How do you think she's doing?"

"What? With you back?"

"Yeah," he said, sounding very vulnerable.

The truth was that Tina had noticed how much quieter Stef was when Milo was around, and when he was gone she'd return to her loud, rambling self. It was, Tina had decided, fear—Stef's fear that if she said the wrong thing her dad might pick up and leave again on one of his vague "jobs." Seeing his expression, though, she couldn't tell him this. So she lied. "You know Little Miss. She's beside herself with joy having you back."

"You think so?" Hope slid into his voice.

"Absolutely. But let's not say you're heading out on a job. Let's say you're going somewhere to interview for work. *Capisco?*"

"*Capisco.*"

They remained on the roof a minute more in silence; then he gave her a kiss, and they descended again to find Stephanie still at the computer. Tina told her to say good-bye to Unity, then stepped over to her window and pulled back the blinds. She didn't see the man inside the Chevy, but from this slightly lower angle she did see the window roll down and the quick flash of hand—white, long-fingered—as it tossed out a cigarette that streamed smoke in the middle of the street.

3

That Thursday morning, Alan Drummond raised the window between himself and Jake, and as they struggled through midtown traffic he called Stuart Fossum at Federal Plaza. They'd known each other in the marines, and each had followed a slightly different route into intelligence, Drummond into the CIA, Fossum into the FBI. When he heard Drummond's voice, Fossum laughed aloud. "Alan! Whenever something's about to fall on my head, it's always preceded by the sound of your voice."

"Am I really that predictable?"

"Come be a G-man," Fossum told him. "Leave those back-stabbers to their games."

Though they hadn't spoken since Drummond had taken over Tourism, Fossum acted as if they were still lunching once a week. "Listen, Stu. I need a favor. And I need it quiet."

"What kind of favor are we talking about?"

"Background files on seven people."

"Heavy clearance?"

"Shouldn't be. They're the aides to a senator."

Fossum paused, considering this. "Sounds too easy. Makes me wonder why a man as important as yourself can't just ask his secretary to do a Google search."

"Let's just say it's not as secure as we'd like it to be. If the senator in question finds out I'm looking into his people . . ."

"Gotcha," Fossum said, cutting him off. "You got the names for me?"

After he recited them from the list in his head, Fossum demanded an expensive meal as repayment, and they settled on Le Bernardin on Fifty-first. Then Fossum sighed. "I don't suppose you're ever going to tell me what office you work in, are you?"

"For the price of lunch at Bernardin, I don't need to tell you anything."

"Not even what this is about?"

Drummond had that story ready. "Somebody's been sticking his hand in the campaign cookie jar. We found out about it before the senator, and we'd like to clean it up before he even knows it's happened."

"Sounds like the CIA wants to keep the senator sweet."

"Now you're with the program, Stu."

When he got out of the elevator on the twenty-second floor, he first gazed at the far wall to see that Irwin and his sidekicks weren't around—they seldom arrived before noon, their mornings filled with legislative conference calls—then wound his way slowly through the cubicles, fielding occasional requests along the way. Sally Hein wanted an ergonomic keyboard; she feared carpal tunnel syndrome was encroaching. Manuel Gomez wanted the Company to reimburse him for an expensive lunch he'd had with a source over at the NSA to compare notes on an Iranian mufti. Only Saeed Atassi, a Syria specialist he'd stolen from Defense, had a work-related request. He'd received disturbing intel from a Tourist in Damascus about a Syrian general liaising with an Israeli colonel to derail secret peace talks between the two countries. He'd worked up a Tour Guide on the issue but requested that, because of time constraints, a version be leaked to both governments, thereby skipping the usual route to the Senate committee that took forever to decide what to do with such things. Drummond promised an answer by day's end.

His secretary, a heavyset brunette with a telescopic eye for detail, brought a stack of mail and a coffee to his large oak desk. He thanked her and opened his laptop, starting up a program called Tracker, which was exactly what the name suggested. It tracked the cell phones and shoulder chips of all his Tourists on a world map, giving him a God's-eye view of the breadth of his influence. Red spots peppered the planet, most remaining still while others, on planes or high-speed trains, moved incrementally. When he dragged his cursor over a dot, a simple heads-up display gave him the work name and any recent notes attached to it. A counter along the bottom gave him the total number: thirty-seven.

He'd finished going through his mail and fielding fresh intelligence reports and delivering orders when Irwin breezed into his office. He'd been doing this more often recently, walking through the door without knocking, even when Drummond was on the telephone. The senator approached the windows overlooking Manhattan. To the city, he said, "I don't know how you do it."

"Do what, Nathan?"

"This. Working a mile up above the city. A bubble." He stepped back and frowned at Drummond. "It's not healthy. If you're not mixing with the rabble, then how can you even protect the rabble's interests? You can say a lot of bad things about politicians, but we never forget who we're representing. They have our e-mail addresses, know our names and faces, know where we live. Everything—well, most of the things we do are there for public display. Step out of line, and someone's standing nearby with a sledgehammer."

Drummond pushed back from his desk and examined the senator. Despite the premature whitening of his hair, the man was full of the kind of nervous energy Drummond had seen a lot of in the military. He had youth in his mannerisms, perhaps a result of mixing with the rabble. "You might be right," Drummond admitted. "Instead, we mix with people like you, and trust that you're reporting back on what the rabble really want."

"Not just what they want. What they need."

"Of course. You here about Hang Seng?"

"Later," Irwin said, waving that away. "You seen Milo Weaver recently?"

The question was ill placed because Irwin wanted to see its

effect. Drummond understood this. He'd been expecting the question, though, and it proved that Weaver had at least been right about Irwin's goons following him. "As a matter of fact, he came by last night. Looking for a job."

"He wants back in?"

"Not in a million years. Wanted advice on where to look. I'm sending a recommendation over to Cy Gallagher over at Global Security. You know him?"

"Think we've crossed paths before."

"Well, it's just a recommendation. I have no idea what he's looking for these days."

"I'm sure that even Cy could find a use for Weaver's skill set," Irwin said, then gave him a nod of greeting and wandered out again.

Later, walking to the lunch he'd promised Stuart Fossum, he used his personal phone to call two Tourists. Practicing bad security, he'd scribbled their six-digit go-codes on scrap paper before leaving the office, and read them off. One Tourist he recalled from Bolivia, the other from Mauritania.

He paid for the lunch—Fossum's insistence on seared Kobe beef with a truffled herb salad made the expensive meal ludicrous—with his own credit card. His guest handed over the folder of seven files without a word, then launched into an extended harangue about the CIA. Drummond played along with it, but cut the meal short when his phone rang and he was called back to the office. In fact, it was Milo who called. Sticking to their prearranged signal, Milo said, "Did you talk to your friend Gallagher yet?"

"Not yet. Later in the afternoon."

"Look, I put together a CV last night that I think you should show him. Little more fleshed out. Can I bring it by now?"

"I'm not in the office."

"Can we meet at the Staples in Herald Square? I'm heading there to do up a copy. Then I'm off to Jersey."

"Not staying at home anymore?"

"Just meet me, will you?"

He hopped a bus to Thirty-fourth, three blocks north of the office, and found Weaver in the hectic, crowded store, sitting on a bench with an open knapsack full of stapled sheets. Drummond settled beside him, his open briefcase between them, and started leafing through one of the copies. He was almost surprised to receive an actual CV for Milo Weaver, with dates and fake CIA departments listed, charting a fictional but appropriately slow career advancement. While he read through it, unfolding pages in an elaborate and noisy game of distraction, Weaver removed the seven FBI files from his briefcase and slipped them into his knapsack.

As they went about their ruse, Drummond tried to get a sense of who among the crowd were Weaver's shadows. The blond girl with the pigtails and the backpack? The biker with the handlebar mustache? The effeminate male duo holding posters for a rave? He had no idea.

Weaver was already getting up, telling him he didn't need advice on the CV. He just needed a job. "You get that to Gallagher and let me do the rest, okay?"

"Sure, Milo. I'll do just that."

When he returned to the office, he gave Saeed Atassi the go-ahead to leak his Tour Guide, then went to Harry Lynch's cubicle. The nervous Travel Agent looked terrified by the personal visit. Drummond squatted beside him. "Harry, I hear you're a whiz with the machines."

"I'm all right, sir."

"Well, I need a little wizardry. Soon you're going to see Tourists Klein and Jones start to move. They're coming here. Is there a way you can arrange it so that no one else knows?"

A smile appeared on Harry Lynch's face.

4

In alphabetical order, they were:

Derek Abbott (Legislative Assistant)
Jane Chan (Scheduler)
Maximilian Grzybowski (Chief of Staff)
William Howington (Legislative Assistant)
Susan Jackson (Press Secretary)
James Pearson (Legislative Director)
Raymond Salamon (Legislative Assistant)

It was a small staff by congressional standards, most of the legwork accomplished by a disproportionately large army of interns. What that meant, Milo realized, was that each staff member had a larger share of the federal administrative and clerical employee allowance—and a senator that paid better than others knew he was buying loyalty.

Each of the seven was represented by a manila folder he laid out on the card table in the dusty safe house on Grand Concourse, across from Franz Sigel Park. It was nearly five, and he'd spent the hours after his meeting with Drummond on four different forms of transport, leading his shadows over into New Jersey and then evading them by bus, boat, taxi, and back alleys before doubling back by bus via the George Washington Bridge and heading up to the Bronx. With the evening came a chilly breeze that leaked in through the fire-escape window he'd broken in order to get inside, then covered with cardboard from a still-full crate of toilet paper. Only now could he begin to go through the files.

Each contained biographical information. The one whose name he had obviously zeroed in on, Jane Chan, did still have family in the old country, but in Hong Kong, not the mainland. Still, since China's takeover in 1997, it wasn't inconceivable the Guoanbu had made her family's continued safety contingent on its American relative's cooperation.

Of the rest, Chinese connections were either unknown or, in three cases, tangential. Derek Abbott had previously worked for Representative Lester Wharton of Illinois, until Wharton was arrested for receiving gifts from the Chinese honorary consul in Chicago, in exchange for trade legislation.

Susan Jackson had studied Chinese culture in college and was semifluent in Mandarin—which made little difference when she was arrested in Beijing in 2005 for joining with farmers to protest their land being taken to make room for the Olympic Stadium. China had since denied her any more visas.

James—Jim, he remembered—Pearson had visited Shanghai twice in the last decade for vacations with a Chinese girlfriend he had since broken up with and whose calls he avoided entirely.

At eight, Drummond called to ask if he was making any progress with his job search, and he gave a halfhearted yes but pointed out that there were still too many options. "Well, narrow it down," Drummond said, stating the obvious.

"I could do that," he answered, "but that doesn't mean my criteria are any good." The job search metaphor wasn't perfect, but with a little imagination it could work.

"Maybe you need some help."

"You got anyone?"

"A couple of guys who specialize in placements. They should be in touch by tomorrow afternoon."

"Thanks, Alan."

He put together a dinner of what the safe house had available:
canned cannellini beans, frozen stir-fry vegetables, and rice. For some
reason there was no salt in the apartment, so he made do with a bottle of soy sauce.

As he ate his heavy, bland meal, he felt a wave of doubt. What
did he really have? An inconsistency between stories. A time problem. That was all he really had, in the end. He was acting like Henry
Gray, starting with a conspiracy and rereading all the known facts
so that they fit his theory. It was bad journalism; it was bad intelligence.

Not only were his clues scarce, but he began to question his own
motives. Was he really through with Nathan Irwin? Or was his unconscious taking charge now, creating phantoms in order to target
the senator?

He really didn't know. Regardless, though they were scarce, the
facts did exist, and even Drummond agreed they should be looked
into.

The files, he realized with some despair, would tell him nothing.
There were three primary ways of gaining an asset in a competing
agency: threats, bribery, and ideology. No matter the aides' connections to China, Xin Zhu could have visited any of them with blackmail material, an offer of money, or even an appeal to their political
philosophy. Ever since the start of the Iraq War, plenty of Company
men and women had grown disillusioned with their own employer.
Even Milo had had enough, making him a prime candidate for some
other country's attentions—so why not some senatorial aide?

So if the mole couldn't be discovered, it had to be provoked into
showing itself.

To provoke a mole into showing itself would require his complete involvement.

Though he wanted to believe otherwise, he was already involved. He'd been neck deep in it ever since he chose to sit down and
read that extensive file on Xin Zhu, and he voluntarily submerged
himself when he brought the story to Drummond. He'd even stepped
out of his own life to look into it, while Irwin's thugs kept trying to
track him.

He called Drummond back but heard Penelope's voice. "Hello, Mr. Weaver. He's on the toilet."

"Pen!" Drummond shouted angrily in the background.

"Can you tell him I'm coming by?"

"I suppose so."

"I'll be needing a lift to JFK."

"Are you kidding me, Mr. Weaver?"

"It's Milo. And I'm sorry, Penelope."

"You know what?"

"No. What?"

"It's nice hearing that from someone other than Alan."

On the way to Eighty-ninth Street, he called home. He chatted unspecifically with Tina about his day, then listened to Stephanie describe hers in unending specifics. She wanted to know when he was coming back; she wanted him to teach her karate.

"Karate?"

"Sarah Lawton pushed me on the ground today."

"Did she use karate to do it?"

"I don't know. What does it look like again?"

Drummond was waiting in the foyer, dressed in a long evening coat. Together they took the stairs to the underground parking lot, and Drummond said, "You know this will be noticed, don't you?"

"I'm betting on it."

They climbed into Drummond's personal car, a breathtaking Jaguar E-Type convertible from 1974, and remained quiet until they were out on the street, dealing with the nighttime traffic. "You should probably tell me what's going on."

"The files won't do us any good, Alan. The only way to bring out a mole is to scare him and make him run. From now on, we're going to do this in the open, but make it look as if we're trying to hide it. This is the first step—you driving me to the airport before I fly to Germany."

"Germany?"

"If we were searching for a mole while hiding our movements, we would go to outsiders for help."

"Oh, Jesus. Don't tell me you mean—"

"Exactly. That's the second step. The third step will be the difficult one. For you, I mean."

"How do you mean, difficult?"

Milo had considered not telling him until the last minute, but he had to know that Drummond was going to follow through. Otherwise, there was no point in beginning. "Do you own a gun, Alan?"

5

It was around two on Friday when he reached the stone arch that spanned the creek running through this quaint neighborhood of Pullach. Oskar had been very specific about the locations of the cameras when he led Milo out, and so he knew to drive beyond the bridge and park in the lot of a tiny grocery store, where he bought two premade ham sandwiches as a middle-aged man with a mustache watched him from the cereal aisle. In English, Milo asked for the toilet and was directed outside. Milo passed the mustached man and went around the rear of the building, but instead of entering the bathroom continued ahead and into the damp woods. He worked his way slowly back to the road, then jogged toward the bridge as he reentered the woods. He followed the dry creek bed.

It wasn't as obvious as he'd hoped. From the rear, most of these houses looked deceptively similar, and once he had to wait for twenty minutes in the underbrush as a pair of children played with plastic guns in a yard. When he finally got to Erika Schwartz's house, it was nearly four and he was desperately hungry, so he settled in the bushes around the rear of the house and ate.

Four hours passed. Rain fell intermittently, then darkness, and by the time the headlights appeared in the driveway he was soaked and cold. He waited until the lights switched off and he heard her go inside alone. He rapped steadily on one of the rear windows. It took a while, but he didn't think it was because she couldn't hear; it was simply because she moved so slowly. By the time she switched on the light in the utility room and got him in focus, his knuckles were stinging. She approached but didn't open the door.

"You look like hell," she called through the glass.

"You look radiant, Erika."

She grinned crookedly. "You really shouldn't be here. I could have you killed."

"I've no doubt. You might want to listen to me, though. I told you I'd help you if I could."

"This is how you come to offer help?" She shook her head. "No one stands in the rain just to offer help. You're standing in the rain because you want something from me."

"I'm standing in the rain because I'd like to offer an exchange of services."

She blinked slowly, as if she had all the time in the world, then unlocked the door and stepped back. He came inside, dripping all over the concrete floor. She opened a dryer beside a front-loading washer. "Clothes in there," she said. "I'll bring down a robe." Slowly, she made her way out and closed the door.

As he undressed, the doubt returned. Was this really the only way to scare a mole? He'd used his real passport at JFK, and before his flight took off he saw one of the shadows running to the gate to catch it in time. That one—a young woman with red bangs—had remained with him in the Munich airport before handing him off to the mustached man they must have called ahead to prepare. The man had followed his rental car all the way to the Pullach grocery store, and was probably still there, watching his abandoned car in the darkness.

Maybe it wasn't the only way, but it was having the desired effect. Irwin knew exactly where Milo Weaver was. Thus, the mole did, too.

The robe Schwartz brought down was soft and thick and very pink, and as he slipped it on she turned on the dryer, ignoring his nakedness. "Do you have something to drink?" he asked.

"I only bought one wine."

"Just water, Erika. I'm thirsty."

They went upstairs to the living room, passing the steel door to the panic room, and settled in the darkness. Schwartz made no move to turn on any light. She went to the kitchen and brought out a bottle of Evian, two wineglasses, and her bottle of Riesling. "So," she said as they each began to drink. "You have come to offer me your wonderful service."

"Something like that."

"Well, I'm flush with excitement."

Milo didn't launch into it yet. Instead, he said, "I hear Conference Room S is finally in service."

"How did you hear about that?"

"You did tell me to ask my own people, didn't you?"

She raised her eyebrows. "A delegation of Americans arrived today. You know what I told Oskar when they arrived with their bright ties and big smiles and vigorous handshakes?"

"What?"

"That we've finally learned the value of a girl's life."

Milo nodded into his water. "When's the next delegation due?"

"Monday. They have a lot of catching up to do."

"Good."

"Is it?"

Milo examined her heavy, damp cheeks in the light from the street, then noticed that on the cushion beside her hand was a small pistol. She looked exhausted. He said, "Everything stays in this room. Agreed?"

Erika Schwartz shrugged.

"A few weeks ago," he said, "there was a scare in the department. We had reason to believe there was a double agent working among us."

"Double agent?" asked Schwartz. "For whom?"

"For the Chinese."

She waited.

"We followed the clues, but they didn't add up. Or, they did, but they proved there wasn't one at all."

Schwartz waited patiently.

"Now, though, it appears that we were twice fooled. We believe we do have a mole."

Schwartz appeared unfazed. "We? I heard you had left the CIA."

"It's a figure of speech."

"Sounds like a CIA problem to me."

"I'm afraid it's your problem, too, Erika. Which is why I've come to you. The Company now has access to a lot more of your secrets than it did a month ago, and, ergo, so do the Chinese."

"Thanks to a young girl."

Milo didn't say a thing.

She said, "Are you here just to deliver bad news?"

"We'd like your help with this problem."

"We, again. Who is this abstract pronoun, exactly?"

"Myself, and Alan Drummond."

Schwartz blinked at him, blank, her eyelids a confusion of tiny wrinkles when they closed. Then, even in the darkness, she found a loose hair on the thigh of her slacks and brushed it away. "The CIA employs twenty thousand people—that's the number it will admit to. Is there really no one else you can go to? Not one?"

Milo didn't answer.

Schwartz took a long breath. "You began this conversation by suggesting you had something to offer me. Maybe you should start with that."

"We'll give you the means to bring down Theodor Wartmüller. The videotape."

"Of him with the girl?"

Milo nodded.

Schwartz found another hair on her slacks, picked at it with her stubby fingers, and said, "If you'd asked me a week ago, I would have told you that the videotape was the only thing I wanted. Now I've had some time to think. If it goes public, it'll cause more grief than solutions. Theodor knows that, too. I'm not sure it's of any use to me now."

"You don't want it?"

"I didn't say that. I'd rather I held on to it than you. I'm simply saying that it won't solve my troubles. And it certainly won't bring down Teddy."

"Then I'll give you other means," said Milo.

"You have other means just sitting around?" A slow grin grew on her face, and she sighed. "Of course you do. Frame-ups are child's play for the Department of Tourism."

Milo felt her watching his face for some reaction. He gave none, and Schwartz finally shook her head.

"That's not enough."

"What is enough?"

"The person who broke her neck."

"That's not up to me."

"Then call Alan Drummond right now and ask him."

They both knew calling wasn't an option, so Milo said, "I'll give you the name myself. All right?"

Schwartz nodded slowly, very serious. "So, to be clear. I will receive the original videotape, the identity of Adriana Stanescu's killer, and the means with which to prosecute Theodor Wartmüller."

Milo wondered if it was really worth it. He supposed it was, but for all this she would do only one small thing. "Yes," he said. "That's right. Now can I tell you what you're going to do to earn all these riches?"

"I am breathless, Milo. Really, I am."

6

He landed at noon and took a taxi back into town, thinking over his escape route. The woman with the red bangs had been on his flight, ten rows up, and while he wanted them to know where he'd been, he didn't want them knowing his destination: the Bronx safe house, which would now be housing two Tourists.

He peered back at the highway. It was a busy time of day, and any of the cars could have been on him—or none. So he asked the driver to take him to Williamsburg and the Hasidic neighborhood he and Tina used to visit for Israeli specialties—any shadow would look as out of place there as he would. However, once they reached the long, lifeless streets, Milo remembered that it was Saturday; this part of Williamsburg was abandoned. It wasn't the kind of place to try to lose a shadow.

"Bedford and Seventh," he told the driver.

As they headed north, the streets filled with hip young Brooklynites at sidewalk tables, munching bagel sandwiches and sushi. He got out in front of a Salvation Army thrift store, then crossed Bedford and bought a Coke at a corner market beside the L-train subway stop. He peered out the window.

"Twenty-five cents," the woman behind the register said as she handed over his change.

There: An old Suzuki pulled up in front of the Salvation Army.

A tall black man got out and stood beside his door, watching faces. If he was irritated, he didn't show it.

"You need something else?" asked the woman.

The man left his car and walked left, toward Sixth, and Milo hurried out, took the corner and descended into the subway. As his head sank beneath the sidewalk, the black man turning, scanning, caught his eye.

Milo used his MetroCard as the train arrived at the station. His shadow ran up to the turnstile, stopping, slapping his pockets. Cursing. The subway doors closed. Milo smiled as the train headed out.

The L-train had the advantage of crossing five different lines inside Manhattan, and he chose one at random, then crisscrossed the island, taking locals and expresses until he was sure he was alone. In the Bronx, he picked up groceries—instant noodles and bread and ham and coffee—and by the time he finally climbed the stairs to the safe house, the sun was setting. He listened at the door but heard nothing. He knocked and waited.

There was a quick shadow over the spy hole, and a man's voice said, "We're not buying anything."

"The Word of God is free," Milo said.

There was an awkward pause.

"Let me in," Milo said. "It's Weaver."

Another pause; then the man unlocked the door and opened it a crack. He had dark eyes. "Riverrun, past Eve," he said.

"And Adam's," Milo answered. "Come on."

The Tourist at the door introduced himself as Zachary Klein. He was a big man who gave off the air of a dunce, though no Tourist is a dunce. The other was a distractingly attractive black woman named Leticia Jones who didn't rise from the cot as she offered a hand. She had huge eyes and a mirthless smile. "You going to brief us, or what? If I have to spend another night with this lout you'll have to call an ambulance."

"Drummond hasn't told you anything?"

"He said to wait for you," Klein told him.

Milo began to unpack his groceries, then saw that the refrigerator and cabinets were already full. "You guys went out?"

"I told her not to," said Klein.

"I'm not eating canned food," said Jones. "That's just not what I do."

"See what I've had to deal with?" said Klein.

"This cracker will eat anything."

Milo almost started to laugh. Despite his easy camaraderie with James Einner, it was a general rule that Tourists should work alone. He'd even tried to explain it in the Black Book, writing, *It's part of the essential nature of Tourism that Tourists cannot abide one another. In the extremely rare instance that two Tourists strike up a friendship, it's over in two weeks, max.*

> We are taught, and we learn through experience, that everything and everyone is a potential hazard. Children, butchers, seamstresses, bank managers and particularly other intelligence agents. We're taught this because it's true. The better the intelligence agent, the bigger the threat. So what happens when two Tourists—two of the most devious models of intelligence agent the world has seen—are in the same room? Paranoia ensues, and the walls go wet with blood.

Happily, though, the walls were still clean, and both Tourists were still breathing. The only way to defuse the situation was to give them a reason to be here, so he took them to the files both of them had already no doubt memorized. "One of these is a Chinese mole."

"Yeah," said Jones. "It's Chan."

"Look who's the racist," said Klein.

"Shut up."

"Both of you shut up, okay?"

They stared at Milo.

"Good," he said. "Now can you please break into these people's homes and find out what's not listed in these files? They have to be done by Monday morning. And please don't leave a mess. If the mole thinks we're tossing his apartment, he's going to walk before we've identified him."

"What exactly are we looking for?" asked Klein.

"Use your imagination."

As if they'd been replaced with new people, Klein and Jones were suddenly professional and efficient. That was how Tourists worked—with a job in front of them, they were swift and effective; lacking any work, they were destructive and wasteful, many turning into prima donnas. In this case, Klein and Jones began with a map of the Washington, D.C., area, charting a path from Montgomery County down to Charles County. Despite their animosity, they decided to work together on each home in order to move more quickly. By eight, they had settled on the details and had left the safe house to take separate trains to D.C., and Milo was alone again. He called home and chatted with Stephanie, and then Tina, who asked if he didn't want to just come over for a few hours. She said that he was missed. It was intoxicating stuff, and the lure of their shared bed, just a subway ride away, was incredibly tempting.

Afterward, he called Drummond.

"Your friends are gone now. They should be done by Monday."

"But they'll be in touch in the meantime?"

"They've got my number."

"Let me know if the skies open up for you at any point."

"Are you still on board, Alan?"

"Ask me again after you've collected your information. Maybe I won't need to do a thing."

"Don't bet on it."

"I'm not betting on anything anymore."

Milo's phone woke him at five in the morning. Klein and Jones had gotten to work quickly, and it was Jones who called in their first report. Milo looked for a pen and paper while she rattled off her information. "William Howington. Twenty-eight, white male—"

"Don't tell me what I already know," Milo cut in.

"The man's got a serious cocaine habit going on. Plus a bucket of ecstasy—looks like he uses them as breath mints."

Drugs were a compromising habit, but enough to make someone spy for a foreign power? "What else?"

"He's writing a novel. Roman à clef, if I understand the opening.
Who do you think Representative Albert Sirwin could be?"

"That's interesting, but not what we're looking for."

"Too bad," said Jones. "Six more to go."

They called in Raymond Salamon's search by noon Sunday, and
Susan Jackson's by three. Salamon's apartment was clean—"*too* clean,"
Klein suggested—while Jackson's was stuffed with Chinese artifacts.
She was the one who had studied Chinese culture, had visited Beijing,
and even been kicked out of China for her demonstrations in support of landless farmers. There were letters and postcards in Mandarin stacked on her desk, and Leticia Jones—who, it turned out, was
fluent—went through them quickly, checking for obvious signs of
clandestine communication. Of course, it's the nature of clandestine
communication that it's not obvious, so she settled on taking snap-
shots of a representative selection for later perusal. From photos and
postcards, they did learn of a lover—Feng Liang, a Beijing University student who had been arrested with her. There were letters from
him and aborted drafts to him, and on her computer they found an
entire romantic history in the form of e-mails.

Maximilian Grzybowski and Derek Abbott were roommates,
sharing a loft in Georgetown. Klein and Jones waited for them to
head out for their Sunday night thrills and spent a couple of hours
perusing an extensive DVD collection of pornography and action
thrillers, then worked their way through the laptops. Neither kept
any sensitive information, though Grzybowski did have a hidden
folder that, once Klein figured out the password, turned out to be
full of more pornography—gay pornography. A decade or two ago,
the threat of this becoming public might have been reason enough
to spill classified secrets, but no longer.

After one on Monday morning, they made it to Jane Chan's
apartment—curiously empty—and discovered what they were half-
expecting to find, extensive mementos of Hong Kong. Family pictures, letters and e-mails, and packages of gifts she'd received from
her uncles, aunts, and cousins. Besides Susan Jackson's love affair, it

was the most damning material they had come across. Both women, so far, seemed the most open to coercion.

They also discovered that Jane Chan was carrying on an affair with the last person on their list, James Pearson, the legislative director Milo had met in Drummond's office with Max Grzybowski. She had photographs of the two of them together, sometimes in various stages of undress, dated as far back as December. Jones offered her assessment. "If I was a mole, I'd certainly start screwing someone senior to me. Best way to get what you're not supposed to have."

It was a good point, and when they went over to Pearson's apartment in Alexandria they found that Chan was sharing his bed. Jones left to collect Starbucks coffees for herself and Klein, and when, at seven, Pearson and Chan left looking like a perfect couple and climbed into Pearson's Mazda to head to work, they moved in.

Pearson's apartment, besides the smell of sex in the bedroom, was as clean as Raymond Salamon's had been, so they could focus almost entirely on his laptop, which used two-factor authentication and 128-character pass phrases. Klein, though, had spent part of his youth as a hacker and needed about an hour and a half before shouting, "Eureka!"

His excitement was short-lived. The security was there only to protect Pearson's personal life, his photos and family e-mails and his . . . poems. There were more than two hundred poems, ranging from haiku to terza rima, in a folder named, unimaginatively enough, VERSE. Most focused on history and love. There was nothing damning here, and the best they could manage was to notice what was missing—among the photographs of friends and family and even the Chinese ex-girlfriend with whom he'd twice visited Shanghai, Pearson had no photographs of himself with Jane Chan, though Chan's photos went back three months. "The man's obviously got yellow fever," Jones told Milo during her call, "but Chan's got no future with him."

"Or maybe he doesn't want any evidence of their relationship on his computer," Milo suggested. "Irwin probably frowns on his aides dating."

Jones wasn't convinced. "No, honey. He's just not that into her."

It was peculiar, but in the end not peculiar enough to matter, nor to give Milo any insight. While the two women—Chan and Jackson—were their primary suspects, the truth was that it could be any of them.

7

Oskar had spent Monday morning filing background checks; it was the one dependably steady job since Erika had committed her transatlantic career suicide two years before. He sometimes recalled Franz's advice—*Schwartz has had her time, Oskar. There's no need to be on hand to witness the collapse*—and reexamined his reasons for sticking with a boss whose end was always nigh. Other times, though, he discounted it entirely, seeing Franz for what he really was: Theodor Wartmüller's lapdog, terrified of losing scraps from his master's table. Today, while visiting the office Franz shared with the now absent Brigit, he saw Franz as something in between the extremes.

"Here's last week's vetting reports."

Without looking up from his laptop, Franz said, "It's Monday, Oskar. That makes you a weekend late."

"I was otherwise occupied."

"Were you?"

Franz sometimes sustained entire conversations without looking up, so Oskar wasn't dissuaded by the sight of the man's thinning scalp. "Is Theodor in?"

Franz raised his head. It was that, the attention, that set Oskar's nerves on edge. "He's in a meeting. In S."

"Right. The Americans."

"Yes."

Franz returned to his screen, but Oskar didn't move. Finally, he looked at Oskar again. "Was there something else?"

"Could you call him out of the meeting?"

Franz laughed in a way that suggested laughter was unfamiliar, and not entirely comfortable. "You must be kidding!"

"It has to do with the Americans."

"Then you can tell him after they've left."

Oskar shook his head. "It might be useless by then."

"You really are a riddle, Herr Leintz."

"Well?"

"Well, do it yourself. I'm not taking responsibility for interrupting him."

Oskar withdrew and in the corridor passed the young, pretty secretaries that, despite his devotion to Rebecka, the Swede, he always chatted up in the break room. Now, he gave each a smile that few returned. They knew he didn't belong up here on the second floor. Ahead, he saw old Jan stepping into Conference Room S with a tray of cups. He jogged to catch up and caught the door before it closed.

Inside, men were laughing. He took in their faces, a broad spectrum of American types. The spectacled academic, two big football players, one business elite, even two black faces and an Asian—Japanese, he guessed—face. Seven. Plus Theodor Wartmüller at the head of the table, shaking his flushed face at some joke, and Brigit Deutsch in a knee-length skirt and high heels, leaning against the end of the table, basking in the attention all these men were giving her.

As Jan silently replaced empty coffee cups with full ones, Oskar peered through the slit in the door, finally catching Brigit's eye. Her joy seemed to dissipate, replaced by . . . could it be embarrassment? Then she got hold of herself and gave Oskar a short, sharp shake of the head. He didn't withdraw. Instead he motioned at Wartmüller, and waited.

Finally, she bowed to Wartmüller's ear and whispered. Wartmüller found Oskar in the doorway. His smile remained as he said, "Just a moment, gentlemen," and got up.

There was no anger when he came out into the corridor, just

condescension. "Oskar! I can't say you've chosen the best time for a chat."

"Sorry, sir, but it couldn't wait."

"It couldn't wait another half hour?"

"It couldn't wait until the Americans had left."

A pair of secretaries passed, and Oskar moved closer to the room's window, covered by venetian blinds. Wartmüller followed him. "Well?"

"Listen, I . . . I don't feel entirely comfortable coming to you with this, but I don't have a choice. Loyalty only goes so far, and then you have to start answering to your conscience."

Wartmüller eyed him. "What are you getting at, Oskar?"

"It's Erika. She's been taking things into her own hands. Things that you should be aware of, particularly if you're speaking openly with the Americans."

"Please, Oskar. Time is precious."

He took a long, exaggerated breath. "Last week—Friday—she met with Milo Weaver."

"Milo—why?"

"They've formed an alliance. I can't say what Erika's getting out of it—she won't tell me—but I do know that she's helping Weaver investigate a mole in the CIA."

Wartmüller considered that for a moment, though in the end he simply repeated the word. "Mole?"

"A Chinese mole. When I asked her what this had to do with us, she said that until the mole was tracked down, everything we said to the Americans would end up in Beijing. So I told her—I said that we had to bring you in. Otherwise, you wouldn't know what to hold back."

"And what did she say to that?" Wartmüller said distantly, a finger brushing his chin.

"She said that you would get in her way. Just to spite her. She said that you would stop her from talking to them."

"To whom?"

"To the men in the room right now. She's waiting for them in the parking lot."

Wartmüller rubbed his eyes with the knuckles of his right hand. "You're telling me that Erika's standing outside, waiting to tell the Americans that they've got a mole?"

"Yes, sir."

Then he said exactly what Erika had said he would say. "Listen, Oskar. I want you to tell me everything you know about this mole theory. What department? How long has he been around?"

Oskar shook his head. "She's only told me what I've told you. Except . . ."

"Except what?"

"She wanted me to pull up everything we have on an American senator. Nathan Irwin. Republican."

"Okay," said Wartmüller, thinking through all of this.

"It's hard," said Oskar.

"Certainly is."

"No, I mean this. Going behind her back. I don't want you to think this is how I treat my superiors."

Wartmüller got a distant look again; then he focused and smiled grimly, placing a heavy hand on Oskar's shoulder. "Oskar, listen to me. You have no reason to feel guilty. Understand? You've done the right thing."

"Thank you, sir. That helps."

An hour later, when he was back at his desk, Erika came in slowly, moving her immense body from support to support—the doorway, the back of a chair, the corner of his desk. She said, "It's freezing outside."

"It is," said Oskar.

"Any idea if Wartmüller's visitors have gone yet?"

"I believe they left about twenty minutes ago."

"Hmm." She moved back to her chair, both hands gripping it. "I suppose someone showed them the rear exit. You think that's possible, Oskar?"

"Yes, ma'am," he said, smiling. "Anything's possible."

8

The call came through at 1:23 P.M. on Tuesday, while Drummond was in the conference room, discussing with the fraud section the movement of funds between three banks—Cayman, Swiss, and Pakistani—and its connection (recently discovered by Malik Tareen, a Tourist who'd been in Lahore for nearly six months) to an Afghan tribe known to be hosting Taliban fighters. Unlike his predecessors, Drummond brought in two advisers from the director's office to listen and offer advice on the next step, and it was generally agreed that while Tourism could squelch the money trail, the army should be brought in to deal with the tribe. Since the army didn't know of Tourism's existence, the information would have to flow through the deputy director of the National Clandestine Service, who was one of the few people below the director's office cleared to have knowledge of Tourism.

With Irwin back in Washington, this was Drummond's second day as absolute sovereign, and it had been a beautiful day so far—no bad news had come through, no signs of impending disaster—and then his secretary told him of the call on line twelve. His mind was still on banking when he answered, and his "Drummond here" had none of the force it usually carried.

"It's me," said Milo.

Drummond blinked at Ascot's men, who pretended not to be listening in. "Yes. How's the job search coming?"

"I'm heading to an interview in D.C. right now. You're on."

"Okay," he said, but Weaver had already hung up.

He wrapped up the meeting and returned to the floor to find Harry Lynch hunched over his keyboard, the remnants of a tuna sandwich all over his desk. "Harry, can you come to my office?"

"Uh, sir. Yes."

He got up and followed Drummond to the far end of the floor, and once they were inside Drummond said, "Shut it, please."

Lynch closed the door.

"Sit down. Please."

Cordial behavior always seemed to trouble Lynch, and he lowered himself into a chair slowly, as if anything faster would lead to a reprimand.

"Thanks for taking care of those recalls for me, Harry. Are we still under the radar?"

Lynch nodded. "I've moved them around occasionally so no one will think they're comatose."

"Good idea. I've got one more thing to ask—can you flag seven passports so that no one else in the building knows about it?"

"Virtual keyboard," said Lynch, shrugging.

"Excuse me?"

"I open a virtual keyboard on the screen and use the mouse to type my instructions. That way, the in-house keystroke recorder doesn't pick it up."

"Sounds simple," Drummond said.

Lynch didn't answer either way.

Drummond unfolded his wallet, took out a slip of paper, and handed it over. "Here are the passport numbers. I'll need you to put my personal cell phone down as the initial contact, and the order is to hold the person until I've arrived."

"No problem."

"Or," Drummond began, thinking through everything. "Me, or Milo Weaver."

Lynch blinked a few times. "Milo's still around?"

"Advising. And that, too, stays between you and me. Got it?"

"Yes, sir." Lynch grinned happily, his discomfort gone, and Drummond felt a pang of jealousy—the mention of his own name would lighten the moods of very few people.

Once Lynch was gone, he picked up his phone, but before he could dial, Irwin called on line seven. "That's funny, Nathan. I was just about to call you."

"Hilarious," said Irwin. "Say, do you know how I can get in touch with Weaver? He's not answering his phone."

"No idea, sir. I haven't talked to him since last week."

"He say anything about going to Germany?"

"No . . . Why would he be in Germany?"

"Well, if you do hear from him, tell him I might have found some consulting work. Good pay and benefits. Tell him to call me."

"I'll do that. Say, are you going to be free this evening?"

A pause. "Why?"

"Because I'm heading to D.C. now, and I wanted to go over some departmental issues with you."

"Don't think so," said Irwin. "The Democrats are holding some so-called nonpartisan dinner; they're insisting I come."

"You might want to skip it."

"Why's that?"

"Because I want to talk to you about Milo Weaver."

"Weaver—but you just said—"

"It's not the kind of thing we can discuss over the phone."

Irwin paused. "Okay, then. You come by my Georgetown place at eight."

"I'm going to need you to come to me. I'll be at the Washington Plaza."

"You're being very mysterious, Alan. I don't think I like that at all."

"Sorry, sir. But I'll need you to come to me. It's the only way I'll feel safe."

"Now I'm completely confused. Why wouldn't you feel safe in my house?"

"It'll all make sense this evening. Eight o'clock, like you said, but at the Plaza. I'll call you with the room number so you don't have to ask the desk for it."

Milo reached Union Station by five, then took a taxi to Thomas Circle NW, where he met Klein and Jones in the Washington Plaza's lounge, the International Bar, where *From Russia with Love*—the best of the cinematic Bonds—played on the flat-screen behind the bar. The film matched the sixties decor, but no one among the after-work business crowd was watching it. They took a leather U-shaped booth against the wall, and Milo ordered a round of coffees. Then he handed out cheap cell phones he'd picked up the day before. "Take apart your Company phones and use these."

"You don't think that's overkill?"

"We're not taking any chances. And we'll maintain continual contact," he told them. "These are answered on the first ring."

"He talks like we're schoolkids," muttered Klein.

Jones smiled, her full lips spreading flatly over her teeth. "Hmm. A schoolmaster."

He wasn't entirely sure they were taking this seriously enough, but Drummond had assured him that these were two of his best Tourists. They seemed to enjoy their roles—Klein, the grumpy dunce; Jones, the exotic seductress. "We're going in order of suspicion, least to greatest." Since there were only seven names, there was no need for note-taking. They knew who each was and where each lived, and all that was required of these Tourists was that they locate and follow each one, calling Milo if any strayed from his or her expected route.

Once they'd gone through the sequence, Leticia Jones called over a waiter and asked for a gin martini. In answer to Milo's look, she said, "I'm not staying up all night without at least one drink."

"I didn't say anything," Milo countered.

So Klein started waving for another waiter. "I'm having a beer, then."

Milo resisted the urge, even as he stared jealously at Jones's drink. At seven, he got up to pay the bill, then told them to go. Jones touched his arm as she left, saying, "Chill out, baby. Mommy and Daddy will take care of you."

He watched her sashay around tables on her way out, garnering appreciative male gazes the whole way.

Drummond left work early to take the Acela Express from Penn Station, which got him to D.C. by seven. Stuck on the crowded train, steamy from the heat of so many bodies, he kept wishing he'd taken his Jag. Even in light traffic, though, speeding whenever possible, it would have taken him nearly four hours. It wasn't a day for chancing tardiness. So he endured the trip and waited in line for a taxi to Thomas Circle and checked into the Washington Plaza under his own name. On his way up to the room he called Irwin. "Room 620."

The senator sounded rushed and uncomfortable. "You going to give me a hint, Alan?"

"You'll find out soon enough."

"This better be worth the inconvenience."

When he got to the room, Drummond removed a tiny Scotch from the refrigerator, and as he unscrewed it the room phone rang. Milo said, "Where?"

"Six twenty."

The line went dead.

Drummond threw back the Scotch, then unpacked his briefcase. There were some loose files and, beneath them, wrapped in a gray bath towel, his pistol.

It was an M9 the service pistol the marines had handed him, which they'd switched to in the late eighties in order to create uniformity with NATO firearms. A good weapon, it had never jammed, though when he'd been issued it the etched metal grip had irritated him. That only took a month to adjust to, though, and when he picked it up it felt as natural as grabbing his other hand in prayer.

Yet once he'd rechecked the full clip and cleared the breech, he went back for the second, and last, Scotch. With a background that included two miserable years in Afghanistan, the prospect of using the pistol didn't disturb him; using it in a D.C. hotel room on a senator did. Particularly when the reasoning was based on a single agent's epiphany.

Yet the epiphany was too damaging to ignore, so he placed the M9 on the dresser, behind the television, and checked his watch. It was seven fifty-two.

Downstairs, Milo had watched Drummond arrive, and, after asking the front desk to patch him through to his room and getting the room number, he took a position at the far end of the foyer with a bouquet of flowers he'd purchased at the gift shop. He checked his wristwatch continually so that the staff would imagine he was waiting on a late date and leave him alone.

Irwin arrived focused on the space in front of himself, so Milo didn't need to hide behind his flowers. Irwin, crossing to the elevators, looked like a man with an unpleasant but necessary task ahead of him, someone who wanted to get it over with as quickly as possible.

Milo waited. No obvious shadows had preceded Irwin, and for the next five minutes no one else appeared. He got up and went to the elevators, but stepped back to let a family go up alone. He waited for the next one and took it to the sixth floor. He knocked on room 620 and heard voices—Drummond: "Can you get that, Nathan? Room service"—then the door opened. Senator Irwin, shocked, stared back. Behind him, Drummond was moving to the television.

"What the hell?" said Irwin. "Alan? What the hell have you—" He stopped in midsentence, because he'd turned to find Drummond pointing a gun at him.

Milo stepped inside and locked the door. He said to Drummond, "You didn't tell him yet?"

"Tell me what?" Irwin demanded.

Alan Drummond looked uncomfortable, but he held the pistol like a pro, his hand steady. "Sit down, Nathan. We just want you to make a few phone calls."

9

The first was Raymond Salamon. Despite the fifteen-minute fight the senator put up, threatening them both with things worse than expulsion, he finally called Salamon and put on his most authoritative voice. "Ray, you'd better get your ass down to Thomas Circle. Now. I've got some Company guys who need to talk to you."

"CIA? What—what's this about?"

"You tell me, Ray. What've you been doing that these thugs are looking for you?"

"I—*nothing*, sir."

"Well, if that's true, then there's nothing to worry about. Just get down here five minutes ago, wait in front of the Washington Plaza, and we'll get it all straightened out."

"Okay."

"And Ray? Don't you dare tell anyone else about this. Not yet. We clear?"

"Yes, sir."

Salamon was true to his word. He arrived in a swift ten minutes, and Milo approached him in the drop-off area that was busy with taxis and bellboys. "Raymond Salamon?"

"Uh, yes," he said.

"Right this way."

He led the frightened aide into the hotel, and in the elevator

Salamon tried to ask questions. Milo answered with hard silence. When they finally made it to room 620, Salamon relaxed visibly at the sight of Irwin, and Irwin gave him a grudging wink. "I knew you were a straight shooter, Ray."

"Your phone, please," said Milo.

"Go ahead, Ray. Give the man your phone. And settle down on the chair. We're in for a long night."

Because Maximilian Grzybowski and Derek Abbott lived together, Klein was stationed outside their apartment waiting for one to leave. When Abbott stepped out, Klein called in, and Irwin dialed Abbott's number. The same sternness, but with a few more fraternal quips—Abbott was clearly one of Irwin's favorites. The same orders, though: Come immediately to the Washington Plaza to speak to the CIA. Tell no one.

Fifteen minutes later, Milo was leading Abbott into the hotel, and Irwin was calling Grzybowski. While they waited, Abbott kept asking Salamon what he knew, and Salamon shrugged meekly. Abbott said, "What's the deal?"

"The *deal*," Irwin snapped, "is that I'm being forced to do this, and I'm not going to believe the charges until these men have proved them to me. And if they don't prove them, then their careers are in the toilet."

When Grzybowski joined them, though, he showed none of the patience the first two had been demonstrating. He, unlike them, had spent time in the Department of Tourism, and knew that the man holding the pistol was just another bureaucrat. "Didn't I tell you, sir? Drummond couldn't stand losing control of his department, and he was bound to get you back for the humiliation. Jesus. Like fucking high school."

It was eleven o'clock by the time Milo met William Howington at the opening of the hotel's looped drive, behind a line of four taxis. He was the first not to immediately follow him into the hotel. "I don't know who the hell you are."

"Irwin said to meet him here, right? I'm taking you to him."

Howington wouldn't be convinced until he'd called to receive a direct order from Irwin. When they reached the room, his mouth hung open. "Is this a surprise party?"

Milo had not expected any revelations by this point. Though anything was possible, these four men had nothing in their files to suggest they could be working for Zhu. Of the remaining three— Susan Jackson, Jane Chan, and James Pearson—all had had some sort of connection to China, but only the women still had emotional ties to that area: Jackson to mainland China, Chan to Hong Kong. Of those two, Milo's suspicions rested more with Jackson, who could be used to keep her lover, Feng Liang, safe. Chan had family that could have been used as collateral, but Milo doubted a man with Zhu's labyrinthine mind would choose an Asian to spy for him.

So his preference was to call Jackson last, but there was a problem. According to Leticia Jones, Chan and Pearson were spending the evening in with some DVDs and delivery pizza. If they called Pearson, he would have to tell Chan where he was going, and Chan—if she were the mole—would be tipped off. Call Chan first, and the same would be true of Pearson.

Klein, who had been watching Jackson's apartment for the previous hour, told Milo that she had gone to bed alone. "Go ahead," Milo told Irwin. "Call Jackson."

He woke her up. "Susan, you need to get down here right away."

"I just fell asleep. What is it?"

"It's your career. Now get dressed and meet me at Thomas Circle. The Plaza. The CIA needs to talk with you."

"CIA? Why?"

"They think you've been a bad girl, Susan—and they're doing a hell of a job convincing me. So get down here and start arguing your side, and don't call anyone else about this until it's been cleared up. Understood?"

All the lights in the apartment came on. It took Jackson eleven minutes to dress in sweats and climb into a waiting taxi. Klein followed most of the way, until it let her off on the sidewalk outside the hotel. Milo was already waiting for her, talking with Klein on the phone. "Go join Jones. Once you're in place we'll finish this up."

Jackson, too, doubted Milo was who he said he was, so rather than manhandle her he waited for her to call Irwin. On their way inside, she said, "What do you think I did?"

His phone was ringing. It was Jones. "Pearson is leaving. He looks nervous."

"Panicked?"

"No, just nervous. He's checking his watch."

"The woman's still in there?"

"Yes. But Klein won't be here for another five or ten minutes."

"Stay with her," Milo ordered. If they called Pearson while he was out, the legislative director would likely still call Chan, if only to explain why he wasn't returning—they were lovers, after all. "We'll call Chan next."

He hung up, and as they waited for the elevator, Jackson said, "Jane Chan?"

He looked at her.

"You're going to call Jane Chan next? What kind of game is this?"

They boarded the elevator. Milo said, "It's not a game."

"It certainly isn't. If you think Jane's some kind of criminal, or terrorist, then you're completely insane."

"It's not that simple."

Jackson was angry now. "You wake people up in the middle of the night to interrogate them? That's Gestapo tactics. And the CIA doesn't even have the authority to screw around with people inside the country. What the hell is going on?"

He wasn't sure why—perhaps because he'd suspected her so strongly, or because she had a history of clashing with the Chinese authorities—but he answered her. "We're looking for a Chinese mole. It's one of Irwin's seven aides, which is why we called you."

She blinked as the doors opened on the sixth floor. "Jane?"

"She and Pearson are our final suspects."

"*Oh.*"

She said that with a strange, unexpected despair. "What?"

"I called her."

"Chan?"

She nodded. Milo grabbed her elbow and pulled her out of the elevator. "When?"

"Just before I left. I told her—"

"What did you tell her?"

"Just that the CIA was accusing me of something, and I had to go defend myself. I told her—well, it just made sense—I gave her the heads-up. If you were looking into me, then you might start asking her questions."

"Why?"

"Haven't you ever had a friend?"

Milo opened the door to the room, and all eyes turned to Jackson, who was still stunned. Milo was already on the phone to Jones. "She knows. Go in now."

Drummond, in the corner, looked as if the pistol had become too heavy for him. "What?"

Milo looked around the room. "Everyone, you're free to go. Irwin, you come with me and Alan."

"Well, isn't this fucking anticlimactic," said Max Grzybowski.

It was twelve fifteen when the three men reached Irwin's long black Chrysler parked around the corner on M Street. Drummond got behind the wheel; Irwin took the backseat, Milo the passenger seat. As they left Thomas Circle, Milo's phone rang. Again, it was Jones. "I've got some bad news for you, Milo."

"Go ahead."

"The woman, Chan? She's sitting on the sofa with two bullets in her chest. Stone cold."

10

It took nearly twenty minutes to cross the Potomac, head down the Jefferson Davis Highway, and exit into the Del Ray neighborhood of Alexandria. They found Leticia Jones in Pearson's apartment, standing over Chan's body, shaking her head. Chan was small, eyes closed on her wide face. Her skin was brutally white, the blood having drained out of two small holes in her chest; one of the bullets had struck high and punctured her aorta. The floor around the sofa was black and sticky.

"It's no good," said Jones.

Milo stood beside her. "What's that?"

Leticia Jones didn't feel up to explaining herself. She pointed at the window to the building's courtyard. "That was already open, and here," she said, crouching on the rug, "are the shells." She pointed a long, red fingernail at a 9mm casing moored in the blood, then another. "Super-close range."

"When did Pearson leave?"

"Got to be forty minutes by now. I guess he wasn't just picking up milk."

Drummond approached them from behind. "If I found this on my couch, I wouldn't be back yet either."

Whether or not she was the mole, Milo hated to find her dead.

He tried to work through how this had happened, avoiding the obvious answer: It had happened because Milo had decided to put his plan into action. Aloud, he said, "Jackson calls Chan to tell her about us. Chan panics and calls Zhu, or whoever her contact is. Zhu sends someone to get rid of her. All in—what? A half hour from Jackson's call to when Pearson left?"

No one answered at first. Irwin was standing in a far corner of the apartment, a handkerchief to his mouth, eyes red. Drummond coughed, then said, "They knew you were sniffing around, Milo. You made sure of that. Zhu kept someone on hand in case there needed to be some killing. I would."

Drummond's phone rang, and he stepped away to answer it. Milo looked at Jones. "Clean, isn't it?"

"Sort of."

"The shooter got all the way from that window to here and put two bullets in her chest—and she didn't even try to get up? She may have been asleep when he came in, but when she was shot she was sitting up."

"Like I said," Jones reminded him, "it's no good."

Klein wandered in from the kitchen, a pint of Häagen-Dazs in his large palm, eating. They both looked at him. "What?" he said.

Drummond came back holding his phone aloft. "It's Reagan National. They've got Pearson."

He had been picked up in Terminal B with a ticket for the six fifty-five Air Canada flight to Montreal. Klein drove alone; Milo joined Jones in her car; Drummond drove Irwin, who by now was showing real signs of shock. The ride with Leticia Jones was silent most of the way, until Milo said, "It wasn't supposed to be like this. No one should be dead."

Jones didn't bother answering that.

Reagan National Airport, like JFK, had its own series of back corridors that led to interrogation rooms. The one in which they'd placed Pearson had a table and chairs and a window reinforced with wire mesh. Before going in, they peered at him through the window. The man that Milo remembered from Drummond's office, talking into his cell phone with the easy confidence of young power, was now a mess. Hair awry, clothes disheveled, and a blank, wet stare.

"Who's going to start?" asked Drummond.

Before anyone could argue, Milo stepped inside the room. James Pearson hardly gave him a look as he walked to the table and sat down opposite. "Talk, Jim."

Pearson stared at his hands, which were flat on the table. "I don't know who he was. But she did. She told me."

"Told you what?"

"That they would get her. She knew."

"Who's they?"

"Her masters in Beijing."

"I don't follow."

He kept his gaze fixed solidly on his chewed nails and shook his head. "She called. Susan. She told Jane that the CIA was bringing her in for some questions, and Jane—I didn't understand it at first—she panicked. She told me she had to go. She had to leave. I asked why. She wasn't making any sense. Then she told me. She said she was working for the other side. For . . . it really sounds ludicrous. For the Chinese. She said she's been working for them for years."

"Did she say why?"

Finally, Pearson looked at him. "Her family. She was protecting them. Do you know what that means?"

Milo didn't answer.

"She said—and she kept telling me how sorry she was—she said that she used the information I shared with her. I mean, we talked about everything, Jane and me. Everything."

"Tell me what happened next."

"Well, I was angry. You can imagine. Can you?"

"Sure."

"I told her I couldn't speak to her. I walked out."

"Outside?"

"No. To the bedroom. She was in the living room, and I went to the bedroom and slammed the door. And this . . ." He trailed off. "The last words I spoke to her were in anger. My God."

"Go on."

He finally took his hands off the table and put them in his lap, which made him look cold, though his face was shiny with sweat. "After some time—ten, fifteen minutes? I don't even know. I came out again. And there she was, on the couch. The window was open—it was cold in the room—and she was dead."

"You didn't hear anything?"

Pearson shook his head. "The TV was on. No, I didn't hear any gunshots." He frowned, as if this had never occurred to him. "Do you think they used a silencer?"

Milo stared at the corner of Pearson's mouth, which was twitching uncontrollably.

"What happened next?"

"I ran. Stupid, maybe. But I thought . . . well, I thought that they didn't know I was there in the other room. As soon as they figured that out I would be next. Witness, that sort of thing. So I wanted to run as fast as I could."

"Why Montreal?"

"Why not?" he said, then shook his head. "Actually, it was the next flight out of the country, so I took it." He frowned. "Am I under arrest for running away?"

Milo got up. "You want anything? Coffee?"

"Alcohol," said Pearson. "Something to settle me down."

"I'll see what I can do," Milo said and left.

In the dim outer room, Irwin had collapsed in an office chair, while Jones and Drummond were standing by the window, arms crossed. They'd heard everything from speakers.

"It's tight," Leticia Jones said. "The story, I mean."

"Think so?" Milo asked, turning to watch Pearson reexamining his fingernails. "What I don't understand is how they did it so quickly. Maybe they had a gunman in the area, but the decision? That had to be Zhu's call. And it's—what time is it in Beijing?"

"One in the afternoon," said Jones.

"She calls—who? Not Zhu directly. Her controller. Wakes up her controller. The controller contacts Zhu. Zhu makes a decision, relays it back to the controller, and the controller contacts the gunman. The

gunman climbs up into the apartment and kills her. All this in . . .
twenty minutes, a half hour? It's efficient; I'll give it that."

Pearson had moved on to his wristwatch, removed it, and begun
to examine it.

"The television was off," said a voice, and they all turned to find
Irwin, white-faced and old, staring through them. "He turned off the
television after finding her body."

No one spoke for a moment. It was a small thing, but it reminded Milo of something else. "And he didn't say anything about
Chan making a phone call. She received the call from Susan, they
argued, and he stormed off. Fifteen minutes later she's dead. When
did she call her controller?"

Irwin made a long exhale, like a deflating tire. "Jesus Christ."

11

There was no point giving him what they knew and didn't know, so when he returned to the room he lied. "We just heard from our people—your prints are all over the shell casings. You killed her."

Pearson looked shocked. "What? No!"

"Did Zhu tell you to kill her? Or was that your idea? I'm guessing it was your idea, because Zhu would have done it properly. He would have moved her body so that it looked like she had run away from an intruder. Shot her in the back. Or he'd simply hide her body. But not you. You were in a panic; you did it all wrong. You walked right up to her, and she sat up—she trusted you, of course. Then you whipped out the pistol and did it. *Then* you turned off the television and opened the window and dreamed up the story of the assassin."

Pearson's eyes were drier now, but he still held on to his confusion. "You don't understand anything. I loved Jane. We were going to be married."

Milo wasn't listening; he was too taken by his own thoughts. "That was Zhu's idea, wasn't it? The relationship. He probably told you from the beginning—stay close to Chan. If you're ever discovered, you can shift the blame to her. Pillow talk. Yes," Milo said, now sure. "You both knew everyone would buy her as a mole—but a round-eye like you? Never."

"Shut up!"

"We were watching your place when you left. You came out walking. Like a man who'd just killed someone, not like someone afraid for his life. You checked your watch, because you wanted some grounding. But you still had your head on your shoulders. People who've just committed murder still have their heads. People who've just discovered their fiancée's corpse—they don't."

At some point, Pearson had begun to shake. It started with the left hand, where he wore his watch, then moved to the right. Milo could hear his foot tapping the tiled floor and noticed the occasional jerk of his chin. It was too much for him. Pearson was a white-collar spy; he wasn't used to things like blood and bullets. Few people were. His body was fighting against itself, against Pearson's will, against the act it had committed. Then the body won, and Pearson heaved and vomited clear liquid across the tabletop.

"So," said Milo. "You want to tell me?"

Releasing the truth was not as difficult as Pearson had likely imagined. You begin with one truth, and the rest slides through that open hole with little effort. Yes, he had killed her. Yes, it had been his own idea. "I'd come up with it when I found out that you'd been in Germany, getting their help to track me down. I didn't know if I could do it or not, but I asked Li for a gun and a silencer."

"Li?"

"I don't know if that's his real name. My contact. He gave me one yesterday, left it in my mailbox."

"Where is it now?"

"A Dumpster. Somewhere between home and here. Don't ask me which one."

"Why Montreal?"

Pearson rocked his head from side to side. "That was the plan. If things fell through and I could make it, I should go to Montreal, to the consulate there."

"Was there a Plan B?"

"I hope so. Because that's all I have to depend on now."

Milo stared at him. There were other questions, important ones such as what kinds of information Pearson had given Zhu, and what Pearson was getting from the relationship, but right now Milo was interested in one thing. "Did you ever meet Xin Zhu personally?"

Pearson shrugged. "Twice. Once in Shanghai. Once here."

"In D.C.?"

"Your Ukrainian source was right—he's a big man. Enormous. But he's not a drinker. Not a womanizer. What he is is very serious. He'll do anything to get revenge. He knows what he needs, and he knows exactly how to get it. He's daunting. He knew exactly how to get at me, and he knew exactly how to get me into Tourism. And I imagine that, by now, if there is a Plan B, it's fully in effect. I'd watch out if I were you."

"He wants revenge for the Sudan."

"Yes," said Pearson. "Not all fathers can hold a grudge so intensely."

Milo wasn't sure he'd heard right. "Fathers?"

Pearson leaned back, his fingers tapping out some code on the table. "Yes. You do know about that, don't you?"

"Why don't you tell me?"

"Delun. His son. You know about him, right?"

Milo's scalp began to itch, but he resisted scratching. "Go on."

"Killed last year. In the Sudan. He was working for Sinopec, the Chinese oil company, and got swept up in one of those riots triggered by the murder of Mullah Salih Ahmad. The murder you guys did." When Milo didn't answer, he added, "Machete. He was chopped up by men with machetes."

It was a simple fact, something that a little more research would have revealed—research that Milo had been too distracted to perform.

It changed everything.

The man he so admired, the cool, complicated spymaster directing all the action from abroad was not so cool after all. He was driven in the same way Milo would be driven if someone ever did anything to Stephanie. He wasn't ruled by ideology or nationalism or even the pleasure of the game, not at the moment. Revenge motivated him, and in that case all predictions went out the window. There were plenty of rules governing espionage, but no rules regulating revenge.

And then . . .

Milo said, "Does he know you've been picked up?"

Pearson gazed up at him with huge eyes. "I hope Li told him."

"Li knows?"

"Well, he was here in the airport, wasn't he? Saw those goons around the X-ray machine cart me off."

Milo wasn't sure of anything now. Wasn't sure what Zhu was thinking, nor even what he himself was thinking. He only felt a cool panic stutter into his body. Zhu knew so much more than they did, and had been ahead of them every step of the way. Now—

"Myrrh," Milo said, almost shouting, as he turned to the observation window.

Drummond's voice came disembodied from the darker room. "What?"

Milo pushed open the door to find them all—Drummond, Jones, Klein, Irwin—staring at him. He focused on Drummond. "*Now*. Order them all back. Zhu knows we're going to recall all the Tourists as soon as possible. Their names and codes are the most important thing he's gotten out of this. He might not give them up so easily."

Drummond didn't react at first, only stared. Then he took out his phone and called the office and told the night staff exactly what to do. His hands, Milo noticed, were beet red and trembling.

12

It was after three in the morning, and talking to Pearson was exhausting him. He'd learned, in generalities, that Pearson's cooperation with Zhu had begun three years before, with an offer of money. There was nothing to pull at the heartstrings in his story. Pearson was simply a man who wanted more, who enjoyed the clandestine games that came with the job description. He met semiregularly with Li, who as far as Pearson knew had no direct involvement with the embassy, and passed on files and discussed office gossip. Over the last year, though, since his son's death, Zhu had begun to demand more information, particularly on Tourism, which Pearson had assured him was responsible for the Sudanese unrest. Finally, in December, Zhu showed up in Washington and met Pearson face-to-face to explain that his requests had a personal nature to them, and they agreed on a new payment rate, deposited into a Cayman bank, to prepare for Pearson's move into the Department of Tourism itself. "It was a lot of money—more than I'd even asked for. He wanted the whole farm."

"So that's what you gave him?"

"I'm a traitor, but I'm not a corrupt capitalist. I give a fair return."

As if on cue, Drummond walked in, gripping his phone. He said, "Go ahead."

"What?"

Drummond couldn't speak. He gave Milo the telephone and walked out again, slamming the door behind himself. "Hello?" Milo said into it.

"Uh, where is Mr. Drummond?" asked a young female voice.

"He just handed you to me. What's going on?"

"It's the phones, sir. They're all off."

"They? Who?"

"The phones," she repeated. "All the Tourists, except three, have gone black. I've contacted them directly with the Myrrh code, but the rest . . . I don't know what to do. They've all turned off their cells."

"You still know where they are," Milo reminded her.

"Of course, but there's no way to contact them."

"Thank you," Milo said and hung up. He felt an urge to throw himself across the stained table and strangle Pearson. Instead, he returned to the observation room and told Klein and Jones to turn on their Company phones. "Right now, please."

There were a few seconds of silence as they reassembled and powered up their phones; the small room suddenly came alive with start-up melodies, then the *beep-beep* of messages received.

Each had an identical message, "Myrrh, myrrh," which had been sent more than an hour before that moment. Each also had another message, sent twenty minutes before the Myrrh code. Jones's read:

L: Stanley Wallis, Kasr el Madina Hotel, Cairo. Total silence.

The *L* stood for liquidate, and "total silence" meant that Jones should disassemble her phone and refuse all outside communication until the job was done. Klein's message was identical, though it pointed him to Peter Schiffer, Hotel Belle Epoque, Bern.

Drummond verified that Stanley Wallis and Peter Schiffer were Tourists, muttering under his breath that Schiffer was the new work name for James Einner. Then he got down on his knees, sat, and lay back, flat on the grimy tile floor, eyes shut. "Holy shit," he said to no one in particular. "He's making us kill ourselves."

Irwin, Milo noticed, was in a near-fetal position in his chair, eyes open and round. Only Jones and Klein, the two Tourists, seemed to be holding it together.

Even Milo felt himself starting to lose it. Throughout the world at that moment, thirty-seven men and women had just received orders to murder one another. Any time now the killings would begin, and there was nothing any of them could do about it.

Drummond sat up but remained on the floor, looking as if he'd just woken. He sighed loudly. "So, Milo. Is he still your hero?"

Milo wasn't listening. He wanted to be far away. He wanted to be home. He took out Drummond's phone and dialed an international phone number, and by the third ring Erika Schwartz picked up.

"It's done," he told her. "Alan will mail the tape. For Wartmüller, go to Lugano, to this address," he said and gave her a street and number. "Garage number six, combination 54-12-35. It's probably not what you expect, but with a little creativity you can end his career with it."

Schwartz said, "You sound terrible, Milo. There were problems?"

"Oh, no, Erika. Everything's just fine."

"Then perhaps you can give me the final thing you promised."

"The final thing?"

"The name of her killer."

Milo had forgotten. He rubbed his eyes. "I'll do that—but I don't think it'll do you any good now."

"Why not?"

13

On all the continents they began to move, drawn by words on small screens. An *L* followed by a name, and each name received the reverse order, to take out the one coming to see him. On a large screen on the twenty-second floor of the building on the corner of West Thirty-first and the Avenue of the Americas, the red spots on every continent shifted, and then, over hours, pairs converged. They left cities to find new cities, and those in the countryside and in places with no names sought out the crowded centers.

In the office, the late-morning light spilling in, they watched and zoomed in on individual cities like spectators to a disaster who morbidly replay the same tape over and over again. A red spot moved closer to another red spot until they were atop one another, and then one moved away, leaving behind a blue spot. Then nearby—never farther than a half mile from the point of contact, and sometimes in the same place—the original spot stopped and turned blue.

"Who's doing that?" asked Irwin, wiping at his nose with Kleenex he'd stolen from a cubicle. "One kills another, and who's killing the first one?"

No one bothered to answer him.

Out in the field of cubicles Travel Agents made desperate calls to hotels in the world's cities, asking to speak to people who never answered their room phones or the knocks on their doors. They knew what total silence meant.

Hanoi, Jerusalem, Moscow, Johannesburg, London, Cairo, Tokyo, Mexico City, Seoul, Dhaka, New Delhi, Brasilia, St. Petersburg, Buenos Aires, Tashkent, Tehran, Vancouver, Phnom Penh, Bern.

In Cairo, there was no joining of spots. Just a red spot inside the Kasr el Madina that turned blue. Milo asked Drummond to zoom in on Bern, then smiled sadly as he saw that Peter Schiffer, once known as James Einner, was in Marians Jazzroom on Engestrasse.

Milo used another computer to find the club's Web site. There was a phone number. He called, and after three rings a woman picked up. A trombone wailed in the background. In German he explained there was an emergency. An accident. The wives of two men in the club had been seriously injured. Could he please talk to Peter Schiffer and James Einner? The woman was hesitant. "We're packed."

"Really," said Milo. "This is an emergency."

He could hear her shouting the names. There was a break in the music that helped her project across the small club that Milo knew so well. Minutes passed, and finally she picked up again and said, "I'm sorry, but they're not here."

"You're sure?"

"Yeah, man. I'm sure."

But there he was, in the rear corner. He wouldn't answer, though. He followed orders too well. "One last thing."

"Better be quick."

"Please write down a message. They'll be there. Give it to either one of them."

"What's the message?"

"Myrrh."

"What?"

He spelled it for her. "And put my name on it. Milo Weaver." He spelled that, too.

He returned to the others mesmerized by the spots changing colors in Drummond's office. Irwin was in a chair, his face in his hands. Drummond was hypnotized, keeping score. Klein and Jones stood back a few paces, watching wryly, though when Jones spoke there was no humor in her voice. "That's seventeen. There—Brasilia— eighteen." She looked at Milo. "All this because someone's kid died?"

He didn't answer her; no one did.

Milo stood beside Drummond, who made a soft whimpering sound each time a spot changed color. He sometimes zoomed back so that the world became pockmarked with red blemishes slowly overwhelmed by blue. The scales tipped, the blue winning, but that didn't slow the color's brutal forward march. Milo kept his eye on Switzerland. Bern.

Red.

Red.

Red.

While he stared he remembered another of those insipid rules of Tourism that had come from his own pen:

A TOURIST KNOWS FAILURE BETTER THAN HE
KNOWS HIS MOTHER

Which was what Peter Schiffer, or James Einner, read at that moment.

He was sitting in Marians Jazzroom, pressed into the soft purple couch that ran the length of the back wall, hardly even listening to the trio on the bandstand—drums, bass, trombone. He squinted in the dim light, reading the pamphlet that he'd spent two months tracking down. Malmö, Toulouse, Milan. Now Bern, where the hand-written child's notebook had been hidden behind this very seat.

He'd discovered it before the club began to fill up for the seven thirty show, so distracted by his search that he wasn't even concerned by the order he'd received some hours before—L: ZACHARY KLEIN. WILL COME TO YOU AT BELLE EPOQUE. UNTIL COMPLETE, TOTAL SILENCE. While he had followed the order by disassembling his phone, he wasn't about to sit around in his hotel, even one as pleasant as the Belle Epoque, when the Black Book was within his reach.

Someone knew he was here—the barmaid had called out both his work names—but not even that mattered. He maintained his absolute silence and continued to read as the woman shouted rudely above the horn solo. Einner glanced at her irritated face (someone on the phone in her hand was insisting), then returned to reading.

He wasn't entirely sure what he thought of the book, but he supposed it wasn't the kind of thing you could digest in one reading. Some of the advice seemed strangely pedestrian, while other bits made him pause and think back over his own actions. Did he, as the Black Book stated was crucial, know empathy? He wasn't sure.

Did he know failure better than he knew his own mother?

No. He hadn't failed enough to be so familiar with it, but the Book had words even for his situation:

If you're new to the game and have only known success, you won't want to hear this. Sure, you'll think, some Tourists run into failure, but there's always a chance I'll be that lucky one who slips between the blades.

You're wrong. Sometimes you'll end an operation having achieved all your objectives, only to learn—maybe years later—that you failed in some unknowable way. In fact, it's more likely you'll fail as often as you succeed.

It was, like a lot of the Book, depressing stuff, and he ordered a locally distilled grappa to cut the edge off of it.

Don't be dismayed; you're still better than most agents. On average (based on a classified 1986 study) a Tourist succeeds 58% of the time, whereas a regular Clandestine Service Operations Officer succeeds 38% of the time. You'll be happy to note that FBI agents tend toward the 32% range, though the KGB—in 1986—had a success rate of 41%. Although the numbers for MI-6 agents have never been released, the State Department estimates something in the high thirties, while as of 1995 (according to a leaked French report) DGSE agents had an appalling success rate of 28%.

As a Tourist, there is only one way to deal with failure—
treat it as if it were success.

On his left, an attractive blonde sat waiting for her boyfriend to
return from the bathroom. She was bored with the music, had been
for their entire stay, while her boyfriend—a sandy-haired twenty-
something who was all elbows—had bounced and bobbed to the
rhythms like a spastic duck. It was the season for the International
Jazzfestival Bern, and there were a lot of his type around. The blonde
leaned toward Einner and said in German, "You come a club to read?"

He gave her a smile. "I come to pick up girls, but the only good-
looking one here has a date already."

"Really? Where is she?"

He maintained his smile until she blushed, pleased. He finished
his drink and left, feeling warm and whole and decided to walk back
to the hotel rather than calling a taxi. If this poor, doomed Klein
was waiting for him, then so be it. He walked up Engestrasse, then
crossed the bridge over the railroad tracks to reach Tiefenaustrasse
and continued toward the Aare, where he passed the occasional wan-
derer and necking couple along the banks of the river. He pressed his
hands into his pockets, the chill refreshing after the stuffy club, and
remembered a story from the Book, the bleakest one.

True story, Tourist. Listen up.

There was a man who, if legends were allowed in our profession, would have been the Paul Bunyan of Tourism. Sixteen
years of continual work—seven years longer than a Tourist's
life expectancy—and even the opposition admitted that he
did his work with panache. He had friends on their side,
friends who'd do anything for him, even as he worked to
destroy them. He had an exceptional life, a woman in every
port—though he stuck to airline stewardesses because they
were the only ones who could relate to him. They understood that he had no base, no home, and that his country
was his feet.

Airline employees are the only ones who get that—remember.

After sixteen years he decided it was time to turn in his spurs.
He'd collected enough scars for three grandfatherhoods full
of stories, and he'd put away enough money to buy a small
island. But it was love that really did him in, as it does most
of us.

Don't turn the page. It gets better.

"Better" was a poor word to describe what followed, he thought
as he passed an old man on a bench, gloved hand propped atop a cane
beside his knee. Einner gave him a welcoming nod, but the man
didn't seem to notice him. He, too, was elsewhere.

He forgot, this Tourist. He forgot that what we do, everything we do, sticks to us. He bought that house in the city,
then a second one in the Rockies. He married that last stewardess who, fortuitously, had also tired of all the air miles.

And they did it. Five years went by. There was a child, then a
second. His old comrades tried now and then to get in touch,
but he sent them away. This was a new life, unlike all the little lives he once lived in all those cities. Some friends worried; they warned him that it wasn't that easy. It couldn't be.

"But it is," he told them, and returned to his soft bed with
his soft wife and children and acres of peace.

Then, five years, seven months, and six hours into this grand
experiment of living, he wakes in a sweat. His wife, dozing
beside him, is no longer his wife. She's reverted to a Face.
Just a Face. Like the ones he remembers from all those airports and train stations and bus terminals, it's filled with
every possibility of betrayal. Because that's what Faces are to
the Tourist. Each Face is an opportunity to be caught, turned

in, tortured, ransacked, slugged. Betrayed. It's the sweet paranoia that keeps us alive.

James Einner had been a Tourist for three years. He liked his
job. He enjoyed that sweet paranoia that kept him alive. To say he
enjoyed the killing would have been a stretch, but there was real
pleasure in planning a murder and, more importantly, assembling
the escape plan. He enjoyed gaining people's confidence, and the
adrenaline rush when someone let slip the crucial secret nugget
that, had he not been working so well, never would have slipped out
of their lips. They were all Faces, sure, but they were people, too.
Adversaries demanded some level of respect, even when he was
about to kill them. Even when they did that one thing that brought
him no pleasure, and in fact cut him off at the knees: begged for
their lives.

This can't be happening, right? What about those five wonderful years? He goes to look in on his children. Children.
At least they don't betray. But he remembers a job in Tang-
ier, another in Beirut, a bad time in Delhi. Cities where they
use children to carry explosive devices and messages and
collect information. Everyone betrays. That's the nature of
living. And children, they're just more Faces.

So he goes down to the basement, where he keeps his guns
locked up, and grabs the old Walther PPK that was his protection of choice in the old days. Then he takes them out.
One by one. And it's a mess. It's a damned shame. Once it's
done, he knows, because violence has cleared his head again.
He remembers that he ignored their screams as if they were
the statistical screams of passengers in a plummeting jetliner.

His friends were right; they all were. But a Tourist is vain,
particularly retired ones, and this one can't bear to stay
around and admit his error. He sucks on the Walther that
once was his best friend.

On both banks the city rose up, and he headed back inland, finally reaching the art deco Hotel Belle Epoque. He preferred modern monstrosities, but an acquaintance in Paris had suggested the place. The acquaintance, however, was obviously more of an art lover than he was.

He collected his key from the charming girl at the front desk, who told him there had been no visitors. However, there had been one phone message. She handed it over.

Myrrh
—Milo Weaver

"Any idea what this means?" he asked the girl.

She had no idea—the caller had said he would understand—and as he took the stairs to his room he worked over what to do. Return yet again? It seemed impossible. The mole had been disproved, and he had been ordered to wait for a contact. But what if his cell phone had been compromised? Perhaps that order had been a ruse? Either way, one or both of the orders were wrong.

The hair he'd slipped into the door was still where he'd left it, so he went in and turned on the television instinctively. There was only one thing to do—call in and get Drummond himself to issue his order. So he lowered the volume on the television and picked up the hotel phone. There was a knock on his door. He put the phone back in its cradle and took a revolver out of the closet and said, "Yes?"

"Seven two six oh three nine."

Einner looked down at his gun and slipped it into his waistband. He opened the door to find a small Asian man—not Chinese; Malaysian, perhaps—looking sternly back at him as he said, "Four two—" He didn't get any further. The man was holding an old Croatian pistol, a PHP, with a short suppressor screwed into it. He pulled the trigger, and the force of the bullet in his stomach knocked Einner back a few steps. There was no pain, not yet, just a weight in his gut that made it hard to reach around to the small of his back to get at his revolver. Nevertheless, he tried as the man took a step forward and shot him once more in the forehead.

His vision went first; then everything began to shut down. But death, like love, is relative. In those final seconds so much can come, and like a judgment he never even knew he had made against himself, his last thoughts replayed a road and trees to the south of Gap, France. The accident he'd set up. Finding the French agent dead against the steering wheel, the girl in shock. Offering his help. Carrying her to his SUV. Her saying nothing. Stopping again and telling the girl that they needed to get out. "A friend lives right through there. Through those trees. He's a doctor." Then carrying her because her legs weren't working well enough. Her slow questions, and the smell of her surprisingly pungent sweat. Holding his breath and thinking only of the next step. Walking, until he saw the two trees, crossed, as if they'd been waiting for years just for this. "Sit down here a sec. I need to rest."

"Where is this house," she said flatly.

"Right through there," he said, and when she looked away he stepped close and reached out, but she had already turned back, eyes large. Thinking only of the next step, he turned her away again and lifted her up and grabbed her jaw and pulled sharply until the crack came and his legs were liquid and he fell with her and all was finished.

I know what you're thinking, because each Tourist reacts the same way to this story. You don't believe it. Or, if you do, you think this man was unbalanced from the beginning. You'd be wrong. He was the best. He was better than you can ever hope to be.

If you think this could never happen to you, you're as much of a fool as he was.

14

Two weeks later, on the day after the final Panikhida, which ended the forty-day mourning period within the Eastern Orthodox Church, Andrei Stanescu touched down at John F. Kennedy Airport in New York, United States. His single beat-up handbag, bought at a market in Ungheni for their move west, held some basic toiletries, one change of clothes, and a crumpled map of Manhattan and its boroughs marked up by his indecipherable shorthand. He showed his Moldovan passport to a brisk and humorless border guard behind Plexiglas, who asked him some questions about his visit. They were nothing. In his life he'd been asked serious questions by border guards and militia and government officials. This was nothing.

"What is the purpose of your stay?"

"Excuse me?"

"Your stay. Why are you here?"

"For to see America."

"So you're a tourist?"

"Yes. A tourist."

He peered at the fresh visas—the Schengen visa that had recently been renewed, as well as the American tourist visa that would allow him two months to do as he pleased. In fact, there was only one thing he was pleased to do, and besides, the two hundred and fifty dollars in his pocket would not last him two months. It would last long enough. Then? Then he would either use the return ticket or he wouldn't; that part wasn't up to him. It was up to God.

He was better now than when he tracked Erika Schwartz and cornered her at that convenience store in Pullach. He hadn't been thinking straight. He'd come off three days of no sleep, and in that time he hadn't even called in to work; his taxi had sat unused until he drove it to Munich to demand some kind of satisfaction. Though, as promised, she did call in the morning with the unfortunate news that there were no tenable leads on his daughter's murder, he knew the sound of a brush-off, and knew that this was what she was giving him. He didn't know why, because when they'd talked outside the church he'd believed that this was a woman who wanted to make a little justice in an unjust world. He'd been wrong.

He'd prepared in advance and knew to go to the AirTrain station. The price, as expected, was five dollars. At Howard Beach, he bought a plastic two-dollar subway ticket from an angry Negro behind another window, who kept telling him to use the machines against the wall. But Andrei was firm. He pushed the five-dollar bill through the window and repeated, "Ticket. Hoyt Street Fulton Mall."

"Okay, man. Here's the MetroCard. Now you find Hoyt your own self," he said, pointing at a map on the wall.

He understood far more English than he could speak, most of it learned from subtitled movies that filled the television back in Moldova. He also understood maps, for during his two years of obligatory military service he'd excelled in all forms of navigation. So finding Hoyt Street station from where he stood was not difficult. There, he saw, he could change trains and change again after another stop until he reached Fifteenth Street–Prospect Park in Brooklyn.

"It will be easy," Rick had told him in slow, watery Russian—a language Andrei knew all too well. "Getting there is the easy part. Getting prepared is easy. After that, it's up to you. It's your show. You know what they say about the pure-hearted, Andrei. You have nothing to worry about."

It had been a surprise when the Alligator dispatch operator radioed him with a pickup from Tegel and said that the caller had requested him in particular. "Me?"

"Yes, you, Andrei."

The smiling, fat Chinaman waiting with no luggage at all decided to take the passenger seat—carsickness, he explained—so Andrei cleared off his loose receipts, his jacket, and the paper bag that had held his lunch, and the man settled in with a loud series of grunts. "Tiergarten, bitte."

While Andrei drove, the man rested his gloved hands on his lap and asked in Russian if Andrei spoke Russian. That should have been a sign, but Andrei just shrugged. "Da."

"Dobriy," said the Chinaman. "Mr. Stanescu, you don't know me, but I requested you be my driver today."

"I heard that," Andrei answered.

"Your story has been heard around the world, even in my country."

"If you're a journalist I'll let you out here."

"Please. I'm no journalist." He reached into his coat and removed a square purple envelope and began to unseal it. "I'm a friend. Or, at least, I hope you'll consider me one. I'd just like to help you."

The Chinaman hadn't been the first person to recognize him. Sometimes in the middle of a ride, a passenger would get a fresh glimpse of him in the rearview mirror and gasp as his memory clicked. Usually his fares chose silence, though sometimes—and it was more often women who did this—they opened their mouths and began long, pointless monologues on what he must be feeling, and how they felt when they learned of his daughter's death. He never knew what they expected from him in return—appreciation? He doubted they understood that what they really provoked from him was hatred.

So he said, "Help isn't possible, sir. Please don't trouble yourself."

"I'm not the only one, am I?" said the Chinaman, reading his mind. "Forget about the others. They're fools. There's only one way to help a man in your position. Here," he said, nodding at the side of the road. "Pull over a moment."

They had just left the highway and entered Charlottenburg, not far from Sophie-Charlotte-Platz. "Why?" asked Andrei.

"Because I don't want you to have an accident when you see this."

He pulled over, wondering how much time he should allow before kicking this bastard out of his taxi. He didn't need to see anything to risk having a wreck. All he had to do was be reminded of Adriana. The man opened the envelope and removed a single photograph. It was familiar, too familiar, but clearer than the one Erika Schwartz had shown him. The man—*that* man—talking to Adriana by the entrance of the courtyard. She was beautiful. He touched the photograph, touched her, and then the Chinaman took it away, saying, "He killed her."

"No," Andrei answered, not even wondering how a Chinese man had gotten hold of the image. "It was someone else."

"Who told you that?"

"German intelligence."

The Chinaman smiled and shook his head. "Spies protecting spies. This man, the one who killed your daughter, is an American spy."

"No, he's a tourist."

"That's what they call them. But he's a spy."

"How do you know this?"

"I know everything about this man. If you'd like, I can share that information with you."

Andrei looked again at the photo in this stranger's hand and felt as if he might vomit. Confusion was beginning to set in. He swallowed, wondering why all the spies he knew were obese. "Who are you?"

"Call me Rick. And know that I'm sickened by what this man did."

"Where is he now?"

"Back in America."

"Then it's no good. I can't go there."

"I can help with that."

It was too stuffy in the car, and Andrei got out to light a cigarette, but the rush of traffic kept blowing out his matches. He moved to the sidewalk and got it lit and took a deep drag. The Chinaman didn't bother getting out, just rolled down the window and stared at him with his Asian eyes. Andrei walked away, puffing on his cigarette, then returned. Above the roar of traffic the man called Rick began talking, and he had to squat beside the window to hear. He, too, was a father. Or he had been until those same spies had killed his only son. "I felt like you, but I knew the only way to ever get back my life was to deal with it. You can stay here, Andrei. You can forget we ever talked. But it will never leave you—trust me. It will make you sick at night when everything is quiet and you remember her again." Rick's eyes were wet, as if this were how he had spent his own nights, but perhaps that was just the wind. "The only way to make some kind of peace is to know that you've done everything you can do."

"Are you religious?" Andrei asked.

"I believe in the order of things."

Andrei nodded at this, then tossed away his cigarette and got behind the wheel again. Rick rolled up his window. Andrei said, "You're talking about revenge."

Rick thought for a moment, then quoted: *"And if any mischief follow, then thou shalt give life for life, eye for eye, tooth for tooth, hand for hand, foot for foot, burning for burning, wound for wound, stripe for stripe."*

That had been six days ago. Now, as he switched trains in Brooklyn, examining the signs above his head to make sure he didn't lose his way, he repeated that verse. It was busy here, and he was just another speck in the mass of many nations that poured through the New York transportation system every day.

Until Prospect Park, everything had been predicted, for he had sat down with Rick and gone over each moment in his journey westward. He'd made his illegible notes on the map Rick supplied, and circled the corner of Garfield and Seventh Avenue. First, though, he had to go to the park.

He'd taken an early flight, and with the change in time zones it was still only a little before three in the afternoon. The day was bright but chilly, and as he settled on a bench he saw couples and people with dogs, some on leads and others running loose. Dogs of a confusing variety of breeds. There were also businessmen on cell phones. It was, he realized, much like Germany, and he wondered why so many Moldovans he knew were desperate to come here. He thought of Vasile, another taxi driver, who would be sick with jealousy if he knew where Andrei was. But no one knew. Rick had been insistent about this. "Not even Rada."

Poor Rada, who woke up that morning and couldn't help but dress in black again, despite the end of the official mourning. This man, Milo Weaver, hadn't just killed Adriana. He'd killed Rada. He'd killed Andrei, too.

So when he left that morning with his small bag he'd explained that he was taking over Vasile's morning shift. As if she knew, she'd asked him to call someone else to take it over. She wanted him at home, with her—she had already called in sick again. She wasn't sure she could bear the empty apartment alone today. He'd had to be firm—"Calling in sick like this, you're going to lose your job. Someone has to earn money"—but he'd given her the kindest kiss he could manage.

"Andrei?" said a voice with an accent that skipped over the rolled *r* in his name.

He looked up to find another Chinese man. A skinny man, taller than he'd expected, wearing a trench coat. He carried a paper shopping bag with

BARNEYS
NEW YORK

written on it.

"Ja?" he said, then remembered where he was. "Yes. I am Andrei. You are Li?"

"About time," the man said, then launched into a stream of English Andrei couldn't understand at all and set the bag at his feet. He ended with "Okay?"

Andrei nodded. "Yes. Thank you."

For a second the man stared at him, his face full of doubt, then turned and walked away.

Andrei waited, breathing through his mouth because his nose had become stopped up, and watched the dogs racing across the park, stumbling and jumping over one another and chewing on each other and pinning each other down. Tongues lashed against their faces as they ran, and their eyes were huge with pleasure.

15

She recalled Venice. After all, it was the three of them again—the three of them and a strange man. Angela Yates was the only missing actor, and she was dead. She'd been dead for eight months.

That was later. At the moment it occurred, she recalled nothing. It was a moment unto itself, with no past or future, and her instincts took over: She reached for Stephanie and pulled her close.

They had just left the apartment. It was nearly seven—they were running late for their reservation at Long Tan, and Little Miss was talking. "If you park in a driveway and drive on a parkway, then . . ." She didn't finish her sentence. Not because of what happened, but because she couldn't find the words to express how much the English language had let her down. A minute later, Tina would share her inarticulateness.

He didn't stand out. In a city like New York few people stand out, but the small man in the soiled, waist-length jacket sitting on their stoop with a leather bag and a shopping bag from Barneys looked like any number of visitors in this city of visitors. Beyond him, a black couple pushed a baby carriage along the sidewalk, and across Garfield the Vietnamese florists were checking on the breathtaking variety of flowers arranged on the sidewalk outside their convenience store every day. The man, hearing them come out, turned to look. He had a round, flabby face and deep-set eyes, and besides the stubble that went nearly up to his eyelids he had plenty of hair. The hair on top of his head looked oily.

Tina turned to lock the door while Milo told Stephanie, "Language doesn't always make sense. Take Russian, for example—"

He stopped because he, too, had noticed the man now staring at them. With a hand that moved as if it were a separate creature entirely, Milo grabbed Stephanie by the arm and pushed her behind him, placing his own body between this man and his girls.

"It is you," the man said in heavily accented English.

With a voice harder than any she'd heard in her life, Milo said, "Go back inside, Tina."

Tina had already locked up and pocketed the key. "What?"

"Inside. Take Stef."

"Milo Weaver," said the man on the steps.

"*Inside*, Tina."

Her hands were shaking, but she got the door open and pulled Stephanie, who knew better than to ask questions right now, inside. They shut the door and watched through the window as Milo took a step down and began to speak softly to the man.

The window was thin, and they could catch phrases: . . . *should go home . . . can't solve anything . . . not at my house . . .* Then they switched to German. The word "Stanescu" came to them, and Tina realized with an unsettling shift in her stomach that Stanescu was the name of the European girl who'd been killed.

Then she recalled this man's face (it looked so different in reality) from some video on CNN, with the weeping mother. *The poor man,* Tina thought, looking down at him over Milo's shoulder. Then the poor man reached into the Barneys bag and removed a small pistol. All the air left her and she reached for Stephanie, who was glued to the glass, saying, "He's got a gun! He's got a gun!" Tina pulled her tight to her stomach and tugged her backward. "Stop, Mom!"

Tina wouldn't stop. She understood enough about bullet trajectories to know that if that man tried to shoot Milo and missed, the bullet would come at them. She wouldn't have her daughter in the way of that. Nor would she have Stephanie watch her father get shot. Tina had watched that before, in Venice, and knew how horrible it was.

She was hardly thinking as she lifted Stephanie, kicking, onto her shoulder, and with strength she didn't know she had carried her up two flights and used her free hand to unlock the door and get inside. Stephanie ran for the window to look down, and Tina took out her phone and dialed 911. "There's a man with a gun," she told the bland emergency operator as a single gunshot rang out. She dropped the phone and ran to the window, where Stephanie was screaming for her father. Tina looked down—the little man was rushing around the corner onto Seventh, and Milo was sitting on the front steps.

She rushed to the door and spun around, pointing at Stephanie, who had begun to cry. Frail girl, shaking hands. "Stay here!" Tina shouted, then fled downstairs, thinking, *I'm a terrible mother.* She couldn't help it. She was what she was.

By the time she reached the front steps three people were standing over Milo, two with cell phones to their ears, one holding Milo's arm and speaking calmly to him. Milo was hunched forward, a bright red hand clutching at his stomach. Blood was all over the three concrete steps, and he was making guttural sounds. She pushed the stranger aside and got close to Milo's face. His lips were too red, and so were his teeth, and when he coughed, bloody spittle shot out onto her blouse. "Honey," she said. "Hey, baby. Look at me."

From somewhere in the sky, she heard Stephanie calling to her, and looked up to see her head poking out of their window. "It's okay!" Tina called. "He's going to be fine! Just stay there!"

Milo was speaking. It was a whisper, so she leaned close. "It's okay," he said, as if he were repeating her words.

"It's not okay," she told him, "but it will be. The ambulance will be here."

"Ambulanza," he said, smiling as a drop of blood rolled down his chin. It was the Italian word for ambulance, she realized, then remembered Venice just as he was remembering it.

When a fresh wave of pain hit him, he leaned forward and squeezed her arm so hard it hurt. He buried his face in her breasts. She was calmer now—panic had given way to shock—and she asked if anyone (there were now a dozen people standing around) could see the ambulance. Two stout men ran to the corner to look. She held on to Milo's head as he whispered something into her cleavage. She tilted his head back. "What, hon?"

"I deserve this," he said.

"No. No one deserves this."

"You don't," he said. "Little Miss doesn't." He coughed up more blood.

When she looked down she saw that so much blood had come out that it looked as if they had both been shot, and she knew that wasn't good. She took his face in her hands and made him look into her eyes. "Lover? Lover. Stay awake. Okay?"

He nodded, but closed his eyes as he did so, which terrified her. She slapped him once on the cheek, hard, and his eyes opened again. "Dominatrix," he said, smiling. Then: "Push me back."

"What?"

"To see her."

She pushed his shoulders slowly, but when his face contorted in pain she asked for help from one of the men standing uselessly around. Finally, his back against the steps and his head leaned all the way back, he was staring skyward. Stephanie was still looking out the window, crying, and he gave her a smile and tried to call up to her, but couldn't get the breath for it. So he told Tina what to say.

"Little Miss! Your dad's going to be all right! He doesn't want you to worry, and doesn't want you to crack your knuckles any-more!"

Stephanie paused her tears to look at her hands, which were clasped together, cracking maniacally. She released them.

By the time the ambulance arrived, nearly two dozen people were standing on either side of the street in front of their apartment, and the driver had to shout at them to get out of the way. A pair of Latino medics got out of the rear with a stretcher, and while one examined Milo's stomach the other talked quietly with him about the sequence of events that had led to his injuries. Sometimes Tina cut in with her own version—"I went upstairs, to protect our daughter," she said defensively, and the medic waved her away. Soon Milo was strapped into the stretcher and Tina was telling him that they would be right behind him.

She then changed and found a new shirt to replace the one Stephanie had ripped on the windowsill, the crowd had dispersed, leaving only a few curiosity-seekers staring at the bloody front stoop, which Tina tried to distract Stephanie from. Though New York Methodist was just up the street, she still used the car, chatting away in what she thought was a calming voice while Stephanie sat silently beside her, peering out the window.

They had spent an hour in the waiting room, receiving occasional reports from a tired doctor who assured her that Milo would live, but there would be a long recovery time. The bullet had entered the small intestine. After she left, Stephanie sank into a disturbing silence, and Tina remembered something from their last session with Dr. Ray. Milo had begun to fade again, worrying her, but then he launched into a non sequitur. "Back when I was still working, I sometimes had these lapses. I'd be in some city, and some unexpected detail would throw me. A dog, a car, some music—always something different."

"How do you mean, throw you?"

"Divert me. I'd suddenly feel a physical need to call home. To talk to Tina and Stephanie. I even called a couple times, but luckily they didn't answer."

"You never mentioned this," Tina said.

"Because it was reckless," he told her. "Which is why it disturbed me. I didn't want to call, but I had to." He looked at Dr. Ray. "Any idea what that was?"

Dr. Ray frowned, then shrugged as if the question were entirely preposterous. "Well, it sounds like love to me. Doesn't it?"

The memory faded as a man in a gray suit with disheveled hair and pink hands stepped into the room. He looked around the crowd of waiting families, finally alighting on them, and came over. He gave Stephanie a smile and nodded at Tina. "How's Milo?"

"Who are you?"

"Oh, sorry. Alan Drummond. Milo used to work for me."

"In the Department of Tourism?"

His face went blank. "I'm not sure what you mean."

Stephanie leaned against Tina's arm and yawned.

"I've finally made an honest man of him," Tina said. "Not that it matters now. The department doesn't exist anymore, does it?"

Alan Drummond moved his mouth as if he were trying to find a way to spit out his tongue. "Are you going to tell me how Milo is? I heard he was shot."

"Stomach. He'll pull through."

"Good. I'm glad."

"Are you?"

A flash of anger passed through his features; then he took the free chair beside Tina. "Yes, Tina. I happen to like the guy."

"Then maybe you should be out catching the guy who did this."

"As you pointed out, I'm unemployed now. But for the sake of argument, who did this?"

"A little man. His name is Stanescu."

"You're sure?"

"Milo said that name when they were talking."

"They talked?"

"Not long. In German. I recognized the man from television. Then he shot Milo."

Remembering, Tina looked down at Stephanie, whose eyes were closed. She was listening, though; Tina was sure of it.

She said, "The name—does this have to do with . . . you know. The girl?"

Drummond didn't look like he understood, then he worked back in his memories and finally got it. "Oh, no. I'm sure it doesn't."

Christ, but these people could lie so well.

16

Though she picked up a bottle as usual and even exchanged a few words with Herr al-Akir, when her home phone rang at nine thirty-five, she hadn't even opened the bottle. Instead, she was sitting at the kitchen table, her cell phone beside her landline, staring at the two phones. Waiting.

She had expected the call to come later, and when she heard Berndt Hesse's hoarse voice—he'd never been used to long bouts of talking—she thought he sounded confused. "Can you get over to Schwabing?"

"If it's necessary, Berndt. What's wrong?"

"I'd rather tell you in person. Come to Theodor's house. You . . . you know where it is?"

"It's been a long time, and it'll take me a while. Could you remind me of the address?"

She drove the half hour to the northern Munich suburb without speeding, and on the way considered calling Oskar. She wanted to at least know if she should be prepared for failure, but there was no point to it. Either it had gone according to plan, or it hadn't.

Instead, she thought of Milo Weaver, and the unexpected connection that had come to her after their brief phone call two weeks ago. She'd hung up, and like a spotlight the realization had swept over her body. No, she had never known Milo Weaver, but his name had come up during an interrogation with an American woman, a terrorist. Three decades ago.

Ellen Perkins, in 1979, had been stewing in a German prison because she was one of those many young people who believed that with a gun, Marx, and some catchphrases, an entire civilization could be torn down. However, this one had a son she had secretly shipped off to America to live with her sister. Over the interrogation table, Erika had explained that she knew about the boy, Milo, and tried to use this knowledge to leverage a little cooperation.

Perkins had been harder than she looked, and the day after the interview she hanged herself in her cell, using the pants of her own prison uniform. She knew how to kill a conversation.

Then, almost thirty years later, she'd interrogated the son. What a truly remarkable world it was.

Theodor Wartmüller's Potsdamer Strasse apartment was high up in one of the many postwar buildings that had been rebuilt to prewar specifications. Two blue Bundespolizei BMWs were parked at awkward angles on the sidewalk in front of it, and farther down the street was a van from N24, the twenty-four-hour news channel. There were also people who, having seen the police and the man outside the building with a huge camera on his shoulder, were standing around, full of dumb curiosity. It took her ten minutes to find a parking space on the next street and walk back, passing Teddy's MINI and cutting through the crowd, waving her BND card to the policeman on duty at the front door. A reporter she recognized from television asked if she believed the story about Wartmüller. She said, "No comment," and continued inside.

The entryway was empty, though another policeman—a local one—stood at the elevator and checked her ID again before letting her take it up to the fifth floor. It was there that everyone had collected. Berndt, Franz and Birgit, Gaby from the public relations department, Robert from Administration, Hans from Operations, Claudia from Fraud. No one was speaking aloud. Only whispers filled the living room of Wartmüller's immense apartment. They were grouped around objects—an art nouveau floor lamp, a Restoration sofa, the drinks cabinet. When she entered, they all looked at her, but only Berndt detached himself from Hans to come over.

"About time you got here."

"What's going on?"

He shook his head. "Paintings. From the E. G. Bührle Museum."

"The robbery in February?" she said, trying to sound shocked. "What does that have to do with Teddy?"

"Two paintings. The final missing ones. They were found here in his apartment."

Erika shook her head. "What do you mean, *found*? No one just *finds* something. You come in and search for it. How did that happen?"

"Anonymous call to Interpol. Interpol brought it to the Feds. They arrived with a warrant a few hours ago."

"Where were the paintings?"

Berndt opened his mouth, then closed it, as if his next words couldn't be believed. "Under his *bed*. Theodor says he's never seen them before in his life."

She exhaled loudly. "The real question is who contacted the press."

He shrugged.

She found Theodor in the guest bedroom—the master bedroom had been taped off for forensics to go over—guarded by two policemen. She didn't bother asking them to leave, because they wouldn't anyway. The bedroom, like all the rooms, had a huge window through which he could easily escape—and through which anyone who knew the alarm code could easily get in.

He was sitting at the bottom of the bed, feet on the floor and elbows on his knees, staring at a large, very dark photograph. It was too dark to make out the subject, and she wondered if it was one of those postmodern works, called something like *Blackness #23*.

He finally raised his eyes to look at her; they were full of red veins. He'd been crying. He knew, just as she knew, that his career was over. Maybe he could get himself out of this, maybe not. The rumors were enough. His face on international television; his biography suddenly of public interest. He would have to start again. The knowledge of this was all over his face, and she was impressed that he had put it together so quickly.

She considered things to say. She could play so many different roles. She could tell from his eyes that he knew, though, and there was no point going through the motions. She was too tired for that, and so was he.

So without a word passing between them, she returned to the living room and joined various conversations about how to control the damage. Even out here, no one was wondering if Theodor had stolen those paintings. No one cared, not even Franz and Birgit. He'd been abandoned so quickly that even as someone—Claudia, perhaps?—suggested that Erika take over the department for a while, she could only feel a dull, quiet sympathy for the lonely man in the other room.

Her phone rang. It was Oskar. He was breaking the rules, and she almost didn't answer. She carried the phone to the doorway, where another policeman was standing with an unlit cigarette, wondering if he could smoke in the stairwell. "Oskar. It's a surprise to hear from you so late. Is everything all right?"

"Yes, but that's not why I'm calling."

"Tell me."

"It's Milo Weaver. He's been shot, but lives. Alan Drummond claims Andrei Stanescu did it."

"Andrei? The father—not the uncle?"

"They're sending over CCTV footage from JFK Airport. He's on a plane now, headed back to Berlin."

"The father," she said again. "That's a surprise."

She fell silent, watching the policeman finally give up and slip the cigarette into a box and put the box into his pocket. She wondered if violence lived in the blood, passed from mother to son, dooming both to abrupt, early deaths.

Oskar said, "What's your order? Drummond wants him arrested when he lands."

She'd stopped thinking of Milo Weaver, languishing in some American hospital, and had moved on to Andrei Stanescu, and the fact that he would risk everything for a single shot at the man who had taken his daughter. *There's violence in us all*, she thought, but only said, "Can you blame him?"

"As rich and intriguing as the best of le Carré, Deighton or Graham Greene...."
—*Los Angeles Times*

The arrest of a long-sought-after assassin brings burnt-out CIA agent Milo Weaver back into the fold to uncover who's been pulling the strings once and for all.

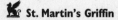